Text copyright ©2010 Crouch & Konrath
All rights reserved
Printed in the United States of America
No part of this book may be reproduced, or stored in a retrieval system, or transmitted in any form or by any means, electronic, mechanical, photocopying, recording, or otherwise, without express written permission of the publisher.

Published by Thomas & Mercer
P.O. Box 400818
Las Vegas, NV 89140

ISBN-13: 9781612181462
ISBN-10: 1612181465

STIRRED

A Jacqueline "Jack" Daniels/
Luther Kite thriller

by
CROUCH & KONRATH

PART I

MARCH 31

"Midway upon the journey of our life I found
myself within a forest dark,
For the straightforward pathway had been lost."

DANTE ALIGHIERI, *THE DIVINE COMEDY*

Jessica Shedd
March 31, 1:45 a.m.

H e wasn't her type.

For starters, too old. Forty-five or forty-six, she guessed—almost fifteen years her senior—and as a rule she didn't date men with long hair. Blame it on the lingering, private shame she still harbored from her early-nineties Michael Bolton phase.

Worse, he'd come at her with no game at all.

Had simply sidled up behind the vacant chair beside her and asked, "Would you mind if I sat here?"

And yet, here she was, almost four hours later, still talking with him at the bar in the Publican and letting him buy her another glass of the excellent New Zealand sauvignon blanc she'd been drinking all night.

As the bartender set a fresh glass in front of her and poured from the bottle, she figured it was Rob's eyes that had kept her in the chair, kept her from just slipping out the next time she excused herself to go to the little girls' room, a trick she'd pulled so many times before. Rob's eyes were black and intense for sure, but they were also listening eyes. She hadn't met a man like him in years. Most of the bores who hit on her might have presented a better exterior package—thousand-dollar suits and cologne and all the metrosexual accessories a single, successful man in Chicago was expected to flaunt—but they were also, almost without exception, unimaginative, self-obsessed bores.

Admen, lawyers, executives, the occasional fund manager who apparently thought she'd come downtown to hear every excruciating detail of his new boat and winter condo in Aspen, or what an adrenaline rush it was—"like a drug, like sex, you know, babe?"—to do whatever it was he did with other people's money.

No, Rob was different.

Most nights when she took herself out looking for Mr. Right, she rarely spoke. Just sat there and sipped wine and listened politely until she couldn't stand another moment of feigning interest.

But tonight *she'd* done most of the talking, and he'd seemed genuinely interested as she rambled on about her job at Fireman's Fund Insurance Company, where she worked as a claims representative.

He'd asked smart questions, and not just about the current job, but about her future goals, where she wanted to be in five years, in ten.

And he wasn't *that* bad looking.

Could've dressed a little nicer for a place like this, but in truth, his faded jeans, black cowboy boots, and plaid button-down only underscored the overall vibe she was getting from Rob.

Real.

This was a real guy and probably out on the town for the same reason she was—to meet someone who might bring meaning to what had become the almost unbearable monotony of her day-to-day existence.

The bartender, a heavily pierced and tattooed young man who barely looked old enough to sell alcohol, stopped in front of them and said, "Just to let you guys know, we'll be closing in ten minutes. Get you anything else?"

Rob glanced over at Jessica. "One more before they kick us out?"

Jessica looked at her wineglass—still a few sips left, though she would've loved one more since the bursts of passion fruit and lime were going down all too smoothly. But she didn't want to come off as a lush on what was turning into their first date.

"I think I'm all done."

Rob paid their tab with a big wad of cash and then stood and helped her into the pre-owned Martin Margiela jacket that still embarrassed her when she thought about what she'd spent on it.

"Thank you, Rob," she said.

"My pleasure, Jessica."

She could feel the awkward moment coming as they made their way through the empty restaurant, the servers already setting the tables with fresh linens and clean glass and silverware for tomorrow. In ten seconds, they were going to be standing on the sidewalk, the question of whether the night was over or just beginning hanging in the air.

She wasn't going to sleep with him—she knew that.

But maybe a quick nightcap back at his place or hers? No harm there.

Rob opened the door, and then they were out on the sidewalk in the cool spring night.

Jessica stopped near the street, her hands in her pockets, half-looking for a cab, half-wondering if she needed to.

"I'm really glad I took a chance asking if I could sit next to you," Rob said.

"Me, too," Jessica said. "It was a really lovely evening."

Come on, continue it. I'm sending you the signal. If I'd wanted our time together to be over, I would've already said good—

"Any chance I could interest you in a late-evening walk?"

Rob extended his arm, the boldest move he'd made yet, and she melted a little bit.

"That sounds very nice."

She took his arm, felt a cord of muscle under his shirt.

"I was thinking maybe we'd walk toward the river," Rob said. "It's so beautiful at night."

They headed east on West Fulton, the clouds glowing with the reflection of the city lights.

"It's funny," Rob said as they walked under the Kennedy Expressway, "past three Mondays I've gone out, just like tonight. You're the first woman who invited me to sit down."

"And I'm glad I did," Jessica said. "I go out a lot, too."

"By yourself?"

"Yeah. It's just...well, you know...so hard to meet people."

"To meet the *right* people."

"Exactly." She laughed. "Everyone's so fake."

"It's an epidemic," Rob said. "People never say what's really on their mind. It's all a game these days."

"I'm right there with you, Rob."

The streets were quiet, the last of the revelers stumbling out of bars in search of their cars or a late-night cab.

Straight ahead, the downtown rose into the night like a range of luminescent mountains, and Jessica could smell the river. The breeze had taken on a cold, dank component as it swept toward them across the water.

They walked up North Canal, the river flowing like liquid glass.

Halfway across the bridge on Kinzie Street, Rob stopped, and they leaned against the railing.

Watched the current pass beneath them.

Watched the lights of downtown twinkling in the dark.

A comfortable moment of silence, she thought. And a good omen, perhaps, that they could share one on a first date.

Rob pointed toward the old Kinzie Street railroad bridge. "You ever see it up close?" he asked. "From the shore, I mean?"

"I've never walked over to that side of the river."

"Well, come on."

"Really?"

"Yeah, let's go."

He took her by the hand, his grip firm and dry, and they moved at a brisker pace across the bridge and then south down the river walk. His stride was brisk, purposeful, and it challenged Jessica to keep up with him.

"Are you sure we're allowed to be here?" she asked.

"Of course. The city is ours."

It was two fifteen when they arrived at the base of the old railroad bridge. It soared into the sky, locked open in a raised position at a forty-five degree angle over the Chicago River.

Sirens wailed somewhere in the distance, but otherwise the city stood as quiet as one might ever hope to hear it.

Snowstorm quiet.

Not another car nearby except for a white van parked near the path.

Rob put his arm around her.

She let her head tilt over and rest against his shoulder, wanting to kiss him, thinking if it was going to happen, now was the moment—standing by the river and feeling like they were the only two people still awake in this gorgeous city.

He was staring up at the steel girders of the bridge, and if she could only get him to look down at her, she felt sure it would happen.

The perfect culmination to this glorious surprise of an evening.

"A penny for your thoughts?" she said. She could feel her heart thumping—hadn't kissed a man in more than six months.

Finally Rob looked down at her.

"I was thinking," he said, "how beautiful you're going to look hanging from the end of that bridge over the water."

The wine buzz vanished.

She stared up at Rob, trying to replay what he'd just said, certain she'd misunderstood, but his grip on her shoulder tightened.

"Wondering if you heard me right, Jessica?"

A strong, metal ache filled her mouth, her heart pounding now, something clenching up inside her chest as the strength flooded out of her legs.

"Happy to repeat myself," he continued. "I said, you're going to look so beautiful hanging from the end of that bridge."

"Rob—"

"That's not my name. I'd prefer you call me Luther. Luther Kite. Perhaps you know me by reputation? I've killed a lot of people."

She screamed for less than a second before his hand covered her mouth, everything happening so fast and with such brute force, her head caught in the crook of his arm as he muscled her toward the base of the old railroad bridge, toward the shadows.

Mace. I have Mace.

The can was in her purse, probably buried at the bottom. She hadn't even touched it since she'd bought it two years ago after taking that self-defense class with Nancy and Margaret.

He dragged her into the shadows, and Jessica felt him lift her—airborne for two seconds—and then her back slammed hard into the ground, the breath driven out of her.

Motes of light starred her field of vision, pure panic and oxygen deprivation, but her left arm—thank God—was free. She felt her purse underneath her, got two fingers on the zipper, tugging it open as he whispered in her ear, "No more screams, Jessica. You understand me?"

Frantic nodding.

"Screaming will only make it worse on you. So much worse."

She jammed her hand into the purse, the back half inaccessible, crushed into the grass under the weight of her and this monster.

"If I take my hand away from your mouth, will you be quiet?"

She nodded again as her fingers grazed the top of the canister, fighting for a workable grip, her chest blitzing up and down. Even her hardest workouts, when her pulse redlined for several agonizing minutes, could never achieve this level of cardiac frenzy.

The man took his hand away, and she stared up at him, her fingers clutching the top of the canister, straining to pull it out from underneath her.

He clamped one hand around her throat, still pinning her under his weight, and with the other grabbed something out of a black duffle bag that she'd failed to notice until now. He couldn't have had it with him. Which meant he'd planted it here.

"I'll let you do whatever you want to me," she said, trying to steady the quiver in her voice. "Just don't hurt me. Please, God, don't hurt me. I won't tell anyone, I swear to you. I just want to live."

Luther grabbed her right wrist and said, "Give me your hands."

He was reaching for her left when the canister of Mace broke free.

She found the trigger.

Swung it up in a single, fluid movement, and then she was pointing it in Luther's face, her finger squeezing, not even certain if she had the damn thing pointed in the right direction, just praying she wouldn't Mace herself.

A burst of pepper spray exploded sideways out of the nozzle as the man swatted the canister out of her hand.

Luther smiled down at her, Jessica so frozen with concentrated terror that she didn't even react as he turned her over and bound her wrists together with a thick loop of plastic.

When he rolled her back over, she said, "Please...is there anything I can do?"

She was crying now, and the acrid stench of urine in the air belonged to her.

"Try not to throw up. You'll choke to death and miss all the fun."

He reached into the duffle and took out a roll of duct tape.

Tore off a strip, slapped it down over her mouth just as it occurred to her to scream again.

For a moment, the tears blinded her.

When she blinked them away, she saw a knife with a curved blade, and on some plane of consciousness removed from this moment, it occurred to her that it resembled the talon of a bird of prey.

Moaning through the tape now, begging him not to do this, making desperate promises.

He sat on her waist, her hands bound behind her back, and no amount of squirming could jolt him off.

Luther glanced over his shoulder—a quick look up and down the river walk.

She turned her head as well and through the blades of grass saw the path still empty.

"Like I told you," he said, "the city is ours."

He grabbed her chin, turned her head back toward him. She stared into his eyes, trying to make some connection through the pitch black, but there was nothing in them approaching compassion or sympathy or anything human.

"It's coming," he said. "Are you ready?"

She shook her head, tears welling again.

"Fighting it isn't going to stop a thing. This is your last moment. I suggest you try to meet it with grace. If it helps, I didn't pick you because of any perceived flaw. You were a nice woman, and I'm sure you'd have made Rob, or anyone else, very happy. Just your bad luck is all. You were just one of many that I've been watching. If any of the other Shedds had been receptive, you and I would never have met."

But all she could think was, *I'm sorry*. For the things she'd failed to do or been too scared to try. For the people she'd mistreated, for the relationships her pride had destroyed, for the stone wall of a daughter she'd been to her parents over bullshit that didn't matter, but mostly for the years she'd wasted waiting for someone to complete her when she should have been working on completing herself.

The tears came freely now, and Luther's dark eyes crinkled.

"I wept not, so to stone within I grew," he whispered.

His voice ripped her away from all the stunning regret, and raw fear enveloped her. She began to scream, her eyes closed, her voice gliding out over the river, becoming lost in the gentle water.

"They're going to write about you tomorrow," he said. "They're going to make you famous."

She opened her eyes and saw him pointing that talon toward the glowing *Chicago Sun-Times* sign, looming above the both of them like a neon cloud.

Then he turned the knife on her.

And the cutting began.

Jack Daniels
March 31, 9:15 a.m.

"Nervous?"

I glanced over at Phin, sitting next to me in the ER waiting room, and then back down at my gym shoes, my toe tapping so fast the Velcro straps were a blur.

I hated these shoes. Velcro was a way of shouting to the world, *"I give up! I don't care about my appearance anymore!"*

But it was true. I'd traded a four-hundred-dollar pair of Yves Saint Laurent pumps for some thirty-five-dollar Keds because my feet were too swollen to fit into anything remotely sexy. Worse than that was the XL T-shirt stretched taut over my waist, pulled over the no-belly shorts, which were still so tight I had the first two buttons undone. My body had become a hideous travesty, courtesy of the alien living inside of me.

An alien that was also trying to kill me, apparently not satisfied with mere physical ruination.

"Why should I be nervous?" I said. It came out clipped and more high-pitched than I would have liked. The air-conditioning was lukewarm, and the smell of lemon bleach was giving me a headache. "I either got better or I didn't. Either way, I still look like Humpty Dumpty."

"You look beautiful, Jack." Phin reached over and took one of my sweaty hands.

"I hate when you say that."

"You do. You're glowing."

His blue eyes shone in a pure, wholesome, loving way that made me want to smack him in the mouth. I turned away, staring at the other unfortunates in the waiting room.

ERs were the worst. An impromptu collection of people brought together by bad news and circumstance. Not that I preferred my ob-gyn's office. Her waiting room was filled with women half my age who liked to chat. Invariably their first question was always, "How old are you?"

Old enough to have known better than to get pregnant this late in life.

Phin's fingers caressed my hand and then sneakily rested on my wrist.

I pulled away.

"Just checking," he said.

"You don't need to check again. That's the reason we're here, isn't it?"

When we took my blood pressure this morning, it had been 160/100—dangerously high. So now we were at the ER checking my urine for protein to see if the preeclampsia had gotten worse. If it had, both Phin and my doctor were going to insist on inducing. But I was still three weeks early. Much as I wanted this kid out of my body, I feared *getting* this kid out of my body even more.

At forty-eight years old, I was still too young to be a mother. If I had three weeks left of being childless, I'd take them, even if all I was fit to do was eat fried pork rinds and watch soap operas with my feet propped up.

"Phin, you got any pork rinds?"

In preparation for my birth, Phin had begun carrying around a diaper bag, which, instead of diapers, he kept filled with various unhealthy snacks and several equally unhealthy firearms. It had gotten to the point where my shoulder holster didn't fit anymore and my ankle holster was too far down for me to reach, so Phin stayed armed for the both of us.

He fished around in the bag—a hideous accessory with Kermit the Frog on it—and came up with a bag of BBQ Fritos. Not as good as pork rinds, but they'd do in a pinch. I tore the bag open with my teeth and dug in.

Phin slapped his jeans, dug out his cell. He squinted at the screen.

"All clear," he read. "How about Mezcal?"

My business partner, Harry McGlade, was waiting outside the emergency room, standing guard. Many months ago, I'd run into a very bad man who'd promised he'd look me up again. Harry, Phin, and my old partner from the force, Herb Benedict, had taken that threat seriously, to the point of keeping a twenty-four-hour watch on me. As gallant as the gesture was, after more than half a year of tripping over them, I'd had enough of my trio of protectors. This was compounded by the fact that McGlade had taken it upon himself to name my forthcoming baby. Because I had the unfortunate moniker of Jack Daniels, McGlade figured the child should naturally be named after some kind of liquor.

"Text him back," I said. "Tell McGlade I'd rather name my kid Helga or Fanny than anything alcohol-related."

"I kinda like Mezcal," Phin said.

"You also liked Peppermint Schnapps."

"Pepper is a cool name for a little girl."

"Sure it is. Why don't we just buy her a little stripper pole for her crib?"

Phin smiled. He had two days' growth of beard and wore a white T-shirt and faded jeans. Last year he'd been bald from chemo, and even though he was in remission, he'd kept the look and had taken to shaving his head. All he needed was a gold hoop in his ear and he would have resembled a sexier version of Mr. Clean.

"This drink-name idea is growing on me," he said. "I can see myself as the proud papa, pushing along a baby carriage filled with little Stoli."

"Not gonna happen."

The image of Phin with a stroller popped into my head. But rather than picture him in a park or at a shopping mall, my mind's eye saw him pushing our baby into a bank, pulling a gun out of her diaper, and robbing the place. Phin was ten years my junior, and I'd first met him in a professional capacity, back when I used to be a cop. I'd arrested him. Though I believed he'd stayed on the right side of the law since knocking me up, I wasn't one hundred percent sure of it.

The nurse called my name, and I heaved myself out of the uncomfortable plastic chair and waddled my way into one of the exam rooms, where I was ordered to disrobe. Phin had to help me with my shoes. I stripped down to my sports bra—uncomfortably tight—and an enormous pair of granny panties that were the single most unflattering piece of clothing ever designed. But I'd lost all of my dignity shortly after the second trimester, so I didn't mind Phin seeing me like this. I plopped myself onto the exam table and lay there like a beached whale waiting to be rolled back into the sea.

A good-looking doctor came in through the curtain, holding a chart. "Mrs. Daniels?"

"Miss," I said. I almost corrected him with *Lieutenant*, but that had been a long time ago.

"I'm Dr. Aguier. I've got the urinalysis results. Your protein level is at three hundred and sixty milligrams, and your creatinine clearance is dangerously high."

Phin's face tightened. "That's worse than before."

"Any headaches or blurred vision?" the doctor asked.

I squinted at Dr. Aguier, pretending not to see him. "Who said that?"

"She's been having headaches," Phin tattled. "And tingling in her hands and feet."

"Any pain in the upper abdomen?"

"Even worse than the pain..." I lowered my voice to a whisper. "I think I have something growing inside of me."

"Jack, can you please be serious?" Phin had taken on a stern, almost parental tone. But I couldn't be serious. If I were serious, I wouldn't be able to hide how scared I truly felt.

"You're at thirty-seven weeks," the doctor said, glancing at the chart. "Has your primary care physician talked with you about inducing?"

"Yes," Phin and I answered in unison. But I added, "I won't do it."

"Eclampsia is a life-threatening condition for both you and your baby. Have you had any seizures?"

"No," I said.

"Yes," Phin said.

I turned to him. "When?"

"Last night, while you were sleeping. You began to shake really bad."

"It could have been another nightmare."

"I've seen enough of your nightmares. This was something else. Your whole body locked, and you were..." He trailed off.

"I was what?"

"Your mouth was foaming, Jack. Scared the shit out of me. Lasted about twenty seconds. You slept right through it. One second longer and I would have called nine-one-one."

Jesus.

Phin tugged out his phone again, glancing at the screen.

He began to walk away.

"Hey!" I called after him. "What is it?"

Phin stopped, and I saw a look on his face that was unfamiliar—fear. Not much scared Phin.

"What?" I demanded.

"It's from Herb. He's at a crime scene near the river."

I knew where this was going, but I asked anyway.

"Luther?"

Phin nodded once. "He's back."

Luther Kite
March 31, 9:30 a.m.

So much to do.

So very little time to do it.

But Luther is pleased.

After months—strike that—*years* of preparation, this is all coming together as smooth as smooth could be.

He stares at his iPhone.

So tempting to call.

To leave another clue. Another breadcrumb.

Getting her number had been child's play. One of the many times he visited her house to watch her, he helped himself to her mail and copied down her cell phone number from a bill. Luther was pleased to discover Jack also had a monthly charge for a portable WiFi hotspot. It was such a smart idea, carrying the Internet around with you, that Luther bought one for himself.

His fingers hover above the keys, poised to text, but then he thinks better of it.

Later, Jack.

No point in rushing anything.

Gratification is so much better when delayed.

A tapping on the driver's-side window pulls Luther's attention away from his iPhone.

A traffic cop is twirling his finger, motioning for Luther to lower the window.

Luther's breath catches in his chest.

If this cop sees what he has in the back of the van...

Luther rolls down the window, forcing his features to relax. "Yes, Officer?"

"You can't park here, buddy, unless you want a hundred-dollar ticket. It's a loading zone."

Luther's finger eases up on the trigger of the Glock he holds down between the door and the seat. "No problem, I'll move."

The officer leans in closer. "Mind if I ask you a question, buddy?"

Luther's finger again tightens on the trigger. "Sure."

"How much did this Mercedes Sprinter set you back, man? It's one sweet van."

"About seventy-five grand."

The cop edges in even closer, trying to peer into the darkness of the cargo area behind Luther.

"A friend of mine has one of these. Totally pimped out the back. Turned it into a little love mobile, if you know what I'm saying."

Luther allows himself a small smile. He's pimped this van out as well, but not for love.

"Yeah, I've made some modifications."

For an excruciating second, he thinks the officer is going to ask for a tour.

"But it's a real expensive vehicle," Luther adds with a hint of condescension in his voice. "I'm not sure a civil servant could afford a ride like this."

The cop's face hardens.

"Move it along."

"Have a nice day, Officer."

As Luther shifts into drive, he sees the professor enter the building.

Goddamn it, now he's going to have to pay for parking.

Jack
March 31, 9:30 a.m.

Against the tag-team protests of the doctor and my boy-friend, I dressed and got the hell out of there. Phin wasn't pleased. He refused to let me use his phone so I could call Herb and also refused to give up the diaper bag, which had my cell in it. I stormed outside, a cool, needling drizzle forcing me to squint, but then Phin made an even bigger mistake: he grabbed my wrist to hold me back.

"Jack, I can't let you go. You need to—"

I twisted my arm, breaking his hold, and then clamped onto his wrist and used momentum and leverage to put him in an armlock. He dropped to his knees, not because he was begging forgiveness, but because if he didn't, his elbow would hyperextend.

Or maybe it was for forgiveness. Angry as I was, we both knew I wouldn't hurt him.

"You don't tell me what I can and can't do, Phin. And you don't try to physically restrain me. Ever. Are we clear?"

Phin stared up at me, his expression resembling a dog who'd been kicked. "In your condition—"

"Luther is probably the most dangerous psychopath I've ever met, and I've met more than my fair share. I'm not going to spend the rest of my life peering over my shoulder, waiting for him to make his move."

"Let Herb handle it. He's good."

"I'm better."

"I couldn't take it if anything happened to you, Jack." He reached up, put his palm on my belly. "To either of you."

I felt his child kick in response.

I released Phin's wrist and headed toward the red Tesla Roadster 2.5 parked in a handicapped spot. The car was Harry McGlade's latest toy, fully electric and capable of zero to sixty in under four seconds. McGlade was sitting in the driver's seat, fiddling with his cell phone. I tapped on his window, startling him. He rolled it down and a frown creased his unshaven face, so much grayer now than when we'd been partners in Vice more than twenty years ago. Fate didn't like me much, and somehow I once again wound up as his partner, this time in the private sector. Working five hours a day with Harry McGlade now made me nostalgic for working eighteen-hour days in Homicide without Harry McGlade.

"You look angry," McGlade said. "Did the doctor tell you that you really aren't pregnant, just morbidly obese?"

"Is this how you watch my back? Playing games?"

"It's TowerMadness. The aliens are trying to take all of my sheep."

"Give me your phone."

He held it away from me. "You're going to break it."

"I'm not going to break it."

"I don't believe you. You've got those crazy preggo eyes. Like you're in a hormone rage."

"Give me your fucking phone or I'm going to rip your face off."

He gave me the phone. I called Herb.

"You're not coming down here," Herb said.

"If one more man in my life tries to tell me what I can and can't do, I'm going to scream."

"She's in a hormone rage!" McGlade yelled at the phone. "Run for the border! Save yourself!"

I didn't hear Herb's reply, because McGlade was being a loud idiot.

I walked away from the Tesla, trying to get out of loud idiot range.

"And she stole my phone!" McGlade yelled again.

"Can you say that again, Herb?"

"The Kinzie Street railroad bridge. It's a bad one, Jack."

"How do you know it's Luther Kite?"

Silence.

"Herb? You there?"

"He...uh...Luther left something. Something with your name on it. You really don't need to come here. I'll drop by your place when I'm finished."

"See you in ten."

I pressed the end call button.

A vehicle pulled up alongside me—Phin in his new Ford Bronco.

"I'm sorry," he said. "Need a ride?"

I put my hands on my ever-expanding hips. "Will you take me to the crime scene? Or are you going to try to control me again?"

"I think I can restrain myself."

I was still ticked-off at Phin, but the alternative was riding with McGlade. Being stuck in a car with Harry McGlade was slightly less pleasant than having cavities drilled.

"Okay. Hold on." I returned the phone to Harry and told him where we were headed.

He frowned. "You sure you want to do this, in your condition?"

"I'm pregnant, McGlade, not helpless."

"What about your precognition disease?"

"It's preeclampsia."

"For some reason I knew you were going to say that."

I sighed. "That's precognition."

"I thought you said it was preeclampsia."

"It is. You're the one with precognition if you knew what I was going to say."

He shrugged. "I probably picked it up from some call girl. I should have seen that coming."

It was always a puzzler whether McGlade just liked to mess with people's heads, or if he truly was that stupid. I voted for stupid.

"You're stupid," I told him.

"And you're huge. I can actually feel the pull from your gravity. Shouldn't you be home in bed letting things orbit you?"

I frowned. "I'll still have preeclampsia whether Luther Kite is on the loose or not. I'd prefer for him to be out of the picture."

"Okay. Lemme beat the Dice level on TowerMadness and I'll meet you there. Shouldn't be more than twenty minutes."

My crazy preggo eyes bored into him.

"Kidding," he said. "I'm on my way."

I hoofed it back to the Bronco, and Phin and I drove in a strained silence to the police blockade on Kinzie—six black-

and-whites, lights flashing. A traffic cop tried to wave us past, but I spotted a tall guy I knew standing among the uniforms.

"I'll get out here," I told Phin.

His mouth became a tight line. "I don't like you being out of my sight."

"They won't let you on scene."

"Why are they letting *you* on scene? You aren't a cop any-more."

"I have friends in high places. Besides, the Chicago Police Department owes me."

He continued to give me a pained look. "You know how worried I am about you?"

"There are two dozen cops here," I said. "I'll be fine."

"That's not what I'm worried about, Jack. The doctor said—"

"It was just one seizure, Phin. You're overreacting."

His eyes went hard. "Overreacting? He was talking about the possibility of your liver rupturing. Kidney failure."

"The odds are against it."

"Coma."

"Not going to happen."

"Death, Jack. You *and* the baby."

"No one is going to die," I said. This worrywart, senti-mental side to Phin was off-putting. I preferred the guy who beat up gangbangers and stole cars.

"Jack..."

"Just give me my phone."

Reluctantly, he reached into the diaper bag, and I spotted another bag of chips. I was tempted to ask for those as well, but managed to control the craving. Besides, eating chips at a mur-der scene was probably bad taste, no matter how delicious they were and how much every cell in my body screamed for them.

Pregnancy sucked.

"Be back in ten minutes," I said, and then exited the vehicle and walked into the fray.

One of the uniforms stopped me, and I asked him to get Detective Tom Mankowski. After a brief exchange, the tall guy sauntered over, his face breaking into a smile when he saw me. He had longish hair, a strong nose and chin, and in profile bore a striking resemblance to Thomas Jefferson on the nickel.

"Hey, Lieut. Congrats on the baby."

"Thanks, Tom. And you don't have to call me Lieut anymore."

He grinned. "Old habits. You want to take the tour? They already cut the body down."

"From where?"

He pointed to the Kinzie Street railroad bridge, jutting over a hundred feet into the air at a forty-five degree angle, just one more architectural erection in a city filled with them. The rusted bridge had been locked into a permanent raised position years ago, when it fell out of use. Constructed of crisscrossing girders, it shared the same antique, utilitarian look as the Eiffel Tower. Tom was pointing to the bridge's midsection, where I saw a length of rope dangling down into the river below. Beneath the bridge, on a wooden walkway, I spotted several paramedics and the obligatory sheet-covered body. Behind them, in the parking lot of the *Chicago Sun-Times* building, media vans and reporters had gathered behind yellow crime scene tape.

Tom led me through the chaos, down some concrete steps, and over to the body. It was windier, and a good five degrees cooler, on the pier. A river smell—partly water, partly muck—wafted up at me. My old partner and good friend, Sergeant Herb Benedict, was leaning against one of the bridge supports. He wore a gray, off-the-rack Sears suit, a tie too wide by several decades, and a large mustard stain on his lapel. When he saw me, his walrus mustache turned down.

"Damn it, Jack. You shouldn't be here."

"Time of death?" I asked.

Herb sighed. "ME says between two and three a.m."

I looked around, didn't see the medical examiner.

"Where's Hughes?"

"Getting coffee. Jack, you really should—"

"Don't start, Herb." I clasped my hands, discreetly rubbing away the pins-and-needles sensation that had begun during my walk over. "How was she hung up there?"

"By her wrists. Rock-climbing rope, looped over one of the girders."

"Traceable?"

"We're checking it out. But probably not. You can buy parachute line anywhere. I got some on Amazon.com that I use for shoelaces. Unbreakable."

I peered up into the gray, overcast sky, drizzle speckling my face, squinting at the underside of the bridge. "How far up?"

"About forty feet."

It was too steep to climb. "Grappling hook?" I asked.

Tom shook his head. "Implausible."

"How do you know?" I asked.

"They tried it on that show, *Mythbusters*. Can't throw one more than twenty feet high."

"So how'd he get the rope up there?" Herb asked.

While they looked up, I looked down, searching the scarred, wooden dock. After ten seconds, I bent over, spotting something that looked like a gray stone.

"Got your gloves on?" I asked Tom. "And a bag?"

Tom fished out a pair of latex gloves and snapped them on. Herb provided him with a plastic evidence bag. Tom nudged the lead weight inside, using a knuckle. It was teardrop shaped, about the size of a walnut, weighing several ounces. On the end, a brass clip, with a bit of monofilament knotted on.

"Fishing sinker," Herb said.

Tom nodded, getting it. "Tied to a thirty-pound test line. He threw it up there, hooked it around a support beam, then tied it to the rope and pulled it up."

"Threw it," I said. "Or cast the weight with a pole."

"Think he talked the vic into coming down here to do a little night fishing?"

I shook my head. "Not with a hundred feet of climbing rope wrapped around his chest." I stared back at the reporters. "Does the *Sun-Times* monitor its parking lot at night?"

"They've got a watchman," Herb said. "No cameras."

"Killer probably parked there, had his gear in the trunk. Or he had it waiting for him on the scene when he arrived with the vic. You check the walkway with an alternate light source?"

Herb nodded. "No blood."

I clucked my tongue, thinking. "So he lured her down here, or brought her down unconscious, and killed her on the spot. Fingernails?"

"Clean," Herb said.

Often victims would scratch their attackers, giving us DNA evidence. Clean nails meant the murderer had been in control for the duration of the crime.

I eyed the climbing rope swaying in the breeze. Trying to haul up a body attached to one end would have required a great deal of physical strength and effort. Or...

I spotted the other end of the rope, wound around the railing near the stairs. "Ask the watchman if he saw any trucks or vans with a trailer hitch. I bet he tied the other end to his vehicle, pulled the vic up by towing her."

Now to the part I'd been dreading. I turned my attention to the body under the bloody sheet. "We have an ID?"

"Jack." The tone in Herb's voice wasn't a warning. He was pleading with me not to continue.

"ID?" I repeated.

He sighed. "Purse was on her. Jessica Shedd. Lives in Wrigleyville."

"Cause of death?"

"Hypovolemia."

Blood loss. I felt the baby kick, or maybe it was my stomach doing flips. Much as I didn't want to view the victim, I asked Tom to lift up a corner of the sheet. Since I was a civilian and couldn't interfere with the chain of evidence, I might mess up the prosecutor's case if I touched anything.

Tom complied, and I forced myself to remain detached.

"Jogger spotted her this morning at dawn, called it in. When I got on scene, I thought she had some extra ropes hanging from her. But they weren't ropes…"

Herb's voice trailed off, and I tried not to look at the loops of intestines snaking out all over the dock. She was naked, on her side, her wrists bound together with plastic zip line. I focused on her face. Eyes wide. Mouth hidden under a strip of duct tape. I backed away, the stench commingling with the rank smell of the river.

I took out my iPhone.

"Sorry, Jessica," I whispered, taking a few pictures. Then I turned to Herb. "You said the killer left me something."

"It's still, uh, in her…"

Herb glanced down, and I forced myself to stare at her slit-open belly.

It had been partially buried in the offal—a paperback book in a zippered plastic bag, so covered with blood that it almost looked like another organ.

I squatted, holding my breath, squinting through the gore.

Written on the bag in permanent black marker:

JACK D—THIS ONE WAS A REAL SWINGER—LK

Herb took some pictures. Tom knelt beside me and tried to lift the book, but met resistance.

"It's wired to her ribs," he said, his expression a mixture of revulsion and anger.

It took a few minutes to locate a pair of wire cutters, and the paramedics did the job while I stared out over the river, rubbing my belly, thinking back to my last encounter with Luther. Remembering the promise he'd made me.

"I'll be seeing you. Soon."

I shivered, suddenly very cold. Herb stood beside me.

"Did Phin and Harry talk to you about Lake Geneva?" he asked.

"Lake Geneva? In Wisconsin? Why?"

"There's a spa there, specifically for pregnant women. We were all thinking...maybe it would be a good idea for you to take it easy these next few weeks. Get out of town."

"My doctor is here in Chicago."

"The spa has some of the best doctors in the state, Jack."

I eyed my friend, saw true concern on his chubby features. "If I ran away every time some lunatic made me a target..."

"She was alive, Jack. When Luther hauled her up. Hughes says she could have been struggling for a few minutes, maybe even half an hour. It looks like raw butchery, but there was actually a lot of skill involved. She didn't die right away."

I wiggled my toes, which felt like they'd fallen asleep.

"I quit the force to get away from all of this," I said softly.

"I know. Hopefully this will be the last one."

"Yeah. Hopefully."

"So, Geneva..."

I shook my head, willing my strength to return. "While it's flattering to have the three of you try to decide my fate, I'll pass. And I kindly caution you not to do anything like that ever—"

"Enough," Herb said.

I turned to him, surprised by the anger in his voice.

"You've been playing this macho mother bullshit for too long, Jack. We're trying to help you, and you're fighting us every step of the way. You *cannot* do this alone. All you're accomplishing is hurting yourself and the people who care about you."

I was unsure of how to answer. Herb and I rarely fought about anything, and him scolding me like that left me at a loss for words.

"Got it!" We turned to look at Tom, who was holding up a paperback book like a trophy. He eased it out of the bloody bag.

"*The Scorcher*, an Andrew Z. Thomas Thriller," he read off the garish cover, which depicted the face of a demented man grinning while holding up a lighter.

"Thomas?" Herb said. "He was that infamous writer. Allegedly killed a bunch of people and then vanished."

"I read this one," Tom said, tapping the book's spine. "A pyro is setting all of these people on fire. Got this one scene where the bad guy fills one of his victims with lighter fluid by sticking a hose down his throat. Then throws lit matches into his open mouth until he ignites."

"Nice," I said, wondering what sort of warped mind could think up something like that. I'd hate to meet one of those thriller writers in person.

"It was actually pretty good," Tom said, apparently sensing my distaste. "Held back on the really gross stuff. Sort of like Stephen King–lite."

"Check if anything is inside," I told him.

Tom flipped through the book, found a dog-eared page around the midpoint.

Chapter thirty-one, page 102.

Strangely, the letter *p* in the word *cops* had been circled.

I gave it a quick scan.

The Scorcher ~ Andrew Z. Thomas

The cops were everywhere. Sizzle could see the lights from the pigs' cars flashing through the windows. They had the warehouse surrounded, their pig-voices blaring through the bull-horns, ordering him to come outside, to surrender.

Huh. Surrender.

Stupid, stupid pigs.

He glanced back at the only bargaining chip he had. Revise that: *had* had. The FBI agent was still cuffed to the metal folding chair, but he looked like a marshmallow left smoldering over the campfire too long. Pitch black. A tar baby. Still smoking. What a sad thing. The last person he'd ever have the pleasure of burning.

"Christopher Rogers..." That pig-negotiator again. "We just want to talk to you."

Hmm.

Or maybe not.

There was still a half-can of gasoline remaining.

A book of matches.

Sizzle sat down on the oil-stained concrete. Truth be told, he'd never considered this. Probably because of the unimaginable pain involved, but there were things worse than pain. Like being locked up away from what you loved most.

He opened the gas can, poured it over his head, those beautiful fumes encompassing him as the pigs droned on outside about surrender and "establishing a dialogue."

Now the fun part. The easy part. The hard part.

The matchbook was from a swank hotel he occasionally treated himself to in Asheville, North Carolina...The Grove Park Inn. Sizzle flipped it open, plucked a match.

No self-reflection, no reminisces.

He just wanted to smell it, even if the smell was his own flesh burning.

He struck a match, stared for three long seconds at the gorgeous yellow flame.

"A little spark is followed by a great flame."

102

Knowing I wouldn't have easy access to the book again, I asked Tom to hold it up and took pictures of that page and of the cover. Then Herb passed it along to the lab guys.

"So who is LK?" Tom asked me. Herb apparently hadn't briefed him.

"We think it's Luther Kite," I said.

Tom nodded solemnly. Everyone had heard about my encounter with Kite. I had to testify at the inquest of the person I'd watched him murder. At the time, I'd sustained a broken leg. That had healed, but the things I'd been forced to watch...

Let's just say I'd rather have both my legs broken than see that again.

Phin had no idea how bad my nightmares actually were. Though I'd managed to stay clear of shrinks, some late-night Internet research supported my suspicion that I exhibited many of the symptoms of post-traumatic stress disorder. It was something I planned to attend to, after I gave birth and got Kite out of the picture. Until then, sleep and I had never been on good terms anyway. And it wasn't like my hypertension could get any worse.

"Now that I think of it," Tom said, rubbing his chin, "there's rumor of a connection between Luther Kite and Andrew Z. Thomas."

"What connection?"

"I read a lot, and sometimes I'll check an author's Wikipedia page. I went to the Thomas Wiki a few months back, after I read his book *The Passenger*. There are some old, unsolved crimes where both Thomas and Kite were at the same place at the same time. It's been fodder for a lot of wild theories on Thomas's website."

The paramedics came with a body bag and began to take away Jessica.

I knew there was nothing more I could do here. I wasn't a cop anymore.

But I could begin researching a connection between Kite and Thomas. Kite, evil though he undoubtedly was, didn't have much of a police record. He was wanted for questioning in connection to a handful of crimes, and there was an arrest warrant out for him in Chicago, but surprisingly little was known about him.

I tried to text Phin, to tell him I was ready to leave, but my hand refused to work. I watched it for a moment, shaking in a palsy, and then it suddenly seemed like none of this was real, that I was in a dream and just waking up. But I couldn't wake. Instead, everything got smaller and smaller, as if my mind was falling into a deep well.

Then it all went black.

Luther

March 15, Sixteen Days Ago

Eighteen Hours After the Bus Incident

"*A*nd what's your name?"

"*Patricia.*"

"*Patricia what?*"

"*Reid.*"

"*May I call you Pat?*"

"*Um, yes. Are you going to let me go?*"

"*I'm going to be asking the questions here, Pat.*"

"*Oh. I'm sorry.*"

"*It's quite all right. Pat, do you believe you're perfect?*"

"*No. Not at all.*"

"*Are you afraid, Pat?*"

"*Yes.*"

"*That's good. Fear of me is the beginning of wisdom. I'm going to ask you a few questions. I want you to answer honestly and with complete candor. You heard the screaming next door, I take it?*" He gestures to the concrete wall.

"*Yes.*"

"That gentleman didn't think his private sins were any of my business. He made me hurt him. I wouldn't mind hurting you, Pat."

"You won't have to."

"Then you must tell me...what's the worst thing you've ever done? Your deepest, darkest, gravest sin."

"I don't know."

"Well, take a moment to think about it."

He watches her eyes flick to the bare lightbulb shining overhead.

"I don't want to say."

He lifts the Harpy off the metal table, opens it. Usually, just seeing the wicked, curving blade is enough. Pat's eyes get wide.

"My husband..."

"Yes?"

"I cheated on him."

"Once, or..."

"Several times...many times."

"Did he ever find out?"

She shakes her head, and he can see that she's telling the truth, that a nerve has been struck, because her eyes have begun to well up with tears.

"He died last year," she says.

"Sudden?"

"Yes."

"So you never got the chance to come clean."

"It kills me. It eats at me. Every single day."

"But maybe it's better he died not knowing? Died believing you were the perfect, faithful wife?"

"I don't know. He was my friend. I shared everything with him."

Luther reaches across the table and touches her hand.

"Thank you, Pat. Thank you so much."

Jack
March 31, 10:30 a.m.

"She has preeclampsia," someone said.

The voice sounded familiar. I opened my eyes, but instead of being home in bed, I found myself strapped to a gurney in the back of an ambulance. Phin was holding my hand.

"No, she doesn't." A woman. Paramedic. Bulging cheeks and a stern expression. "That was a tonic-clonic seizure. This isn't preeclampsia. It's full-on eclampsia. Why isn't this woman on bed rest?"

"This woman can hear you," I said, though my tongue felt thick and the words came out more slurred than I'd expected.

I heard a rapid *beepbeepbeepbeep* and saw some sensors on my enormous, protruding, bare belly. I traced the sound to a machine.

"Cardiograph looks okay," said the medic. "The fetus doesn't appear to be in distress. But you should be at home, resting. Has anyone talked to you about inducing?"

I tried to sit up, but the strap around my shoulders wouldn't let me. I could see Herb, Tom, and McGlade all staring at me through the rear ambulance doors, each practicing their expressions of intense disapproval. Though McGlade's looked more like a hangover.

"Can I leave?" I asked.

"We should take you to the hospital for observation. Your husband said—"

I shot Phin a glance. "He's not my husband. Unstrap me. Now."

The medic didn't move.

"Look," I said. "I promise I'll go straight home and rest. I know all about eclampsia. There's nothing that can be done to treat it, other than giving birth. And I've still got three weeks before that happens. So there is absolutely no reason for me to go to the hospital. I'm fine."

"You're not fine," the paramedic said. "The next time you have a convulsion, you may not ever wake up again. If you know all about eclampsia, then you're familiar with the term *multi-organ failure.* Both you and your baby are in serious danger. You should go to the hospital."

"That's my choice," I said. "Not yours." I met Phin's eyes. "And not his." I noticed I had an IV in my arm. "What's that?"

"Magnesium sulfate. For the convulsions."

"It's making me sick."

"No, that's your toxic body making you sick. You've basically become a factory for manufacturing poisons. Until you have this child—"

I nearly lost it. The tears welled up suddenly, and almost erupted in a sobbing jag to end all sobbing jags. I was stubborn, but I wasn't an idiot. I knew I was acting like a selfish asshole. I knew inducing labor was the right thing to do. I knew I needed to apologize to Phin and everyone else.

But I managed to squeeze my eyes shut and keep everything inside. It was more than just my unpreparedness for motherhood. There was a very bad man after me. A bad man who no doubt knew my doctors, knew my due date, and might very well be watching me right now.

I wasn't prepared to fight that man while a baby suckled at my breast. And as vulnerable as I was, I couldn't rely on my friends to get me out of this mess.

But maybe I could compromise a little.

"Geneva," I said, my voice cracking. "I'll go to Geneva."

I felt Phin grasp my hand.

"You're sure?" he whispered.

I nodded, no longer able to trust talking without blubbering.

"Thank you, Jack," Phin said, kissing my forehead.

I somehow managed to mumble, "Please take me home," without having a complete breakdown.

Reginald Marquette
March 31, 11:30 a.m.

Midmorning on the third floor of Lewisohn Hall, the dismal light crept in through the blinds into the cluttered, cramped office of Reginald Marquette, PhD, Department Chair of Ancient Literature at Columbia College.

The knock at the door drew Marquette's head up from the paper he'd been reading—a twenty-five-page thesis on William Blake's *Proverb of Hell* that was so well-done he was almost certain the author hadn't written a single word of it. She'd been a solid C student all semester, and had never produced anything approaching this caliber of excellence. Her mistake was in not buying the B version and keeping this quantum leap in academic performance plausible.

Marquette set the paper aside and worked his way between stacks of books and papers and prehistoric correspondence, some of which bore postmarks from the previous decade. But the disorganization didn't bother him. He thrived in chaos. As he moved toward the door, his only thought was how much he was looking forward to locating whatever website this

William Blake scholar had used to purchase her term paper. Maybe he'd surprise her with a rigorous oral exam on her two dozen sources next class.

Watch her twist and blush and stutter.

You had to make an example out of cheaters.

A painful, public, humiliating example.

Marquette opened the door to a man with long, black hair tied up in a ponytail, who sported a black blazer over blue jeans. Black cowboy boots completed his unusual costume.

"May I help you?" he asked.

"Professor Marquette?"

"That's right."

The man extended his hand.

"Rob Siders from Ancient Publishing. I e-mailed you last week regarding our interest in publishing your work on Dante."

Marquette smiled as he shook the man's hand.

"Of course. Yes. I'm sorry. You mentioned you'd be stopping by, didn't you? Please, come in."

Marquette ushered him inside and closed the door after them.

He lifted the stack of his embattled TA's student reviews off a chair, said, "Have a seat. I apologize for the mess, but there is actually a system in place here, as unlikely as it may appear."

When they were finally sitting across from each other at the desk, Marquette said, "May I offer you a cup of coffee or tea or water? I could probably wrangle something up in the faculty lounge."

"No, I'm fine, thanks. It's a great honor to meet you, Dr. Marquette."

"Please, Reggie."

"Your work is amazing, Reggie."

Marquette puffed his chest up. "Oh, thank you."

"Busy morning?"

"Just catching up on some grading for my eighteenth-century English lit class. I have to say, your e-mail was intriguing, but would you mind telling me a little more about you and your company? I couldn't find much information on the Internet."

"We're a boutique publisher of academic work of the highest quality. I'm the editorial director and co-founder, and I've been searching for someone like you for quite a while."

"What do you mean, 'someone like me'?"

"A true scholar who can bring *The Divine Comedy* to twenty-first-century readers like it's never been presented before."

"Wait...you're talking about a translation? Didn't Pinsky already knock that out of the park back in—"

"I'm not talking about another inaccessible translation. I'm talking about an adaptation."

Marquette straightened in his chair. "I'm not following."

"We're looking for something written in modern language. Possibly even using modern historical figures."

Marquette laughed. "You mean like putting Bill Clinton in the second circle?"

"Exactly. And Bernie Madoff in the eighth, and so on."

"Who's in the ninth?"

"I have no idea. That's where you would come in with your vast knowledge of the mood and intent of the original text. We want a book that can communicate to present-day American masses, just as Dante's masterpiece reached his Italian countrymen back in the fourteenth century."

Marquette felt a shudder of excitement.

An adaptation for the masses could mean recognition. Serious recognition, beyond the handful of academics who subscribed to the same six scholarly journals.

And he did have a sabbatical scheduled for the fall term.

"Of course, you don't have to decide right now," Siders said, rising from his chair, buttoning his blazer. "Are you free for lunch? I can lay it all out for you. We are offering a sizeable advance."

Marquette leaned back in his chair and scratched under his chin at the salt-and-pepper goatee. His wife, an economics professor at Northwestern, did have a midday mixer for her department faculty that he had kind of promised to attend, but the last thing he wanted to do was spend several hours mingling with a bunch of accountants dressed up like teachers.

"That'd be lovely," he said.

The pale man smiled. "Perfect. And I brought the company credit card, so lunch is on me."

Jack

March 31, Noon

Home was a house in a secluded, woodsy area in the western suburb of Bensenville. I moved there with my mother a while back, but my mom had since gone on to a Florida retirement community (where, according to a phone call from her last week, she had to buy a new mattress because she wore the other one out with sexual escapades). Now I lived there with Phin, an ill-tempered cat named Mr. Friskers, and a basset hound named Duffy who was a gift from a friend also named Duffy.

Phin pulled into the driveway and hit the unlock code for the garage door. When he parked inside, I entered the disarm code for one of our three burglar alarms. I walked into the house, disarmed the second alarm, and patted the third one on the head. As usual, Duffy was barking his head off, and truth be told, I trusted him more than I trusted the electronic systems. Though he only weighed about eighty pounds, his bark was loud and deep, and sounded like it sprang from a giant Rottweiler.

Duffy gave my hand a lick, his tail wagging furiously. With his stunted legs and sagging belly, he looked like someone had stepped on a very fat beagle. Duffy the guy had dropped Duffy the dog over at my place a few months ago when he caught wind of my current situation with Luther Kite. I'd grown quite fond of the hound, who liked to sing whenever I took a shower, and he was the only creature on the planet that Mr. Friskers seemed to tolerate.

Phin locked up behind me, and I waddled into my office, kicked off my shoes, and plopped my fat ass into my computer chair. I was exhausted and hungry. But before I could rest or eat, I had some work to do.

First item on the agenda was calling Duffy the guy—Duffy Dombrowski. I met him some time ago on a trip to New York. He was a counselor who moonlighted as a pro boxer, and I guessed he might have had a crush on me. Or vice-versa.

He answered on the third ring. "Yeah?"

"Duff, Jack Daniels."

"Hey, Jack. How's stuff?"

"Stuff's fine. I need you to take Duffy for a few weeks."

"Everything okay?"

"I'm going to this pregnancy spa, and I don't want to kennel him. I can give you some money for food."

"You'll do no such thing. And I'd be happy to take him for a while."

"He eats his weight in dog food every five hours."

"That little? You trying to starve him to death?"

I smiled. "I can ship him to you. You still living in that trailer?"

"Chateau Dombrowski is still my summer home. In winter, I've got a Swiss chalet."

"You can't even spell *chalet*."

"I can't even spell *Swiss*. When can I expect the beast?"

"I'll text you."

"Looking forward. Everything else, uh, okay?"

"Fine," I lied. "With you?"

"Life's a banquet, and I've got forks for hands."

"Thanks, Duff. I owe you one."

I hung up, then started up Firefox and logged onto the NCIC. The National Crime Information Center was a database maintained by the Feds. Since jurisdictions were local, a cop in Milwaukee had no way of knowing that the killer he was after had the same MO as one in Boston. But if both precincts filled out NCIC reports and uploaded them to the server, then bad guys who crossed state lines could have their movements tracked.

With Duffy sitting under my desk, drooling on my bare feet, I accessed the NCIC data on Andrew Z. Thomas.

While it printed, I refreshed myself on Luther Kite. As I remembered, there was nothing solid. His sister was abducted at a young age and never found. His parents had been killed several years ago. According to NCIC, he was wanted for questioning or warrants in connection with the following:

November 7, 1996 shooting at Ricki's Bar in Scottsbluff, Nebraska

October 27, 2003 murder of Worthington Family in Davidson, NC

October 27, 2003 abduction of Beth Lancing in Davidson, NC

October 28, 2003 murder of Daniel Ortega in Wal-Mart, Rocky Mount, NC

October 28, 2003 murder of Karen Prescott on Bodie Island, NC

Undated murders connected to numerous bodies uncovered in the basement of the Kite residence on Ocracoke Island on November 14, 2003

November 11, 2003 or thereabouts murder of Sgt. Barry Mullins and Max King

November 11, 2003 murder of Beth Lancing and Charlie and Margaret Tatum

November 12, 2003 Kinnakeet Ferry Massacre

Plus the arrest warrant for the murder of August 10, 2010, with which I was intimately familiar.

Thomas's data was even slimmer.

October 30, 1996 murder of Jeanette Thomas, his mother

Disappearance of Walter Lancing in early November, 1996

Heart Surgeon Murders, including boxes left at Ellipse in Washington, DC, and the bodies unearthed on Thomas's lakefront property on Lake Norman, NC, including schoolteacher Rita Jones

November 7, 1996 shooting at Ricki's Bar in Scottsbluff, Nebraska

November 12, 2003 Kinnakeet Ferry Massacre

Disappearance of Davidson Police Department Homicide Detective Violet King

Duffy the dog fell asleep on my feet, snoring like a chainsaw. I chewed my lower lip, mulling over the data. The connection between the two was the Ricki's Bar shooting and the Kinnakeet Massacre. I was about to Google them both when I realized that someone, or many someones, might have already done the work for me.

I surfed over to Wikipedia and looked up Thomas, and as expected, user-aggregated content gave me more information than I could have found on my own in an hour of surfing.

Settling back in my chair, I began to read, learning more than I ever wanted to about the world's most mysterious mystery writer.

Reginald Marquette
March 31, 12:15 p.m.

"I'll drive," Rob Siders said as they walked down the sidewalk away from Lewisohn Hall, toward a white Mercedes van with tinted windows, parked on the curb. "Any favorite spots?"

"There's a great sushi place a couple miles up on State Street. Why don't you follow me up there? That'd probably make more sense."

"No, I'm staying down at the Blackstone. I've got to come back down this way anyhow."

Siders disappeared around the front of the van, but Marquette hesitated for a moment on the sidewalk adjacent to the curb. It was stupid and irrational—he knew this—but there was still this voice in the back of his head asking why an editor from Ancient Publishing was driving around in what he and his wife had always laughingly referred to as "a serial killer ride." A stark white cargo van, nondescript, and possibly filled with horrors.

Of course, that wasn't the case, but still, some small part of him felt unnerved at the prospect of getting in.

The driver's-side door slammed.

The engine roared to life.

Hell with it. Life is about taking chances.

He reached for the front passenger door, tugged it open.

As he climbed up into the seat, a strange smell wafted out of the back of the van—something astringent like Windex or ammonia.

"Buckle up for safety," Siders said, glancing over at him and smiling.

Marquette pulled the harness across his chest and clicked in the buckle.

Siders shifted into drive, eased out into the street.

Marquette stared through the deeply tinted glass, watching as they passed groups of students lounging in Grant Park.

A typical spring day—wet and chilly. It was the first of April, the grass and the trees just beginning to pop with pale baby greens and yellows. He'd always loved this time of year.

Classes winding down.

The blessed summer just within reach.

"How long has Ancient Publishing been in business?" he asked.

"About two years. Mind if I borrow your cell phone?"

Little weird, but whatever. "Um, sure."

Marquette dug his HTC Thunderbolt out of his pocket, handed it over.

"Thinking about getting one?" he asked.

"No, I don't like the Droid operating system. More of an iPhone guy myself."

Siders's window hummed down halfway, Marquette watching in astonishment as he tossed the phone outside and then held the button to scroll the window back up into the door.

"Why the hell did you do that?" Marquette said.

Siders's black eyes remained hidden behind a pair of shades.

He stared straight ahead through the glass and drove on without speaking.

"Stop the car. I want out."

Marquette reached down to unbuckle his seatbelt and found no button. Just a smooth, square face of metal, inset with what appeared to be a hole for a small-gauge Allen wrench. And the belt remained tight when he tugged on it, no play at all.

He glanced at the door—no handle, no mechanism for lowering the window.

The blast of fear hit him like a freight train.

He turned and looked at Siders.

"What do you want with me?"

"Let's just say, I love your name."

The man shot him a quick, smirking glance, and Marquette noticed for the first time the black curtain that separated the two front seats from the rear of the van.

"Curious to know what's back there?" Siders asked. "Go ahead. Have a look."

Marquette swept the curtain back as Siders flicked a button in the ceiling.

A dome light illuminated the back of the van under a hard, clinical glare.

Dark windows.

No carpeting.

The ceiling and the sidewalls had been reinforced with black soundproofing foam.

In the center of the white metal floor, he spotted a drain capped with a large, rubber plug.

Along the driver's-side wall, a tool cabinet had been bolted into the floor, holding shelves of surgical tools—forceps, saws, scalpels, steel retractors, clamps.

He looked back at Siders.

"You're him, aren't you? The man who hung that woman off the railroad bridge."

Siders smiled. "You saw that, huh?"

"That was you?"

"That was all me."

Marquette squirmed in his seat, attempting to slide out of the lap belt.

"Don't do that," Siders warned.

Marquette cocked his left arm back and punched the passenger's-side window, crying out as his hand bounced off, leaving a blood smear across the glass.

Siders began to laugh.

Through the fear, Marquette managed to blurt, "I can take you to an ATM right now."

"Yeah? What's your daily limit?"

"Two thousand. And I won't tell a soul, I swear to God."

Marquette knew his knuckles were broken, but he scarcely felt the pain. The overriding sensation was a tightness like a dumbbell sitting on his sternum, turning each breath into a quick, shallow gasp that was making him dizzier and more lightheaded by the moment.

"I have a family. A wife..." Tears beginning to sheet over his eyes. "A daughter."

"Good for you. Will they miss you?"

"Very much."

Siders gave him a sideways glance. "It's a good thing to be missed, don't you think?"

"Please."

"Don't you beg me. That's the only warning you'll get. And don't try to hit me." Siders showed him the pistol in his left hand.

Marquette looked out his window, saw that they were heading south on Lakeshore Drive. A few strands of sunlight had finally broken through the cloud deck, slanting down into the surface of the lake. Subjected to the onslaught of the sun, it didn't even resemble water. More like a field of shimmering jewels.

They skirted Solider Field.

Traffic was light.

Marquette considered his life. He had family, friends. His feelings for them were pure, but nothing extraordinary. Nothing about his life was extraordinary. He'd spent endless hours at a liberal arts college, teaching uncaring teenagers who needed the credit to graduate, and in his spare time he'd studied the writings of people who had died hundreds of years ago.

Still, it was *his* life. Marquette had lived it as best as he could. Made some mistakes, had a few regrets, but there were still things he wanted to do. Stand in a castle in Scotland. Swim with dolphins. And though it was cliché, he'd always planned to get around to skydiving someday.

But now, all he wanted was to see his family. One last time.

"Can I call my wife?" His lower lip quivered, the tears starting to come. "Tell her goodbye?"

"No."

Siders parked near Adler Planetarium and killed the engine. The sun coming through the windshield made it tough to see anything.

"There is some good news here," Siders said.

"What?"

"All those scary-looking tools you saw back there? That's postmortem entertainment."

"What are you talking about?" He was having a hard time following, his thoughts coming at him in fractured streams of fear and sorrow and regret.

"You're getting off easy is what I'm saying. See this?" Siders held up a cheap-looking paperback book with a garish cover. The title was *The Killer and His Weapon*. "The girl on the bridge? She became intimately familiar with another book by the same author. Ever read him?"

Marquette squinted at the writer's name. "Andrew Z. Thomas? No, no I haven't."

Siders smiled. "Trust me. This one will *really* get under your skin. Look here."

Marquette looked at the man's other hand, saw he was holding a syringe.

"What's that?"

"One hundred milliequivalents of potassium chloride. It's the final stage of state-sponsored lethal injections."

Marquette looked at the needle. At the clear liquid in the cylindrical tube.

"What does it do?" he asked.

"Stops your heart."

"How long does it..." He couldn't get the words out.

"To die? Between two and ten minutes."

"Does it hurt?"

"I'm not going to lie to you. Having your heart stop hurts. But not nearly as much as what's behind the black curtain."

This conversation had gone from surreal to positively insane. "Will...will I be conscious after my heart stops?"

"I don't know, brother. That's part of the mystery of what lies beyond, that you're on the verge of knowing. It's kind of exciting, actually."

Marquette looked out over the harbor, the skyline standing indistinct in the haze.

"I'm not ready," he said.

His heart beating so fast.

"No one's ever ready," the man said. "I could've done this anywhere, you know. Figured you loved this city. That you'd want to go sitting back, staring at the skyline across the water."

"I haven't talked to my daughter in two years. A stupid fight."

"Most fights are."

"Do you...have family?"

"Not for a long, long time."

"I need to apologize to her."

"Okay."

"Okay?"

Marquette turned away from the window.

"I'll let you call her."

"You're serious?"

The man pulled an iPhone out of an inner pocket in his jacket, glanced at it. "Sure, we've still got a little time. And a friend of mine once told me that murder shouldn't be without its little courtesies. What's her number?"

"Oh, thank you. Thank you." He had to think for a moment, years since he'd dialed it.

As the man punched it in, he prayed for the first time in ages.

Prayed her number hadn't changed. Prayed she'd answer.

The man held up the iPhone screen, her number displayed.

"You understand what the purpose of this call is *not*, correct?"

"Yes."

"If you try to save yourself, give away our location, anything like that..."

"I understand. Completely."

The man pressed the green call button and handed him the phone.

"One minute."

It rang.

Twice.

Three times.

On the fourth, he heard his daughter's voice, and he had to fight with every atom of his being not to break down.

"Hello?"

"Carly?"

"Dad?"

"Baby."

Figured she could hear the tears in his voice, but he didn't care.

"Why are you calling? Is Mom okay?"

"She's fine." He turned away from the man who was going to murder him and leaned into the tinted glass. "I'm sorry, Carly. For everything. You are my—"

"Dad, I'm kind of in the middle of something...could I give you a call back in—"

"Listen to me. Please. I was wrong, Carly. So wrong."

"Have you been drinking?"

"No. No. Carly, you are my princess. You always have been, and I love you beyond words. Do you hear me?"

On the other end of the line...silence.

"Carly?"

"I hear you. Dad, is everything okay?"

"Yes. I just..." He shut his eyes, tears streaming down his face. "I need you to know how I feel about you. How I've always felt. Those summers up in Wisconsin with you and your mother on Lake Rooney...best times of my life. I would give all the treasure in the world to go back there for a single day. I'm so proud of you, Carly."

Now, he could hear her crying.

"Ten seconds," the man said.

"I have to go now, sweetheart."

"I want to see you, Dad. I'll be in Chicago week after next."

"I'd like that very much. I'm sorry, Carly. I'm so sorry."

"Dad, are you sure everything's—"

He felt the phone get snatched away from his ear.

Marquette wiped his eyes, stared for a moment across the harbor.

When he looked back at the man, he said, "I should've done that a long time ago."

"But you did it. There were people in my life, now long since gone, that I can never have a conversation like that with. Count yourself lucky."

But Marquette didn't feel lucky. He felt devastated.

"It's time, Reggie. Roll up the sleeve of your left arm."

Marquette's fingers trembled so badly that he fumbled with the button on his cuff for thirty seconds before he got it undone.

"Are you strictly a scholar or is there some real belief behind your work?" the man asked as Marquette slowly rolled up the sleeve of the cream button-down shirt his wife had given him the Christmas before last.

"I don't know."

"I've studied quite a bit of Dante's masterpiece myself. It fascinates me. I have a question for you."

"Yes?"

"To which circle of hell will you be taken?"

Marquette stared into the man's black eyes—such terrifying emptiness.

"The fifth circle."

"Anger?"

"It's the root of all my failings."

"You're a very honest man, Reggie."

The rolled sleeve was above his elbow now, and the man said, "That's fine. Turn your arm over. Let me see your veins."

Marquette hesitated, but only for a second.

"Are you feeling the urge to resist?"

"Of course I am. This is my life you're taking."

"I understand that as long as you understand what's behind the black curtain. If you want to go out screaming and in agony, the option is there."

"I don't want that."

The man with long, black hair held the syringe, his finger on the plunger, and moved it toward the pale underside of Marquette's forearm.

"Try to keep it steady."

Marquette grabbed his wrist to keep his arm from shaking, watched the needle enter a periwinkle vein with a stinging pinch.

"Speedy travels, brother," the man said, and his thumb depressed the plunger.

When he'd shot the full load into Marquette's system, he tugged out the needle and leaned back in his seat.

Marquette sat with his palms on his knees.

Waiting.

Heart racing.

Lines of icy sweat trilling down his sides.

He didn't feel anything yet.

Out the window, he saw a couple in their thirties walking along the shore with two small children.

An old man sitting on a bench twenty yards away, smoking a cigar.

A half-mile out—a sailboat gliding shoreward.

He whispered the names of his wife and his daughter, and then it hit him—like someone had dangled his beating heart over the fast lane of an interstate and a sixteen-wheeler had slammed through it at full throttle.

He heard himself gasp.

The pain of molten rock being pouring into his chest cavity. He had a faint understanding that he was thrashing about in the front passenger seat of the van, eyes bugging out, and then he was still, crumpled against the door and staring out the window one last time, the world turning into a negative of itself.

He wasn't moving, couldn't move, not even to close his eyes, and he thought, *I'm going to die with them open*, and he stared at the familiar profile of the Hancock Building, five miles away, until it ceased to mean a thing.

* * *

Wikipedia Entry for Andrew Z. Thomas

Andrew Ziegler Thomas (born November 1, 1961) is an American author of contemporary horror, suspense, true crime, and thriller fiction, and a suspected serial killer. His stories have sold more than 30 million copies and have been adapted into feature films, television movies, and comic books.

Early Life

Thomas was born in Winston-Salem, North Carolina, in 1961 to James and Jeanette Thomas, along with his fraternal twin brother, Orson. His father, who worked in a textile factory, died of lung cancer in 1973, when Thomas was eleven.

Education and Early Career

Thomas attended Appalachian State University with his brother beginning in 1980. He graduated with a BA in English in 1984. Orson Thomas left during their junior year for unknown reasons.

1980s Work

After finishing college in 1984, Thomas began submitting short stories to horror and suspense magazines. His first short story, "An Ocean of Pain," was published in *Ellery Queen's Mystery Magazine's* December 1986 issue. At this time, Thomas had already begun work on his first novel, *The Killer and His Weapon*, a story about a man coming to terms with his homicidal instincts. With that novel, he landed renowned literary agent Cynthia Mathis, who still handles rights to his work. *The Killer and His Weapon* was published in 1988. Although not a critical success, it sold over 100,000 copies in hardcover and 500,000 copies in paperback, big numbers for a first horror novel containing depictions of graphic violence.

1990s Work

Thomas's second novel, *Sunset Is the Color of a Broken Heart (1990)*, was a critical and commercial flop. Straying from the page-turning horror and suspense of his debut, *Heart* was a tender, autobiographic coming-of-age story about a young boy growing up in the piedmont of North Carolina. Following the disappointing performance of his second novel, Thomas released a string of commercial successes that were seen as a return to the thrills of his debut, while also incorporating elements of true crime. These included *The Way the World Ends (1991), Blue Murder (1992), Plan of Attack (1993), Midnight: Collected Stories (1994),* and *The Passenger (1996). Blue Murder, Plan of Attack,* and *The Way the World Ends* were all adapted for film, with *Blue Murder* becoming a box-office hit. By the time Thomas released *The Scorcher* in 1996, he had established himself as one of horror fiction's rising stars and the heir apparent to Stephen King and Dean Koontz.

The Heart Surgeon Murders and the Unraveling of Thomas's Career

On October 31, 1996, a box containing human hearts was left in Washington, DC, at the Ellipse, near the site of the national Christmas tree. Some of the bodies those hearts had been taken from would later be unearthed at Thomas's wooded property on Lake Norman in North Carolina. It is widely believed that Thomas was responsible not only for planting the box of hearts at the Ellipse, but for the Heart Surgeon Murders as well.

Murder of Jeanette Thomas

Thomas's mother was found strangled in the basement of her home, the same house where Thomas had lived as a child, on November 2, 1996. An arrest warrant was issued for Thomas, as he had been seen visiting her close to her estimated time of death, on the evening of October 30, 1996.

Disappearance and Presumed Murder of Walter Lancing

Walter Lancing, editor of the Charlotte-based nature magazine *Hiker*, had been a close friend of Thomas since Thomas's relocation to Lake Norman following the success of his first novel. Lancing's white Cadillac Deville was found one week later, parked beside a Dumpster behind the Champlain Diner in Woodside, Vermont. The interior of the Cadillac was covered in blood, which testing later proved to be Walter Lancing's. His body has never been found.

Incident at Ricki's Bar in Scottsbluff, Nebraska

On November 7, 1996, a shootout occurred at a rural bar on the outskirts of Scottsbluff called Ricki's. Eyewitness accounts support the theory that the incident involved Andrew Z. Thomas and an unidentified man with long, black hair, both of whom fled the scene.

First Extended Disappearance of Thomas: 1996–2003

The shooting at Ricki's Bar was the last public sighting of Thomas for almost seven years. In the wake of his disappearance, four bodies were exhumed from Thomas's lakefront property in North Carolina, and warrants for his arrest were issued in connection with these killings. Thomas had been a successful writer leading up to 1996, but with newfound infamy, his books became massively popular, resulting in reissues of his backlist, remakes of his movies, and the emergence of a cult following devoted to unraveling the mystery of what led a successful writer to murder. In addition, much speculation abounded regarding his disappearance—was he dead or alive? If the latter, was he still writing?

Reemergence and North Carolina Killing Spree #1: October 27–28, 2003

On October 27, 2003, Zach and Theresa Worthington, and their two children, were murdered in their home on Lake Norman,

North Carolina. Their next door neighbor, Beth Lancing (widow of Walter Lancing), was abducted from her home by a man later described by Jenna Lancing as tall, pale, and with long, black hair. The next day, October 28, a clerk was murdered in the men's restroom of a Wal-Mart in Rocky Mount, North Carolina. The photograph taken of the murderer by Wal-Mart security cameras is the only good photograph in any law enforcement database of the man believed to be Luther Kite. While Kite is believed to have been aboard ship during the Kinnakeet Ferry Massacre, the images don't confirm this. The night of the 28th, Karen Prescott, former book editor and girlfriend of Thomas, was found hanging from the lighthouse on Bodie Island. Thomas was immediately suspected of these murders, with rumors spreading that he had come back out of hiding.

Disappearance of Detective Violet King

Violet King, a homicide detective with the Davidson Police Department, traveled to Ocracoke Island on November 4, 2003, to investigate a lead in the murder of the Worthington family and abduction of Beth Lancing. A partial fingerprint belonging to Luther Kite had been lifted off a laser pointer found in the hand of the Worthington's youngest child. Kite's family lived on Ocracoke. King last contacted Davidson PD on November 6, and was not heard from or seen again, with the brief exception of her appearance in North Carolina Department of Transportation video footage of the November 12 Kinnakeet Ferry Massacre.

Kinnakeet Ferry Massacre: November 12, 2003

On the morning of November 12, 2003, six vehicles boarded the 5:00 a.m. Kinnakeet ferry traveling north out of Ocracoke. For reasons unknown, a slaughter ensued. The ferry captain was killed, along with five passengers, and when the ferry finally ran aground on the shoals off Hatteras Island, Rufus and Maxine Kite were also found dead, crushed to death against the railing by a Chevy Blazer. The final death count was eight. Video footage on the ferry showed some of the carnage, including shots of what appeared to be Andrew Thomas, Violet King, and a man with long, black hair whose identity could not be positively confirmed as Luther Kite. Their bodies, however, were never located among the dead, and it is assumed that they were either killed and thrown overboard, or escaped.

Controversy and Second Extended Disappearance of Thomas: 2003–present

Up until his reemergence in 2003, the prevailing theory (also held by prominent state and federal law enforcement officials involved in the Thomas investigation) was that the writing of *The Scorcher*, Thomas's most violent book to date, had pushed him over the edge, beyond the realm of fiction, into an attempt to experience and embrace violence in the flesh. However, in light of the 2003 murders in North Carolina, culminating with the footage of the Kinnakeet Ferry Massacre, competing theories have emerged, some supporting Thomas's innocence—whether in fact he could have been the victim of a massive frame. Other theories debate whether or not Thomas is still alive and writing, and if so, under what popular pseudonyms he may still be producing fiction. Some believe he continues to release new work under the name Jack Kilborn, a writer who emerged on the scene in 2009 with the popular horror novel, *Afraid*.

Writing Style

Thomas employed a sparse, clipped writing style, punctuated by scenes of hyper-violence, which, despite many complaints that it was gratuitous, in reality left much to the reader's imagination.

Influences

Thomas has been frequently compared to King, Koontz, Richard Laymon, Edward Lee, Jack Ketchum, Clive Barker, and other horror and pulp fiction masters.

Critical Response

Thomas was never a critics' darling. Over the nine-year span of his career, none of his books received a starred review from either *Publishers Weekly*, *Kirkus Reviews*, *Library Journal*, or *Booklist*. His prose has been described by the *New York Times* as "ranging from careless to wretched" and *Kirkus Reviews* famously bemoaned the planned continuation of his first novel, *The Killer and His Weapon*, "sadly, a sequel is in the works." Recent critical analysis, however, has begun to take the view that with another decade or so, Thomas might have reached the broader audience enjoyed by stalwarts of the horror genre, such as King and Koontz, finally earning him wider recognition and acclaim for his intense characterizations of depraved human behavior, and provocative plotting.

Bibliography

The Killer and His Weapon (1988)
Sunset Is the Color of a Broken Heart (1990)
The Way the World Ends (1991)
Blue Murder (1992)
Plan of Attack (1993)
Midnight: Collected Stories (1994)
The Passenger (1995)

The Scorcher (1996)
The Dark Heart (unfinished) (1998)

Personal Life

Even prior to the events of late 1996, Thomas was known as a reclusive writer and rarely seen in public outside of bookstore events and the occasional mystery convention (Bouchercon 1995 in Indianapolis being his last). For several years, he was romantically involved with Karen Prescott, an editor at Ice Blink Books, but their relationship ended prior to Thomas's 1996 troubles. His literary agent, Cynthia Mathis, was also a close friend, and although she denies having had any physical contact with Thomas since 1996, she maintains her belief in her client's innocence, even to this day.

* * *

Jack
March 31, 12:50 p.m.

When I'd finished perusing Thomas's Wikipedia page, this prompted me to check out the unofficial AZT website, which was run by fans. Though *fans* might have been a misnomer. On his message board, Thomas had dozens of haters who were convinced he was a monster. There was also an entire section devoted to theories speculating on whether or not Thomas was still alive and still writing.

I searched the site for "Luther Kite" and got more than a hundred hits on the message board. I spent an hour reading through them. The vast majority referenced Thomas's Wikipedia page, the disappearance of Detective Violet King, and the murder of Luther Kite's parents. There were theories that Andrew and Luther were partners, that Andrew killed Luther, that Luther killed Andrew, and that aliens had abducted Andrew and put an implant in his brain, turning him into Luther. None of them had even the barest shred of authenticity, until I came upon five entries by a poster named "ALONEAGAIN."

Everyone here is off base. The Andy Thomas I knew is long gone. His killer, Luther Kite, is alive and well and continues to thrive.

and

Luther Kite took Andy. My lovely Andy. The poison he spreads lasts for generations. It consumed my baby.

and

Luther Kite is the devil, and the devil's greatest trick is to convince us he doesn't exist. The only thing worse than a devil is a devil in disguise.

I searched for info on ALONEAGAIN, but the bio page hadn't been filled out. However, he/she did have two more entries on the message board. I clicked on the first.

Luther can do anything. He once swallowed a bus.

Whatever the hell that meant.

And:

He's coming for you, Jack. There is no place you can run. He took my baby. He'll take your baby, too.

I stared at the screen, feeling all the hairs on my arms stand erect. The message was dated five months ago, and it was obviously intended for me.

Was ALONEAGAIN a screen name for Luther?

It seemed that way. But talking about yourself in the third person, unless you were schizophrenic, was highly unusual. Nothing I'd learned about Luther led me to believe his particular brand of insanity was schizo-related.

So this might have been someone else discussing Luther. Someone who knew him? Someone who knew Thomas?

Maybe Thomas himself?

I let my mind grapple with it. What if Thomas hadn't committed those murders? What if he'd been framed, by Kite, and had been in hiding ever since?

I went back to the Wikipedia page for Thomas and wrote down the name of his literary agent as I overheard Phin on the phone in the kitchen, making Geneva arrangements.

I Googled the Cynthia Mathis Literary Agency.

She had over a hundred thousand hits, most linking to her blog, *The Agent Knows Better*. I took a cursory look and found it was filled with posts where Cynthia belittled new writers, trashing their query letters and telling them they stunk. Authors were apparently a masochistic bunch, because they ate up her abuse like candy and asked for more.

The blog was part of her website, and I found the contact info and dialed her New York office. Got a phone tree and punched in the number for the head honcho.

A secretary picked up. "May I ask who's calling?"

"My name is Lieutenant Jacqueline Daniels," I said, hoping the name would be familiar. "I'd like to speak with Cynthia Mathis."

"Hold please."

I endured new-age Muzak.

In the meantime, on a whim, I booted up the voice stress analyzer program McGlade had installed on my computer, switched to speaker phone, and waited for the agent to pick up.

"Lieutenant Daniels? I'm delighted you called, darling. I've followed many of your cases. Are you thinking of writing true crime, or more of a memoir? If you're worried about the writing part, I know several excellent ghostwriters."

Her voice was low, her delivery fast, pure Manhattan.

"I'm not sure anyone would be interested in reading about my exploits, Ms. Mathis. I'm calling about a different matter. Your client, Andrew Z. Thomas. Have you been in touch with him?"

I moused over the BASELINE button and clicked.

"No one has heard from Andy since Kinnakeet back in 2003." Her tone had become frosty, defensive. "And frankly, I'm tired of defending him from police officers who insist on his guilt."

I waited, needing more in order to hammer out a baseline. Voice stress analysis was basically a lie detector, and in order to establish if a person was lying, it needed a sample of normal speech to compare it with.

"Are you there, Lieutenant? I said I no longer answer any questions about Andy. Everyone seems anxious to accuse him of murder, but no one has made any effort to find him or clear his name."

The program flashed ACCEPT. I hit the pause button.

"I don't think he's guilty," I said quickly. It wasn't a complete lie, because I wasn't sure. "I'm trying to find him, and I may have a lead on his whereabouts." Now that was a complete lie, but so was introducing myself as Lieutenant.

"You know, I've insisted upon Andy's innocence since—"

"I'm sort of pressed for time, Ms. Mathis. If you could just answer a few questions for me, I'd really appreciate it. And who knows, maybe there's a book in this after all."

"I understand. Go ahead."

"Do you know anything about a man named Luther Kite?"

I clicked on ANALYZE.

"Never heard of him," she said.

The machine blinked TRUTH.

"Do you know anything about Mr. Thomas's brother, Orson?"

"No. Andy never spoke of him."

TRUTH.

"How about Walter Lancing?"

"I never met him, darling, but I knew he was Andy's friend. He was one of the victims. Andy would never have hurt Walter."

TRUTH.

"Have you ever used the screen name ALONEAGAIN?"

A short pause. Then: "No, I haven't. What would I use a screen name for?"

TRUTH.

"How about Karen Prescott?"

"Of course I knew Karen. I'd met with her dozens of times. She was Andy's editor for a time. And he didn't kill her, either."

TRUTH.

I glanced at the Wiki page in another window. "Do you know the whereabouts of Violet King?"

"Violet King? I'm sorry, but I can't place the name."

LIE.

I sat up a little straighter. "She was a cop who disappeared when Andy did, right after the Kinnakeet Ferry Massacre. Are you saying you don't know where Violet King is?"

"I have no idea where she is."

LIE.

"Ms. Mathis, I think it's imperative that you be honest with me here. Locating Andy isn't going to be an easy task, and I think Violet may be essential to finding him."

"I don't know her."

"Yes, you do, Cynthia. I'm a cop. I'm an expert at detecting lies."

Especially with the right software.

Cynthia sighed. "I've never met Violet, and have only spoken with her once."

TRUTH.

"What did you speak with her about?" I asked.

"After Andy's disappearance, I got a letter. Written in his handwriting. It asked me to forward all of his future royalty payments to Ms. King. I called her to ask what their relationship was, but she'd been in some sort of accident. She was in a lot of pain, couldn't answer my questions. I followed up with a letter, got a nice note back saying she didn't know where Andy was, and didn't want any of his money. But she cashes the checks I send her twice a year."

TRUTH.

"Do you still have the letters? From Andy and from Violet?"

"Probably. I never throw anything away."

I gave her my fax number and then asked if she suspected Violet of anything.

"You mean did she force Andy to write that letter? Of course I suspected that. I represent a large number of mystery writers. But I checked the postmark on Andy's letter. It was stamped several weeks after Violet's tragedy."

"What tragedy?"

"The poor girl was horribly burned and disfigured. So if you're thinking she had Andy tied up in her basement and forced him to turn over his rights, there's just no plausible way."

"Do you have Violet's contact information?"

"I do. I can fax it along with the letters. Now I have a question for you, Lieutenant."

"Go ahead."

"I know there were several books and a TV movie based on that Gingerbread Man case you were involved in, but you never told your side of the story, darling. For a small fee, I could have you partner with a ghostwriter, and I'm sure it would be a huge bestseller."

LIE.

"Thanks for the offer, Cynthia. I'll call you if I have more questions."

I hung up, feeling a little bit dirty, and then scrolled through my iPhone contacts for an old friend.

Well, perhaps *friend* wasn't the proper word. But we'd crossed paths a few times in a professional capacity, and we trusted each other as much as a cop could trust a reporter.

Make that a *former* cop and a *former* reporter. Last I heard, he was no longer with the *Chicago Record*. Fired, would be my guess. But if he still had access to their online archives, I might be able to find some Andrew Z. Thomas and Luther Kite info that wasn't on Wikipedia.

I did have his number, listed as *Chapa*. I pressed the name, listening as it rang four times. Just as I figured I was going to be bounced to voicemail, he picked up on the fifth. I forced myself to sound upbeat.

"Hi, Alex. Jack Daniels. How's retirement treating you?"

"Lieutenant, who told you I'm retired?"

"Word gets around. I heard about that little blow up in Oakton. Hairy."

Chapa laughed. "Blow up? Nice choice of words, Jack. Actually, I'm just taking a break from it all down here in the Florida Keys. How 'bout you?"

"Still fighting the good fight in Chicago. I'm calling because I need a favor."

"Again? How many times am I going to have to—"

I cut him off. "If I recall correctly, you're the one who owes me a few."

"Apparently age is starting to have its way with your recollections, Lieutenant."

I frowned. "Let's get this dance over with, Chapa. I need a log-in for the *Record's* archive database. Lives are at stake."

There was a pause. I could hear thunder in the background.

"Chapa? You die on me?"

"Quit with the wishful thinking, Jack. That's a hell of a request you're making."

"You heard the lives at stake part, right?"

"Tell me more. Pique my reporter's natural curiosity."

"In a nutshell, I've got a psycho named Luther Kite after me. I need background on him and an author named Andrew Z. Thomas. They've both made headlines in the past. But if you're making me jump through hoops, I'll just pony up the money for an online subscription. It won't—"

"All right, Jack, enough already. I'll help you. You got something to write on?"

"Write on? What is it, 1965? I'll use Notes on my iPhone."

"Okay, cop of the future, here goes."

I put Chapa on speakerphone and he gave me a six digit password for someone named Wormley.

"Thanks, Alex. Now we're even."

I moved my thumb to hang up.

"Even my ass, Jacqueline. First of all, you owe me a drink the next time we run into each other, which hopefully will be no time soon since I always seem to get shot at whenever we're together."

"Done." I could buy the old hack an Old Style. "What else?"

"And not Old Style, either. There's going to be some quality rum involved. I also need some info from you."

"I'm flattered, but I'm seeing someone. And you aren't my type."

"Save that thought for a lonely night, Lieutenant. What I need is a name."

I snapped my fingers. "Peppermint Schnapps."

"Peppermint Schnapps? Are you drinking, too, Lieutenant?"

"That's what my boyfriend wants to name our baby."

"I prefer mojitos, myself, but that's only because Gale keeps bringing pitchers over. That's another story. I need the name of a man. He was involved in some sort of kidnapping in Chicago about a decade ago."

"Sure thing."

Chapa described the guy, and I accessed the CPD criminal offender database. After a bit of back and forth, I got him a name and emailed him a photo.

"Just one more thing, Jack. You've got two hours to access the Record's database, and then my sense of journalistic duty will kick in and I'll have to let them know their system has been breached. Good luck."

"Take care, Chapa. I owe you an Old Style."

I hung up and then logged into the *Chicago Record*, courtesy of Wormley's password. I searched for Kite, Thomas, and Violet King. For the first half hour, I scrolled through all the same info I'd already gleaned via Wikipedia. But I did find something interesting, and possibly relevant, from the November 11, 2003 issue.

After Violet King went missing, her husband Max and her supervisor Sgt. Barry Mullins visited the home of Maxine and Rufus Kite on Ocracoke Island, searching for her. Their bodies were recovered two days later, along with numerous others, hanging from chains in the basement of the Kite residence. Also on site was an elaborate, labyrinthine basement consisting of rooms of torture, what appeared to be a homemade electric chair, and in the deepest section, ten bodies hanging from chains in the ceiling, among them Max King and Barry Mullins.

I couldn't find any further references to Violet King. But apparently she and Thomas disappeared, and remained hidden until years later when she was burned.

If Thomas was the killer, would she have run off with him knowing he may have killed her husband and her boss? Or perhaps her finding out triggered his rage, and then his guilt caused him to pay her off?

Then again, I wouldn't peg someone who built a home-made electric chair as capable of guilt. Thankfully, there were no descriptions of the *labyrinthine basement consisting of rooms of torture*. I didn't even want to imagine what the playroom of a sadistic psychopath looked like. It gave me the creeps.

I logged out just as Phin walked in carrying a lovely roast beef sandwich and a plate piled high with pork rinds. I don't think I ever loved anyone as much as I loved him at that moment.

"Whatcha doing?" he said.

I clicked on my screen saver as he crouched next to me. "Some research." Then I managed to fit so much of the sandwich in my mouth at once that I could have successfully auditioned for porn.

"What kind of research?"

Telling him I was trying to find a link between Luther Kite and Andrew Z. Thomas would no doubt provoke disappointment in my boyfriend, but at the same time I didn't want to lie to him. So I grunted something noncommittal as I voraciously chewed.

"Jack, I hope you're not pursuing this Luther Kite thing."

I made another generic grunt.

"The spa has an opening day after tomorrow. I told them about your condition and arranged to have your medical records transferred. I had to claim I was your husband in order to get permission. Which brings me to something I've been thinking about."

I managed to swallow the food in my mouth, and narrowed my eyes at him. "What are you getting at?"

"Do you like the pork rinds?"

"The pork rinds are fabulous. Now what are you talking about?"

"I was thinking..."

"You were thinking..."

"It might make things easier..."

I shook my head, knowing where this was headed. "Phin, don't..."

"For both of us..."

"Phineas Troutt..." Don't say it. Don't.

"If we got married."

Luther

March 15, Sixteen Days Ago

Twenty-Two Hours After the Bus Incident

*H*e has been uncooperative thus far, so Luther is stretching him on the rack, cables beginning to sing with tension, the man's forehead popping beads of sweat like a newly waxed convertible.

Luther finally stops the pulleys from turning and steps away from the control panel.

He stands next to the gurney and stares down at the man named Steve, a tall, scrawny guy with the underlying core muscle strength of a life-long manual laborer.

"Look at me. Look at me, Steve."

Steve's head is immobilized, so he can only cut his eyes toward Luther, grunting against the unbearable strain.

"Are you ready to talk to me now?" Luther asks.

"Yes," the man grunts.

"For the last time...the worst thing you've ever done...tell me, and I'll know if you're lying."

Steve hesitates.

"Steve, I know you're strong, but trust me...my machine will literally pull you apart."

"I...killed a man."

Luther stifles the beat of surprise. The man's reluctance to speak at all was the first indication that he was holding on to some secret, but Luther never expected this.

Never expected to get so lucky.

"You killed a man."

"Yes."

"Who was it?"

"I don't know his name. No one knows about this. Not even my wife."

"Tell me what happened. Tell me everything."

"Three years ago, I was driving home from a bar—I'd been drinking—and this guy...he pulled out in front of me. Cut me off. I'd never reacted like that before. Never since. But I lost it. I followed him for twenty miles."

"You were angry."

"Very much. I don't understand...looking back...it was such a stupid thing. So pointless. I'd lost my job the week before. I'd been drinking. I was in a bad place. I tailgated him until he finally pulled over and jumped out of his car screaming, calling me a psycho."

"What did you do then, Steve?"

"I popped my trunk, took a two iron out of my golf bag. I only hit him once. I didn't expect him to die."

"We all do things we regret. And no one ever saw you?"

"No. It was just a country road on a quiet summer evening. And it was...it was a kid, too. When the newspapers started covering the murder, it came out that he was only twenty-two. He'd just finished college, had been on the verge of starting a teaching job at a local elementary school. Sitting there, watching those news reporters as his

family begged anyone with information to come forward...it was so awful. It still is so awful."

"Thank you, Steve."

"Are you going to kill me?"

"No, but it almost sounds like you want me to."

"We all have evil in us," Steve says. "Some more than others. I never knew I had this in me, and it scares me, because I wonder how much of it is still inside. Waiting to come out."

Luther pats him on the shoulder.

"Don't worry, sir. There's a special circle of hell for people like you."

Jack
March 31, 1:45 p.m.

*I*t *might make things easier for both of us if we got married.*

That had to be the single most unromantic proposal in the history of matrimony. I was fat and disgusting, with au jus all over my chin, and the man I loved had just asked a lifelong commitment of me with the same passion and intensity as when he asked what DVD I wanted to watch that evening.

"You're kidding," I said.

He flinched a little. "I'm serious. We're living together anyway, and for insurance, and taxes, and for the baby, I think it's a—"

"Hold on." I held up my hand. Phin knew I'd vowed to never get married again. I'd been engaged not long ago, and it had ended badly. My previous marriage had also ended badly. For him to ask me, especially like this...

My fax machine chirped.

Phin took the opportunity to break eye contact and walk over to the printer. I watched him read the cover sheet and frown.

"Andrew Z. Thomas, Jack? I thought you promised to give this up."

"I promised to go to Geneva. Not drop this case."

He shook his head and spread his hands out. "It's not just this case. It's everything. You were supposed to retire from police work altogether. But ever since you quit the force, you've been doing the same damn thing. It's like you never even left."

"Excuse me if I've got some psycho chasing me."

"Excuse me for caring about you."

He walked to the door, but stopped before leaving.

"Is this ever going to end, Jack? Even if Luther gets caught or killed, there's always going to be one more case that the famous Lieutenant Jack Daniels needs to solve."

"That's what I'm paid to do, Phin. I work with Harry now. I'm a private eye. I'm very good at it."

"It's going to get you killed one of these days. I don't want to see that."

"No one's forcing you to stay."

Probably a mean thing to say to someone who just asked for my hand in marriage.

"Wow. How's it feel to be the President of the United States of Super Bitch?"

Ouch.

"I thought we had boundaries, Phin. You don't ask me to stop being me. I don't ask you to stop doing whatever dumbass criminal activities you do..."

"Nice. Real nice."

"...and you don't ask me to marry you. Those were the rules."

"Enjoy your sandwich," Phin said.

Then he left. Duffy gave me a sad, backward glance, and went with him.

I hated myself for a few seconds and then rolled my chair over to the printer and quickly read the letters the agent had faxed over. They didn't reveal anything new, but Violet King apparently lived in Peoria, about a three-hour drive from me.

I was eating my sandwich and weighing my options, deciding if a personal visit would be better than a phone call, when I found the biggest diamond ring I'd ever seen hidden under the pork rinds.

Oh...shit.

I immediately got up, realizing what a jerk I'd been, and padded into the living room in time to see Harry McGlade pull into the driveway and Phin drive off in his Bronco, right over my lawn.

I called him on my cell, but he didn't pick up.

The tears came fast and hard.

I was still sobbing when McGlade pressed the security code and strolled in.

Duffy—who apparently hadn't been let into the Bronco— was all over him, jumping up and down, wagging his tail.

"What's up with Phin? He looked pissed. You do something?"

I sniffled. "I'm...I'm the...I'm the President of the United States of Super Bitch."

"No shit. You have been a bit bitchier than normal. But I wouldn't call you the President of the United States of Super Bitch."

"Thanks, Harry."

"You're more like the Master of the Bitchiverse."

I waddled into the kitchen and grabbed the box of tissue. Empty.

"Or Bitchzilla. You're such a giant bitch that you stomp through cities, crushing smaller bitches."

I looked around for another box of tissue and spotted Mr. Friskers on the counter. He hissed at me.

I wiped my nose on my sleeve and turned to face McGlade. "Do you want to go to Peoria?"

"Can't. The Tesla can only go about two hundred miles per charge."

"We can take my car."

"What's going on in Peoria? Some kind of Bitch Convention? Are they voting to make you Queen?"

"Goddamn it, McGlade! Enough already!"

Mr. Friskers was apparently tuned into my feelings, because he launched himself at Harry with a terrible screech and attached himself to my partner's chest. McGlade tried to pull him off, but that was the wrong move, as it just made the cat dig his claws in deeper.

Duffy the dog, excited by—well, all the excitement—ran up and bit McGlade on the leg.

I yelled at Duffy and then looked for my squirt bottle that I used when Mr. Friskers got nasty. It was next to the sink, empty. Mr. Friskers got nasty a lot.

"I'M SORRY I SAID YOU WERE A BITCH!" McGlade cried out. "CALL FOR HELP!"

I reached over to swat Duffy. He gave me sad eyes and peed all over McGlade's leg.

"THAT'S EVEN WORSE THAN THE BITING!"

I grabbed Mr. Friskers by the scruff of his neck and twisted. He detached from McGlade and took a swipe at me, but I released him.

He landed on the dog.

What happened next could best be described as *basset hound rodeo*.

The dog howled, running around the kitchen, the cat clinging to his back like a jockey.

"I'm bleeding," McGlade wailed. "This was a new shirt. Do you have stain remover?"

As Harry unbuttoned his shirt, Duffy began to buck, but his stunted little hound dog legs weren't suited to the task. Mr. Friskers hissed and spat, clinging to Duffy in a wholly unnatural way, his cat eyes so wide they looked like they were about to pop out. Eventually, Duffy's floppy ears blocked his vision, and he ran full force into the refrigerator with a *thud*.

The ride finally over, Mr. Friskers bounded off, straight at McGlade.

The cat leapt up just as Harry took off his shirt and clung to his bare chest, claws sinking in.

"BOTH NIPPLES!" McGlade screamed. "HE'S GOT BOTH NIPPLES!"

Duffy, excited by the commotion, trotted over and bit McGlade's leg.

"HE BIT ME IN THE SAME EXACT SPOT! THE PISS-ING WAS BETTER!"

I grabbed another bottle from under the sink and squirted all three of them until they parted ways.

"IT STINGS! GODDAMN IT, JACK, IT STINGS!"

That's when I realized I'd accidentally grabbed the bottle of vinegar I used to polish windows.

Both Duffy and Mr. Friskers seemed fine, but McGlade was pounding on his bleeding chest like it had caught fire.

"Why don't you just rub salt on me?" he accused. "Or squeeze on some lemon juice?"

"Sorry," I managed. But it had improved my mood. A lot. Seeing McGlade in pain appealed to my baser instincts.

"JESUS HOLY MOTHER LOVING EVERLASTING CHRIST IT BURNS LIKE ACID! WHAT THE...AW, SHIT! MY NIPPLE IS GONE!"

I looked at Mr. Friskers to see if he was chewing on anything. Or playing with it. He once batted around a Skittle for two hours, and nipples didn't seem that different.

Luckily, McGlade hadn't lost a nipple. It was just covered with blood so he couldn't see it. I offered him a kitchen towel and then sent him to the bathroom to clean up. Then I locked Duffy in my office and mopped up his pee.

"I may need stitches," McGlade called from the bathroom.

"Do you want to go to a doctor?"

"No. But what if I get an infection?"

"The vinegar probably cleaned the wounds out," I said, not knowing if that was true or not. But it sounded plausible. If something stung that badly, it was probably killing germs.

"Your pets suck. You got an extra shirt?"

"Bedroom closet. Use one of Phin's."

I went back to my office to check on Duffy and found him happily polishing off my beef sandwich and pork rinds.

My beef sandwich and pork rinds...

"Down! Bad dog!"

I raced for the plate, not concerned for the food, but for what was under the food.

What *had been* under the food.

It was too late. The food, and my engagement ring, were in the dog.

"You call him a bad dog for eating your food, but not for biting your guest?" McGlade had come into the office pulling on a white T-shirt. "You need to get your priorities in order."

I collapsed onto my chair, which groaned in protest. "I really need to go to Peoria."

"I'll go with you, on one condition."

"What?"

"You euthanize both animals."

"McGlade..."

"Euthanize them with the cleansing fire of a 450-degree oven. And some gasoline. And a gun."

"My car's in the garage," I said.

"They have to die, Jack. Especially that cat. It's like a reincarnation of Jack the Ripper. I swear the little bastard was smiling at me the whole time."

I wrote Phin a note saying I was sorry and not to let Duffy out until I returned.

Then McGlade and I headed off to Peoria to see Violet King.

Luther
March 31, 1:45 p.m.

He's sliding a copy of *The Killer and His Weapon* into a clear plastic bag already bearing a note to Jack—black Magic Marker prewritten on plastic—when his iPhone buzzes like an angry yellow jacket.

Luther glances at the caller ID. Swears.

Unfortunate timing for someone to be calling, with Marquette wide open, and Luther sitting in the back of his van. He can see people passing by on the sidewalk through the one-way glass—at least several a minute. He hadn't expected there to be so many out on a rainy spring day. Hopes choosing this location hasn't been a critical mistake.

The phone is still ringing.

He sets the bag down and wipes the blood off his arms, answers on speaker, "Hello?"

"Yes, I'm trying to reach Rob Siders."

"Speaking."

"This is Peter Roe's secretary." The patent attorney. Spectacularly bad timing. "Mr. Roe asked that I call you to reschedule your appointment."

Alarm bells go off in Luther's head. "Reschedule?"

"Yes, he has a conflict tomorrow afternoon, but I could slide you in the day after at ten a.m."

Luther's mind works feverishly. No. No, no, no, no, no. This will ruin everything. Must remain calm.

"But I'm only in town for a limited time," Luther says, trying to keep his voice under control. "It's mandatory that I see him tomorrow."

"Well, if I switch some things around, maybe I could fit you in at noon."

"Listen to me very carefully. Noon will not work. One thirty is the only acceptable time."

"Hang on. Let me put you on hold for just a second."

Muzak kicks in. If this doesn't work out, there are no other options. He'll have to show up at one thirty regardless. Wing it. That will be trickier, and more people will have to die, but he's up to the task.

The secretary comes back on the line. "Good news, Mr. Siders. Mr. Roe has agreed to squeeze you in at one thirty, but it will have to be an abbreviated meeting. He has something at two—"

He cuts her off. "Fifteen minutes is all I need."

Luther ends the call.

He seals the plastic bag containing the book and slips it into Marquette's abdominal cavity. Peeling off his latex gloves, Luther reaches for the Handi Wipes. Then he puts on his special gloves, noting they're due for an oiling. He undoes the bungee cord on the side panel, freeing a much larger plastic bag and a gigantic cardboard box.

The next part will be fun, Luther muses.

Better than wrapping presents at Christmas.

He goes to work.

Hector Ramirez
March 31, 2:00 p.m.

Clutching his father's hand, Hector Ramirez fought the urge to run to the steps looming ahead of him, steps that climbed toward the pillars of his favorite place in the city. He loved the Shedd Aquarium. He loved the dolphins. Loved the turtles. Loved the sharks. He loved all marine life, even barnacles. The season pass was the best gift he'd ever received. When Hector grew up, he wanted to be a marine biologist.

"Hey buddy, can you give me a hand here?"

Hector was pulled to a stop. He stared at the man talking to his father. A pale, dark-haired man dressed in overalls, standing at the top of a ramp extending down out of a big white van.

The man had an enormous cardboard box on a handcart.

"I just don't want this box to break open and spill everywhere," the man said.

"Wait here, *hijo*," his father ordered Hector, and then released his hand and started walking toward the van.

Hector watched the two men wrestle the big box down the ramp, noticing with great delight that it said *FISH FOOD* on the side.

This drew him over.

"What kind of fish is it for, Mister?"

The pale man winked at him.

"A jackfish."

Hector's brow furrowed. "What's a jackfish?"

"It's one of nature's greatest predators."

"And they have it here at the aquarium?"

"Yeah, one will be here very soon."

The man pushed the hand truck back up into the van, hopped down onto the pavement, and raised the ramp.

"You're just leaving it here?" Hector asked.

"Someone will come get it." The pale man winked. "Trust me, the jackfish will be here soon. It can smell the blood, you see."

Hector watched the man climb back into the van and pull away.

"*Hijo! Zapatos!*"

Hector looked down at his shoes and saw that he was standing in a widening pool of blood.

Jack
March 31, 4:30 p.m.

After half a lifetime of driving a Chevy Nova, I'd traded up and purchased a Nissan Juke. It was an odd-looking vehicle that resembled a cicada, but it contained a turbo engine and all-wheel-drive, and because it was an SUV, it would accommodate family vacations.

That is, if Phin ever forgave me.

McGlade drove to Peoria, since neither of us wanted to risk me having a seizure while behind the wheel. He spent most of the time complaining about the pain in his chest. A few years back, McGlade had been captured by a serial killer, had his fingers sliced off one by one, and I didn't recall him complaining about that half as much as he was complaining now.

But then, vinegar in an open wound probably stung like a bastard.

I didn't bring my Kindle along, but using the Kindle app on my iPhone, I'd downloaded the Andrew Z. Thomas e-book, *The Scorcher*, and read a good chunk of it before we arrived.

While I wouldn't qualify Thomas as a psychopath based solely on his writing, the guy had a creepy imagination. He certainly wrote realistic villains. Sizzle, the book's antagonist, read like an amalgamation of several murderers I'd known. All bad guys thought they were the good guys and were able to justify their warped crimes in their own minds. Thomas nailed it.

"How about Goldschlager," Harry said, interrupting my reading.

"Huh?"

"As a name for the baby."

"Goldschlager?"

"It's cinnamon schnapps."

"I know what it is. And no."

"You sure? Goldschlager is hot." His smile was as wide as a zebra's ass.

"I'm not naming her after alcohol, McGlade. That's my final say on the subject."

I went back to the e-book.

"Kahlua."

"No."

"Baileys."

"Is she plural? No."

"Budweiser."

"Hell, no."

"Wild Turkey."

I stared at McGlade. "You're not even trying."

"What guy wouldn't want to nail a chick named Wild Turkey?"

"That's what I want for my daughter. Guys trying to nail her based on her name."

"You sure she's a girl?"

"No penis on the ultrasound. That's usually the giveaway."

"Penis could have been hidden. Or really tiny. Terrible thing to be born with a small penis. So I've heard."

"It's a girl," I said again, wondering why I felt so strongly about it.

"Maybe it's one of those half-boys, half-girls. A hermaphrodolt."

"You got the dolt part right."

"If your baby has both male and female genitals, I've got the perfect name. You want to hear it?"

"Christ, no."

"Yes, you do."

"No, I don't."

"Brandy Alexander," he said, beaming.

I shook my head. "You are one troubled son of a bitch. I swear, you sit at home all alone and think of this stuff, don't you?"

"I will never admit to that. How about something retro? Like Zima?"

"Why not just name her Ripple?"

"Nah. That's stupid."

"Is there anything I can do to make you stop?"

"Probably not."

But he was blessedly quiet for a few minutes. Hopefully he'd run out of names.

"Jagermeister," he finally said.

"That's the one, McGlade. I'll name her Jagermeister. It took a while, but you finally struck gold."

He raised an eyebrow. "Are you serious?"

"I'm serious," I lied. "Jager is a perfect name. Now we can finally move along to other things, like silence, and not talking anymore."

"Well, I'm happy to be of service, Jack."

"Thank you so much for your hard work."

"You're welcome."

I managed to read through two full paragraphs before he said, "How's Glenfarcas for a middle name?"

I rubbed my eyes. "Don't you have an off switch?"

"Jagermeister Glenfarcas Troutt."

Obviously, I wasn't going to get any reading done. "First of all, you're an idiot."

"It's catchy. She won't be in fourth grade and have another student named Jagermeister Glenfarcas Troutt in the same room as her. I'd put good odds on it. Two to one, at least."

"Second, why do you think my daughter will have Phin's last name?"

He gave me a WTF glance. "He's the father."

"Phin and I aren't married." This made me think back to my terrible reaction to his proposal, and Duffy eating the evidence. I was a horrible human being.

"Babies get the father's last name," McGlade said. "I think it's the law."

"You do understand this is the twenty-first century, right? I can name her whatever I like."

"Don't go bringing up all that feminist mumbo-jumbo. When a guy plants his seed in some hot-to-trot floozy, the baby takes his name. It goes along with the other rights a father has, like having to pay child support, and teaching the kid about sports and finger-banging. When my baby is born, he'll take my name."

It was an unhappy coincidence that McGlade had recently gotten some poor woman pregnant. When he wasn't trying to come up with names for my baby, he was giving me poor child-rearing advice. Stand-outs included: "Never hit your baby with anything thicker than a car antenna," and "To make sure your baby doesn't drown when she's alone taking a bath, tie a few fishing bobbers around her neck," and "The latest diapers are superabsorbent, and are easily good for a few days before they have to be changed."

"Just what the world needs. Another Harry McGlade."

"Maybe you can babysit sometime. Harry Junior should get to know his Auntie Jackie."

Now I made the WTF face. "Don't call me Auntie Jackie."

"You know, I just read that if your baby doesn't stop crying, she's never too young to get started on Ritalin."

"And stop giving me parenting advice. In fact, can you stop talking altogether? Please?"

"Okay, but I get to say one more baby tip."

I sighed. "Fine."

"You should never raise your voice at your child. It means you've lost control."

I considered it. "That's actually pretty good, McGlade."

"Thanks. And make sure to drill a few holes in her Punishment Box, so she can breathe a little bit."

I knew McGlade was joking. Probably. Hopefully. And thankfully, he kept his word and was mostly quiet for a while, except for his annoying habit of humming old Neil Diamond tunes.

"You need to pee-pee?" McGlade finally broke the semi-silence.

"What?"

"Piss. Urinate. Drain the clam. I thought you crazy preggos had to pee-pee every five minutes."

"I'm fine, and though I'm touched by your interest in my bathroom habits, why are you asking?"

"There's a truck stop coming up."

I tried to suppress a shudder, but it came anyway. "I hate truck stops."

McGlade glanced at me and then slowly nodded. "Oh, yeah, I remember. Some assholes attacked you at a truck stop a while back."

My mind involuntarily conjured up an image of a serial killer named Donaldson, his corpulent face leering at me.

"Yeah, two of them almost killed me."

"What happened to those guys?"

"One of them's in jail. The other ran into a bigger badass than he was."

That run-in had happened shortly after my encounter with Donaldson. Supposedly, he'd been tortured for hours and then burned. It was a miracle he'd survived, though Donaldson probably didn't consider it miraculous in the least.

"Where is he now?" McGlade asked.

"Last I heard, in an institution, in terrible pain, under constant medical care."

Harry said, "Sounds like he got what he deserved. What was his name?"

"Donaldson."

Harry snapped his fingers on his good hand. "I heard about that guy. He was hanging out with some young chick. They were both killing hitchhikers or some crazy shit."

"Can we not talk about this? You promised not to talk about anything."

"Someone tied them up and went at them with antique farm implements."

"McGlade..."

"Didn't Donaldson have a bunch of pictures in his car of people he'd killed?"

"McGlade! Enough!"

He glanced at me, saw how serious I was.

"Jesus, Jackie. What's the problem?"

"Pregnancy isn't easy, McGlade. It's especially difficult when you're staring over your shoulder the entire time, waiting for some psycho to kill both you and your baby. Do you have any idea what it's like to be afraid all the time?"

McGlade didn't answer. I hoped that had finally shut him up.

But after a few miles of silence, I began to feel shitty for snapping at him. Was that who I'd become? A gigantic bitch who treated the people who cared about her like trash?

"I understand fear," McGlade said, jolting me out of my self-pity party.

I stared at him. "I know."

"Do you?" He briefly met my eyes. "You've been through the wringer, Jack. No doubt. No one ever said you had it easy. But how much do you know about what Alex did to me?"

Alex Kork was another psycho from the past I didn't want to think about. But she'd hurt McGlade as much as me. Maybe even worse.

"I remember being tied to that chair, helpless. Phin ever tell you about it?" McGlade asked.

"Not in detail." Phin had been there as well. They'd been bound, back to back, at Alex's mercy. And Alex had no mercy.

"She was cutting my fingers off," McGlade said, holding up his mechanical hand. "Stopping the bleeding with a blowtorch. Lemme tell you—the pain was unimaginable. But you know what was worse than the pain? The loss of all hope. Knowing I was helpless, that it wasn't going to end. That was worse. I'd take a bullet for that man of yours. Phin is the only thing that kept me sane while it was happening. And then you came in, saved my ass. I owe you both. And I'm sorry I piss you off all the time. You're family to me, you know."

Ah, hell. I hated Harry when he got real. It made me feel even worse about myself.

"Got any more of those parenting tips?" I managed to say, trying to break the maudlin mood.

"Just one. Love your kid. Love her as hard as you can. Because you don't have forever. You only have a short time." He frowned. "It's always too short a time."

I let that sink in. Then said, "Christ, McGlade. That's almost profound."

"Yeah. And also, teach her how to suppress the gag reflex. That's the single most important trait in chicks."

I felt a headache coming on. "You can go back to shutting up now."

The GPS piped in to inform us that our exit was coming up. McGlade turned off the highway, and soon we were cruising through a residential area. Townhomes and cul-de-sacs. The neighborhood wasn't affluent, but it had a homey Mayberry, USA, vibe going on. It was nice to see trees again after an hour of flat, barren plains.

We were nearing the residence of Violet King, and I was thinking about what I was going to say to her when McGlade broke my concentration.

"Promise not to freak out?" he asked.

I didn't like his tone, and it made me freak out a little. "What?"

"I've been keeping a close eye on the rearview mirror, for obvious reasons, and the same beat-up Monte Carlo has been behind us since we left Chicago."

Donaldson

March 28, Three Days Earlier

The pain was constant.

Unrelenting.

It didn't even let up during sleep—what little sleep he could get between nightmares.

That's how it had been for years.

He was hooked on narcotics. Always wore two codeine patches on the ruins that were his legs. Thrice-daily Vicodin and Norco. Ativan to help him sleep. His lungs were scarred, making each labored breath a wet, raspy wheeze. He had six fingers left, and only four of them still worked properly.

Sometimes, it got so bad he couldn't stop trembling, shaking for hours on end. If he'd been the type of man to believe in karma, or justice, or some higher power that dished out retribution, he might have drawn the obvious conclusion and realized this was what he deserved.

That's what the judge, and the jury of twelve, had said while sentencing him to this hellhole.

Him and his partner.

Partner. What a joke.

A joke that became a self-fulfilling prophecy.

Though he'd killed many, and was widely known as a monster, the extent and permanence of his debilitating injuries deemed him no longer a threat to society, so this medical facility wasn't even maximum security. Sometimes, they forgot to lock the door to his room at night. One of his doctors even had the balls to tell the court that there was zero concern about escape, because that would mean being away from the pain meds.

The court agreed. Their mistake. One they'd pay dearly for.

Groaning, he shuffled down the hospital hallway, supporting himself with the rolling IV stand, his backless gown exposing the latticework of scars covering him from neck to heels. Nurses didn't even bother looking at him. To them, he was as harmless as a toothless puppy. Even with full doses of various medications swirling through his system, walking was agony, each step an electric jolt of pain, firing the nerve endings he still had left—an unremitting reminder of the horror he had endured.

He reached the end of the hall and then paused to catch his tortured breath, which rattled in his chest like a BB in a can of spray paint. He was getting close to his stamina's limit and contemplated leaning against the wall to rest for a moment. But rather than give in to the fatigue and pain, he pressed onward, turning the corner, limping down four more doors until he reached her room.

She was sprawled out in bed like a broken, violated angel. Pretty once. Now an apocalypse of scar tissue and skin grafts and tubes and stitches. Her latest operation had been a week ago—a setback that had cost them a lot of precious time.

He pushed his way inside, seeking the nearest chair, collapsing into it with a sigh of relief even as his nerves flared in unison.

"Hey," he rasped. "How you doing?"

She peeked her remaining eye open. "Aces. You?"

He cupped a hand to the hole where his ear used to be and said, "Louder."

She repeated at a higher volume. "Aces. You?"

"Each sunrise is a gift from the Lord. We still on for two days from now?"

"Yes."

"You sure?"

"Yes, I'm sure. As long as your fat ass doesn't gobble up all our pills."

The *fat ass* comment was a nod to the past. He hadn't been fat for some time. Fat required the ability to eat solids.

"Two days then," he said, nodding to himself. "Then we're out of here."

Over the last six months, the duo had been stockpiling medication. Soon they would have enough to survive on the outside for two weeks without needing to find another supply.

Two weeks would be more than enough time to do what needed to be done.

"You scared?" she asked.

"Of getting out? Or of what we have to do?"

"Both."

"Hell no. It's my only reason for living."

"Me, too."

He stood up, waited for the pain to abate a bit, and then headed for the door.

"Just two more days, Donaldson."

"Two more days, Lucy. Then we go after the bitch."

He twisted what was left of his face into a smile.

Jack Daniels, here we come...

Lucy

March 30, One Day Earlier

When the knock finally came, Lucy opened her remaining eye and struggled to sit up in bed. She took several shallow breaths, waiting for the lightheadedness to abate, but it wouldn't leave. It was the three codeine patches, she figured. Had to be. Enough narcotic-punch to knock out a good-sized dog. But for someone like her, who needed pain relief more than oxygen, it only made her dizzy. She typically got by on two patches. It didn't kill the pain—nothing could—but at least it brought the level down to a point where it wasn't *all* she could think about, where she could sleep, and sometimes, dream. But tonight was a three-patch night, because finally, after three years, she was getting out. And this meant walking.

She scooted her toothpick legs off the side of the bed and eased the soles of her feet down onto the cold linoleum.

He was knocking again, the impatient jerk. Wasn't like she could just hop out of bed and scamper over to the door, and he knew it.

This was work.

Slow, agonizing work.

The first two steps were the worst—like someone driving spears up the middle of her legs, but by the fifth and sixth steps, she had steeled herself to push through the oceanic pain.

She crossed the dark room, moving slowly toward the door.

The only light came from a streetlamp outside her window, filtering in through the glass behind her and casting eerie shadows of the bars across the floor.

Lucy reached the door, panting and already more exhausted than if she'd run a marathon back in her prime.

The door was unlocked—their angel had seen to that— and she turned the handle with her three-fingered claw.

Donaldson stood in the low-lit corridor just outside her door leaning against the wheelchair, looking positively naked without the rolling IV stand that had come to define them both as much as the hideous hospital gowns.

"What took you so long?" he whispered.

"That's a good one, fat ass," she said.

"You ready?"

"Hell, yes."

Lucy had been through the more recent surgery—just nine days ago—and as bad a shape as they both were in, the skin grafts had left her far weaker.

She took three agonizing steps and then collapsed into the wheelchair, every last nerve she still owned screaming out in a chorus of blinding, white-hot pain that was so intense, she leaned over the armrest and vomited on the floor.

"Lovely," Donaldson said and started to push.

"How we doing on time?" Lucy asked, wiping her mouth on the sleeve of her gown.

"About a minute behind, thanks to you."

"But he'll wait...right?"

"What we're paying this asshole, he better."

The progress down the corridor was slow, and after ten feet, slower, Donaldson panting, and Lucy feeling drips of cold sweat raining down off the end of his prosthetic chin implant onto her hairless skull.

"You gonna make it, D?"

"Go to hell."

The clock over the nurses' station read 7:15 p.m., and Donaldson nodded to the young nurse writing in her charts, wrapping up the tail end of second shift.

"Evening," he rasped.

She ignored him.

Donaldson pushed the wheelchair down the hallway and into the rec room. As usual, it was mostly full after dinner. Various formerly dangerous psychopaths with various physical health problems huddled under an old TV that never played anything stronger than PG-rated comedies. A few glanced at Lucy as she rolled in. One, a paraplegic named Briggs, who'd killed his caregiver for making him green beans instead of his preferred creamed corn, flicked out his tongue at Lucy like a serpent. She would have loved to have finished the job God had begun and fully paralyzed the prick, but there were more pressing things on her mind at the moment.

They passed the empty table with the painted-on checkerboard. The checkers were still absent, having been confiscated by the staff a month prior, following a fatal bludgeoning over a disputed move. Why couldn't habitually violent and insane criminals just play nice?

They headed toward the door at the back of the room, Lucy watching the large, mean orderly named Gary out of the corner of her eye. He wasn't paying attention to them, engrossed instead in an issue of *US Weekly*.

Donaldson wheezed heavily as they approached the door. Felt like cold, salty drizzle pattering on the top of Lucy's bald head, and though it disgusted her, she didn't say anything. In truth, she felt sorry for him.

Which was odd. Lucy hadn't thought she was capable of pity. She leaned forward, struggling to push in the door handle.

"How's the coast, D?"

"All clear."

As rehearsed, Lucy said loudly, "I really have to pee."

"Seriously? You take forever."

"Screw you then. I'll do it myself."

Donaldson grunted a "whatever" as he pushed the wheelchair into the bathroom.

Their angel, a dour-looking Cuban named Henry, stood waiting behind a laundry cart.

Henry quickly shoved a screwdriver in the door jamb to stop it from opening.

"What took you so long?" he said.

Lucy flashed a smile—one that had once been inviting, but was now monstrous. "We came as fast as we could."

"Yeah, well, the price just went up."

"What are you talking about?" Donaldson rasped. "We paid you everything we have."

"I'm not talking about money."

Lucy glanced back at Donaldson.

"I know you guys have been hoarding meds. I'll take your Vicodin."

Lucy felt a sudden rush of panic. "Henry, no."

"I got no sympathy for you, bitch. How many poor bastards did you torture to death? The both of you are scum. Only reason I'm helping in the first place is to take care of my mother."

Lucy knew Henry was full of shit. Ward gossip spoke of his chronic gambling problem, owing big money to a Chicago hood named Dovolanni. That's how they'd known to approach him.

"Just give him the Vicodin," Donaldson rasped.

Reaching beneath her flimsy gown, Lucy fingered one of the toilet-paper wrapped bundles, squeezing it to determine the type of pill inside. Roundish...that meant Ativan. She tried the next bundle, felt the long pill, and produced the Vicodin.

Henry tore open the toilet paper, dumping vikes into his palm.

"Daaaaaamn. You two been busy."

"You said we'll have some civilian clothes," Donaldson said.

"Yeah, man. In the hamper, under all the sheets."

The Vicodin disappeared into the pocket of Henry's scrubs, and he pulled out a pair of rubber gloves. He squeezed into them and started pulling linen out of the hamper, stacking it on the floor.

The stench of urine wafted up at Lucy.

"Those are *soiled* sheets?"

"Pissed in them myself," Henry said. "We get stopped, no one's going to search through pissy linen."

Lucy had never wanted to kill someone so badly before in her entire life, and that was saying something. Also, it was the first time she'd been glad for the incineration of her nasal cavity. She could still smell, just not as potently. Donaldson's nose, on the other hand, was fully intact. It was the only thing on him that was fully intact.

The orderly pulled out the last of the linen, and then a pair of bib overalls which he handed to Donaldson, and a hideous flower-print dress for Lucy.

"Hurry up," Henry said.

Lucy struggled onto her feet and took the dress from Henry. She staggered over toward the sink, experiencing a moment's hesitation at the prospect of stripping in front of these two. Just as she tugged her head through the neck hole of the gown, she glanced back at Henry, half-expecting him to be leering at her from across the room. But he wasn't even watching. He had turned away completely, and not out of any sense of respect. She knew it was disgust. He was repulsed by her body.

Christ, she wanted to kill him.

But at least he wouldn't see the other pills, wrapped in toilet paper, which she'd set on the sink.

The dress swallowed her tiny, emaciated frame. She stuffed the packets of pills into the front pocket and limped back over to her partner.

"Need help, D?"

"Little bit."

Lucy had more control of her three remaining fingers than Donaldson had of his four. As he stepped into the overalls, Lucy tried not to look at the small, plastic tube between his legs, but she couldn't help herself. Another jolt of compassion. *What the hell is wrong with me?*

It took her forty-five seconds to get the shoulder straps on Donaldson's overalls buttoned.

When she'd finished, Henry tapped the laundry cart—a huge canvas bag cloistered in a metal frame on wheels.

"Your carriage awaits."

The orderly grabbed Lucy under her arms and lifted her over the side, dropping her onto a rope and something else—a broom handle, which had been snapped into two pieces.

Donaldson practically fell on top of her climbing in, and Lucy gummed her arm to stop herself from crying out in pain.

Her partner had barely had a chance to settle in when the first piss-stinking linen fell on top of them.

She heard Donaldson gag.

"Is it bad, D?"

More linens rained down on them—soiled sheets and pillowcases.

"There's goddamn diarrhea on this one."

It was so awful, Lucy had to fight the urge to laugh.

She huddled next to Donaldson under the weight of thirty pounds of filthy linen as the wheels to the laundry cart squeaked underneath them.

She heard Henry say, "Wassup, my man?" to someone as they rolled along.

Her left leg was crushed under Donaldson's, the pain brilliant near the site of one of her grafts. She could feel the salty sting of someone else's urine pressing against the open wound.

But she couldn't cry out. Couldn't make a single, goddamn sound if she ever wanted to see the outside again.

The cart banged against what felt like a wall, jolting Donaldson against her.

She found his hand in the darkness.

Their claws embraced and squeezed through the pain.

After a moment, she heard the sound of elevator doors spreading apart.

They rolled several feet into the car, and as the door closed back, Lucy realized she wasn't going to be able to stand this much longer. Aside from the pain of Donaldson's weight on her and the burning in her skin graft, she was having trouble breathing in the confined space.

They ascended one floor and then rolled along again, Lucy beginning to panic, *I can't breathe, I can't breathe, I can't breathe, get these blankets off me!* She was going to scream. Absolutely lose it. Screw the plan and getting out, she just needed oxygen.

The cart stopped.

Henry was pulling the linens off of them—she could feel the weight lessening, and then she saw a light in the ceiling.

Lucy wriggled herself away from Donaldson and clambered to her feet, taking deep, penetrating breaths.

They'd come to an empty patient room, and Lucy saw where Henry had once again jammed a screwdriver into the doorjamb as an added precaution.

The black iron bars that normally covered patient windows had been cut through with a blowtorch, which still lay on the floor underneath the window frame.

Would be so much fun to grab that torch and...

"Hurry up," Henry said. "Let's go."

"Where's the harness?" Lucy asked. "We paid extra so you could buy one."

"Didn't have time. Come on."

She staggered over to him and he lowered what resembled a lasso over her head, cinching it snugly around her chest under her armpits.

Oh, sweet merciful Jesus, this was going to hurt.

"Up and over," Henry said, patting the windowsill. Lucy climbed up, and as she squatted on the perch, Henry said, "Oh, yeah, almost forgot."

He walked over to the laundry cart, reached in, and lifted one of the broken broom handle pieces.

"Bitch, if you so much as make a peep, I will simply let go of the rope, bolt out of the room, and get the hell out of dodge. You understand what I'm telling you?"

"Yes."

"Open up."

"Why?"

"Open your mouth."

Lucy opened her mouth and Henry jammed the broom handle into the hinge of her jaw.

"When the pain comes and you want to scream, just bite down. And remember, if you do scream, I'll drop your sorry ass."

It was only twenty feet down, but it might as well have been two hundred. First time Lucy had been outside in years, and the night was cold, the wind wandering up her dress like the finger of a dirty old man. Henry faced her on the other side of the window. He stood braced against the wall with the rope wrapped around his waist, the line already taut.

She eased off the ledge, and as the rope dug into her armpits, she understood that she had not fully contemplated this moment. She'd known it was coming, known the pain would be horrendous, but still she had glossed over just how excruciating the next minute of her life was going to be.

Henry began to lower her.

Slowly.

Inch by inch.

Blood poured down her neck, and she realized she had already bitten into the broom handle with enough force to split her gums. Her claws clenched, sweat dripping down her face, burning her remaining eye.

Scream. I gotta scream. I can't hold it in.

Her surgery of nine days ago had involved skin grafts on the undersides of her arms, and if the rope tore the skin, which it felt like it was doing, she would bleed out.

She whimpered in her throat, loud enough for Henry to hear, and almost hoped he would go ahead and make good on his promise.

Drop me. Let me die now. At least the pain will be over.

But then her toes were touching the ground, and she was lowered onto what was left of her ass, the edges of her vision narrowing into blackness as unconsciousness took her.

* * *

When she awoke, Donaldson was on the ground next to her, writhing and moaning.

"I need some pills," he groaned.

"Where's Henry?"

"Bringing his truck around. Gimme some damn pills."

Lucy reached into the front pocket of her dress.

Oh shit.

"Donaldson, they're gone."

"Gone?" he screeched, crawling toward her. "You're holding out on me, you skank, aren't you? You want to keep them all for yourself."

"They must've fallen out. Help me find them."

Lucy heard the grumble of an approaching vehicle.

"You stupid idiot, I need my goddamn pills."

"Help me look!" she whispered, her hands groping through cold blades of grass.

"I'll kill you if you've lost them."

There. Near the base of the building, she spotted something white—toilet paper.

Headlights coming. Henry, or maybe one of the guards patrolling the grounds.

"I found the patches," Donaldson said. "But no pills. We gotta get the pills."

A truck pulled up on the road behind them.

Henry said through the open window, "Time to go. Get in the back, under the tarp."

"Just a second," Lucy whispered, crawling toward the toilet paper.

"Or I could just leave."

She reached the building, grabbed the bundle containing the pills—unsure if they were the Norco or the Ativan—and stuffed them down into the front pocket of her dress.

It took everything she had to stand.

Donaldson was already climbing into the truck bed.

She wiped the tears out of her eye and followed.

* * *

Lucy huddled under the tarp in the bed of the truck, gritting her remaining teeth together as it began to move. She felt every bump, every jolt, in every nerve of her body. It was worse than being lowered by the rope. She heard a keening sound above the roar of the motor, realized it was Donaldson, sobbing in pain.

They reached the guard post at the prison's exit, and Lucy held her breath. It could all fall apart here if the guard checked under the tarp.

"Good evening, Henry."

"Hey, Ron."

"Got anything under the tarp back there?"

"Nope. Go check if you want."

Lucy heard footsteps coming around to the tailgate.

Her bladder spasmed as the tarp lifted.

"Okay, man," Ron said, looking right at her. "You can go."

Henry's bribe had obviously worked. The gate opened, and they drove off the prison grounds, to freedom. But it wasn't over yet. Lucy knew that if Henry wanted to double-cross them, this was the time to do it. He was supposed to have bought them a car with the money Donaldson had transferred from his bank account. But he could have kept it all, and was now planning to just dump them along the road somewhere. Or, worse, kill them. Because if he dumped them, and they got caught, they could finger Henry as an accomplice in their escape.

If it had been Lucy, she'd kill them both.

The truck stopped, and she heard the driver's-side door open.

This is it. The execution of a flawless plan, or a double murder.

In either case, she would be relieved.

The tarp lifted, and Henry scowled at them. "Ride's over. Get out."

Lucy painfully scooted across the truck bed, pushing herself onto her feet. They were in a wooded area. Looked like a forest preserve. The only other vehicle was a beat-to-shit Monte Carlo. Black, at least a decade old, missing hubcaps and a right fender.

"This is the car you bought me?"

In the moonlight, Lucy glimpsed tears glistening on the scar tissue of Donaldson's face.

"This is it, man."

"I gave you over fifty thousand dollars, you son of a bitch."

Henry puffed out his chest. "It runs, and the title is clean. If this ain't acceptable, I can take you back to the institution."

"It's fine," Lucy said, grabbing D's hand. "We're fine, aren't we, D?"

"Aren't you forgetting something?" Donaldson asked.

"What?"

"You were supposed to get us a gun? And some cash?"

"Glove box," Henry said. "Beretta. Serial numbers filed off. Even threw in a full magazine."

"Does it even shoot?"

"Guess you'll find out, right? Keys are under the floor mat."

"How about money?"

"Yeah. About that. I forgot to make a trip to the ATM this morning." Henry teased out his wallet, handed Donaldson some bills.

"Twenty-six dollars?" Donaldson began to shake with rage. "How far are we supposed to get on twenty-six bucks?"

"We'll manage," Lucy said. She was feeling just as betrayed, but there was nothing they could do about it. At least they still had the Norco.

"You won't be reported missing until lights out, in an hour and a half," Henry said. "You get caught, and mention me, I'll track you down and end both of you."

"You think it's easy, killing someone?" Lucy said. "Looking them in the eyes as they fade away? Listening to that last bit of air hiss out of their lungs? You know what that air tastes like?" She smiled, knowing it made her look like a skull when she did. "It tastes like cotton candy."

"Screw both of you," Henry said. Then he hurried back to his truck, hopped in, and sped away.

"I need some Norco," Donaldson said.

Lucy did, too. They should ration it, especially since that prick took their vike stash, but right now the pain was so intense it was impairing her ability to think. She carefully unrolled the ball of toilet paper. It was the Norco, thank Christ. It had been a bad piece of luck to lose the Ativan, but losing the Norco would have been far worse. She gave Donaldson two pills.

"Three," he demanded.

Lucy noted a flare of anger, but it immediately subsided. She gave him one more and then took three for herself, chewing hers so they'd take effect faster.

The powder tasted like battery acid, coating her throat with pointy little bits.

"Will you look at this piece of shit?" Donaldson gestured to the car. "That asshole."

"It's okay, D. We're free."

He grunted and then opened the driver's door and located the keys. There was a small plastic frog attached to the ring, and when its belly was pressed, a tiny flashlight beam came out of its mouth. With a moan, Donaldson heaved himself into the seat. Feeling playful, Lucy stuck out her thumb.

"Give me a ride, mister?"

Donaldson's face softened. "As long as you promise not to sing any show tunes."

Lucy limped around to the door, climbed in.

"Take the gun out of the glove box," Donaldson said.

Lucy pulled it open, had to dig under the owner's manual to find it.

She held the Beretta up under the globe light. "This ain't its first rodeo. It looks older than shit."

"Give it here," Donaldson said.

There was a moment's hesitation, but Lucy handed it over. Donaldson ejected the magazine.

"Seven damn bullets. That cheap-ass son of a bitch. At least it's a forty-five." He tugged back the slide. "Okay, here's one more."

"All we need is one," Lucy said.

He popped the magazine back in. It took a considerable effort, but Donaldson opened the door and aimed the Beretta at the nearest tree. The noise of the report filled the car, set Lucy's ears ringing. It had been ages since she'd heard a firearm discharge. She'd never been a fan of guns. Her beauty, her wits, and sadistic creativity had comprised her arsenal.

She said, "You just wasted a bullet, dumbass."

"No, I'm making sure this piece of shit will actually fire when we need it to."

He gave Lucy the gun and cranked the engine.

Phase one of their revenge plot now complete, it was time for phase two.

The pain Lucy felt would be nothing compared to the pain they were going to dish out.

She grinned like a skull as Donaldson hit the gas.

Luther

March 16, Fifteen Days Ago

Two Days After the Bus Incident

"*Take a few deep breaths, Amena. That's good. That's much better. What's your last name?*"

"*My maiden name is Haman. My current name is Haman-Bowers.*"

"*Current? How many names have you had?*"

She smiles a smile that twenty years ago would have launched ships. "*Always on the lookout for another one, cutie.*"

"*That's a beautiful ring you have on your finger.*"

"*Which one?*"

He points to it. "*Tell me about it.*"

"*Oh, it's just a four-carat diamond.*"

"*Your husband gave that to you, I assume?*"

"*Yes.*"

"*He didn't come on the trip with you though.*"

"*No, we're divorced.*"

"*Oh, I'm sorry to hear that.*"

Another smile. "It's quite all right."

"How about this one. The green stone."

"Oh, that's my emerald. Platinum band. Surrounded by twenty-nine diamonds."

"It's lovely."

"My second husband, Peter, gave this to me for our first anniversary."

"What about that necklace? Those real?"

"Of course." She touches the sapphires. "These were from Chance, my fourth."

"How many times have you been married, Amena?"

"Five."

"You took them for everything, huh?"

An elegantly restrained smile. Amena reaches across the table, fingers glittering with bling under the bare lightbulb hanging overhead, and touches his hand.

Ballsy. He has to give her that.

Luther can see that she believes she is getting a toehold, perhaps beginning to take control of her situation. This amuses him.

And even though she's in the neighborhood of sixty, there's an undeniable sensuality still present in spades.

No question, she's about as smoking hot as a grandma can get. Much rarer than a MILF.

A GILF.

"I have money," she says.

"Then what were you doing on that shitty bus?"

Amena doesn't respond.

He continues, "Lot of older gentlemen on this bus tour. Maybe you were looking for husband number six?"

She smiles. Coyly. "Every dime I've gotten in a divorce settlement, I've earned. I may be older than you, but trust me, hon, I could show you some things."

"No doubt, but that's not what I'm interested in."

"Money then?"

"I already have plenty of money, Amena."

"So what do you want? I'm sure we can work this out to our mutual satisfaction."

"Actually, you've already given it to me. Exactly what I want. The greatest gift of all."

"I'm sorry?"

Now it's his turn to smile. "Confirmation that you're a gold-digging bitch. And I know just where to put you."

Jack
March 31, 4:45 p.m.

I craned my neck, trying to peer into the rearview mirror.
The angle was wrong, so I adjusted it.

There.

Three cars on the street behind us, and I spotted the Monte Carlo McGlade had mentioned, about a hundred yards back.

"See it?" he asked.

"Yeah."

"Is it Luther?"

"I can't tell. Slow down."

McGlade tapped the brakes. After a few seconds, the two other cars passed, but the Monte Carlo stayed back, maintaining its distance.

"Can you get the plate?" McGlade asked.

"No, they slowed down, too. I can't even tell how many people are in the car. Turn here, see if they follow."

McGlade hung a right, passing an elementary school.

The Monte Carlo made the same turn.

"Try pulling over," I said, "letting them pass."

"What if the car doesn't pass? What if they try something?"

I tugged my Colt Detective Special out of my purse and spun the cylinder, double-checking that all six chambers were full. "I'd be okay with that."

"Rock out with your cock out," McGlade said, easing over to the side of the road and coasting to a stop on the gravel shoulder.

I eyed the rearview mirror.

The Monte Carlo had also pulled over, now two hundred yards back.

McGlade reached under his jacket, pulling out his .44 Magnum.

He checked the side mirror, said, "You're a better shot than I am. My Model 29 has a drop-out range of about eight inches from this distance." He offered me his gun. "You could put a few through the driver's-side windshield."

"I don't even know who they are."

"If it's Luther, we can end this now."

"And if it's someone else?"

He shrugged. "Oops."

"I'm not going to shoot into a car when I don't know who the target is."

"How about putting a couple rounds in the engine block?"

More cars passed.

I didn't notice any pedestrians, but a ricochet could easily hit someone's home. "No," I said. "This is a residential area. Too risky."

"Then I'll do it." McGlade opened his door.

"What if the driver has a rifle?" I asked.

McGlade closed the door. He also scrunched down a little in his seat. "Well, what's the plan then, Sherlock? Wait here for the rest of our lives?"

If I'd still been a cop, I'd have called for backup, and they could have approached the car. I could still call Phin or Herb, but it would take several hours for either of them to show up.

"Nine-one-one," I said. "Tell them we're being followed and suspect the individual is armed. Let the local fuzz approach the car."

I reached for my iPhone.

"It left," McGlade said.

I checked the mirror, saw the Monte Carlo speeding off in the opposite direction.

"Now what?" he asked. "Should we troll around?"

I considered it. "Yeah, do it."

I wanted this over and done with. If this was Luther, I'd get the license plate number, call the police, and end this.

But we circled the neighborhood for ten minutes and couldn't find the vehicle again.

"Maybe it was just a coincidence," McGlade said, finally pulling into a parking spot against the curb in Violet's town-house subdivision.

"Maybe." But my gut didn't think so.

McGlade had his smart phone out. "You see pics of this Violet King chick? Smoking hot. You know I love blondes."

He was looking at her on Google Images—Violet's photo in an old Reuters story from 2003 when she was in pursuit of Andrew Z. Thomas during the North Carolina murders.

"You love anything with boobs," I said.

"She's a cop?"

"Used to be."

McGlade opened his door as I reached for mine.

"Why'd she quit?" he asked.

"I guess we're about to find out."

Donaldson

March 31, 5:00 p.m.

After fleeing the neighborhood when Jack Daniels had spotted their tail, Donaldson had returned ten minutes later. They'd spent another five minutes circling, but there was no sign of Daniels's car.

"You blew it, D."

Lucy's bitching was starting to get on his nerves. He considered the Beretta. Maybe not killing her, just a bullet somewhere non-fatal. To shut her the hell up.

"What was I supposed to do? Just sit there while they called the cops? You wanna go back to the hospital?"

"You shouldn't have let them out of our sight. That was stupid."

"They were going to come after us. That was a new car Jack was in. We're riding around in a piece of shit from the nineties. They'd catch us, no problem."

"Well, maybe you should have—"

"There! Look!"

Donaldson slammed on the brakes, and they both moaned in pain as the Monte Carlo jerked to a stop.

Lucy leaned forward in her seat, staring intently through the windshield. "I don't see it."

No shit. She only had one eye. Donaldson pointed. "Parked over there beside the Dumpster." He realized he'd driven right past it. The Juke was a small car, and it had been blocked from view by a Chevy Astro the last few times they'd circled.

"So, how are we going to find which townhouse they're in?" Lucy said. "There must be like forty of them."

"We stake it out."

Donaldson drove around to the other side of the lot and parked out of obvious sight. It was the perfect spot. Far enough away from Jack's car to avoid easy detection, while allowing him and Lucy a clear view of nearly every townhouse in the complex.

"We don't want to miss them coming out," Donaldson said. "So Lucy?"

"What?"

"Keep your eye open."

Jack

March 31, 4:55 p.m.

Five Minutes Earlier

I huffed and puffed my way across the parking lot toward a townhouse set off from the others, surrounded by overgrown shrubs that came halfway up the windows.

There was no name on the mail slot, just the number I'd gotten from Cynthia Mathis—813.

"Try not to say anything stupid or offensive," I said as I rang the doorbell. "Tell you what...just don't say anything at all. If you have an idea for a question, write it on a piece of paper and I'll consider it."

"Sure thing, Mom. Want to hand me my crayons so I can play quietly in the corner?"

"Like I'd trust you with crayons."

The doorbell didn't work, so I banged hard on the glass door, almost said "This is the police" out of habit.

I heard a television set blaring on the other side of the door. The rain had begun to pick up again, and I was overcome with a sudden craving for Ben & Jerry's Chocolate Chip Cookie Dough Ice Cream, and, incongruously, dill pickles.

I needed to write to Ben & Jerry and ask if they'd make a cookie dough pickle flavor.

"Did your stomach just say something?" McGlade asked.

"Pretend you're still a cop. Act copish."

The door creaked slowly open.

Even before I saw her face, I smelled the smoke and nicotine.

I smiled. "Violet King?"

I could only see a thin panel of the woman's face through the four-inch crack between the door and the doorframe.

"Who's asking?" Southern drawl—faint but unmistakable. The sour odor of beer mingled with the cigarette stench.

"I'm Jack Daniels. This is my partner, Harry McGlade. We'd like to ask you some questions about Andrew Z. Thomas."

Her eyes narrowed. "I don't think so."

The woman started to close the door, but stopped. She glanced at my baby bump and then back up into my eyes. Her features softened. "Tell you what...you can come in for a minute."

Violet opened the door, and for a brief moment, the bleak, gray light from outside flooded into the front room of her townhouse. A haze of smoke lay upon everything like mist on the surface of a lake. An old-school tube television droned on from the far side of the room—a soap opera, the characters yelling at each other in a hospital room, debating whether or not to pull the plug on someone.

Violet stood less than five feet tall, but she must have weighed close to three hundred pounds. Her housedress was faded and expansive, and it took Violet more effort to waddle back across the room than it did for me to follow her inside.

"Is this her?" McGlade said from the corner of his mouth. "Or the beast that ate her?"

"Be nice, McGlade."

The living room was small and cramped and dark. Aside from the illumination of the television, there was only one other light source—a weak lamp on a marble-topped table next to the couch. A cigarette burning in an ashtray sent blue coils up into the dusky light.

Under the eye-watering reek of new and old tobacco smoke, I detected another, more offensive odor—rot. Spoiled vegetables or meat, or possibly both.

As my eyes adjusted to the lowlight, I saw the walls were covered in baby pictures—photographs of a cute little boy. In many of them, a gorgeous, young blonde held the baby, her smile radiating love and joy. Violet's hair was still blond, but she no longer seemed to be the woman in those pictures. I wondered if it hurt her to look at them.

Violet backed up carefully to the couch, and as she settled her bulk down onto the cushions, the frame creaked.

"Sit down." Violet motioned to a leather love seat. She lifted a remote control off the sofa cushion and muted the soap opera. The floor at her feet was littered with bags of potato chips and Chex Mix and enough Sam Adams Cherry Wheat bottles to make me wonder if she owned stock in the company. Something crunched under my Keds—mouse droppings.

"You have a lovely home, Miss King," McGlade said.

"What is it you two want?"

My bare arm touched the couch, layered with so much smoke residue I could practically feel the nicotine buzz seeping in through my pores. I forced a pleasant smile.

"I understand you were a police officer back in North Carolina."

"Homicide detective. But that was a long time ago."

"Was there a reason you left?" I asked.

"I'm on disability."

"Something weight-related?" McGlade chimed in.

Violet gave him a dismissive glance. "Injured on the job."

On the table, amid the garbage, was a keychain with a Toyota fob.

"Tough to make do on a disability income," I said. "But then, you have supplemental income as well."

I kept silent, hoping she'd fill in the details.

She said nothing.

"How do you know Andrew Z. Thomas?" I asked.

"Well, it's no secret I was involved in an investigation eight years ago."

"Where he was the subject?"

"Correct."

"And this investigation took you out to the North Carolina Outer Banks?" I asked, recalling the Wikipedia page.

"Yes."

"How did that investigation end?"

Violet let out a long sigh. "There's been a lot written about what happened on Ocracoke Island. I'm sure you can find books and Internet websites to answer all of your questions."

"I've had quite a bit written about me as well." I smiled. "It doesn't always tell the whole story. Or even the truth."

"I don't talk about that anymore."

"Have you been in touch with Andrew?"

"It's been a long time since I've seen him."

I noticed a photograph on the wall.

Grunting, I struggled onto my feet and walked around the couch as Violet tracked my movement with thinly veiled suspicion.

I reached up and lifted the framed photograph off the nail, studied it for a moment, and then showed it to Violet.

"When was this taken?" I asked.

The photograph was of a younger, much thinner, happier Violet, standing arm-in-arm with Andrew Thomas. A snow-covered mountain range loomed in the blurry distance behind them. I could tell this was Violet only by her green eyes. Otherwise, the woman in the photograph and the woman sitting on the couch looked nothing alike.

"That was taken seven years ago," Violet said. She heaved her bulk forward and snatched a partially full bottle of beer off the table, raising it to her lips.

"You had a relationship with Mr. Thomas."

"What makes you say that?"

"You look like a couple here."

"We were close for a little while. That was a long time ago."

"But still close enough that his agent sends you his royalty checks. From what I understand, his books have become quite popular since the controversy. Lots of money, I hear."

Violet shrugged. As a former cop, she knew how to play the game, to only offer information that I already knew. She'd be tough to crack.

I asked, "Where was this photograph taken?"

Violet gave the faintest smile. "Paradise."

"Where's paradise?"

She shifted her bulk on the couch. "You're here about the murder, aren't you? That woman killed on the bridge."

"What makes you say that?"

"I saw you on the news. Not too many pregnant women go to crime scenes. The TV showed you collapse." Violet's eyes lit up. "I hope the baby is okay."

"Do you know anything about that murder, Violet?"

She shook her head, reached over to the table, and lifted the cigarette which had nearly burned out. Violet brought it to her lips, took a long, hard draw until the ember flared back to life.

"Only what I saw on the news," Violet said, letting the smoke out through her nose.

I watched her eyes closely. "Have you ever used the screen name ALONEAGAIN?" I asked, referencing those messages I'd seen on Thomas's website message board.

"Huh?"

The confusion I saw told me she had no idea what I was talking about.

"Are you familiar with a man named Luther Kite?"

Violet's face hardened. She turned and spit over her shoulder, a glob of mucus running down the wall. She raised her hands and exposed the bare undersides of her flabby arms. The skin resembled spiced ham—mottled and rubbery. Burn scars.

"I have Luther Kite to thank for this," Violet said.

"I don't remember reading anything about your involvement with Kite."

"And you won't."

"Did that happen after the Kinnakeet massacre?"

"I don't talk about it."

"We believe Luther Kite is the one who murdered Jessica Shedd."

"I wouldn't doubt it."

"Any information you give us could be helpful. It could save lives."

"I'm afraid I'm not going to be helpful."

McGlade leaned forward. "So you and this writer guy were knocking the boots?"

"Excuse me?"

"Was he parting the pink curtains?"

Violet looked at me for some interpretation, but I could only close my eyes and shake my head.

"Was he slipping you the bloatwurst with the special sauce? Had Captain Wonder Worm invaded Panty Land?"

"Were you sleeping with Andrew Thomas?" I finally translated.

She drained the beer and let the empty drop to the carpet. "That's none of your business."

"That means yes," McGlade said. "And since he's still giving you money, I bet you probably have some idea where he is."

"I want him to leave my house right now." She pointed at McGlade. "Neither of you are cops. You're here at my invitation."

McGlade leaned forward, opening his coat, showing Violet the butt of his revolver. "Maybe I'll just look around anyway."

She folded her arms. "You won't find anything. Go ahead."

"Really?" McGlade said. He apparently hadn't been expecting that answer any more than I had.

"I've got nothing to hide. Andy and Luther were from a lifetime ago. I haven't seen either of them since I got burned. Just because I don't like to talk about a terrible part of my past doesn't mean I'm covering for anyone. You can search wherever you want, waste all the time you'd like. Just try not to mess my house up."

McGlade and I exchanged a glance, me wondering if it was even worth looking around. But he stood up and immediately began to snoop. I stayed seated. Not because I believed Violet would suddenly open up, but because I wanted to keep an eye on her. She was probably armed, and I didn't want her doing anything to us or to herself.

McGlade started in the kitchen.

I heard him open the fridge, say, "Mother of God, the smell is unbearable," and slam the door shut.

I realized he was the wrong person for this job. What was he looking in the fridge for? What clues did he expect to find there? Bologna and Cheez Whiz?

McGlade opened and closed a few kitchen cabinets, making a lot of racket, and then eventually worked his way upstairs.

After ten minutes of me watching Violet light one cigarette after another, McGlade returned, carrying a stack of CDs.

"Where did you get these?" he asked her.

"What are they?" Violet said.

"Bootleg Rolling Stones concerts."

"I don't know. I used to be really into music."

"Can I borrow them?"

"Excuse me?"

"I've been looking for some of these for years. I promise to return them in good condition."

I rolled my eyes.

"You can keep them," Violet said. "I already ripped them to my computer."

"Really? Thanks!"

"That's all you found?" I asked, incredulous.

"Are you kidding? This is an epic find. You know how rare this one is? From 1997, taken directly from the soundboard."

"That's a great concert." Violet began to beam. "I was at that show. Front row. Jagger actually sweated on me."

"That's awesome. So where's your baby?"

Violet's expression went from soft to pained.

"There's a nursery upstairs," McGlade continued. "It's the cleanest room in the house. But no baby food in the fridge. No bottles in the cabinets. This house boasts a wide variety of unpleasant odors, but dirty diapers aren't a part of the bouquet. So where's the kid?"

Violet said nothing, but her eyes had begun to glaze over.

"Dead?" McGlade asked.

I glared at him. This was taking good cop/bad cop too far. I didn't feel a threatening vibe from Violet. The only emotion she stirred up in me was pity.

"Now I'm going to *insist* that you leave."

"Was it the writer's baby?" McGlade pressed. "Is the royalty thing really child support?"

"The state took my baby, Mr. McGlade. Some neighbors made false accusations. I've spent close to a million dollars on lawyers trying to get him back." Her voice was cracking. "They won't even let me see him."

"How old is he now?" I asked gently.

"Almost seven."

"What's his name?"

"Max. After his father, my husband, who was murdered by Luther Kite and his family." Violet gave me an imploring look. "If I knew anything that would hurt Luther, I'd tell you. I swear I would. He destroyed my life. But there's nothing I can say that will make my situation any better. Not a damn thing."

"Maybe what you know can help save someone else," I offered.

Violet sat silent for a moment before answering. "There's no saving anyone, Jack. I'm surprised you haven't learned that by now."

I fished a business card out of my purse and handed it to her. "If you change your mind or think of anything, call me. Anytime."

"And thanks for the CDs," McGlade said, smiling and holding them up. "You can also call that number if you find any more Stones bootlegs."

We let ourselves out. The rain had stopped, and it felt colder than before.

"Well, that was pretty much a waste of time," I said, heading for the car.

"Are you kidding? I'm going to make a few hundred bucks selling these CDs on eBay."

I scanned the parked cars, searching for the Monte Carlo.

My iPhone buzzed.

A text from Herb.

Just four words, but they hit me like a slap across the face.

THERE'S BEEN ANOTHER MURDER.

Lucy

March 31, 5:45 p.m.

Movement in her peripheral vision, such as it was, pulled Lucy's attention away from the Juke. Two thirteen-year-old boys—one tall and scrawny, one fat as a little doughboy—stood ten feet away, staring at her through the glass, their mouths hanging open, a look on their faces caught between ridicule and disgust.

They approached, and one of them knocked on the window.

Lucy looked over at Donaldson, who said, "Just tell them to get lost."

She turned and stared at the boy through the glass. "Go away."

"Holy shit, she's only got one eye!"

"And this dude looks like Freddy Krueger!" the other boy yelled.

"Give me the gun," Lucy said. "I'm killing them both."

"We don't have time."

"How about just one of them?"

The taller of the two boys, a white kid wearing a black parka with a bandanna tied around his head, said through the glass, "What happened to you? Some kinda accident?"

Lucy lowered her window. "I was hanging out with my stupid friend, and we asked these very bad people too many questions."

The tall boy's friend punched him in the arm. "Damn, dawg, let's skate."

"Sure you don't want to have a little fun?" Lucy asked. "I've played with boys like you before. I would do things to you that would blow your minds."

"Yo, she's psycho, Chris, come on, quit messin."

"I'm coming around to your way of thinking," Donaldson said. "Lots of cornfields around here. Maybe we could take a little siesta." He turned to the boy. "Do you youngsters like beer?"

"You got beer?"

"We also have candy," Lucy said. "We're going to a party. All your friends will be there. Your parents said it was okay. I just talked to them."

"Chris, this is whack, let's bounce."

"Oh shit," Donaldson said. "Jack's coming out, look."

Lucy glanced through the windshield, spotted Jack and some man walking out of a townhouse on the far side of the complex.

The two teenage wiggers had made what was probably the only intelligent decision in their young, white trash lives, and had taken off.

"Too bad," Donaldson lamented, watching them go. "My tube was getting hard."

He started the car.

"What are you doing?" Lucy said.

"Following Jack."

"No."

"No?"

"Don't you want to know who Jack was visiting?"

"Yeah, but we'll lose Jack."

"We know where she lives. We can always pick her up again. But who's so important that Jack drove all the way out to Peoria to see them? This might be someone we need to talk to. Or someone to use as leverage."

Donaldson grunted. "Yeah, all right." He killed the engine and jammed the Beretta down the chest pocket of his overalls.

Jack Daniels's Juke hauled ass out of the parking lot, tires squealing.

"She's going somewhere in a hurry," Lucy said.

Donaldson opened his door and struggled up out of the Monte Carlo.

It took Lucy three tries to muster enough inertia to hoist herself out of the seat.

Finally standing on her pushpin legs, she felt lightheaded. A wave of crippling pain swept through her. She braced herself against the car, took a deep breath.

"You all right?" Donaldson asked.

"Yeah. I'm gonna need a new patch soon."

"How many we got?"

"Fifteen." And it had been a hard-fought fifteen. Lots of pain-loaded nights in order to save them up.

"We'll apply fresh ones when we get back to the car. Or maybe we'll get lucky, and our little home invasion will result in some meds."

They limped across the parking lot together like a pair of crippled demons, and by the time they reached the stoop to number 813, they were both panting so hard they had to stand there for two full minutes, recovering from the exertion.

"You ready?" Donaldson gasped, pulling the Beretta out of his overalls.

"I don't have a weapon."

"If I recall, your weapon was dragging people behind your car for miles, then spraying them with lemon juice."

"*Organic* lemon juice," Lucy corrected.

"You're such a tree-hugging hippie. Do you want to go out and score some lemonade before we bust in? Or maybe some granola?"

Lucy shook her head. "Just don't mess it up, fat ass."

Donaldson made a sad, three-fingered fist, and pounded on the door.

After a while, slow, heavy footsteps approached from the other side.

As soon as the door cracked open, Donaldson shoved the Beretta into the homeowner's face.

"Who are you?" he asked.

"Um...Violet."

"Are you alone?"

A hesitation, then, "Yes."

"We'd like to talk to you, Violet. You can open the door, or I can blow your brains out the back of your head. Your call."

The door opened.

Lucy's heart rate accelerated. It was an even bigger rush than morphine. God, she missed this shit.

They forced their way inside, Lucy deadbolting the door behind her.

The place stunk of stale cigarettes and beer and desperation. She turned to look at Violet, amused to find a morbidly obese woman in a housedress so big it could've been a circus tent. Except there wouldn't be any customers who'd pay to sit under that big top.

Lucy remembered back to a guy who'd given her a ride. Before she'd met Donaldson. A long time ago. A lifetime ago.

The driver had been fat.

He'd also been a lot of fun.

Every extra pound of fat a person carried required an extra three and a half miles of veins and arteries to supply it with blood.

Which meant that fatties bled.

A lot.

And Lucy loved blood.

Luther
March 31, 8:30 p.m.

L uther stands glaring at the desk clerk.

"No, that won't work. I need a room on the twelfth floor."

"Sir, here at the Renaissance Blackstone, we strive to make—"

"Yeah, I don't give a shit about that. I just want a room on the twelfth floor."

The desk clerk sighs but maintains her pleasant exterior. She turns her attention back to the computer screen, fingers tapping furiously at the keys. "Sir, all we have is a suite, but—"

"I'll take it."

"—it's four seventy-five a night."

Luther reaches into his wallet and throws down the stolen plastic.

* * *

It takes him five minutes to get the screws out of the windowpane in his suite on the twelfth floor, and even then, the window will only crack open six inches—suicide prevention measures.

But it's all he needs.

He reaches down into his duffle bag and lifts out the bubble-wrapped package. Sitting on the windowsill, he has to press his face into the glass to get a decent look down the twelve floors to Michigan Avenue.

Lots of cars out, but pedestrian traffic on the sidewalk is fairly light.

He shoves the package through the opening in the window and watches it fall.

* * *

Three minutes later, Luther pushes through the revolving doors and walks outside.

A fine drizzle is falling.

He moves twenty feet up the sidewalk and stops where the package has finally come to rest after a hard bounce that had nearly taken it into Michigan Avenue.

Reaches down, lifts it, cuts through the packing tape with his Harpy.

It takes him a moment to unwrap the numerous layers, but he finally gets down to the device, which looks intact.

Moment of truth.

He slides the release button to power it up.

He smiles.

Damn sturdy piece of engineering.

Jack
March 31, 9:00 p.m.

I stared at my computer screen, looking at the crime scene photos Herb had e-mailed me, trying to make sense of it.

Two people killed for no apparent reason, beyond sending me some kind of message.

But what was the message? For me to be afraid?

Got that. Loud and clear.

"Hungry?" Phin asked, poking his head through the door. He was still mad at me, and had refused to accept my apologies or even discuss what happened earlier.

I could have gone for some ice cream, or nachos, or sardines—better yet, all of the above mashed into a single bowl—but I told him, "I'm okay."

He left without replying.

I'd walked Duffy when I got home from Violet's, but he hadn't given up the goods. I wondered if feeding a dog a box of laxatives was dangerous. I also wondered, after the ring appeared, if I'd even want to wear it knowing where it had been.

Assuming I said yes to Phin's proposal.

Assuming that proposal was even still on the table.

I turned back to the monitor, staring at the photograph of the large cardboard box labeled FISH FOOD.

There had been another book, this one the Andrew Z. Thomas thriller *The Killer and His Weapon*, found in a baggie in Marquette's stomach. The baggie read:

JD, HE DEVOURED THIS BOOK IN ONE SITTING, LK

Luther Kite had again bent over a corner to bookmark a section from chapter one, page 151, and another letter *p* had been circled—this time, the one in the word *pleasure.*

The Killer and His Weapon ~ Andrew Z. Thomas

He saw it at once—a revelation.

Walls coming down all around him.

Restraints unlocking.

Chains falling away.

Good and evil, these contrived lenses through which humanity viewed itself, was a fraud. There was no law. No law but that to which he chose to hold himself. Anything less was weakness. Adherence to illusion. He was above all, above everything, the God of his own world, and in that moment he knew how he would live henceforth. To which code of ethics he would subscribe and none other.

The world was wide and life was short and there was so much beauty to be had.

He would honor *his* will.

Seek the means to his pleasure.

He rose up from the rock where he'd been sitting, lost in thought for the last seven hours, and roared from the top of the twelve-thousand-foot mountain, the sun blinding in his eyes, awash in pure mountain light, his voice reverberating off the surrounding peaks, racing down into the vast green forest. He had never in all his life felt so strong, so filled with joy, so invincible.

Tonight, he thought, as he started down the mountain, so light on his feet he half-believed he could take flight, glide down over the valley like some terrible bird.

Yes.

He would begin his new life tonight.

Remember tonight...for it is the beginning of always.

Start by embracing that impulse he'd shunned just yesterday when they'd stopped by his campfire to say hello.

Start by killing that young couple in the tent across the stream.

151

I read the page again and again, and then went back and reread the excerpt from *The Scorcher*, trying to understand why these pages had been marked. What was Luther telling me? Were these clues? Or was he just playing mind games?

There had been witnesses at the aquarium who saw Luther drop off the cardboard box. He'd been wearing a blue work uniform and driving a white van, though no one could recall the make, model, or license plate number.

Herb had already interviewed both of the families of the victims, and at first blush, there didn't appear to be any connection between the two, other than the curious fact that Marquette had been dumped at the Shedd Aquarium, and the first victim had been named Jessica Shedd. But Jessica had no association with the aquarium at all.

It puzzled me in a needling sort of way, like I was missing something as it stared right in my face.

Fingerprints found on the box belonged to Luther Kite.

Fingerprints found on the book belonged to Andrew Z. Thomas.

I mulled that over. Had Luther somehow gotten one of Andrew's personal copies in an attempt to make it seem like Thomas was involved? Or perhaps Thomas wasn't locked up in Violet's basement, as the literary agent had suggested, but in Kite's.

The thought of being the captive of a psychopath since 2004 made me shiver.

I had another thought. I'd forgotten to take a picture of the plastic bag that read *JACK D—THIS ONE WAS A REAL SWINGER—LK* in black marker. Since I had a sample of Thomas's handwriting from the letter he'd sent his agent, it was possible to compare the two and determine if they matched. If they did, that was pretty solid evidence that Andrew Z. Thomas was still alive.

I texted Herb, asking for pics of both bags.

Then I reread the *Scorcher* excerpt, my eyes lingering on the last line of the page.

"A little spark is followed by a great flame."

That sounded like a quote I'd heard before.

I Googled it.

Hmm.

It was from Dante Alighieri, writer of *The Divine Comedy*. Curious, I went through the remainder of the text, feeding each sentence into Google, but the remaining hits were all bootleg e-book excerpts from *The Scorcher*. I repeated the process with the second book and came up with similar results until I searched on the line: *Remember tonight…for it is the beginning of always.*

Dante again.

I doubted that was a coincidence. I perused Dante's Wikipedia page, wondering what connection a poet from the Middle Ages might possibly have to these murders. Then I surfed over to Amazon.com and found a free copy of *The Divine Comedy* for my Kindle app. I also checked out the page for *The Scorcher*, which was $12.99—a ridiculous price for an e-book, especially one so old. But I bought it—even cognizant of the fact that the royalties went straight to Violet King's beer-and-cigarette fund—and then spent ten minutes scanning through the several hundred customer reviews.

The Scorcher averaged three stars. Many were five-star praises, but an equal number were one-star wonders from people who seemed shocked that a thriller about a serial killer who burned his victims alive contained scenes of graphic violence.

Halfway into the fourth page of reviews, I came across one that made me do a double-take.

> Thomas wrote this book as an ode to the seventh circle of hell in Dante's Inferno, illustrated through the anti-hero's journey away from God and toward this inner ring. By embracing violence, he embraces his own downfall.

While that review seemed more insightful than most, it was the reviewer's name that caught me by surprise.

ALONEAGAIN.

Same screen name as the one who left those messages to me on Andrew Z. Thomas's message board.

I clicked on the name, but it took me to another screen which informed me that "This customer has not created a profile yet." I checked for other reviews by ALONEAGAIN, and found several, all of them for Andrew Z. Thomas novels.

I surfed over to the review for *The Killer and His Weapon.*

Thomas continues the Alighieri allegory (grin), focusing on the fifth circle of the inferno, anger. How are your anger issues, Jack?

I reflexively looked around my office, suddenly feeling as though I was being watched. I almost called out to Phin but managed to keep the fear in check.

The review was dated five months ago.

I read the others, but they were all older, and none of them addressed to me.

Wrapping a blanket tightly around my shoulders, I plunked down another thirteen bucks, brought up the file on my computer, and began to read *The Killer and His Weapon.*

Literary Agent Cynthia Mathis
March 31, 9:50 p.m.

Cynthia sipped the last of her espresso, courtesy of the seven-hundred-dollar machine occupying much of her kitchen counter, and then attacked her keyboard. She was finishing up her weekly post on *The Agent Knows Better,* her wildly popular blog.

Your query letter is one of the most terribly uninteresting things I've ever read, and even if your novel is ten times as good it would still be unsalable, unpalatable, and unworthy of my time. I encourage you to read my book, Golden Query Letters, *and start over from scratch. But first, go back to high school and get that GED. Hopefully English is not your first language.*

Cynthia smiled. Snarky and funny, yet truthful. The thousands of wannabe newbies following her blog would love it. She cut and pasted the next e-mail into her blog, a simple question from one of the clueless asking if self-publishing e-books was a viable career alternative. She heard her cell phone ringing but didn't pick up, eager to correct the mindless dolt on the realities of e-books.

No one makes money self-publishing, Cynthia typed. *There are a few loudmouth, know-it-all writers who blog about their successes, but they are no doubt liars. The only legitimate way to publish is through a respected publishing house. E-books are a fad, and the fools who jump on that bandwagon will blacklist themselves in the traditional publishing world.*

She saved the entry and then went to Twitter to announce her latest entry to her myriad of faithful followers.

Too bad they were all talentless hacks who would never sell anything.

It would be a few minutes before she started receiving comments, so she turned her attention to her cell and listened to the voicemail.

"It's me. I need you to get on the next plane to Detroit. I'll text you instructions when you arrive."

Cynthia's heart rate doubled. She listened to the message again, to make sure she'd heard correctly, and then hopped onto Priceline.com to find a flight from LaGuardia to Michigan.

Luther

March 31, 10:30 p.m.

He checks out of the Blackstone and stands outside in the cold mist, waiting for the valet to bring his Mercedes Sprinter. God, he loves this vehicle, but it's time to get it out of sight. Off the streets. News of the little package he deposited at the Shedd Aquarium is out, and numerous people saw his van pull up. If not already, the word on his ride will be out very soon.

He tips the valet a quarter and climbs in and speeds off down Michigan.

Swings around onto Lake Shore Drive and barrels north eating Lemonheads and listening to Miles Davis. He likes Miles. Lemonheads, not so much. But he's all about embracing bad habits.

Luther registers a palpable sense of relief when, a half-hour later, he's finally off the main roads and driving through a quiet, mostly deserted neighborhood.

He's safe here.

The lights of the Sprinter slash through the fog and strike the rear of the semi-trailer. He brings the van to a stop and leaves it running as he opens the door and steps outside.

The ramp is a bitch to drag down but he manages.

He drives the Benz up into the trailer and parks it against the front wall. The fit is too tight to open the driver's-side door, so Luther climbs back through the cargo area and exits out the rear doors.

It has been a big day, a perfect day, but tomorrow will be even bigger.

Historic.

The culmination of thousands of hours of work.

But there is still much work to do, he thinks as he strains to lift the auto ramp, *and miles to go before I sleep.*

And I have promises to keep.

APRIL 1

Donaldson
April 1, 1:23 a.m.

They'd spent the measly twenty-six dollars Henry had given them on gas. Goddamn pay-at-the-pumps made it impossible to steal fuel. And that fat bitch Violet King, useful as she was, had only had ten bucks on her, which they'd also put into the tank. That meant, if they wanted to eat, they'd have to steal food or money.

Shoplifting seemed to involve less risk.

Why hadn't they thought to eat back at Violet's place? She wouldn't have missed the food.

As it was, this 7-Eleven would have to do.

Donaldson went in first, the big pockets of his overalls much better at concealing foodstuffs than Lucy's ugly-ass housedress.

She distracted the Indian clerk at the counter by asking for bogus directions.

The convenience store no doubt had closed circuit cameras, but they were a long way from the institution. If the clerk happened to catch them, they both looked pathetic enough to probably get away with just a warning.

Donaldson pinched two packages of Twinkies, a handful of Slim Jims, some candy bars, and was reaching for something *he* could actually eat—a cup of apple sauce—when he heard, "You! What are you doing!"

He froze, feeling a sense of humiliation that took him back to his youth and being scolded by his father.

The clerk shoved Lucy aside and stormed over, his expression pure anger.

"Empty your pockets! Right now!"

When Donaldson didn't move, the prick actually put his hands on him, taking out all of the stolen snacks. Donaldson stared over his shoulder at Lucy, who was reaching for the gun stuffed into the back of her underwear. She'd been holding it so Donaldson had more room for food. He shook his head—shooting would bring the police. Instead, he lowered his eyes and apologized to the prick.

"I'm sorry. I was hungry. I haven't eaten in—"

"Then get a job and earn some money, you freak. If I see you in my store again, I'm calling the cops."

After removing the last Snickers bar, he grabbed Donaldson by the bib strap and escorted him out of his store. Pain flared all over Donaldson's body, but he dared not resist.

Once outside, he followed Lucy, the two of them limping toward their piece-of-shit car parked across the street.

"You were supposed to distract him," Donaldson said.

"He was onto you, D. Nothing I could do about it."

"We gotta come up with a better plan for next time."

"Don't need to. While he was busy with you, I helped myself."

"Food?" Donaldson's mouth began to water at the thought of it.

"Better."

"Cash?"

"Register was locked, but I got these." Lucy reached into her dress, pulled out a long, accordion string of cards.

Scratch-off lottery tickets.

"Goddamn it, girl, no one ever wins at those things. Why didn't you grab something we could actually use?"

Then Lucy did something that Donaldson hadn't seen in all the time they'd been institutionalized.

She began to cry.

Donaldson didn't know how to react. Once upon a time, he'd tried his damnedest to kill this girl. And she'd returned the favor. But these last few years, rehabilitating, plotting, planning their revenge, Donaldson realized he'd formed a relationship with Lucy that was as intimate as any he'd ever had. Looking at her, so obviously distressed, he felt bad for his comment.

They climbed painfully into the front seats of the Monte Carlo, and Donaldson gave her one of the car keys.

"Look. Let's scratch these babies off. Maybe we'll win the lottery after all."

After spending ten excruciating minutes scratching off all seventeen cards, they'd only won a single free ticket.

"I hate you," Donaldson told Lucy.

It grew cold, and with no money for a motel, they were forced to sleep in the car, the situation only compounded by the fact that Lucy had lost the Ativan, the drug that helped them to sleep. Without it, it would be damn near impossible to drift off.

Donaldson didn't believe in karma, but when he considered the many people he'd ruthlessly murdered, he wondered if sitting there shivering, hungry, and in terrible pain might actually be what he deserved.

Jack
April 1, 7:30 a.m.

I didn't have any seizures that night, because I didn't sleep. Too much on my mind.

Insomnia and I were old, familiar enemies.

Even though Phin was still angry, he'd insisted on staying in my room and had only fallen asleep an hour before dawn. Now, as the sun came up, he was still sleeping in the easy chair, Duffy at his feet.

I read Andrew Z. Thomas long into the morning.

The Scorcher was a violent little potboiler that had surprisingly held my interest, despite the fact that it had no hero to root for. But having read it, I still wasn't sure what it was supposed to teach me. When I'd finished *The Scorcher*, I dove into *The Divine Comedy*, and the only thing I learned from that one was that Dante was nuts. Thinking up tortures for sinners and then writing an epic poem about it struck me as the ultimate in poor taste. That so many religions and people took what Dante said about hell as a universal truth was a scary proposition.

After the reading binge, I walked Duffy in the backyard.

When he finally pooped, I stared at the pile, wondering what my next course of action should be. Arriving at no pleasant way to solve the problem, I put on a latex glove and played pinch and squish, which was every bit as revolting as it sounded, the smell so bad I actually took off my sports bra and tied it over my nose and mouth. After a thorough examination, I deemed the ring wasn't there. It had been a disgusting waste of time.

On the plus side, it was so terrible, I didn't see how changing a baby's diaper could be any worse.

When I walked back inside, Phin was up.

"Let's take your blood pressure," he said, sleep still pulling on his voice.

"Later."

"Now."

I was too tired to fight with him, so I took a seat while he pumped and calculated.

"One sixty-five over one ten. It's gotten worse."

"I feel fine."

"We need to take you to the ER, Jack. This is a serious—"

"Feel."

"What?"

I grabbed his hand, placed it on my belly. "Feel. She hears your voice, and she's saying good morning."

Phin held his palm there, our child's little feet tapping against him. For that brief, crystal moment, I could picture being married to him, and the white picket fence fantasy hit me full force. No more chasing killers or carrying guns. Just the three of us, being stupidly, happily domestic.

Phin pulled his hand away. "I'm calling the doctor, asking him what to do about your blood pressure."

"Can you just sit with me a little, first?"

He left, and I felt a pang of guilt dead center in my chest, questioning yet again why I simply hadn't said yes to his proposal.

Waddling back to my office, I plopped down behind my desk and stared at my computer. I considered opening up Notepad to jot some things down, but instead went analogue and took out a piece of paper and a pen.

I made a list of data points on the first murder.

Vic Name: Jessica Shedd
Location where body found: Kinzie Street railroad bridge, hanging over the water
Time of Death: March 31, approx 1:30–2:30 a.m.
Cause of Death: blood loss, with extensive premortem mutilation
Found 6:40 a.m. by jogger
Book found in plastic bag wired to ribcage
Writing on bag: For Jack D—This one was a real swinger—LK
Book: The Scorcher by Andrew Z. Thomas
1 page dog-eared: page 102
1st letter "p" on the page circled
Dante line: A little spark is followed by a great flame.

Something occurred to me. I grabbed my Kindle and found the corresponding page which had been earmarked. Then I backspaced until I came to the beginning of that chapter. Wrote it down.

Chapter 31
Relevance of excerpt...unknown.

Okay, next murder.

> Vic Name: Reginald Marquette
> Location where body found: Shedd Aquarium
> Time of Death: March 31, approx 1:00–2:00 p.m.

I went online and logged into the Chicago PD database, checked the police report to see if the coroner had determined cause of death. Yep.

> Cause of Death: potassium chloride
> poisoning, postmortem mutilation
> Witnesses say body dropped in cardboard box at entrance to
> aquarium at approx. 2:00 p.m.
> Book found in plastic bag in the stomach
> Prints on bag belong to Luther Kite
> Prints on book belong to Andrew Z. Thomas
> Writing on bag: JD, He devoured this
> book in one sitting, LK
> Book: The Killer and His Weapon
> by Andrew Z. Thomas
> 1 page dog-eared: page 151, in part 1
> 1st letter "p" on the page circled
> Another Dante line: Remember tonight...for it is the
> beginning of always.

I studied the similarities first.

Obviously, a victim named Shedd and a crime scene at the Shedd Aquarium. Two Thomas books. Two Dante quotes. Two notes to me written on plastic bags. Fingerprints from both Kite and Thomas.

As for differences...

One younger, single woman; one older, married guy.

She was a claims adjuster; he was a professor.

She was tortured; he died relatively fast and painlessly.

I checked their birth dates and addresses, but didn't notice anything that linked them.

I scribbled *Two different murderers?* on the pad, and then called up Phil Blasky at the county morgue.

"Phil, Jack Daniels."

"Hey, Jack. How's retirement treating you?"

"You're bullshitting me, right?"

"Absolutely. Calling about these Kite murders?"

"Yeah. Style seems different. One was torture, one was poison."

"You thinking two different killers?" he asked.

"Crossed my mind."

"I can tell you the mutilations appear consistent. Same weapon used—a curved, serrated blade. The cutter was right-handed in both cases. Entry cut was at the same location, just above the belly button. The cutter has some knowledge of anatomy. No unnecessary damage to the internal organs."

"A doctor? A butcher?"

"Possibly. Or could be someone who has simply gutted a whole lot of people."

I crossed out my *Two different murderers?* note. "Thanks, Phil."

He hung up.

I stared at my notes, my mind drifting, and wrote down:

Jessica.

Sara.

Amanda.

I scratched those out, and then wrote:

Maria.

Lisa.

Carla.

Carla Daniels.

Carla Daniels-Troutt.

But I hated the name Troutt. I didn't much care for the name Daniels either. That was my ex-husband's name, and I just kept it for professional reasons.

Though my maiden name, Streng, wasn't much better.

Did I have to use my name or his name? Couldn't I pick something entirely new?

I wrote:

Carla Einstein. Carla Aristotle. Carla Hemingway.

And I realized I hated the name Carla, too.

I heard Phin coming back, quickly turned the paper over.

"The doctor said to take you to the emergency room immediately."

"Of course she said that. She could be sued otherwise."

"Put your shoes on."

I reached for his belt, tugged him closer. "I know something that can lower my blood pressure."

"I'll meet you in the car."

He pulled away, rejection prickling me like a blush.

Which was probably how I'd made him feel yesterday.

I hoisted myself out of my desk chair and then went to find my shoes.

This was shaping up to be a really shitty day.

Luther

March 17, Fifteen Days Ago

Three Days After the Bus Incident

"Name?"

"Christine. Christine Agawa."

"How much do you weigh, Christine?"

"What?"

"Did you not hear my question?"

"Yes, I just don't understand—"

"Your understanding is not integral to this conversation. Answer the goddamn question."

Her eyes lower. She stares into the table.

He can practically smell the shame and the self-hate radiating off of her.

"Three hundred and seventy pounds."

"Is that accurate? Or are you keeping a few pounds from me?"

"I haven't weighed myself in a while. I'm probably heavier."

"Have you been heavy all your life?"

"Since I was…" She wipes a tear from the corner of her eye. "Since I was ten."

"What prompted this?"

"I don't know."

"But it isn't some thyroid condition or anything like that beyond your control?"

She shakes her head.

He slides his chair back and stands.

"Thank you, Christine."

"Why am I here?" she asks as he reaches for the door. "Please." Crying now. *"I'm so worried."*

"It's okay, Christine. Quite healthy in fact. But you shouldn't be worried." He smiles. "You should be terrified."

Peter Roe
April 1, 1:30 p.m.

It was his first appointment after lunch, a "potential client" intake with a man from Champagne. Their first telephone call had gone well enough to schedule an in-person meeting. The product at issue was a glass-cutter implementing some state-of-the-art, design-around technology that Mr. Siders seemed confident would be a goldmine once brought to market. Then again, that was the trouble with inventors. Seventy-five percent of them were certifiably, batshit crazy, and ninety percent harbored delusions that their invention would make them millions. But one of Peter's strengths—he liked to think—was his gut-check when it came to accepting new clients. Knowing whether or not to sign them up. Having that innate sense about whether their product had enough potential to make dealing with their mental instability or neuroses, whatever you wanted to call it, worthwhile.

Peter's phone rang.

He answered on speakerphone, "Yes, Kelly?"

"Mr. Roe, Mr. Siders is here for his one-thirty."

"Thank you, I'll be right out."

He disconnected and lifted the microphone to his dictation machine, entered a 3.25-hour time billing for the response to an office action of the United States Patent and Trademark Office that he'd completed before lunch.

Rising from his desk, he slid into the Versace jacket he wore in court and for initial meetings—had to impress on every conceivable level when you billed out at $625 an hour.

He met Mr. Siders in reception, found a tall man with long, black hair bundled up under a White Sox baseball cap, wearing dark sunglasses, black boots, black jeans, and a long-sleeved black tee from Slayer's *Hell Awaits* tour. Not exactly dress-to-impress attire for that first meeting with your patent attorney, but it wasn't unusual. In Peter's experience, inventors were a quirky bunch, and most dressed to fit that mad scientist vibe they put out into the world like a Mace-blast of pheromones.

"Rob Siders," Peter said with a smile he'd honed to perfection over the years—confident, comfortable, wealthy, and friendly without being too open. Important to send these subtle messages to establish the appropriate attorney-client boundaries from day one.

Roe extended his hand, and the man stood up and shook it.

Limp-wristed, cold-fish grip, and something was wrong with the man's skin. He glanced down.

What the hell?

Siders was wearing latex gloves.

"Mr. Roe, nice to finally meet you."

"What's with the gloves, Mr. Siders?" He tried not to make the question sound rude or prying, but Jesus, talk about strange.

"I don't want to freak you out."

"You won't."

"I have psoriasis. It's not contagious or infectious, but it's not very pretty either."

"Understood. Did Kelly offer you coffee or water?"

"Yes, but I'm fine. Just had lunch."

"Excellent, come on back."

Siders grabbed the black duffle he'd brought along— probably contained a prototype he wanted to show off—and Peter led him down the hallway, past the large office where his paralegal and two associates slaved away in cubicles, before arriving at the corner digs he called home.

He stood in the doorway, ushered Siders through.

"Nice office," Siders said.

"Thank you."

And he had to admit it was—horizontal bay windows with spectacular views of The Loop. The rent was scary, but with what he pulled in annually, and his churn-and-burn approach to associate mentoring, he could swing it, and would continue to do so for the foreseeable.

Instead of artwork, his wall-space was devoted to his Illinois and Minnesota law licenses, his license to practice in the USPTO, his law degree from Duke, his master's in mechanical engineering from Iowa State University, his Best Lawyers in America plaques, and row after row of the face pages of every patent he'd prosecuted through to issuance.

Siders, as most clients did stepping into his office for the first time, stopped a few feet in and scanned the array of credentials.

"Impressive," he said, nodding his head.

"Please, have a seat, Rob."

Peter unbuttoned his jacket and took a seat in the leather chair behind his desk. He'd never admit this to a client in a million years, but this meeting was merely a social inspection. He'd already undertaken some quick research, had one of his associates prepare a memorandum on the twenty most-recently issued patents in the field of glass cutting to get an overview of the current state of the technology. To be honest, he was hopeful. There were some holes, and with the guidance of a legal supernova like himself, Siders might actually have a shot at staking out his own piece of the market.

"Would you mind shutting the door?" Siders asked.

Roe kept an open-door policy in his office—not so much out of any atmosphere of sharing or generosity he wanted to foster, but more out of his inclination to "pop in" on his paralegal or associates at any time to confirm they were on task instead of surfing the Internet or taking personal calls. In truth, it didn't matter—he monitored their web-browsing and had a secret program that logged their every keystroke and sent daily reports to his e-mail—but he liked to remind them that he was always watching.

"Mr. Siders, I can assure you—everything we discuss is subject to attorney-client privilege, and in fact, some of my associates may be assisting with all aspects of your portfolio if we go forward."

"I understand, but it's what I'd prefer. At least on the first occasion I set foot into your office."

"Of course. But on one condition."

"Name it."

"You take off your sunglasses."

Siders smiled and complied.

Strike one, Roe thought as he walked to his door and closed it. All inventors had a reasonable paranoia of having their intellectual property stolen, but distrusting your attorney was the stuff of mental illness.

"I've taken the liberty of performing some preliminary research," Roe said as he eased back into his chair. "It looks promising. You told me a little about what you'd designed, but just so you know, my approach is to work with my clients from square one. If you can build something from the ground up that takes into account all existing technology and pending patents, I find that the success rate of getting a quick Notice of Allowance is much higher."

"I brought my prototype, if you'd like to see it."

"Absolutely."

Siders knelt down by his duffle and unzipped the bag.

He lifted out a fire ax.

"Is this a joke?" Roe asked as Siders set it on the sheet of glass that protected his desk.

"Not at all."

"Your glass-cutting technology is an ax?"

"It's very effective. Perhaps it would clarify things if I gave you a demonstration."

"By all means."

Siders stood and lifted the tool.

He went around to the plate of glass behind Roe's desk.

Strike two.

"Excuse me, Mr. Siders." He swiveled around in the chair. "Just what the hell do you think you're doing?"

"I'm demonstrating."

"On my goddamn window?"

"Well, yeah. You got any other glass around here?"

Strike three.

Roe stood, rage overtaking him. His time had been wasted. The hour he'd spent dealing with this meeting, instructing his associate on the research, reviewing his memo. He'd been on law review, been voted one of Chicago's top patent lawyers four years running. He was better than this, and his time far more valuable.

"Mr. Siders, I don't think that I'm going to be able to help you."

"Why is that?"

"I'd like for you to leave now."

"But I have to show you how this works. Once you see it—"

"I'm asking you for the last time to leave."

"But you've got to see this. It'll blow your mind."

Siders had the ax cocked back over his shoulder, Roe fast coming to the realization that the man was massively unhinged. Mentally unstable. With genius often came debilitating emotional baggage, but this wasn't genius. This was psychosis.

Roe lifted the phone, punched in Kelly's extension, and brought the receiver to his ear.

"Kelly, I need you to get security up to my office right..."

He pulled the phone away from his ear and stared at the severed cord with a mix of shock and growing terror.

Holy shit.

Siders, probably when Peter had gone to close the door to his office, had cut the cord.

He needed to get out of here. Right now.

He turned and started quickly around his desk, but Siders blocked his path, smiling now.

The elbow came fast, and he didn't so much feel the impact to his jaw as register that he was suddenly sitting on the floor.

Siders said, "Relax, and this will go quickly and without much pain."

"You...you can't...you..."

Peter was trying to stand up when he saw the steel tip of a black cowboy boot on an intersecting trajectory with his jaw.

Jack
April 1, 1:40 p.m.

As I scanned the ER for the second time in two days, I wondered how many people actually died in the waiting room before being seen by a doctor. Supposedly my blood pressure constituted enough of an emergency to warrant this trip to the hospital, but was not so critical that I didn't have to wait an hour. Add in the forty minutes it took to get to Chicago from Bensenville, because Blessed Crucifixion was the nearest hospital in my insurance network. If my condition had truly been life-threatening, I would have been dead by now.

"If my condition was truly life-threatening I'd be dead by now," I told Phin.

"I'll check with the nurses' station again."

He got up and walked off. I sighed. No doubt I was going to be given the labor induction talk again, but today was April 1, and there was no way I was having my baby on April Fool's Day.

My iPhone rang.

The screen said Blocked Call, but I hit the accept button anyway.

"Jacqueline Daniels? We regret to inform you that Herb Benedict is dead. He ate so many double cheeseburgers that he exploded—an explosion so powerful it also killed sixteen other people."

McGlade often blocked his number when he called me, because when I knew it was him I usually didn't pick up. "Are you here yet, Harry?"

"Pulling into the parking lot. Remind me again what I'm supposed to get out of watching your back all the time. Money? Fame? Are you setting me up with some close friends of yours who are twin strippers?"

"You get the satisfaction of knowing I've lived for another day."

"I'd rather have the twin strippers."

"I gotta go. My water just broke."

"Seriously?"

"No. Two can play that stupid April Fool's game."

I hung up. Phin wasn't back yet. I was thinking about texting him something dirty when my iPhone rang again. Another Blocked Call, and this one asked if I wanted to use FaceTime—an app that allowed the people talking to also see each other's faces. Just like the Jetsons. Phin had insisted upon it, in case of emergencies, and to use it I carried around a rechargeable WiFi hotspot, which cost slightly more per month than my annual electric bill.

I tapped the button, allowing FaceTime, annoyed at the prospect of having to look at McGlade while talking to him.

But it wasn't McGlade staring up at me.

It was a pale man with black hair.

Someone I hadn't seen in quite some time.

Someone I'd hoped to never see again.

The repulsion was so intense that part of me—a very large part—was tempted to hang up and throw the phone away. But that's not what cops do.

Luther smiled into the camera.

"You're looking very pregnant, Jack."

"You're looking ugly as ever. Wouldn't this be better in person? I've got some friends who are itching to say hello to you."

"All in good time. I've got a little game for you. If you win, you save a man's life. Interested?"

"I'm not playing any game with you, Luther."

Luther pressed the second camera button, and the video on my iPhone switched from Luther's face to an image of another man in a nice suit, unconscious, a strip of duct tape over his mouth, and his wrists and ankles zip-tied.

I'd played a sick game like this before with a serial killer who sent me pictures of people she was about to kill. But those were just still shots. This was live video.

"Can you still hear me, Jack?"

I didn't answer. I felt like vomiting and then running away to someplace where this lunatic could never find me.

"Answer me, Jack, or I'll cut out this man's eyes."

"Yes. I can hear you, Luther." I was going to add, "Let him go," but I knew that would be pointless. Luther had something in mind, and my only option was to wait and see what happened next. "Where did you come up with this idea?"

"I learned it from a mutual friend of ours. You remember Alex Kork. The most beautiful woman I've ever met."

"Alex was a monster," I said. "Like you."

"Birds of a feather. Here's how the game works, Jack. It's very simple. I ask you one question. If you don't have an answer for me, I'm going to murder him. Ready? Do I have your full attention?"

"I can't play your game right now, Luther. I'm in an emergency room."

Now I hit my camera button, showing him the waiting room. Then I looked frantically around for Phin. If I could let him know what was happening, he could find Herb and maybe we could figure out where Luther was.

Luther said, "Blessed Crucifixion? Is it the preeclampsia again?"

If his knowledge of my condition was meant to unnerve me, it worked. I took in a quick breath through my clenched teeth to steady myself.

"How about we do this another time? Let that guy go. You can always find someone else to kill later on."

"That won't do. It has to be this man, at this time. But he has one chance. You. If you hang up, he dies. If you don't want to play, he dies. If you get the wrong answer, he dies. Are you ready? Tell me you're ready, Jack."

Phin still wasn't back. I set my jaw. "I'm ready."

"Where am I?"

"That's the question?"

"That's the question."

"I don't understand."

"I've been giving you clues, Jack. If you've been paying attention, you should know where I am right now. I've practically spelled it out for you."

I closed my eyes, thoughts racing so fast I felt dizzy.

My feet and hands tingled.

My blood pressure was probably off the charts.

But I focused. I focused hard.

I considered the two previous murders.

The data points I'd written out this morning.

The similarities and differences.

"Where am I, Jack?"

Where was he?

"You have ten seconds."

The first murder had occurred at the Kinzie Street railroad bridge.

The second was at the aquarium.

What did they have in common?

"Oh, look who's awake."

The camera switched from Luther back to the suited man on the floor, whose eyes were bugging out.

"Mr. Roe, let me introduce former Chicago police lieutenant Jack Daniels. Jack Daniels, this is Mr. Peter Roe. Peter, if Jack doesn't answer this question correctly, you're going to die. How's that sound? All she has to tell me is where we are."

The man screamed through the duct tape and writhed on the floor.

"Six seconds, Jack."

The first two murders had taken place outside.

But this was inside.

"You have four seconds, Jack."

Jessica Shedd was killed at the Kinzie Street bridge...

Reginald Marquette was killed at the Shedd Aquarium...

Marquette.

Is he killing people at locations based on the last name of the previous victim?

"Two seconds, one second, and—"

"Marquette," I screamed into the phone.

"—we're all out of time."

The man on the floor was nodding violently.

"What was that, Jack?" Luther asked.

I thought about locations in Chicago with the name Marquette, and could only come up with one.

"Marquette Park."

Luther smiled. "Epic fail, Jack. Does this look like a park to you?" He panned the camera around what appeared to be an office. Diplomas and certificates on the walls. "Do you see any pigeons or squirrels running around? Were you really a lieutenant? Don't they make you take some sort of intelligence test for that?"

Shit. Of course.

"The Marquette Building," I said. "You're in the Marquette Building, downtown, on Dearborn."

Luther nodded, looking off to the side. "Yes, but that wasn't your first answer. We'll have to go to the judges, see if it's acceptable. Can we accept that answer?"

The camera switched to Mr. Roe, nodding so frantically that he was probably giving himself whiplash.

"Looks like the judges will allow it. Which means that now we have the bonus question."

I heaved myself onto my feet and started through the waiting room. Where the hell was Phin?

I said, "You told me you'd let him go if I got it right."

"I said no such thing. I told you I'd murder him if you got it wrong. And that applies to this question as well."

"Is this the last one? Or will you just keep doing this over and over until I get one wrong?"

"We'll make it three questions total. If you get all of them correct, Mr. Roe will live to see the fall. Here's number two. Precisely what time was Reginald Marquette killed?"

I passed the check-in window and spotted Phin hunched over a water fountain at the end of the corridor.

"How precisely?" I asked, stalling for time.

"Down to the minute."

I was practically jogging down the corridor now, waving an arm, trying to get Phin's attention, but he was taking the longest drink of water ever.

"Hello, Jack? You seem distracted. Are you walking around?"

"Stretching my legs a bit," I said, breathing heavily.

"Switch cameras. Show me what you're looking at."

I stood next to Phin, and then hit the camera change button, showing the waiting room. Into Phin's ear I whispered, "Luther is killing a guy named Roe at the Marquette Building."

Phin nodded and whipped out his phone.

"Okay, Jack, switch back to your chubby little face, and hit me with that answer."

"I'm thinking."

"You either know it or you don't."

Time of death.

Time of death.

Marquette.

Dropped at the aquarium around two.

Come on, come on.

I pictured the page of notes.

"Ten seconds, Jack."

Jessica Shedd's murder pointed to Marquette's death. Her name was the next location—the Shedd Aquarium. So then what clue predicted the next time of death?

"Seven seconds."

The book itself?

No, too broad.

The dog-eared page. It had to be.

The dog-eared page found in Shedd's stomach was from chapter thirty-one of *The Scorcher*.

"Five seconds."

The page number.

What was the page number?

102.

The coroner had said that Marquette had been killed just prior to being dumped at the aquarium at two p.m. Probably within the hour.

"Four...three...two—"

"You killed Marquette yesterday at one oh two p.m."

Luther nodded, looking somewhat disappointed. "Maybe you aren't as slow as I thought. Okay, last question. How does the novel *The Killer and His Weapon* end?"

"I haven't read that one yet. I only read *The Scorcher*."

"Really? Did you like it?"

"I did. The author was really able to get into the head of a psychopath. Is he still alive, by the way? Andrew Z. Thomas?"

"Andy will live forever, through his words. Now answer the question."

"At the end of *The Scorcher*, the hero burns himself alive."

"That wasn't the question. I asked about *The Killer and His Weapon*."

Goddamn it. Why didn't I read that one instead? I closed my eyes, remembering the back jacket copy. It was about an everyday Joe who embraces his homicidal instincts. Thomas wrote nihilism. He had a thing for Dante.

"Five seconds, Jack."

"He..."

"Yes?"

I took a shot, hoping I was right.

"He goes to hell," I said.

Luther stared at me for a moment, and then nodded. "Not bad. You figured that out without reading it?"

"I took a guess."

"Good guess. You're correct. And now Mr. Roe will live to see the fall."

Luther switched the camera view to Mr. Roe, and I realized with a sickening clarity exactly what was going to happen next.

Peter Roe

April 1, 1:45 p.m.

The man calling himself Siders set his iPhone on the desk and stared down at Roe with pitch-black eyes. He drew a folding knife out of the front pocket of his jeans and pried open the blade.

Silver. Gleaming. Laughably sharp.

It looked more like the talon of a bird than a knife.

Roe said, "Please don't do this," but it came out only as a muffled scream through the duct tape covering his mouth.

As Siders lowered the blade toward his leg, Roe tried to say, "Oh, please, God, no."

Felt himself begin to pass out.

A slap brought him around again.

"These are your last moments of life, Peter. You want to sleep through them?"

Roe whimpered as Siders made an incision in his seven-hundred-dollar pants and tugged the blade through the wool, cutting all the way down to his knee. Then he pulled out a roll of duct tape from his duffel and went to work taping

182

something encased in bubble wrap to the inside of his leg, winding the tape around and around and around.

Siders finally set the tape aside and took hold of Peter's leg, gave it a good shake, said, "I think that'll work."

He walked around the desk and Peter heard his footsteps trailing away toward the door, followed by the sound of the lock clicking into place.

Siders returned and hoisted the fire-ax off the floor.

"Glass cutting at its finest," he said.

Swung.

Jack
April 1, 1:45 p.m.

I grabbed Phin's phone away from him and yelled at Herb to hurry.

He said, "Cops are on their way. Roe is on the twelfth floor. Security is already on their way up."

"I'll see you there."

"Jack—" Both Herb and Phin said it at the same time, but I was already storming out the automatic exit doors, looking for McGlade.

His Tesla was parked in a handicapped spot.

He was playing TowerMadness.

"Hiya, Jackie. Almost beat the Dice level."

I tugged open the passenger door and slid into the seat. "How fast does this bucket go?"

"Zero to sixty in three point seven seconds."

"Show me."

Peter Roe
April 1, 1:48 p.m.

The pick end of the ax head punched through the office window, which spiderwebbed into a million fractures but stayed intact. Siders ripped the ax head out and struck again, and again, and again, tiny squares of plastic-coated safety glass raining down on Peter's face as the cool April air streamed in.

Peter was screaming against his gag, wondering if Kelly and his associates could hear the noise, but in truth, it wasn't that loud, and it didn't matter if they did.

He recalled the speech he gave to every new hire (which, considering his turnover, was a frequent occurrence) where he preached his open-door policy, with one caveat: *Never, under any circumstance, come into my office when the door is closed. Don't even knock. Because I'm either sleeping or naked.*

That policy had sure come back to bite him in the ass.

Bound and gagged and watching this maniac tear a hole through his window, Peter Roe realized he was an asshole. Greedy, selfish, demanding. He'd been okay with it up until this moment, because of the money. That balm of being rich that soothed so many of life's ills, including a guilty conscience. But soon, he was going to be dead, that money unreachable, and so now he only had the knowledge of what an asshole he'd been. A douche bag, as his son would say, and it was his douche baggery that had landed him in this spot.

Siders tossed the ax onto Peter's sofa and wiped the sweat that was pouring off his brow.

The hole he'd created was ragged, irregular, about three feet across at its widest point, and as Peter stared through it, it occurred to him for the first time what was about to happen.

For some reason, he'd assumed this psycho was going to stab him to death, but that wasn't it at all.

Siders grabbed his legs and dragged him across the carpeting toward the hole, Peter squirming, fighting with everything he had to break free, but all he accomplished was digging the plastic zip-ties so deep into his skin he could feel fresh blood begin to flow.

His feet moved through the opening, dangling out over Dearborn Street, and then he was out up to his knees, the awful tug of gravity already beginning to pull him the rest of the way through.

Siders sat on his stomach, momentarily halting his progression through the hole.

"I envy you," he said. "'When will I die?' is a question that haunts every man. No one knows the day, let alone the hour. But you do." Siders glanced at his watch. "In seventy seconds, you're going out this window. I promised Jack you'd live to see the fall, which is why I'm not cutting your throat first. I'll shut up now, and give you a moment to pray or make your peace or whatever you feel the need to do."

Peter realized this had to be that madman who'd hung the woman off the bridge near Kinzie Street, the one who'd dropped that professor in a fish-food box at the aquarium.

What were the odds?

"Forty-five seconds, counselor."

He couldn't speak, so he couldn't beg, but he had a hunch his cries and blubbering would make no difference. Roe wasn't religious, and it surprised him that even now, on the literal precipice of death, he had no sudden fear or belief in God. Only a gaping emptiness in the pit of his soul that he recognized as regret.

"Thirty seconds."

Regret for so many things.

But he came back to something he'd told his wife, his son, his friends, so many times—guilt, worry, jealousy, and regret—these were worthless emotions that accomplished nothing.

And so he attempted to clear his mind.

A sudden noise ripped him back into the moment.

He craned his neck, saw the door to his office burst inward.

His staff? His wonderful, disobedient staff, rushing to his rescue?

No! Something even better.

Security from the lobby!

Two men whose names he'd never even taken the time to learn had broken in with guns.

They'd come to save his life.

Jack
April 1, 1:50 p.m.

"Holy...shit..."

"Yeah. Does it feel like eighty or what?"

The city blurred by, the acceleration in McGlade's Tesla reminding me of my younger years, when I thought roller coasters were a good idea. I was actually pinned to my seat by the G-force, and we came up on the tail end of a city bus so quickly I was sure we'd embed ourselves in it.

But McGlade swerved, and the car proved its handling was just as wicked as its speed, narrowly missing the bus, weaving between a cab and an SUV, and then drifting through two El-track posts until we swung out onto Wabash, speeding south.

"Remember *The French Connection?*" McGlade said, a crooked grin plastered on his face. I looked at the tracks overhead, then at the traffic ahead of us, and realized I probably wouldn't have to induce labor. This might just do it for me.

I chanced a glance at my iPhone.

I'd lost the connection back in the hospital and now saw a text from Phin saying he was on his way. I punched the address book and called Herb as McGlade laid on the horn and ripped past a group of geriatrics who toppled like dominoes along the side of the street.

"Jesus, McGlade!"

"Hope they were wearing adult diapers."

"Do that again and I'll need one."

"Please don't do that in my new car, Jack. It's impossible to get the smell out of the leather." He shot me a quick, sheepish glance. "Or so I've heard."

Another burst of acceleration, which was almost surreal since there was no sound of a roaring engine to go along with it. The Tesla was electric, quiet as a church mouse.

"Mile and a half to the Marquette Building," McGlade said, coasting through a red light, swerving to avoid a cab. "Piece of cake."

"Just make sure it isn't an upside-down cake."

The words had barely left my lips when I saw a construction scene ahead—a roped-off section in the middle of Wabash where some city workers were ducking into the sewer main.

There was no conceivable way we'd be able to stop in time.

Peter Roe
April 1, 1:50 p.m.

He'd buy the security guys cars for this. Hell, he'd buy them each a—

Siders reached around his black jeans, pulled out a gun of his own, and shot each of the guards several times in the chest.

They dropped to the floor.

It had all happened in the blink of an eye.

"Twenty seconds, Peter."

Roe felt the spring breeze coming through the broken glass, and it felt like utter hopelessness.

Like finality.

He stared at the face-page of the patent for an emergency egress lighting system he'd shepherded through the USPTO.

At least I made a small difference in the world, he thought.

His heart was racing—

"Fifteen seconds."

—but he fought through the fear and took in a deep shot of oxygen.

"Ten seconds."

He'd lived a calculated life built upon the accumulation of wealth, but he'd loved it, and he'd lived it the only way he knew how, and he wasn't going out that window—

"Five...four..."

—with any—

"Three...two..."

—regrets—

"One."

—but one. He'd never learned the names of those two guards who'd died trying to save him. So he turned his head, staring hard at their cooling bodies, and memorized the names on their tags.

Wilson and Roberts.

Thanks for trying, guys.

"Peter Roe, it is one fifty-one p.m. Godspeed."

Roe felt a jag of glass cut into his back as he went over the lip.

There was a blink of excruciating brightness as he caught a face-full of sunlight, and then his stomach lifted, Dearborn Street rushing up to greet him, twelve floors streaking past in a blast of wind and sun and glimmers of reflected light, and the people on the sidewalk oblivious to what was falling toward them, in particular a street preacher holding a fat, black Bible and shouting that the day of judgment was at hand to every pedestrian who passed by.

Jack
April 1, 1:51 p.m.

"Uh oh," McGlade said as we rocketed toward the construction.

The workers were digging up the asphalt, and an entire fifteen-foot slab that should have been on the street was no longer there, a rocky ditch in its place.

McGlade punched the horn—

—and accelerated.

"Harry! Holy—"

The Tesla hit the edge of the hole, but rather than go in headfirst and cartwheel in a spectacular spinning ball of death, the car took the sloping indentation like a ramp and actually took to the air—

"—sheeeeeet!"

—landing safely on the other side of the hole, kissing the street so gently it felt like the wheels had never left the ground.

"Cool," McGlade said. "They oughta put that in the sales video."

"Jack? Jack, where are you?" Herb's voice.

I looked at my iPhone, realized Herb had picked up.

"We're close," I said, as McGlade wove through a pair of El supports, brought two tires up onto the curb, and then pulled away just before a fire hydrant ripped his car, and us, in half.

"Shots fired on the twelfth floor," Herb said. "Cops almost on the scene. Wait for backup, Jack. What am I saying? Don't you *dare* go inside. We're cordoning off the building. He's not going to get out. So don't do anything stupid."

McGlade jammed his foot into the brakes, skidding onto Adams, heading west.

Traffic was at a standstill, but he powered up onto the sidewalk, horn blaring, and took it all the way to Dearborn, bringing the machine to a screeching stop outside the entrance to the Marquette Building.

"Houston, the eagle has landed," he said.

A black-and-white was already on scene, the officer standing out in the middle of Dearborn, trying to reroute traffic.

I pushed the door open and hauled myself up out of the seat, my hand in my purse, already fingering my Colt Detective Special. I didn't know for certain that Herb had put out the word that I'd be here. It was a hot scene, and I didn't want some beat cop thinking I was just some civilian commando with a gun. Good way to get shot.

Two more cruisers with sirens wailing came tearing around Adams behind us.

"McGlade, go watch that entrance, and don't let any black-haired male out of the building."

"I won't let anyone out. But don't you go in there, or I'll kick your ass."

As he ran toward the main entrance I headed over to the police cruisers.

One of the officers had joined in to help direct traffic away from Dearborn, and the other, a young cop who looked barely out of high school, was just climbing out of the nearest car.

When he saw me, he said, "Ma'am, I'm going to need you to go stand over on that sidewalk. We have a dangerous situation here." He pointed at the building across from the Marquette.

I held up my hand. "My name is Jack Daniels, out of the two-six. Heard of me?"

His brow furrowed, skeptical. "You mean Lieutenant Daniels?" He looked at my belly, dubious.

"You were called here on a one eighty-seven in progress, correct?" I asked.

"That's right."

"The suspect is a white male with long black hair. Armed. He's still in the building, and he's killing a man."

"I need to call this in."

He reached up to his shoulder mike.

I said, "You have to shut this building down and get some men inside, right now, Officer. No one in or out unless your career goals involve riding a Segway writing parking tickets."

My tone must have hit home, because the next words into his microphone were, "Car one-three-five-six, take the rear entrance. No one gets in or out. Suspect is a white male with long black hair. Proceed with caution, he is armed."

And then the cavalry arrived.

A Chevy Caprice roared up behind the two squad cars, and Herb burst out from behind the steering wheel as fast as I'd ever seen him move.

We started walking toward the building.

It sounded like several districts coming at once, a rash of sirens echoing between the skyscrapers, the cranky horn of a fire truck blaring several blocks away.

"You've gotta lock it down, Herb," I said.

"It's happening, Jack. I've got units securing the Adams, Marble, and Clark Street entrances."

"I want everyone funneled through the Dearborn Street exit," I said as we reached the sidewalk. "Nobody leaves the building until I've seen them. Where's SRT?"

The Special Response Team was our version of SWAT.

"On their way, but you have to..." Herb looked over my shoulder and said, "Oh, hell."

A crowd of a dozen or so horrified onlookers had gathered around a brick planter up ahead.

Already, I could see the pool of blood.

Herb had his badge hanging around his neck, and he rattled it as we approached.

"Everyone back! No one leaves until we talk to you!"

We stopped several feet away from the carnage.

I said, "Shit, he hit a pedestrian."

There were two bodies. The first, a suited man—Roe—lay facedown and sprawled in a bed of crushed flower bulbs that had just begun to sprout. He looked like a giant plate of lasagna in a vague man-shape. The poor soul he'd hit was a wreck of bent appendages, and his head had been crushed in against the brick. A thick Bible was open next to him, the pages flipping in the breeze.

Sidewalk traffic had been effectively shut down, so the only onlookers were those who'd been here when it happened.

"I'm going inside to look for him," I said.

"Jack, we've got two dozen cops in the building. They'll find him."

"Did any of those cops just have a face-to-face conversation with the killer?" I asked. "I can help."

"There's a psycho in there who wants to kill you."

"I won't stand here and do nothing."

Herb touched my arm. "Listen to me, Jack. I promise you...no one will leave that building without you saying it's all right."

"Herb—"

"I'll walk you to the entrance."

"Herb—"

"Whose crime scene is this?"

I bit my bottom lip, fuming.

But damn, he was right.

"Yours," I said.

"You respect me?"

"You know I do."

"Then please, Jack, do what I say."

Luther
April 1, 1:54 p.m.

He strolls through the Law Office of Peter Roe, deceased, PC, which has, not surprisingly, become a ghost town following the gunshots.

He can't stop smiling.

FaceTime with Jack was even better than he imagined.

Passing through reception, he opens the heavy wooden door and steps out into the hallway.

For the moment, it's empty, although he can hear approaching footsteps and voices just around the corner.

Police officers coming.

Security arrived faster than he anticipated, and no doubt the cops have already surrounded the building.

The sirens are loud even in here.

Must sound like Armageddon out there.

It's a concern.

But the harder the challenge, the more satisfying the win.

Herb
April 1, 2:04 p.m.

The elevator doors separated and Sergeant Herb Benedict strolled out onto the twelfth floor of the Marquette Building. It was quiet as death.

Everyone had probably fled following the gunshots.

SRT had given the floor the all-clear and were now sweeping the lower levels.

Herb turned to the three beat cops who'd rode up with him, sent a pair down the opposing hallway.

"Check every office. If you find anyone, confirm IDs. Anyone who looks even vaguely suspicious needs to be brought down to the lobby and questioned. This guy is a killer. He could have taken hostages. Stay frosty. Sakey, you're with me."

Officer Sakey, a curly-haired rookie with a unibrow, followed Herb down the main corridor toward Roe's office.

The building itself was a work of art, one of the first steel-frame skyscrapers ever built, with masonry walls and a two-story atrium down in the lobby, loaded with mosaics, sculptures, and bronze.

Sakey covered the door and Herb went in first, gun drawn.

The Law Office of Peter Roe, PC, still smelled of gunpowder.

Reception felt empty, and a quick look around confirmed it.

Herb headed down the hall and walked into the largest, plushest office in the suite.

The stench of shots fired was strongest here, but there were other underlying odors—blood, the lake, stale coffee. Herb stood for a moment in the threshold, letting the awful aura of this room wash over him.

At his feet lay the two security guards in puddles of congealing blood.

Multiple gunshot wounds to the chest.

Behind the desk of Peter Roe, a hole had been chopped through one pane of the bay window. Chunks of safety glass peppered the carpet, surrounding what he figured had been used on the window—a fire ax.

How had Kite even gotten a meeting with Roe? There was probably a firm calendar on the receptionist's computer. Herb turned and started toward reception as the mike on his lapel crackled.

"Sergeant Benedict, Nicholson here, over?"

"Yeah, whatcha got, over?"

"I'm down in office twelve-twelve. Got a guy here who doesn't want to leave, over."

"Keep him there, on my way. Out."

Herb picked up the pace and hollered for Sakey to follow.

They made their way back out into the corridor, where every office door stood open, a few having been kicked in.

Around the corner from another set of elevators, he saw Officer Nicholson standing outside an open door. Nicholson didn't have his weapon drawn yet, but he had unsnapped his holster and his hand was resting on the square composite butt of a Glock.

Herb sidled up beside Nicholson and stared into the small office.

The occupant was a Caucasian with short brown hair, wearing a white shirt and blue tie. Since the response team had already cleared the floor, Herb wondered why the hell this guy was still here.

"Sir, I'm Sergeant Herb Benedict. Put your hands where I can see them."

The guy scowled as he raised his hands above the monitor.

He said, "I just went through this with those other cops."

"Didn't those other cops order you to leave?"

"I know my rights. You can't make me leave."

Herb made a mental note to take the SRT to task for not forcing this moron out of here.

He said, "Sir, do you understand what just happened in this building, not two offices down from yours?"

"Yeah, someone got shot. I saw the guy run off. Ran right past here."

Herb shook his head, amazed. How stupid were some people? "Aren't you worried about being killed?"

"You want to know what I'm worried about?" The man pointed at a stack of manila folders sitting on his desk next to the keyboard. "Do you know what happens in fourteen days, Officer?"

Herb noted the plaque on the doorway: David Dean, JD, LLM. Master's of Laws in Taxation.

Ah. He was a tax attorney.

"Filing deadline is two weeks away," Dean said, "and I'm up to my armpits in work right now. My clients come first."

Herb took a quick look around the sparsely furnished office, saw a few ferns that needed watering, generic art on the walls. He noticed sawdust on the floor. Probably some recent remodeling. The only personal items were on Dean's desk—a smiley-face coffee mug, a crystal paperweight, and a framed picture of Dean shaking hands with Bill Clinton.

Herb said, "Sir, I'm going to ask you to leave the building. We're clearing everyone out."

"That's bullshit, I—"

"You'll be able to come back tomorrow. It is within my power to arrest you if you don't comply."

Dean pulled a big, dramatic sigh, rubbed his temples, and then powered off his monitor.

"I don't get it," Dean said. "Isn't this the safest place I could possibly be right now? That guy you're looking for is outta here."

He snatched his jacket off the chair as he stood, and Herb escorted him to the elevator, watching to make sure it didn't stop until it reached the lobby.

Then Herb and Sakey returned to Roe's office.

Luther
April 1, 2:07 p.m.

Jack Daniels is surrounded by cops, and she's scanning the crowd in the Marquette Building's gorgeous lobby.

It's all terribly exciting, and Luther struggles to keep the smile off his face.

She stares right at him, locks eyes for a delicious moment, and then moves along to the next person in line.

Luther waits patiently for his turn to leave.

Herb
April 1, 2:07 p.m.

Not for the first time since she had retired, Herb wished Jack was with him. She had an almost supernatural knack for finding clues at crime scenes, for figuring out things that didn't add up. He understood why Jack had needed to retire, and supported her decision, but he hoped the building would be fully cleared soon so Jack could come up here and offer her impressions.

When Herb stared at Roe's office, he didn't see clues. He just saw an office.

Desks, chairs, plants, too many file cabinets to count...

File cabinets.

All offices had file cabinets.

But that tax attorney Herb had shooed out of the office down the hall, the one with the Clinton photo...where were *his* file cabinets?

Herb hadn't noticed any.

Odd. So odd, in fact, that it made Herb uncomfortable.

Feeling a little spurt of adrenaline, he led Sakey back to 1212 and made a quick tour of the tax guy's office.

It was small. No reception area. Just a desk and a computer.

And no file cabinets.

Herb grabbed his walkie-talkie.

"This is Sergeant Benedict. Put me in touch with the SRT leader. Over."

"This is Lieutenant Matthews, SRT. What's up, Sarge? Over."

"When you swept the twelfth floor, why didn't you escort the tax attorney down? Over."

"What tax attorney?"

Luther
April 1, 2:08 p.m.

Unwinding his tie and tugging it off his neck, Luther eyes the exit. The atmosphere is electric. A touch of fear in the air. Confusion. Excitement. Lots of chattering, questions, complaining. A few jokes, some of the nine-to-fivers obviously excited that something interesting is happening in their drab, dull lives.

Something to tell the kids about over dinner. Maybe they'll even get on the six o'clock news.

There are now only four people ahead of Luther in the exit line, and police are waving a metal detector wand over each person before allowing them to leave the building.

He checks his watch, trying to appear impatient.

A minute, two tops, and he'll be out of here.

Herb
April 1, 2:08 p.m.

Herb checked the nameplate on the door and spoke into his radio, "David Dean, in twelve-twelve, over."

"There was no one on the floor, Sarge. We checked every doorway. Even broke into a few offices. I don't know about Homicide, but my team doesn't make mistakes. When we do something, it's done right. Over."

The little spurt of adrenaline became a giant spike.

Herb walked behind Dean's desk and turned on his monitor, still half-expecting to find a spreadsheet or an Excel document—some evidence of tax work.

Dean had been playing the videogame Angry Birds.

Herb lifted the Clinton photo, saw the blur lines around the president's head—a mediocre Photoshop effort.

"Attention!" he yelled into his mike. "Suspect is in the lobby. He's a white male, mid- to late forties, short brown hair, wearing a white shirt and a blue tie. He's claiming to be an attorney named David Dean. Repeat, the suspect has short brown hair and is using the name David Dean."

Luther
April 1, 2:09 p.m.

J ack stands less than six feet away.

She hasn't glanced at Luther again, having already dismissed him.

He's tempted to clear his throat, make a noise, see if she'll notice, but he's already cutting it too close.

Instead, he takes out his iPhone, hits redial, and slides the device into his breast pocket.

Jack paws at her phone, distracted by it, as the cop at the exit begins to check Luther for weapons.

Jack

April 1, 2:09 p.m.

I accepted the Blocked Call FaceTime request, but the screen was black.

I held the phone to my ear, heard the sound of numerous, muffled voices.

"Hello?" I said.

A second later, I heard, "Hello?"

But it wasn't an answer.

It was my voice coming through the iPhone speaker.

An echo.

An echo meant another iPhone was picking up my voice.

It meant that Luther was here, in the lobby, with me.

Near me.

"He's here!" I yelled, a big mistake.

While panic didn't break out, there was an uptick in movement and commotion.

Since I wasn't a cop, I didn't have a radio.

I grabbed the lapel mike from the uniform standing next to me at the same time I heard Herb's voice shouting through his earpiece that Luther was in the lobby.

As I scanned the crowd, I pressed the iPhone to my cheek, hoping to hear something that would give me his location. I plugged my free ear with my finger, focusing on the sounds coming through my cell.

It was faint, but unmistakable.

"Okay, you can go."

I looked to the exit as a thin, brown-haired man left the building.

"Stop him!" I yelled, but all the cops in the lobby were already in motion, closing the door after the man who had just left.

I hurried to them, trying to push my way past, but one of the officers grabbed my shoulders.

"He just walked out!" I yelled.

We both pushed through the door—

—into chaos.

Outside the building, the scene was bedlam.

Firemen, paramedics, cops, swarms of people waiting for their coworkers to emerge, a slew of media sticking microphones and cameras at anyone who stood still long enough...

But no sign of the brown-haired man.

Herb

April 1, 2:10 p.m.

Herb listened to the radio chatter. Orders were barked. Men complied.

No one found Luther.

Chewing his lower lip, Herb eyed the sawdust on the carpeting in Dean's office. He looked at the paneling on the wall directly above it, saw that the color didn't quite match on either side.

Herb put his fingers in the seam along the top and pulled.

The panel tore easily away, revealing a small, dark bathroom.

Herb saw a gun on the sink. A black T-shirt. Boots. A black wig.

It all came to him in a rush. Luther had planned the Roe murder perfectly. Had rented an office near him, built a fake wall over the bathroom, and after the murder, he'd simply walked to his office and hid behind the panel, waiting for the cops to leave.

With his hair recently cut and dyed, Luther had strolled through the lobby, right past Jack, and walked out of the building as David Dean.

The son of a bitch had been right there, talking about April fifteenth.

And Herb hadn't just let him go.

He'd *insisted* he leave.

Jack
April 1, 2:12 p.m.

I did my best to rally some officers to search in all directions, but Luther was gone.

The FaceTime disconnected without so much as a gloat from the killer, but I expected him to be in touch.

When Herb found me amid the commotion outside the Dearborn Street entrance, he had such a look of defeat on his face I thought he was going to cry.

I felt the same way.

"I screwed up," he said.

"I screwed up," I said a millisecond later. "I was too focused on black hair."

"We both were."

He gave me the quick rundown of a fake tax attorney named David Dean.

"Damn." I shook my head. "He played us good. Don't blame yourself, Herb."

"Do you blame *your*self?"

I didn't answer.

"You can't hog all the guilt, Jack."

"Let's beat ourselves up later. We still have a crime scene to work."

I followed Herb down the sidewalk to the brick planter which had been cordoned off. The crime lab team was already working what was left of Mr. Roe.

"There should be a book in a plastic bag inside of the man in the suit," I said.

"There is no inside," one of the techs said. "It's all on the outside."

"You haven't found a plastic bag?"

"Not yet."

I glanced down into the devastation. In the tier of ugly corpses, jumpers were a close second to burn vics.

"Got something," another tech said. His gloved hands were running along the surface of Roe's pants. "There's an object on the side of his leg. A bulge."

"Cut the pants off," Herb said.

The tech trimmed away the pant leg below Roe's waist with a pair of scissors to reveal more blood and bone, but amid all the wreckage, I saw where a bubble-wrapped package had been duct-taped to Mr. Roe's thigh.

The tech stumbled back.

"What are you doing?" I said.

"Could be a bomb."

I hadn't considered that.

"We need to get the bomb squad here, let them secure this." He started to pull me away but I jerked my arm free.

"It's not a bomb," I said.

The tech looked at Herb, who said, "Jack, I gotta be honest. I'm not feeling real comfortable standing here right now. You know what this perp is capable of."

The techs had already backed off and were helping to clear a perimeter around the two bodies.

"Herb, this is a game for him. If that's a bomb, and he's watching right now, with his finger on the button, he pushes it, and then what?"

"We're blown into a thousand pieces."

"Exactly, and where's the fun in that?"

"I'm not following. This guy wants to kill you. And now you're standing here, and you've never been more vulnerable."

"Yes, he wants to kill me, but he wants to look in my eyes while he does it. He wants to take his time with it, drag it out. To be there, talking to me when it happens. This isn't his style."

I reached into my purse, pulled out my miniature Swiss Army knife, and stepped over the side of the planter.

"Jack!"

"We don't have time for a bomb squad, Herb. There are clues in this body, and more people are going to die and it will be on our heads."

He put his hand on my forearm, but I shrugged it off.

"Goddamn it, Herb! Let me do my goddamn job!"

"It's not your job anymore, Jack. Give me the knife."

The idea of my former partner and best friend doing this made me understand what a stupid idea it had been in the first place.

"Maybe we should wait for the bomb squad," I said.

"I can do it."

"It's a tiny knife. You have fingers like sausages."

"Chain of evidence, Jack. You're a civilian. Give me the knife and get behind the goddamn police tape or I'll have you arrested."

The likelihood of Herb arresting me was nil. But I gave him the knife.

He squeezed into a pair of latex gloves. Then he knelt beside the carnage and opened a blade. The bubble wrap was smeared in blood, and as Herb cut away the tape, my heart stopped. I'd been expecting a book, another paperback, but this wasn't a book. Through the plastic, all I could discern was that it was thin and gray.

What if I was wrong? What if this was an explosive of some kind?

Herb continued to slash at the package.

My apprehension climbed.

Then I heard another voice: Phin's.

He was screaming my name.

I looked back at him, behind the yellow police tape, and gave him an OK sign with my thumb and index finger that was the total opposite of how I felt.

Herb cut through the last of the plastic and peeled it back and then jerked the package free. He unwound the packing tape and pulled out a thin, gray device roughly eight by five inches, less than a centimeter thick, and held in a clear plastic bag.

Herb stood and made his way through the flower bed, back over the brick.

Held it up for me to see.

Written on the bag in black marker:

JD—THIS ONE REALLY FELL FOR YOU—LK

When I noticed what the bag contained, I realized I should have guessed it earlier.

It was a book. An e-book.

More specifically, a Kindle e-reader.

"It's just a Kindle!" I yelled to the lab team. "All you chickens can come back now." Then I asked Herb to hold it face up for me.

"What is it, Jack?" Herb asked.

"It's an e-reader." I used my fingernail to slide the power switch through the plastic bag, and the screen changed from a portrait of Emily Dickinson (who looked disturbingly like the magician David Copperfield) to the text of a book.

A bar at the top of the screen displayed the title: *Blue Murder - A Thriller.*

The progress meter at the bottom of the screen showed it was 4% into the book. The section had been electronically bookmarked, the top corner displaying a dog-eared icon.

I remembered from the Wikipedia entry that this was another Andrew Z. Thomas title.

Taking my iPhone out of my purse, I snapped a quick photo of the page as Herb held it up.

Blue Murder - A Thriller

Walking home on the dark wet street, he glimpsed his apartment building through the trees. The thought of falling asleep tonight in that gloomy bedroom knotted his stomach. It had felt good telling them about the dream. He wished he'd told them everything. Especially about the fear. About waking in the middle of the night, bolting up in bed in that black room, mentally, physically quaking. About not knowing why an image as seemingly benign as the second hand gliding toward the XII, drove terror so deep inside him he'd removed the clock from the wall in his classroom. About not knowing what in God's name was going to happen that afternoon in that lovely town, at the corner of Oak and Sycamore. They think not there how much of blood it costs.

After reading the section, I frowned.

Herb said, "What's wrong, Jack?"

"There's no page number."

He pointed to the 4% at the bottom of the screen. "Page four."

"No, that's the percentage of the book read. There are no page numbers on Kindles, only..." I nodded, feeling the exhilarating rush of discovery.

"What, Jack?"

"There aren't page numbers, but there are locations."

Through the plastic, I pressed the MENU button, and when the tab appeared, the location popped up, centered on the bottom of the screen:

Location 310 of 7647

"Jack—"

"Just a second, Herb." I pressed the page-back button and kept pressing it until the screen arrived at the beginning of chapter two.

"Holy shit," I said.

"What's wrong?"

"What time is it?"

He glanced at his watch.

"Two thirty-three."

I rubbed my forehead. "He's going to kill someone in a little over twelve hours."

"How the hell do you know that?"

"The location is the time: three ten. Before, he was using the page number to tell us the time of death. If we go back to the original screen..." I paged back. "See how the first *a* is highlighted? This had been bugging me. Remember how a *p* was circled in the previous books?"

I could see the light blink on in Herb's eyes.

He said, "He was telling us the murders would happen in the p.m."

"Exactly. And the chapter number..."

"Is the day."

"So a murder is going to happen at three ten a.m., on April second. Tonight."

"But where, Jack? You knew to come here...how?"

"The name of the prior victim indicates the location of the next murder."

"Did Luther tell you that?"

"In a way. First, he killed Jessica Shedd. Then he killed Reginald Marquette at the Shedd Aquarium. Then he killed Peter Roe in the Marquette Building."

"So where's the next murder going to happen, Jack?"

"Roe."

"Roe? What does that mean?"

"I don't know. Might be a park, another building, a museum. Anything."

Herb frowned. "It could also be alluding to something else. *Roe vs. Wade.*"

I let that sink in, felt a chill come over me. *Roe vs. Wade* was the landmark Supreme Court case confirming the right of a woman to terminate her pregnancy.

I remembered the last time I'd seen Luther. I'd been helpless, my leg broken. He could have killed me then. But he'd known I was pregnant, and it was only now that he'd decided to come back into my life.

"I have a bad feeling, Jack, that he's changing the rules."

I really didn't want Herb to continue, but I asked, "What do you mean?"

"Roe? You having a baby? The last names are all about location, right?"

"Yeah."

"So what if he's saying that *you're* the location? That he's going to end your pregnancy tonight at three ten a.m.?"

I took five steps away so I didn't contaminate the murder scene, and threw up all over my Keds.

Luther

March 18, Fourteen Days Ago

Four Days After the Bus Incident

"*A priest, huh?*"

"*Yes. In a Catholic church in Pittsburgh.*"

Luther leans forward across the table, holds a long moment of eye contact. The man is fifty-five or fifty-six. Smooth-shaven. Thinning gray hair. Thin lips. Kind eyes.

"*Let's be honest for a moment, Father. You okay with that?*"

"*Of course.*"

"*You're not married.*"

"*In most cases, the priesthood and marriage are separate paths.*"

"*You're celibate?*"

"*I am.*"

"*Is that difficult?*"

"*There are moments of temptation, but with God's help, I've kept my vow.*"

"*Really.*"

"*Yes.*"

"*Kind of hard with all these delicious little acolytes running around, isn't it? Eager young boys looking up to you for instruction in God's word? Wanting to know the ways of the world?*"

"*Never.*"

"*Really.*"

"*I have never touched a child. That is the gravest of sins, in my opinion.*"

"*But you've been tempted.*"

"*Thankfully, no, not in that direction. True, I've never had sexual intercourse, but if I'm honest, I have been tempted by the desire for female companionship from time to time.*"

"*And you've never acted on it?*"

"*Not once. God has guided me through the temptation.*"

"*Wow,*" Luther says. "*So you're a perfect human being.*"

"*No, I am deeply flawed, as we all are.*"

"*So what are your sins, Father? Just think of me as a fellow priest, taking your confession. Or God.*"

"*You're neither. You're just another lost soul in need of guidance. I'll pray for you.*"

"*It won't help. Tell me what you said during your last confession.*"

"*Confessions are private.*"

"*If you prefer, I can make you watch me kill someone.*"

"*I sometimes...disagree on certain policies the Church demands I endorse. Last month, I questioned when His Holiness, the Pope, spoke out against condom usage for the prevention of sexually transmitted diseases, specifically AIDS, in Africa.*"

"*Did you openly defy him?*"

"*No. My disagreements remain unspoken.*"

"*Ever stole money from the collection basket?*"

"*Of course not.*"

"*Drink too much Communion wine?*"

"No."

"I have no use for you," Luther says.

"Would you consider letting some of the others go? I would happily stay in their place."

"Didn't you just hear what I said?"

"What?"

"I have no use for you."

Luther draws his Glock.

The priest's eyes show a moment of total shock and terror, but they quickly recover, now filling with a deep, horrified sadness.

Finally, they glow with intense purpose.

"Allow me a moment, my son?" the priest asks.

"Take your moment."

The priest shuts his eyes, and with a whisper, begins to pray.

When he's finished, Luther levels the gun on him. "Now you're ready to meet your maker?"

"Yes."

"No fear at all?"

"The Lord is my shepherd. I fear no evil."

Luther nodded.

Then he stood up and shot him five times in the legs. It was only when he was sure the priest did indeed fear evil that Luther put a bullet in his head.

Lucy
April 1, 3:00 p.m.

"How we doing on gas, D?"

Her partner glanced over. "Quarter of a tank."

"We gonna make it?"

"You better hope so. Otherwise, I'm gonna peddle your ass on the street. How many tricks you think you'll have to turn to make five dollars?"

"You're an asshole."

They passed another road sign.

Just fifty-nine miles to go.

They'd be there within the hour.

With what little was left of her tongue, Lucy could almost taste how sweet this was going to be.

Luther

April 1, 5:30 p.m.

Luther stares at his laptop screen, drawing in a deep breath. Then he begins to scream at the top of his lungs, "Oh, God, help me! Please help me! JESUS CHRIST, SOMEONE HELP!"

Jack
April 1, 6:00 p.m.

I didn't bother fighting it.

Not this time.

I let Herb wield his power, and the Chicago Police Department checked me and Phin into the Congress Hotel under fake names. McGlade got the room next to mine. They put two officers in plainclothes down in the lobby to monitor all coming and going.

Phin and Harry had gone back to my house for my clothing and sundries, to ship Duffy the dog to Duffy the person in NY, and to set up Mr. Friskers with the portion-controlled food and water dispenser and automatic litter box cleaner. Once again I tried to talk to Phin about the proposal, but he'd folded his arms and shut me down with a "Not now."

Hell hath no fury like a bank robber scorned.

That made me wonder if the engagement ring had been purchased with ill-gotten gain, which made me wonder how far said ring had traveled through Duffy's digestive tract. I felt my blood pressure skyrocket at the thought of Phin taking

Duffy for a walk before driving him out to the airport. Worst-case scenario, I'd borrow a metal detector from McGlade and spend a few hours hunting through my backyard for buried treasure.

I sat on the queen-sized bed and picked up the phone on the nightstand. Herb had already given me an unneeded lecture about using my iPhone. A techie from the crime scene team had cloned my number, so the cops and Feds would receive every call I did, in an effort to pinpoint Luther's location if he called again.

I knew the inherent difficulty in tracing cell phone calls and didn't hold out much hope. But I didn't want the Feebies recording my private conversations.

I called Duffy the guy and was relieved when he picked up, which made me realize how few friends I had. I wondered if that was by choice, or if I was simply an unlovable workaholic.

"FedExing the beast my way?" he asked.

"Phin is right now. I'll send you the arrival info when I get it. Also...there's a problem with Duffy."

"Is he licking himself too much? That's not a problem so much as a lifestyle choice."

"Phin proposed to me, and Duffy ate the ring."

"Off your finger?"

"It wasn't on my finger yet." I felt awful saying it, and Duffy was kind enough to let it slide.

"So you need me on poop patrol?"

I let out an exasperated sigh. "I'm sorry, Duffy."

"No sweat. My hound, Al, once ate all of my keys. They were on a leather keychain, which he digested. Then he pooped them out one at a time. Took me eight days to get my car key back. I had to take a cab to a boxing match, which cost more than the purse I won."

"What kind of purse was it? Gucci?"

"You sure you're a cop and not one of those stand-up comics?"

"Thanks again, Duff. I really owe you for this."

"No biggie, Jack. Maybe one day I'll need you to pick through some of my dog's poop. You never know."

I thanked him again and hung up.

Then I used my iPhone to access Google and read up on *Roe vs. Wade*.

John Doe and Jane Doe are often used in the legal system as placeholder names for anonymous or unknown defendants. When plaintiffs are anonymous, the names used are Richard Roe and Jane Roe. In 1970, Roe filed suit against Henry Wade, the Dallas district attorney representing the state of Texas. The case eventually went up to the U.S. Supreme Court, which deemed abortion a fundamental right under the Constitution.

Though the hotel room was warm and a bit stuffy, I shivered. If Herb was right, and Luther wanted to kill my baby, I wasn't sure what point he was trying to make. Surely a serial killer like Luther wasn't pro-life. Maybe this was just a coincidence?

I Googled "Roe" and "Chicago" and came up with hits on the late patent attorney's office, a used office furniture company, and the Regional Office of Education on the Illinois State Board. The cops already had people stationed at both the furniture store and the State Board, but neither of these felt right to me. It didn't seem to be the direction Luther was pointing me.

Next I tried "Wade" and "Chicago" only to be inundated with articles about the Miami Heat basketball player Dwayne Wade, who was born in the Windy City.

Finally, I tried "Roe" on its own.

Roe was the name for fish eggs and business speak for Return on Equity. The Environmental Protection Agency also had a Report on the Environment which they called ROE.

Perhaps Luther was going with the first name instead of the last this time, so I tried "Chicago" and "Peter."

Nothing concrete.

I added "landmark" to the search, hoping Google would reveal a Peter building, park, or museum.

Nada. Zip. Zilch.

I rubbed my eyes. The screen was getting blurry, probably from squinting at the small text. The rubbing didn't make things any clearer, and I had a sudden attack of vertigo, the room beginning to spin. I held onto the armrests of my chair so I didn't fall off, and then willed myself not to pass out.

When the dizziness finally passed, I went back to Google. For some reason, Luther kept alluding to Dante's *Inferno*.

I did some additional surfing on the work.

Inferno was the first part of *The Divine Comedy*, and it concerned Dante's encounter with the spirit of the Roman poet Virgil, who takes him through the nine circles of hell to witness the suffering of various sinners. The torments those poor souls endured had been fodder for Christians going all the way back to the fifteenth century, since the Bible was oddly lacking in any detailed descriptions of hell. We had Dante to thank for fire and brimstone and demons who tortured the damned.

Ultimately, *Inferno* is about the path to enlightenment. Dante is lost at the beginning, and witnessing the suffering of those who had sinned helps to put him on the path of righteousness.

Or some bullshit like that.

I wasn't a religious person, but I found the whole idea of a God who allowed people to be boiled in oil for eternity in direct conflict with an all-powerful, all-loving creator. Hell was a concept that helped church officials exercise control over the masses, and ultimately, make money.

Though I didn't believe in hell, I wouldn't have minded a little enlightenment in my life. But I was doubtful I'd get it from anything written centuries ago.

I yawned, rubbing my eyes again.

Then I tried rereading the excerpt from *Blue Murder*, but the picture I'd taken of the Kindle screen was too small to make out. That led me to buying another overpriced Andrew Z. Thomas e-book and searching for the location Luther had bookmarked.

According to Google, the line *They think not there how much of blood it costs* was another Dante quote. There was also mention of the intersection of Oak and Sycamore, but Chicago didn't have any corresponding intersections, although there were about a hundred non-intersecting streets individually named Oak and Sycamore in Illinois.

I wasn't feeling any traction there, had no idea what Luther was trying to tell me, and lacking any other ideas, I put my feet up on a pillow and dove into *Blue Murder*, trying to stay calm and focused in the face of knowing that someone was going to die horribly in—I glanced at my iPhone timer I'd programmed—seven hours and five minutes.

Unlike the stark realism of *The Scorcher* and *The Killer and His Weapon*, *Blue Murder* contained an element of the supernatural.

The plot concerned a man plagued with strange premonitions that kept coming true. I read for an hour, convinced that the hero wasn't seeing into the future at all, but in actuality remembering horrific events from his past that he wanted to hide from himself, when I heard someone at the door.

In an instant, I had my Colt in my hand, my thumb on the hammer.

I heard Phin say, "It's me," before letting himself in.

He carried two suitcases, which he set on the floor next to the door.

"Did you ship off Duffy to Duffy?" I asked.

He nodded.

"Did he, uh, poop before you crated him?"

Phin raised an eyebrow. "No. Just pissed. Any particular reason we're talking about your dog's bodily functions?"

I noticed he said *your dog* rather than *our dog*, even though Duffy had taken a stronger liking to Phin than he had to me.

"I think he's constipated," I lied. "I'm just worried about him."

Phin bent over, unzipping a pouch on my suitcase. He removed the blood pressure monitor and approached me. I was too preoccupied to have my blood pressure taken. But Phin had to touch me to do it, and I wanted to feel his hands on me, if only in a clinical way.

He wrapped the cuff around my forearm and pumped it up.

"I didn't mean to treat you like that," I said. "Your proposal caught me off guard."

He made no response.

I put my hand on his.

"Please, Phin. Talk to me."

"What would you like me to talk about, Jack? I proposed to the woman I love, and she still hasn't given me an answer. 'Will you marry me?' isn't a trick question."

I took my hand back, unsure of how to reply, so I just went with, "I'm sorry."

"I don't want apologies. I want a yes or a no. I think I deserve that."

"It's a bad time," I said. "There's too much going on."

"Look, I know I'm not the most romantic guy in the world—"

"It's not that."

"—and the proposal could have been better. But I was nervous and wasn't expecting to do it right then. I had it all planned out. I was going to take you out to that German place you love—"

My eyes welled up. "Phin, please don't—"

"—get the tuba player to make the announcement. I was going to get down on one knee—"

"—it's not that, Phin. I...I know it's cliché...but it's not you. It's me."

He waited for me to expound, plainly not convinced.

I did my best. "These past few months I've felt like an object, not a person. Something to be guarded at all times. Plus I've got a child growing inside me, which is pretty damn weird, and I'm still not sure how I feel about it. Aren't mothers supposed to instantly bond with their unborn babies? Well, I haven't. I feel more like a stranger has moved into my house, and I'm not sure I want them to stay."

Phin studied me, staring hard.

I had no idea what he was thinking. Probably the same thing I was—*I'm a loser that no one can ever possibly love.*

"I didn't mean to add to the stress in your life, Jack."

"Goddamn it, that's not what I meant."

He glanced at the digital readout. "One forty-five over ninety. Still high."

Phin undid the Velcro, taking his hands back.

Then he walked over to the sofa and sat down, using the remote to turn on the television.

"Will you come to bed?" I asked.

"I'm not tired."

"Then let's go out. It's been ages since we played pool together. A little nine ball?"

"It's not safe. There's a madman after you, and you need to rest."

"Sex?" I tried. I'd never felt less sexy in my life, but I could at least take care of his needs.

"I'm tired, Jack. You aren't the only one with a lot on your shoulders."

"I...we should be supporting each other, not fighting."

Phin sighed. "Yeah. We should be doing a lot of things."

"Phin—"

"Can we talk later?"

"Sure," I said, trying to sound upbeat.

I went back to *Blue Murder*, trying not to let Phin see or hear me cry.

Then I read until I could no longer hold my eyes open, finally drifting off to sleep, in bed alone.

Luther
April 1, 11:48 p.m.

All the planning, all the preparation, all the money, all the hard work—everything comes down to a single moment: this one.

The truck is ready. The van is ready. The gurneys are ready. The remote is ready. The aerosols are ready. The fans are ready.

Luther tests them all one last time, except for the aerosols; he only has a limited amount of each gas, and testing them on himself isn't conducive to healthy living. Or living at all.

He recalls the last time he filled up with gasoline, hearing some jackass at the pump loudly bitching about the $4.06 a gallon, calling it a gas crisis.

Chicago is about to have a gas crisis, that's for sure.

But it won't be what that fool was talking about.

In the course of his research, Luther has learned everything about the catalog of criminals Jack Daniels spent her lifetime hunting down. He's even met a few of them. One of the standouts was a serial poisoner known as The Chemist. Much to be learned from that one. So much, in fact, that Luther took a shortcut. Rather than delve into the science of chemistry on his own, Luther simply kidnapped a chemist from a local lab and applied the necessary persuasion to get what he wanted.

What he wanted was gas.

Lewisite and QNB.

The lewisite was particularly nasty, and the experiments Luther conducted resulted in some spectacularly disgusting symptoms. The helpful scientist who cooked it for him met with a terrible death, being the first test subject for the lewisite, which was followed with a chaser of the potassium chloride he'd also concocted.

QNB is also especially useful.

Luther used it to great effect after the bus incident.

Unfortunately, he's down to his last tank, which is a shame, but the amount remaining will be more than sufficient to get the job done.

Perfect for certain circles in his epic masterpiece.

Also perfect for the upcoming festivities.

Luther checks the time on his iPhone, shivering as an anticipatory tingle of excitement shoots through him.

It isn't sexual in nature. A better comparison might be of winters long past, the night before Christmas. He had a pleasant childhood, at least early on, and that euphoric *waiting for Santa* expectation was quite similar to what he's feeling now.

He's on the brink of unveiling something extraordinary.

Something life-changing.

It's like the grand opening of a new store, or a summer blockbuster movie debut.

Except, of course, for the large number of people who will suffer and die.

But what Luther is doing is art, and no one ever said art is easy. He knows this firsthand. Knows that the best art is written with blood.

He smiles.

"It's all for you, Jack," he says, keeping his voice at a whisper so as not to disturb the dead.

APRIL 2

Jack

April 2, 2:39 a.m.

My iPhone buzzed on my nightstand.

I opened my eyes and squinted at the screen, saw that I had a message.

I reached for my cell, read the text.

The natural law in naught is relevant.
Into the yellow of the Roe's Eternal

The calling number was blocked, but this had to be Luther.

I guessed the passage was another snippet from *The Divine Comedy*, and a quick Google check confirmed it came from *Paradiso*.

Except *Roe's Eternal* was supposed to be *Rose Eternal*.

I Googled "Chicago" plus "Roe's"—

—and on the first page got this hit:

Hiram Roe owned the land that Rosehill Cemetery would be built upon. His farm was called Roe's Hill because it was higher than the surrounding swampy land. Spelling errors turned the name Roe's Hill *to the name* Rosehill.

I checked the time, wide awake now: 2:39 a.m.

The fourth murder was supposed to happen at 3:10 a.m., in only a half hour, and Rosehill Cemetery was at least a fifteen-minute drive from the hotel.

Phin slept on the sofa, snoring softly.

I woke him yelling, "Phin! Get Herb and Harry!"

He shot straight up as if spring-loaded.

I scooted my large butt over to the edge of the bed and fought to squeeze into my newest pair of Keds.

"Luther sent me a text," I said. "He's at the Rosehill Cemetery."

Phin instantly got on his phone and conveyed the news to Herb and Harry.

Then he came over and put a hand on my shoulder.

"Jack, you aren't going anywhere."

I met his loving gaze with venom. "Really, Phin? Trying to tell me what I can and can't do again? How'd that work out for you last time?"

"Luther wants you there. This is a trap."

I folded my arms over my chest, which made me even more aware of how pregnant I was because my boobs had gone up a full cup size, which made me even more irritated. "Damn it, Phin. Herb will call in every cop and Fed in three states. There won't be a safer place to be in the world than that cemetery."

"You don't know what he's planning."

"And you didn't see him do what I saw him do. I need to be there, Phin."

His mouth formed a thin line, and he folded his arms as well.

I clenched my teeth. "It's what I do. It's who I am. You won't ever change that. And if you loved me, you wouldn't even try to."

I forced myself to wait for his reaction. If he still insisted on keeping me in the hotel room, I'd knee him in the balls and mail his ring back to him, along with all of his stuff. Caring for me was one thing. Trying to control me was something I would never, ever accept.

Phin must have understood, because he slowly knelt down and fastened the Velcro strap on my left shoe.

"Promise me you won't take any risks," he said, staring up at me. "No unnecessary chances."

"I'll be fine," I said. "Let's *go*."

We met the two cops on guard in the hallway just as McGlade was leaving his room, bleary-eyed, his suit rumpled, fly unzipped. His shoes—Italian loafers—were on the wrong feet.

"What kind of asshole kills someone at three in the morning?" he grumbled. "It's psychotic."

"I'm driving Jack," Phin said. "You coming with us, or going by yourself?"

McGlade frowned. "My car isn't charged. The hotel didn't have a long enough extension cord. And why is Jack going?"

Rather than reply, I headed for the elevators with the men trailing behind me. Herb texted me, saying he was already en route.

My escorts took their own car.

I rode with the boys.

McGlade was uncharacteristically silent, until I realized he'd fallen asleep in the back seat.

We reached the cemetery at 2:58 a.m. and found a police barricade already in place at the Ravenswood Avenue entrance. After parking on the street under a railroad viaduct, I met Herb at the front gate, a castellated Gothic structure built of pale stone that looked straight out of medieval times, complete with arches and turrets. It was the same color and style as Chicago's famous Water Tower. In addition to five squad cars and SUVs, I counted two ambulances, three fire trucks, plus four unmarked government-issue sedans—the FBI. It was cold, the stinging wind a sign that winter wasn't through with Chicago yet, and I wished I'd brought a warmer coat.

"Damn it, Jack, why are you here?" The first words out of Herb's mouth.

I bit back my anger, forcing myself to accept that he, like Phin, was simply worried about me. Treating me like I was helpless, fragile, and incompetent was just their way of showing they cared.

"What if Luther is tracking me?" I asked, keeping calm. "Am I safer here, or back at the hotel, guarded by two men, while every other police officer in Illinois is here?"

"Fine. But you stay out here. There's no way you're going inside."

Be nice, Jack. "What's the situation?"

"We've got more than fifty cops here, plus Feebies. Hostage negotiator en route, in case Luther has grabbed someone. All exits blocked. Downside—Rosehill is big. Three hundred and fifty acres, including a massive mausoleum in the southwest quadrant. We're searching it section by section, and it's going to take hours."

"Any sign of forced entry?"

"No. Gates were all locked. If he's in there, he broke through the fence or hid inside before the cemetery closed for the evening."

"And what time was that?"

"This main entrance, five p.m. All others at four."

My cell buzzed. I glanced at the screen.

Blocked call.

"It's him," I said.

I answered.

"Hello, Jack." Luther's voice. "I just sent you a picture."

On cue, my iPhone buzzed, indicating a text message. I clicked on it and saw a photo.

Life is because God is, infinite, indestructible, and eternal.
ROBERT E. FRANKS
Sept 19. 1909 – May 22. 1924

Herb leaned in over my shoulder to look.

"The place is surrounded, Luther," I said. "Give up or you'll die here."

"We all have to die sometime, Jack. And this is a lovely place for it. Green, peaceful, some nice scenery. You should come in. I have no intention of killing you today. But you and you alone can save others, if you're fast enough. Here one must leave behind all hesitation; here every cowardice must meet its death."

I guessed that last line was more *Divine Comedy*.

"I'll pass," I said. "But I'll be sure to drop in and say hello when you're locked up in Cook County, being traded for cigarettes."

"Suit yourself. I don't have a Dante quote for that, but Burke should suffice. How about: 'All that is necessary for the triumph of evil is that good men do nothing.' Have fun sitting on the sidelines, watching men die, knowing you could have prevented it."

The call ended.

A cold wind whipped through my hair, stinging my scalp. The trees beyond the gate rustled in the breeze, and I realized I'd been unconsciously rubbing my belly. I took my hand away.

"Is the SRT here?" I asked Herb, not liking the sound of Luther's threat.

"Yeah."

"The bomb squad?"

"We have several K9 units, some trained in explosives."

"Find that grave," I said, but as the words left my mouth I realized I didn't want Herb to be the one looking for it. I believed Luther. Though I knew he was nothing more than a sick, disturbed man, part of me worried he somehow had the power to kill everyone here. I'd faced so many monsters in my career, but none scared me as much as Luther.

He was the boogeyman.

"Is there overnight security?" I asked.

"Yeah, but it's not extensive. Pretty much just a guy driving around. He hasn't reported in."

I glanced beyond the gate into a pool of darkness. "Where are the lights?" I asked.

"No lights inside."

"Caretakers?"

"There was a groundskeeper. Guy named Willie. Tom talked to him a few minutes ago."

"Groundskeeper Willie?" I asked.

Herb shrugged.

Detective Tom Mankowicz approached with his partner, Roy Lewis, a bald guy who looked a lot like the boxer Marvin Haggler.

"Hey, Lieut," Roy said, the smile on his face reaching his eyes. "Terrible situation, but good to see you."

"We need to find the gravesite of Robert E. Franks," I said. "Tell the teams in the field."

"Won't be easy." Tom rubbed his chin. "There are a quarter million people buried here."

"There's got to be some sort of grave map or database."

"Got the family service counselor for the cemetery on the way here, but it'll be a few minutes."

"What about that groundskeeper?"

Rob and Tom looked around, and then pointed to a man leaning against the stone entrance, watching everything going on with wide eyes. As we approached, I noted he was tall, with a pot belly that rivaled mine, short red hair, and a pointy Bob Hope nose.

"Mr. Kneppel, we need to know the location of a certain grave. Robert E. Franks."

Kneppel's wide eyes got wider, and when he spoke, he flashed a gold tooth. "Bobby Franks?" His voice was hoarse. "Uh...we're not supposed to give out the location of that particular gravesite."

Bobby Franks. That was a name I recognized. He was one of the most famous murder victims of all time. Back in 1924, it had been nationwide news, called the crime of the century. Two teenage law students named Leopold and Loeb had murdered the thirteen-year-old boy just to see if they could get away with it. His death was nothing more than an intellectual exercise. But they'd inadvertently left evidence alongside the body and were defended by the most famous lawyer of the day and probably all time, Clarence Darrow. Darrow didn't get them off, but he was successful in avoiding the death penalty, which the public had demanded. It made sense why the cemetery wasn't public about the grave's location—it could draw unwanted attention to a place whose purpose was to provide a quiet venue for the living to visit and mourn the dead.

"It's okay, Mr. Kneppel," Herb said. "We're the police."

"Oh. Yeah. I guess it'll be okay. He's in the Jacob Franks mausoleum. The paths are all labeled."

Willie mentioned an intersection, and Herb immediately spoke into his lapel mike, repeating the caretaker's words.

Then he, Roy, and Tom headed for the cemetery entrance.

"Guys!" I called.

They stopped and turned back to face me.

"Let SRT handle this one," I said. "With K9 support and explosives experts."

"Seriously?" Herb said.

"I've got a bad feeling, Herb."

"We talking cop intuition? Or..." He let his voice trail off, and I got the full meaning of his insinuation. Was I off my game? Had the stress, the preeclampsia, the baby, and Luther muddled my thinking and made me overreact?

"I dunno," I said. "But I would consider it a personal favor if none of you went to that grave."

They spent a few seconds exchanging glances.

"Sure, Lieut," Tom said. "My fiancée, Joan, is big on intuition. I've learned to heed her. We can hang back here. Roy?"

"You're my brother from another mother, man. Ain't going without you. And I'd follow the Lieut straight anywhere, she asked."

I speared Herb with my eyes. "Herb?"

"It's my crime scene, Jack. I'm highest rank on site."

"Highest rank or fattest rank?" McGlade chimed in, apparently grumpy after being woken in the middle of the night.

"Shoes fit okay?" Herb asked him.

McGlade looked down, noticed his faux pas. "I meant to do that. It's a trending topic on Twitter. You did it, too, but your stomach is so huge you can't see your feet."

I heard a *click* and thought maybe Herb had set his jaw. Hard to tell with his chubby face.

"McGlade, one of these days—"

"—you're going to stop eating everything you see?" Harry interrupted. "Don't answer. I'm afraid if you open your mouth you're going to suck all of us in."

"Y'all a punk," Roy said, taking a step toward McGlade. "Didn't your mama teach you manners?"

McGlade sneered. "Nope. But your mama taught me some stuff last night."

Roy took another step, and then Phin moved into the mix as well, backing up Harry.

There was so much testosterone in the air, if I wasn't already pregnant I might have been worried.

"Look." I spread out my palms. "Everyone needs to calm down. Herb, please, do this for me."

His hound dog jowls dropped even farther, his mustache looking like a horseshoe.

"Sure, Jack. I'll let the SRT take over."

He barked orders into his mike, and I released a sigh of pure relief.

"See how I distracted him from going?" Harry whispered to me. "I would have thrown a donut for him to fetch, but didn't have one handy."

Once again I wondered if McGlade was smarter than he acted.

The next few minutes were spent in silence, all of us waiting. Roy and Tom fidgeted. Harry stepped away and switched his shoes. Herb appeared more anxious than I'd ever seen him. I thought about reaching for Phin's hand to hold it, but was worried he wouldn't accept mine. Willie pulled out a flip phone at least a decade out of date and walked away, his finger in his free ear.

Finally, Herb's radio crackled. "We've reached the mausoleum. We're going in."

I checked my iPhone.

3:10.

According to Luther's book code, it was time for the next victim to die.

SRT Team Leader
Lieutenant Matthews
April 2, 3:10 a.m.

Matthews shouldered the M-16 assault rifle and spoke into his shoulder mike, "Sanchez, Williams, you stay with me. Swartwood, Patel, get in position behind us on the edge of the road. This is a potential hostage situation, so sight your targets. Kitt, Strand, I need eyes around back, make sure nothing comes up from behind."

His men fell into position around the mausoleum, a stone building approximately ten feet tall and the size of a small garden shed. Stone flower pots framed the green iron door, where a pair of red roses had been threaded between the handles. The structure was surrounded by trimmed hedges and flanked by similar mausoleums and headstones. It bothered Matthews. Too many places to hide.

"Battles, open that door, and get out of the way. Angelo, get eyes inside and report back. I'll be on your six."

Matthews covered the door as Battles pulled the bolt cutters out of a backpack. The lock on the door gleamed under the LED flashlight mounted beside the M-16 scope—a new lock, no rust, unlike the decades of oxidation on the vault's iron gate.

"Set for bursts of three, and stay sharp," he said.

Matthews heard the metallic *snick* of the pinchers biting through the lock.

Battles slid the bolt cutter into his pack and backpedaled down the steps and away from the entrance, shouldering his weapon as Angelo approached.

It was difficult to see much more than the beam of Angelo's LED light.

"At the door," Angelo said, his voice soft and steady, though Matthews could hear an edge of fear in it. That was a good thing. Fear enhanced the senses.

Matthews expected the iron door to creak, but it opened smooth and silent, as if its hinges had been oiled.

"Stepping inside," Angelo said.

His light played off the stone, shone through a stained-glass window in the back wall.

"Report," Matthews said.

"Clear. There's two vaults, one on top. Bottom one is Robert Franks. Stained-glass window above them, and...we have a device."

"IED?"

"I don't think so. Metal canister. Looks like a scuba tank."

A course of panic flooded through Matthews. "Possible aerosol. Get your masks out and—"

The crack wasn't as loud as thunder nor as bright as lightning, but the explosion knocked Angelo out of the building.

Matthews felt the ground vibrate the soles of his Doc Martins and took an involuntary step back.

The two men flanking the mausoleum dove for cover, but he stayed upright.

For a long moment, nothing happened.

No one spoke, no one moved.

Was that even a bomb?

Angelo had been thrown onto his back, but now he sat up.

Thank God. He appeared to be in one piece, and there was no debris, no shrapnel, no fire, no smoke.

Everything stood perfectly silent—

—except for a hissing inside the crypt.

Matthews caught a sickly-sweet floral odor a half second before Angelo started coughing and screaming, the cop pawing at his face and frantically trying to rip off his vest.

Matthews recognized the odor: geraniums.

Post-9/11, they'd all been given a crash course in chemical agents. A geranium smell was linked to one of the deadliest chemicals used in World War I—lewisite.

Matthews screamed, "Chemical agent, masks on!" He slid out of his pack, and ripped open the zipper, digging for his own gas mask, eyes beginning to burn.

When he tried to call for backup, he suddenly couldn't speak, his throat already swelling.

In his earpiece, he heard a cacophony of choking...screaming...coughing...vomiting...pure panic.

He'd been cold up until this moment, but now his skin grew hot as the invisible gas penetrated his Kevlar, accelerating through levels of increasing pain—first the fast onset of a sunburn, and then a steady sting, and then skin being eaten away.

Snot, mucus, and tears streamed down his face, and before he realized what had happened, he threw up all over himself.

Matthews struggled onto his feet despite the agony—had to help his men—had to make the screaming stop—but when he started walking he realized the problem—the gas had come in contact with his eyes, his corneas.

He could barely see a thing.

His knees buckled, and he hit the ground.

He needed to call for an extraction. Medics. Get his men attended to.

But with every passing second, the pain and the panic was becoming more intense, and all he could do was try to scream.

Luther
April 2, 3:11 a.m.

Luther watches the carnage on his iPhone, which has been synced to several netbook PCs around the Franks tomb, each equipped with a night-vision camera and running on battery power. Yet another trick he learned from Alex Kork, and it works like a charm.

It looks a lot like the biblical day of reckoning.

Screaming.

Hysteria.

Men tearing off their clothes as the lewisite burns their flesh. Coughing and spitting as it sears their lungs. Vomiting. Bleeding. Falling over.

On any other day, Luther would have been happy to watch until the last man dropped.

To watch it again and again and again.

But this is just a warm-up for the main event.

He steps behind a tombstone and calls Jack on his iPhone.

Jack
April 2, 3:11 a.m.

The screams coming through Herb's mike were horrifying to the point where he had to turn down the volume. I was so taken aback by the sound that I grabbed Phin's shoulder so I didn't fall over. First, Luther had emulated Alex Kork with the iPhone contact. Now he was following in the footsteps of another old adversary, a nut job known as The Chemist.

What other bad folks from my past would Luther dredge up?

The second SRT unit went in, wearing full containment suits, to extract the team, and Herb called in more paramedics and the Center for Disease Control.

My cell rang. Blocked call. I answered without saying anything.

"Do I have your ear now, Jack?" Luther purred. "You could have stopped this. You could have stopped all of this death by simply stopping me. That's what I want, Jack. I want you to stop me. Find me, and come alone, or many more will die. I've got this whole place wired with gas. You get safe passage. Anyone else comes in, I'll go all 'Jumping Jack Flash' on them."

He disconnected.

Herb was yelling orders into his walkie-talkie, denying backup until his men were properly equipped. I knew from experience that McGlade had a P4 space suit, suitable for dealing with chemical warfare, but his place was miles away.

"Luther said he'll give me safe passage," I said to Herb in between his orders.

"No way in hell," Herb replied.

Phin and McGlade echoed the sentiment, and both Tom and Roy joined in.

"Look, guys. He doesn't want to kill me. He wants me alive."

Herb frowned even deeper. "Absolutely not. We don't know what kind of gas that is, if it can drift, if it's contagious. I just called in the National Guard. You're not going to go running around a dark cemetery, hoping to bump into—"

"I don't need to hope," I interrupted. "I know where he is."

"Then tell me, Jack."

I shook my head. "You'll send in more cops, and Luther will kill anyone that goes after him. Anyone except me."

Herb shook his head right back at me. "Jack—"

"We have a chance to end this, Herb. To be free of this son of a bitch, once and for all. He's not going to try to kill me. But I'm sure as hell going to try to kill him."

Everyone stared at me, no one speaking.

Once upon a time I had commanded people, and they listened to me. Not only because I had authority. But because they trusted my orders, my judgment. I studied each of their faces in turn, trying to show them I was still the same woman.

Being a target and being pregnant didn't mean I was unfit to lead.

"I'm in," Tom said, drawing his Glock from his shoulder holster.

Roy followed suit. "Hell, yeah."

Phin and McGlade also pulled their weapons.

"We can take this punk," Harry said.

"I'd follow you to hell, Jack," Phin said. "You know that."

I looked at Phin. "Are you serious?"

"Absolutely. You were right."

"About what?"

"Me trying to control you. I love you, and while I hate the idea of you going in there, you actually doing it is exactly what makes you the woman I love. Fearless. All I want is to protect you."

I could feel the emotion coming, but I pushed it back. "I know, Phin."

"You know I respect you, right?" he said.

I did, but damn it felt good to hear him say it. I nodded.

"And you know I'd die for you?"

I nodded again, swallowing the lump in my throat. If he'd proposed to me saying that, I probably would have said yes right away.

I wanted to hug him. I wanted to kiss him. I wanted to apologize for being the Master of the Bitchiverse.

But I wasn't sure how, and I didn't have the time to figure it out. Later, after we were done.

"Are all of you insane?" Herb asked. "I just lost God knows how many men out there, to God knows what."

"Maybe it was mustard gas," McGlade said. "You like mustard, as evidenced by the stains on your shirt."

"Just tell me where he is, Jack." Herb's eyes drilled into mine, his face imploring.

I turned to Groundskeeper Willie, who'd wandered back over and had been watching all of this like a child watches a slasher film, wide-eyed and horrified. "Luther asked if he had my ear. Bobby Franks was killed by Leopold and Loeb. Ear. Lobe. Are either of the killers buried here?"

Willie gave me something midway between a nod and a head shake. "No...no they're not...but their families are. Samuel and Babbette Leopold. Allan, Anna, Albert, and Earnest Loeb."

"Do you know where those graves are?"

"Yeah. They're hard to spot. I can take you."

"Let's end this, Herb," I said. "You've been so gung-ho about protecting me that you've forgotten all the times I saved your ass. I'm not some fragile porcelain doll about to break. I'm still the same woman I've always been, Goddamn it, and if we were still partners I'd be marching in there right now and you know it."

Herb stared at me. "Do you even have a gun?" he finally asked.

Phin dug into the diaper bag, slapping my Colt into my hand.

"Okay," Herb said. "Let's end this."

We all boarded Willie's golf cart, and without even asking, the groundskeeper got behind the wheel and put the pedal to the metal, catapulting all seven of us through the entry arch of Rosehill Cemetery.

Luther

April 2, 3:14 a.m.

He pinches the bridge of his nose and allows himself a small, private smile.

This is perfect.

Even better than perfect.

Jack
April 2, 3:15 a.m.

Though Luther had alluded to Loeb by mentioning the ear, he could have easily been at the Leopold grave. That's where Willie dropped off Tom and Roy, Herb giving them strict orders to maintain radio contact and treat any threat as deadly.

We rode over to the Loeb tombstone, passing through acres and acres of white monuments that gave off a pale, ghostly glow between the trees. We had just begun to slow down when I saw it, parked on the pathway: a semi-truck with the unmistakable logo of the Chicago Police Department—a black-and-white five-pointed star.

"Did we buy a semi-trailer since I retired?" I asked.

"I never got that memo," Herb said.

He got on his mike, asking if anyone had parked a truck in this section of the cemetery. Then he turned to Harry. "You, bonehead, come with me. Phin, stay with Jack."

"We're covering you," I insisted.

"No, you're not."

"Your ability to tell me what to do ended when you armed me," I said. "I'm the best shot here. We'll cover you."

Herb looked ready to deck me, but he managed a curt nod.

We climbed off the golf cart and crept across the lawn toward the semi. It was dark, cold, and quiet except for the occasional scream from the Franks mausoleum, acres away. Sounded almost like birds from this distance.

While I was tempted to focus on the truck, I knew it could very well be a decoy Luther had planted to command our attention. So instead, I surveyed the trees, the headstones, the road that snaked through the cemetery.

There wasn't a single streetlight for hundreds of yards in any direction, and I couldn't see a damn thing.

I also realized I'd been unconsciously patting my belly again.

"Rear cargo door is open," McGlade said as we drew within fifteen feet of the trailer. "And there's something in back. Something big under a sheet. I see wheels. It's a truck or a van."

"Luther's van?" I whispered to Herb.

"I'll check it out," Herb said. "You all stay here."

"How you planning to get in there, tubs?" McGlade said. "There a crane nearby?"

"Give me a boost."

"And get a quadruple hernia? No thanks. How about Phin goes in?"

"I'm not leaving Jack's side," Phin said. "Why don't you go, McGlade?"

"Because I'm not as stupid as fatso here. You'd have to have the IQ of a potato to willingly go into that—"

"Oh, God, help me! Please help me! JESUS CHRIST, SOME-ONE HELP!"

For a half second, we all froze.

The cry emanated from the vehicle under the sheet.

Someone, hard to identify if they were a man or woman, in unimaginable pain.

Herb charged forward, hauled himself with great effort up into the trailer, and flopped into the cargo bay. Despite his size, he managed to scramble to his feet in seconds, rushing in to help.

As I opened my mouth to yell, "Careful!" he fell to his knees and rolled over onto his side.

"Herb!"

In hindsight, it was perfect. Some traps were baited with cheese or meat.

This one was baited with good will.

Seeing my ex-partner and best friend lying on the floor of the trailer flipped an automatic action switch inside me, and I climbed up into the trailer without a second thought, twisting out of Phin's grip. Once inside, I struggled up off my bruised knees and tore ass to Herb, intent on dragging him out of there. I held my breath with my free hand over my nose and mouth so I didn't inhale whatever gas had incapacitated him.

Already, Phin and Harry were clambering into the truck behind me, screaming for me to get back, their hands clutching my arms, but I was fighting them off, still reaching for my partner.

"Oh, God, help me! Please help me! JESUS CHRIST, SOME-ONE HELP!"

The screaming voice repeated.

Verbatim.

No change in intonation or speed.

That wasn't a live person—that was a recording—and it hit me flush in the chest, a sickening realization spreading through me like a flash of blinding heat as I stared at Herb, unconscious on the floor.

I'd put us all in danger.

We needed to get the hell out of there.

The moment I touched Herb's arm, I heard the sound of the metal bay door at the back of the trailer. Two seconds before it slammed shut, I caught a glimpse of the man closing them—Groundskeeper Willie, smiling.

"I'm sorry," I said to Phin and Harry. "I'm so, so, sorry."

But they were already crumbling to their knees, and so was I.

Then my face lay against the cool plank flooring of the trailer, and I heard the voice of another officer coming through Herb's mike: "Sergeant Benedict, we have no trailer on scene. Repeat, no trailer on scene. Over."

I couldn't stop my eyes from closing. Couldn't fight it any longer.

One lingering, awful thought descending as the gas took me.

"Sergeant Benedict?"

Where—

"Do you read me?"

—will I—

"Sergeant Benedict!"

—wake up?

Luther

April 2, 3:22 a.m.

Luther locks the trailer door and lets the QNB gas go to work.

As he waits, he removes the latex nose and the gold cap from his bicuspid, and pockets them both. Then he opens an alcohol swab pack and wipes the spirit gum off his face.

Finally, he un-cinches the pillow belted to his waist, letting it fall to the ground.

Thanks for the assist, Groundskeeper Willie.

Luther puts the gas mask back on, counts slowly to sixty, and then opens the bay door.

All four are sleeping and will stay this way for several hours.

Luther tugs out the steel ramps and then climbs up into the trailer.

He needs to work quickly.

It takes five minutes to load them all into the van. The fat one is especially difficult, and Luther almost considers leaving him, but he can't.

All four—he smiles—it's too much of a coup.

Besides, not only is Herb one of Jack's closest friends, but Luther has a perfect spot for him.

Once they're all inside, Luther splashes around a bucket of blood in the back of the Sprinter, courtesy of the real grounds-keeper, and a bucket of bran cereal mixed with water, courtesy of Kellog's.

Then he carefully backs the van out of the trailer and drives to the nearest cemetery exit on Western.

There's a barricade, natch, but Luther's gas mask, and the new stenciling on the sides of his Sprinter that read CDC—Center for Disease Control—go a long way toward establishing his credentials.

Even so, his van is stopped by cops.

"Don't open the back!" Luther screams through his closed driver's-side window. "Lewisite gas!"

"These SRT guys?" a baby-faced cop asks.

"Civilians inside the grounds, and they're dying."

The cop and his partner shine their spotlights in on his unconscious passengers.

The blood and the fake vomit make it look like a scene from a warzone.

"Gotta move them! Now!" Luther screams.

The cop, who appears to have just achieved puberty, speaks into his walkie-talkie and then waves him through.

Perfect.

Luther pulls out onto Western, mightily pleased.

Now the real fun can finally begin.

INTERMEZZO

"Through me the way is to the city dolent;
Through me the way is to eternal dole;
Through me the way among the people lost."

DANTE ALIGHIERI, *THE DIVINE COMEDY*

Luther Kite

Sixteen Months Ago

*H*e tackles the house first, stripping it down to bare walls and *floor.*

It takes him two days to install the chains—drilling deep anchors into the masonry to hold the leg irons, manacles, and neck collars.

Fifteen Months Ago

"How may I help you?"

"When I make a withdrawal, I can request any denomination, even coins, correct?"

"Yes."

"I need fifty thousand dollars in pennies."

"Excuse me, did you say fifty thousand dollars?"

"Yes. That comes out to five million pennies." He smirks. *"I'm guessing you don't have that many in your cash drawer."*

"No, we don't even have that many in the vault. But we can get them for you. It just may take a bit of time."

"No problem. I have plenty of time."

"Might I ask what they're for?"

Another smile. "I'm going to prove that money can't buy happiness."

Fourteen Months Ago

He stands at the opening to the warehouse all day, watching the trucks back in.

Load after load after load of sand, and the growl of the dozers spreading it around.

He can't remember the last time he's been this energized.

Finally, after all these years...

Creating again.

One Year Ago

The weather comes two days early.

Ten Mole Fan 18" DMX wind machines.

Six thousand apiece.

When the crew has completed the install, he walks through the warehouse with the remote console, pushing buttons, imagining all the fun to come.

Eight Months Ago

Luther watches Jack Daniels from the tree outside her house. He also notices someone else watching her.

That won't do at all.

Jack is his, and his alone.

Six Months Ago

The bill for the monitors, the remote cameras and batteries, and all the cables, comes to a hair over two hundred thousand dollars.

"You opening up a television studio?" Luther is asked as he hands over the credit card.

"Something like that."

Three Months Ago

When the driver for "The Septic Specialist" climbs back into his rig, Luther is sitting in the passenger seat, smiling and holding a subcompact .40 Glock.

"How full of shit is the tank?" he asks.

The driver's eyes narrow with confusion. "Um, about three-quarters."

"Buckle your seatbelt and drive where I tell you."

Two Months Ago

Luther stares into the cage, locking eyes with the enormous beast.

"You sure about this, buddy?" the man selling it says. "He's a vicious son of a bitch. Not a good pet at all. Plus he eats a whole lot of meat."

Luther nods slowly. "Meat won't be a problem."

One Month Ago

It's late in the night.

Two, maybe three a.m.

It has rained all day, and it's still raining—he can hear the patter of it on the roof far above his head.

In a distant corner of the warehouse, under a portion of failed roofing, water drips into a growing puddle on the concrete floor.

He cut the generators for the night, and so he walks in total darkness, guided only by a flashlight.

Down he goes—several flights of metal stairs that echo in the dark—into the basement.

When he reaches the cell, he fishes the keys out of his pocket and unlocks the deadbolt.

Pushes open the door, lets the beam of his flashlight play across the walls, finally landing upon the wretch of a human being that sits huddled in the far corner, chained to the wall by an iron neck collar that looks like something from the dark ages.

The man looks up as the light strikes his face.

Haggard. Emaciated. Toothless.

His beard a foot and a half long.

Luther has been force-feeding him for the last month, the man apparently intent on dying after seven years in captivity.

But he's not about to let that happen.

He still requires Andrew Z. Thomas to wear a helmet, although in truth, he probably no longer contains the strength or wherewithal to bash his head against the concrete wall.

Luther sits down across from him.

"I never hear you typing anymore." He touches the old typewriter he brought down years ago as a sick joke. In the beginning, Andy had written every day. A pile of five thousand single-spaced pages still stands against the wall, and he figures it could probably fetch a small fortune on eBay.

The first several hundred pages are actually decent, but soon after, the strain of captivity having taken its toll, the writing had disintegrated into madness.

Incoherent sentences.

Then incoherent words.

And finally just a single word, typed over and over for five reams of paper...

```
lutherlutherlutherlutherlutherluther-
    lutherlutherlutherluther...
```

"I'm nearly finished," Luther says. "But I need you to hang on a little while longer. You're the centerpiece after all. If you do that, I promise you, I'll give you what you want."

The chain clinks against the wall as Andy looks up.

"What's that?" Andy says.

The words come out at barely a whisper, but Luther stares nonetheless, stunned.

These are the first words Andy has spoken in more than a year. He assumed the man's mind was gone.

"I'll set you free," Luther says, rising to his feet.

Russell Bilg

March 14, Nineteen Days Ago

Fifteen Minutes Prior to the Bus Incident

He pulled the Prevost motor coach into the oasis in Indianapolis at four in the afternoon, following a ten-hour haul out of Philadelphia. He was carrying forty-two passengers on a bus tour called "Sea to Shining Sea." Russell couldn't understand anyone wasting a vacation on this, or even worse, wasting their hard-earned money. It was essentially a northerly-oriented coast-to-coast trek through the Midwest, Dakotas, and Montana, eventually concluding in Seattle. This was day one of his twenty-fourth "Sea to Shining Sea" tour, and already he couldn't wait for it to be over.

The passengers slowly unloaded from the bus, drifting herd like toward the oasis, which contained a giant convenience store, restrooms with full showers, and several fast-food chains.

He'd given them thirty minutes to be back on the bus—they had reservations at an Embassy Suites in Chicago, and he had a reservation for dinner and getting loaded with an old friend at the Hopleaf, his favorite beer bar.

While the bus's bottomless gas tank filled, Russ grabbed the empty, 24-oz. wide-mouthed Coke bottle and walked into the store.

He'd been holding it back all day, knowing this oasis was coming, and it was most certainly worth the wait.

This place had the best restroom in the world, boasting stall walls that dropped all the way to the floor for maximum privacy, and the option (for a five-dollar credit card charge) to purchase twenty minutes in an "executive stall" outfitted with high-grade toilet paper, guaranteed cleanliness, a bidet, and a first-rate magazine selection.

Russ bought an "executive stall pass" and headed back toward the restrooms.

They'd be in Chicago in three hours, and he needed a night of letting his hair down, because tomorrow was going to suck major ass.

On the itinerary...

The Willis Tower at nine-thirty a.m.

Lunch in the Signature Room on the ninety-fifth floor of the Hancock Center.

And then an afternoon drive down to St. Louis, where the first item on day three's agenda was the Gateway Arch.

In his experience, all people wanted to do was have their fat asses hauled to the top of shit.

Russ entered the restroom and made his way down to executive stall number eight.

Punched in the code, stepped inside.

Clean as a whistle, and it smelled like lavender and roses.

He installed himself on his throne, set a magazine in his lap, and pulled the small, velvet bag out of the inner pocket of his vest.

From the velvet bag, he fished out a Ziploc baggie containing a quarter lid of pot, stems and leaves from rolling past joints, and papers.

Driving forty-two people across the country was a stressful proposition.

He tried to always make sure he was good and baked for the last few hundred miles of every driving day, and since he'd been with the bus company now going on twelve years, he had their drug testing schedule pegged down to a science—they tested him twice a year, always before the big Alaska tour. And he wasn't such an addict that he couldn't abstain for a month to turn up a clean UA.

He rolled a tight little number and fired it up right there in the stall.

Took one deep, penetrating hit that nearly cut the J in half, and then twisted it out against the wall.

He held the smoke until his lungs screamed, and then opened the empty, wide-mouthed Coke bottle he kept for just such an occasion and blew the smoke inside, capping it before any escaped.

Leaned back on the toilet.

Shut his eyes.

Let it come like a heavy, warm blanket—

A knock on the stall door ripped him out of his bliss.

"Occupied," he said, coughing.

"Yeah, I know. I was just wondering...um, you think I could have a little toke?"

Shit.

"I don't know what you're talking about."

"Look, we're alone in here, all right?"

"I told you, I don't know—"

"Will you cut the shit, please? I can smell it a mile away. I could turn you in, you know. But all I want is a little puff."

Russ sighed. "Hang on."

He stood and removed the stupid chauffeur's hat and vest his employer required him to wear *at all times behind the wheel*, which not only bore his name but also the Charter Bus USA insignia.

These, he hid behind the toilet.

"You letting me in, or what?" the man said through the door.

Russ turned the lock, pulled it open.

The man who stood before him was tall and pale with a cascade of long, black hair that hung to his shoulders.

"Get in here," Russ whispered, "before someone sees you."

It was a roomy stall, with plenty of floor space for both of them to stand without crowding each other.

Russ took the lighter and the half-smoked J out of his pocket, figuring the best course of action was to expedite the proceedings, just let this guy get his toke and get the hell on his way, out of his life. Count himself lucky that an employee of the oasis, or worse, a cop, hadn't caught him.

"So how many passengers you carrying?" the man asked.

Russ had been on the verge of striking a flame, but this stopped him cold.

He stared into the man's coal-black eyes. "Excuse me?"

"Your bus out there...how many people are on the trip?"

How the hell did this guy know he was driving the motor coach? Had he seen him pull up to the pump? Then followed him in here?

"Forty-two," he said, opting to play it cool, hide the agitation. "Now when I light this, you've got to take a quick, deep hit, and that's it. I don't want to smoke this place up. And be warned...this is good shit. I don't know what your supply is like but this—"

"Forty-two...that's perfect. Now your company monitors your progress in real time with a GPS tracker, correct?"

"What are you talking about?"

"Your bus. The employer tracks where you go. To make sure you're keeping to your schedule and predetermined route. Am I right in this assumption?"

These questions were beginning to harsh Russ's mellow.

"Yeah, why?"

"Because I'm going to have to disable it. Do you know where the GPS unit is?"

Russ felt a sudden coldness spreading through him. It was good pot, he'd taken a big hit, and there was a chance he was just stoned already, had missed the playful, joking tone in the stranger's voice.

But this seemed unlikely. The higher probability was that this man standing in his stall was completely off his rocker.

"That's a good one," Russ said, forcing a smile, trying to just push through the moment, get back to saner ground. "So you ready to hit this?"

The man with long, black hair turned his back to Russ.

He heard the door to the stall lock back into place.

When the man turned back to face him, he held a knife, the blade sharply curved and gleaming under the fluorescent lights.

Fear slashed through Russ's high.

"Look, man, you want my wallet, that's cool. Just...don't hurt me. Please."

"Do me a favor," the man said.

"Anything."

"Pick up the vest and that cap that's stuffed back behind the toilet."

"Oh, yeah, sure."

Russ turned and knelt down, grabbed the burgundy Charter Bus USA vest and cap.

"Here." He offered them to the stranger.

"No, just set them on top of the toilet tank."

"Okay."

Russ did as he was told.

"Many thanks," the man said. "Didn't want to get your blood all over my new clothes."

Russ only caught a fleeting glimmer as the blade streaked across the stall in a broad, fast arc. When it hit his windpipe, there was no resistance, just a brilliant burn, followed by the sharp stench of rust. He saw blood pouring down his chest in shiraz-colored eddies, tried to breathe, but the effort only produced a burbling in his throat, the burn getting more intense with every second, specks of incandescent black beginning to blossom and fade across his field of vision like demon fireflies.

The man with long, black hair wiped Russ's blood off the blade with several plies of that executive toilet paper, and then folded the knife and slid it back into the side pocket of his jeans.

He put both hands on Russ's shoulders and eased him down onto the toilet seat.

"Don't fight it, brother," the man said. "It'll only make the pain worse. Just close your eyes and let the darkness come."

Luther

March 14, Nineteen Days Ago

The Bus Incident

The vest fits more snugly than he would have liked, and the chauffeur's hat is a few sizes too large, but nothing he can't cope with.

He pays the astronomical gas bill with Russell Bilg's company credit card and heads back outside.

A raw March day spitting drops of freezing rain.

Sky overcast and dismal.

Not a trace of discernible blue.

It takes him five minutes to locate the GPS tracker—a metal device the size of a deck of cards, mounted to the inside of the tour bus's back bumper. It's attached by a strong magnet, and he tugs it off and relocates the unit to the undercarriage of a minivan parked on the other side of the gas pumps. Then he jams two screwdrivers into the hinges of the rear emergency exit. There are two window exits on either side of the bus, but he should be able to cover those.

At last, he boards the coach and stands facing the passengers, getting a good first look at his cast.

An AARP crowd for the most part.

Plenty of gray and white hair, but he anticipated this. In fact, he'd hoped for it.

Senior citizens are, by definition, way ahead of the curve when it comes to experience. Experience means living. Living, without exception, means sins.

Sins of every caliber.

It warms his heart to consider the possibilities.

"Good afternoon, folks," he says with a big, toothy smile.

They look tired and bored, scarcely refreshed from the snack and bathroom break.

"My name is Rob Siders, and I'll be taking over for Russell Bilg. I know you probably couldn't tell, because Mr. Bilg is such a consummate professional, but he was becoming very ill today and requested a fill-in. That's the reason for the delay here at the oasis, and I apologize for that on behalf of Charter Bus USA. But now we're back on track, and we're going to keep pushing on for a few more hours. If you have any questions, don't hesitate to let me know."

An older woman, a third of the way back, raises her hand.

"Yes ma'am?"

"Hi, Patricia Reid here."

"Hi, Patricia."

"How much longer until we get to the hotel?"

"About three hours, assuming no traffic snafus." Luther smiles again. "So what do you all say? Ready to hit the open road?"

He receives back only a few half-hearted nods.

"Oh, come on, we can do better than that, can't we? I'm not going to start the engine until you all convince me you're ready to have some real fun. So...I said..." He cups a hand to his ear. "Are we ready to hit the open road?"

This time, a dozen people respond with unenthusiastic *Yeahs*.

"That's what I'm talking about!"

Luther pumps a fist and turns to hide the malicious grin that's creeping across his face.

This is possibly the most fun he's ever had, and it's only getting started.

* * *

He drives north out of Indy on I-69, keeps anticipating that first question about their route change, why they're no longer heading toward Chicago, but two hours into the trip, it still hasn't surfaced. Only as they cross the border does he register the first curious rumblings from the passengers, sees faces glancing out the big, tinted windows at the bleak Michigan farmland scrolling past, draped in the deep blues and grays of a cold, spring evening.

But he drives on, and still no one questions their course.

* * *

Four hours have elapsed since they left the oasis, and night has fallen, and no dinner or hotel rooms have been procured, and finally, on the east side of Lancing, Luther watches a man rise from the back and work his way down the aisle toward the front of the bus.

He stops behind Luther.

"Um, excuse me, sir."

Luther briefly cuts his attention from the giant steering wheel and glances up and over his shoulder at the old man looming above him—bald, thick glasses, fanny-packed. Then he turns his focus back to the pavement streaming under the bus in a long, endless trail of reflective paint.

"Some of us were just curious about where we are exactly."

"Michigan."

"Yeah, see, um...we thought that we'd be in Chicago by now. It's late and we're hungry, and our itinerary tomorrow involves a number of famous Chicago landmarks."

"I'll make an announcement explaining the course change," Luther says.

"That'd be great. People are just anxious to know what's going on."

As the man waddles back to his seat, Luther grabs the microphone off the dash and addresses his passengers.

"Folks, I got word back in Indy that there had been a terrible accident on I-65 outside of Gary, Indiana, so we're on to plan B. I know it's been a long day, but we'll be pulling into the hotel shortly."

"What about Chicago?" some old bag whines from the back of the bus.

"That'll be day after tomorrow, ma'am."

"What's there to see in Michigan?"

Fair question, but it still annoys the hell out of him.

"We're going to tour an old auto factory," he says.

"I don't want to tour an auto factory," says another woman. "I want to see the Sears Tower and the Hancock Building. That's what I paid for."

"Me, too."

Worse than driving a bunch of kids to school. Luther doesn't even bother to correct them that Sears no longer owns the skyscraper.

He exited the interstate five miles back, and they're closing in now, moving through the outskirts of the city, the buildings taking a turn toward abject dilapidation, and with a greater frequency of abandonment.

Luther speaks into the mike again.

"Please trust me, gang. We're staying someplace special. It's going to be very memorable."

He brings the bus to a full stop and digs the remote control out of the duffle bag in the floorboard, watching his passengers closely now, most staring through their windows, trying to glean some level of detail beyond the glass.

Good luck with that. This urban ghost town hasn't seen a spark of electricity in years, except for Luther's personal generators, which are currently off.

"Where are we?" someone asks.

He lets the question hang unanswered as he pulls past the gate into a vast, empty parking lot, riddled with broken concrete and toppled light poles.

"Is this even a road?" a man sitting directly behind him asks.

The first warehouse appears in the distance, the lights of the motor coach striking the door as it slowly lifts.

Luther pulls the bus inside, brings it to a halt, and finally kills the engine.

Reaching down once more into the duffle, he grabs his Glock, two extra, non-factory clips, a plastic bag, and a canvas bag. He tucks the gun into the back of his waistband, stuffs the clips and plastic bag into his pockets, and climbs out of the driver's seat.

He stands, faces his bleary-eyed passengers, half of whom are now openly glaring at him. The other half stare through the glass into the low-lit gloom of the warehouse, bewildered.

"I can't tell you how much I appreciate your patience," he says.

A man six rows back is struggling to his feet—short, red-faced, with tufts of platinum hair between his ears and the bald, pink dome of a scalp riddled with irregular, black patches of skin cancer. He says, "Well, mine's at an end."

"Take your seat, sir," Luther says.

"You go to hell. I want off this bus right now. And I want a refund from Charter Bus USA."

"Where have you brought us?" someone asks.

"Sit down, sir," Luther warns again.

Other passengers have begun to stir, a few toward the back also rising to their feet.

The man's insolence is catching fire, and as he marches up the aisle, Luther estimates that he'll have a full-blown mutiny on his hands within the minute. He has a gasmask and aerosol canister of QNB—an incapacitating agent—but that's only for use as a last resort.

Making an example is definitely the smarter, and easier, play.

When the man is three feet away, Luther draws the Glock and shoots him in the face.

As he topples back into the aisle, dousing the first three rows in blood, the noise of the gunshot is instantly surpassed by the screams inside the bus.

Luther steps back, takes the microphone, and speaks in a purposely calm voice he thinks sounds quite similar to the crazed computer, HAL, from that Kubrick film.

"Please stop screaming, everyone, and return to your seats."

The screaming doesn't stop.

"Please stop screaming, everyone, and return to your seats."

A cluster of people toward the back of the bus are forcing their way down the aisle, and a man several rows back is in the throes of a heart attack.

Luther asks nicely for a third time for everyone to return to their seats, and then he shoots a man fumbling for the side window exit lever, and three others for good measure.

Then he calmly repeats his orders.

Through the wisp of gun smoke, he watches everyone scramble back to their seats, frantic to comply as if engaged in a horrific game of musical chairs.

"Very good," he says. "Very good."

Luther aims his Glock at a large, mustached man sitting two rows back. He and the obese woman across the aisle from him, at forty-five or fifty, appear to be the youngest of the group.

"What's your name, sir?"

"Steve."

Luther tugs the plastic bag out of his pocket and hands it to Steve.

"Collect everyone's cell phone right now, starting with yours. Ladies and gentlemen, our friend Steve will be coming by to get your cellular devices. In the meantime, I want to see both hands on the seat in front of you. This means everyone. You fail to do it, I shoot you."

Luther reaches into the driver's seat and grabs the heavy canvas bag brimming with handcuffs.

He gives it to the nearest passenger, a stern-looking man, completely bald, wearing a Cubs T-shirt.

"Start passing these out. Quickly." Into the mike, Luther says, "Anyone not wearing handcuffs gets shot."

"Why are you doing this to us?" a woman cries.

He levels the Glock on her, says, "Come here. Yes, you, right now." She steps out into the aisle. "Closer." When she's six feet away, he orders her to stop. "What's your name?"

"Lillian. Lillian Slusar."

"Do you know what a double-tap is, Miss Slusar?"

She shakes her head.

He shows her, the two rapid-fire shots puncturing her heart in less than a second.

No one screams this time, the expressions of horror voiced only as gasps and muffled cries.

"Does anyone else have any more questions for me?" Luther gazes out at the silent, horrified stares. "Excellent." He still has three rounds in the clip, but he goes ahead and swaps it out for a freshie. "How we coming, Steve-o?"

The burly man has reached the back of the bus.

"I've got them all."

The woman with the bag of handcuffs is halfway to the back.

"Handcuff queen, how we doing?"

"Fine," she weeps.

"Anyone gives you an ounce of trouble, you just let me know."

"Yes, sir."

An eerie silence falls upon the tour bus, no sound but the clink of steel bracelets clamping over wrists.

Steve returns and drops the grocery bag filled with phones of every make and model at Luther's feet. Then he locks a pair of handcuffs around his own wrists and returns to his seat.

Luther brings the mike to his mouth.

"We have to unload now. We're going to go two at a time starting at the front of the bus. I've prepared some rooms for you. Some even have cots. I don't want to hurt anyone else, but I hope you understand that I won't hesitate. There will be no warnings. I won't ask nicely a second time for you to do what I tell you. If you deviate, in the slightest degree, from my commands, I'll simply kill you where you stand. Now I know this isn't exactly the bus tour of America you all signed up for, but I can promise you this..." He smiles wide. "This one is going to be a helluva lot more exciting."

PART II

"All hope abandon, ye who enter in!"

DANTE ALIGHIERI, *THE DIVINE COMEDY*

Luther

The fat man's suit is stained and torn.

He sits on the floor, peering up at Luther, trying to look defiant, but Luther senses the fear coming off him like radiation, and imagines that his chubby fingers—hands bound behind him with zip line—are trembling.

"How are you, Herb?"

The fat man just glares.

"You're angry with me, that's fair."

"Where's Jack?"

"Jack's resting. She has a big, big day ahead of her. So do you. And your friends, Harry and Phin."

"What have you done with her, you son of a bitch?"

"You'll get a chance to find out firsthand, Herb. Within the next several hours, in fact. You're an important part of everything that's about to happen."

Luther reaches down and lifts a black velvet cloth out of a crumpled paper bag at his feet.

Sets it on the table between them.

"Before we begin, I just want to be clear that I don't have any desire to get into a conversation with you about *why* I need to blind you. Only the method."

He waits for it.

There.

What had been predominately anger and rage in the fat man's eyes gives way to full-blown terror.

Nice. That was fun.

"Blind me?" Herb asks, his voice dripping with disbelief.

"And you have a choice here, which is the good news."

Luther opens the velvet cloth, upon which lay an ice pick and a curved needle and thread.

"I'm going to either jam the ice pick into your eyeballs, or stitch your eyelids closed. It's entirely your call, but if you don't think you can sit still while I do the suturing, you might need to man up and just go the faster, more permanent route."

The fat man has begun to sweat, beads dripping off his double chin.

"Is a blindfold an option?"

"Herbert." Luther says his name like he's scolding a bad dog. "Just tell me the way you'd like for me to go."

"Oh...God." He can see the fat man is fighting to keep it together.

"Choose or I'll choose for you."

Herb's voice is barely a croak. "The needle."

"Okay," Luther says, standing. "Now you have to remain very calm. I can't have you flailing around while I've got a needle near your eye. That could be dangerous. I could poke my finger."

"We're...doing this...*now?*"

"Right now."

Luther kneels down, picking up the surgeon's suture.

"Now, I want you to start practicing," Luther says.

"Practicing what?"

Luther sits down on the table and raises the needle, a twelve-inch length of black thread dangling from the eye.

"Holding very, very still."

Jack

My baby woke me, kicking.

I opened my eyes, found myself staring down into broken pavement, my head as unwieldy as a hot air balloon. Swallowing, I felt a dry tightness in my throat. I had a slightly metallic taste in my mouth and was hot all over.

And yet, I shivered.

The pattering on my windbreaker sounded like rain, and the dirty street smelled of it.

I lay for some time on the wet pavement trying to cobble together my last cogent memory, but I couldn't find it. I remembered the Marquette Building, checking into the Congress Hotel, but everything after lay beyond my mind's reach, lost in a painful, throbbing fog. Something about Phin and maybe Harry. Flashing red and blue lights on tombstones. But nothing concrete.

It took a substantial effort to finally heave myself up into a sitting position.

I rubbed the sleep out of my eyes and squinted until the world came into focus.

I was sitting in the middle of an empty street lined with small factory houses.

Rain fell out of a low, ominous cloud deck.

I had to turn over onto all fours and get my legs underneath me to even have a chance at standing. Once on my feet, I could feel my heart pounding and that disturbing pins-and-needles tingling in my extremities.

The clothes I wore weren't mine—this much I knew. Dark blue rain pants and a matching jacket. Sports bra underneath. White sneakers that squeezed my swollen feet. I patted myself down, looking for my cell phone, any sort of weapon. Found nothing.

I pulled the nylon hood over my head and started across the street toward the nearest house, not realizing until I reached the porch its state of disrepair.

Paint had chipped off everywhere.

The floorboards sagged.

I climbed the steps and banged on the front door and waited.

No one came.

I moved over to the window beside the door, cupped my hands over my eyes, and peered through. Almost all of the glass had been broken out, save for a few sharp jags remaining around the perimeter. The house was dark inside, and by what little light slipped through, I saw that the interior lay in ruin—furniture destroyed and rotted down to the splintered frames. The floor littered with syringes, empty beer cans, broken bottles. I caught a strong waft of mildew from what could only be severe water damage.

No one had lived here in years.

I waddled down the creaky steps, my brain reeling.

Halfway up the stairs to the house next door, I stopped. This one was abandoned too, standing in an even greater state of ruin, with the roof over the front-left quadrant caved in.

I scanned the other houses in the vicinity and saw more of the same—this entire neighborhood of homogenous factory houses was a ghost town.

A crow streaked past overhead, buzzing the treetops, its cawing filling the air with a solitary, haunting echo.

Where the hell was I? How did I get here?

Aside from the bird, there were no other sounds. Most notably absent was the hum of car engines and city noise. It was so quiet here, I could've been standing in a secluded forest.

Stumbling back into the road, I trudged along the middle of the street and cupped my hands around my mouth.

"Hey! Anyone there!"

No one answered me.

An ancient water tower loomed in the distance, and I was trying to make out the faded writing on the tank when I heard someone scream up ahead.

While my memory didn't return, I instinctively knew who was behind this.

Luther.

Please, please, please, don't let the person screaming be someone I love...

Phin

He opened his eyes and found himself strapped to an odd sort of chair, his arms and legs stretched taut, secured with leather restraints. Some sort of pulley-and-gear system had been integrated into the seat. It looked like a high-tech dentist's chair, with more bells and whistles, none of them appearing to be pleasant.

Phin didn't like it at all, and his heart began to do a thrash metal drum solo. He tried to pull free, but the bonds were solid.

The room was stuffy, smelling of mildew and rank blood.

Concrete walls. Low light.

A floor covered in sand.

A dungeon. He was in a dungeon.

How did he get there?

The snatches of memory came rapid-fire, like thumbing through a stack of postcards.

The cemetery.

The golf cart.

The semi truck.

Jack.

JACK.

"JACK!" Phin yelled.

"Phin? That you?"

It wasn't Jack. Phin craned his head and noticed an identical chair across from his, with another occupant strapped to it.

"McGlade?"

"Tell me we got drunk and this is some S&M hooker thing."

"Luther's got us."

"Do you think he's going to be bringing in hookers?"

"I doubt it."

"Kinda figured."

"You see Jack or Herb?"

"No. There's some kind of control panel on a cart. One of the walls I'm facing has a big window, but it's dark behind it. There's a plaque beside it, looks like brass, has some writing. All I can make out are the words CIRCLE and VIOLENCE with a bunch of smaller words. And..." McGlade's voice trailed off.

"And what?"

"Body. A dude. Sitting in the corner."

"Alive?"

"No."

"You sure?"

"You can try to yell, see if he wakes up. But it'll be tough for him to hear without a head."

Phin felt himself grow very cold. "Aren't you going to make some joke about giving head?" he tried.

Harry didn't answer.

"You with me, Harry? Don't freak out on me now."

"I've been kidnapped by a killer and am looking at a corpse without a head. Who wouldn't freak out in this situation?"

"We need to think rationally."

McGlade let out a slow breath. "You want to know what I'm thinking rationally about? Once again we're tied up and waiting for some maniac to torture us to death. I should just go ahead and wet my pants right now."

"Keep it together, Harry."

"It's like déjà vu all over again," McGlade said. "You know how many nightmares I've had about the last time this happened?" His voice cracked. "I...I can't handle it, buddy."

"Yes, you can."

"No, I can't. I went through this once before. I can't..."

"We'll get out of here, Harry. It ain't over till it's over."

But Phin's own words didn't convince him. And they felt even more hollow when he heard Harry McGlade begin to softly sob.

Jack

I rushed through the overgrown weeds in the front yard and up onto the porch. This house, like all the others, was barely standing upright, its entire frame listing to the left. Through the door came the cries of a woman.

A woman. I blew out the breath I'd been holding, ashamed to be grateful that it was no one I knew.

She screamed again.

I had to help her, but I hesitated. Without a weapon, bursting inside wasn't exactly a safe proposition.

I turned the handle anyway and eased the door open.

In the lowlight, it took a moment for my eyes to adjust. When they did, I spotted a sofa on the far side of the living room, the upholstery rotted away, now nothing but a wooden frame and rusty springs. Nature had found its way inside, dirt and leaves and animal droppings and puddles of stagnant water. A coffee table lay smashed on the floor beneath a light fixture that dangled from the ceiling by its wiring, the plasterboard around it bowing down.

I called out, "Hello?"

"Back here!" a woman cried.

The floorboards creaked under my weight as I made my way through the living room, dodging gaping holes where the wood had deteriorated.

I stopped, listening.

I stood in a dark, narrow hallway, rain falling through a hole in the ceiling above me. There was a door at the end of the hall, its frame outlined with threads of light. From behind the door rose a chorus of screams—numerous voices—that soon devolved into groans.

I moved forward.

A floorboard snapped.

My leg punched through into the crawlspace under the house, my right foot sinking down into cold mud.

I fought my way out, the tendons around my elbows straining as I heaved myself back up onto the floor, pushing away from the hole and gasping for breath, sweat popping out in beads all over my face.

People were still screaming behind the door, but I couldn't move just yet, the exertion of hauling myself out of the crawlspace having sapped what little energy I'd had. I was dizzy, achy, exhaustion already tugging at my body even though I'd only awoken a few minutes earlier.

I barely made it onto my feet.

Staggered the last few steps to the door.

Pushed it open and stood in the threshold gasping for breath, the black stars in my field of vision threatening to sweep my consciousness out from under me.

Oh...oh dear God.

It had once been a small bedroom with a window looking out into a backyard at a child's swing set and the factories beyond.

Now the flooring had been stripped down to the plywood. In places, the drywall had been ripped out, leaving the studs exposed. The leg irons and wrist irons and neck collars had been anchored deep in the studs, and four people, one on each wall, stood in chains. A smell not dissimilar to barbecue hung in the air, and I noticed smoke rising from the shoulders of an old man across the room, his corduroy jacket dotted with charred holes, some of which were still ringed with smoldering ash.

His head hung down and he wasn't moving.

He stood on a metal grate, blackened from flames.

A blonde, several years my senior, called my name from across the room.

We locked eyes.

Hers were filled with terror.

I could guess mine were, too.

Luther

He screams into the microphone, "Say it! Say it! This is the start! You mess this up, I'll teach you what pain really is! Say it!"

Jack

Tears streaked down the woman's face, her entire body shaking.

She said in an otherworldly voice, "Welcome to hell, Jack."

"Is Luther here?" I asked.

"I don't know."

"I'm going to help you," I said. "I'm going to get you all out of here."

The woman's face screwed up in a wreck of fear as she shook her head. "You can't help us."

I took a step into the room, looking at the grating on the floor, spying the dancing flames beneath it.

Luther had turned the room into an oven.

I was unable to comprehend how much time, how much money, it would take to build something like this. And why? What was the point of being this elaborate?

Up in one corner, hanging from the ceiling where two walls met, I spotted a surveillance camera. Underneath it, a brass plaque, twelve inches long and three inches wide.

The words "CIRCLE 1: LIMBO" had been engraved into the metal, followed by three numbers:

666

I crossed over to the smoking man, checked for a pulse, knowing there wouldn't be one but trying anyway. Then I walked over to the woman who'd spoken to me and tested the chains.

Heavy-grade iron. Nothing I could do to free them without help or tools. I glanced at the two other shackled men—both twitching as if in the throes of debilitating palsy, their eyes gone wide, vacant.

"I'm coming back," I said.

She mouthed, "Don't leave me."

"I have to find something to break these chains."

"Please," she begged, reaching out for me.

I took one of her hands in mine and gave it a gentle squeeze.

"What's your name?" I asked.

She took a moment to answer, as if she couldn't remember. "Andrea."

"Andrea, I'm Jack Daniels, and I will be back here as soon as I possibly can. I promise you that."

I hurried out of the room, stepping carefully around the collapsed section of flooring in the hallway. Spent a moment in the kitchen ransacking the cabinets and drawers, searching for anything that might help me to get through the chains or the studs they'd been anchored to, but there was nothing of use.

I worked my way through the living room and down the front porch steps into the yard, didn't stop until I'd walked out into the middle of the street.

Luther was behind this, no question, but my head was still spinning.

I didn't understand how—

Something knocked me to my knees, and my ears popped with the sudden change of pressure, a blast of furnace-like heat encompassing me.

For what seemed an endless moment, I couldn't hear anything.

Molten ash drifted down like snowflakes from hell.

Shingles and two-by-fours and strips of siding lay burning in the road all around me.

I looked back over my shoulder, saw the house I'd been inside not fifteen seconds ago, now roiling in flames and coughing up clouds of pitch-black smoke. The overhanging trees, which had also caught fire, scratched the gray, afternoon sky with blazing orange fingers.

My hands—my whole body—wouldn't stop shaking.

The last five minutes had been possibly the most surreal of my life, and that was saying a helluva lot. Truth be told, I wasn't sure any of this was real, and had begun to doubt my sanity when I heard Luther's voice, inexplicably, inside my head.

"Better keep moving, Jack."

I reached up and touched my right ear, felt an earpiece.

When I tried to tug it out, it wouldn't budge.

"It's not coming off," Luther said. "Super glue."

I pulled harder, felt a streak of tearing pain, skin ripping.

Everything came rushing back.

Rosehill. The semi-trailer. The gas.

It all felt like so long ago.

How many hours had I lost?

And then: Phin. Harry. Herb.

My boys. My caring, supportive, heroic boys.

Where were they?

Pain threatened to hobble me. Pain and guilt and anger at this crazy situation that I should have seen coming.

If he'd touched them...

"Where's Phin?" I asked, trying to keep my voice clear of emotion, but it sounded strange—muffled and crowded out by the ringing in my ears.

"Phin's with me, Jack. So is Harry. So is Herb. Everyone's been invited to the party."

I struggled up onto my feet.

The blast had rocked my inner ear, and I stumbled sideways, catching myself from falling by latching onto a mailbox post.

"You see that warehouse in the distance?" Luther asked.

"Which one?"

"The freestanding brick one."

It was big, in similar disrepair to the other buildings in the area. "Yeah, I see it."

"Start walking toward it."

"What do you want, Luther?" My balance was returning and the noise in my ears beginning to subside. I straightened up and started down the middle of the road.

That brick, windowless warehouse stood several hundred yards ahead on the far side of an empty parking lot, and even from this distance, a strange noise seemed to emanate from inside—a soft, machine-like hum.

"I've been watching you for close to a year, Jack. You've lost your way, haven't you?"

"What the hell are you talking about?"

"You used to be a cop. The best of the best. But now you're a nobody. And you feel like a nobody, don't you, Jack? Are you even happy to be bringing this child into the world?"

His question unnerved me, and not only because this nut job was psychoanalyzing me.

But he might actually be right.

I thought quitting the force would make me happy, that I could slip into a domestic life like I slipped into a new pair of Ferragamos. But it had been harder than I'd expected. Even if I hadn't been constantly looking over my shoulder, waiting for Luther to show up, tripping over my 24/7 protectors, I was still unsure this was what I really wanted out of life.

But I was sure of one thing. I was damn sick of Luther Kite.

"Feel free to answer every question I throw your way," he said.

"Go to hell."

The side mirror of a long-abandoned car, missing an engine and sitting on concrete blocks, exploded three feet away from me, and I jumped back as the gunshot echoed between the houses.

It had come from a few hundred meters away.

High-velocity sniper round.

I ducked, covering my head, fear coursing through me like electricity.

Nothing, *nothing*, was scarier than being shot at.

"There's a blast from the past, eh, Jack? Pinned down by snipers. I've gone through great lengths to learn from those you've encountered before."

"What the hell do you want?" I managed, teeth chattering, my whole body a knotted cramp.

"Any time I feel like it, I can end you. Any time I feel like it, I can end Harry or Herb or Phin. Or just hurt them and make you listen. Do you understand me?"

I ground my molars.

"Answer me."

I had no choice. "Yes, I understand."

"Are you even happy to be bringing your child into the world?"

"Under the present circumstances—"

"No, period. Before all this started. Before the first murder."

"I'm...conflicted," I said.

"Why?"

"I don't know." It was an honest answer, and it nearly brought me to tears.

"Are you afraid of being a mother? Or afraid of losing who you think you are? What if I told you who you are, Jack? What if I showed you how to be the person you were always meant to be?"

"What do you want from me, Luther?"

"I want you to appreciate every moment of this, Jack. Most works of art are intended for the masses. For the widest possible audience. But imagine if Picasso had painted something only for the benefit of a single human being. What if Hemingway had written a book only to be read by one person? I've created something just for you, Jack."

I'd heard too many psychos spout off their insane reasons for doing the horrible things they'd done, though admittedly none had put this much effort into it. Luther must have been working on this project for years. It told me something about the scope of his deranged fantasies, and the depth of his depravity.

It also told me that I probably wouldn't get out of there alive.

"Why me?" I asked.

The noise of whatever was inside that brick warehouse in the distance was growing louder.

"Because you're worthy of it," Luther said. "I've followed your career. I know what you've witnessed, the killers you've chased. There's never been anyone like you. There's never been anyone like me. We're like two sides of the same coin."

I found my spine, managed to stand up straight, even though I could feel a dozen bull's-eyes all over my body. I stared in the direction the shot had come from.

"There's nothing special about you at all, Luther. You're scum, just like all the rest of the assholes I've gone after. Just another broken human being, getting your rocks off hurting others."

Another round went off, cracking over my head. My legs went to jelly, and my baby began kicking like crazy, but I stood firm.

"You're wrong, Jack," Luther said, his voice a whisper. "I stopped being a human being a long time ago."

Luther

He lies under a tarp on top of a building, watching her through the scope.

Jack looks so small from four hundred meters away, stumbling through the vast, empty parking lot like a lost soul crossing a desert.

Something undeniably heroic about her.

No question.

She's been tested before—Alex Kork nearly killed her several years ago. Charles Kork, Barry Fuller, that trio of snipers, The Chemist, a fat slob named Donaldson—but Jack has always prevailed. He figures she must contain a carbon core. A soul as hard as a diamond.

So what happens when a diamond finally breaks?

He knows.

It's spectacular.

Catastrophic change.

Nuclear fission.

And he's the man to break her. The only thing that can cut a diamond is another diamond.

He says into his mike, "This is the only help you're going to get from me, Jack. When you reach the door to the warehouse, there will be a keypad. What do you think the code is to get inside?"

"How should I...wait."

He hopes she's putting it together.

"Six-six-six."

"Exactly."

He watches her go, trailing her movement with just the barest movement on the bipod. Nothing rivals following someone through a high-end scope from a quarter mile away. The target's next breath just a finger-squeeze away from never happening.

Back when he was first building this place, he'd occasionally come across a dealer or a foot soldier. The occasional heroin whore who'd made the mistake of wandering out into his urban ghost town to find a quiet place to shoot up.

He'd grab them, explain the rules, and cut them loose.

Supply a bottle of water and a two-minute head start.

If you lasted until morning, you got to leave.

To live.

He'd snipe them with his bolt-action Bor.

7.62 x 51mm rounds.

They'd only play after dark, Luther tracking his prey with night-vision from the top of the water tower, his goal to keep them running all night. The most enjoyable games were those that never even required him to shoot.

Just make them run until they dropped from exhaustion, then go and finish them with his hands.

When he closes his eyes, he can still see the gray-green graininess of the runners, out of breath, hunkered down behind a Dumpster in the pitch black, puking their guts out from sheer exhaustion as he puts another round through the metal beside their heads to keep them moving.

The fear in their faces. The abject fear. Nothing like it in the world.

An acquired taste, sure, but once acquired—pure addiction.

He's so happy he bought this town.

Not the entire town. No need for that. It was abandoned. But he'd snatched up enough of the foreclosed homes for pennies on the dollar, all the factories and warehouses for prices so low it was almost more criminal than the acts he carried out here.

This neighborhood belonged to Luther. Or rather, he owned the rotting carcass of what was once a neighborhood.

It starts with one inciting event. The auto factory dies.

Then the steel mill follows.

People move away.

The retailers, unable to stay in business, go with them.

Finally the state cuts off services and utilities, and all that is left is the decaying, empty homes and buildings.

A perfect location.

He was so lucky to stumble across it. So lucky that his financial situation allowed him to tailor it to his particular needs.

After all this time, all this money, all this effort, it's finally happening.

Jack is almost to the first warehouse.

Luther leaves the Bor under the tarp and heads down to the control room to watch her on flat-screen, realizing as he descends the stairs that everything in his life—the good, the bad, the pleasure, and the pain—has all been a ramp-up to this moment.

To the next several hours.

It's not joy he feels. He's no longer capable of true happiness. But there's a feeling of peace watching this all unfold that remains unmatched in recent memory.

And though he's lived long enough to know it won't last, that this sense of satisfaction will fade and die like everything else in this fallen world, he's also lived long enough to know to enjoy it while it's here.

To be fully, unapologetically, in the moment.

He hopes to teach Jack this feeling.

Even if it takes years.

Jack

I punched in the code.

A green light blinked.

A deadbolt snicked open.

Standing outside the door, the noise on the other side was already loud, but when I finally pulled it open, it became otherworldly.

I paused in the threshold, coming fast to the conclusion that stepping inside couldn't possibly be a good idea, but Luther was barking in my ear to move. I no longer feared him shooting me—it was terrifying to be fired at, but Luther had put in too much time and effort to kill me before I saw everything he wanted me to see.

But I had no doubt he'd hurt and kill my friends.

I stepped inside and the door slammed shut after me, coaxed in by a vacuum.

I shivered.

Total darkness.

Freezing cold.

Screaming wind.

Pellets of ice driving into my face.

I was in the thick of an indoor blizzard.

I spun back around, trying to find the exit, desperate to get out, already disoriented.

Stumbling into a wall, I groped for the door, felt it, but there was no handle on this side.

A jolt of claustrophobic fear shot through me—the panic of being trapped.

The noise became louder, the wind stronger.

I wasn't alone. I heard moaning.

I took deep, slow breaths and willed myself to settle down. I couldn't lose my head, my nerve. Must not let that happen.

There was a strobe in the distance—a cutting blue blink of light every few seconds that looked like electricity in a cloud.

When it flashed, I could see a wall of swirling fog ahead of me.

What the hell? How much money had he spent building this—whatever *this* was? Over the years, I'd had more than my fair share of encounters with monsters, and they all had warped fantasies that prompted their actions. But Luther's fantasies were way off the charts. This guy had built his own psychopath Disney World.

I forged ahead into the storm, holding my left arm out to protect my face.

It reminded me of the worst Chicago winter storms—those handful of times when I'd been forced outside with the snow pouring down and the wind ripping through the trees, and nothing to see beyond five feet in front of your nose but the manic flakes.

I must've made it fifty or sixty steps into the warehouse—I lost count—before hands suddenly grabbed my shoulders.

I screamed and pulled back, but they didn't let go, the cold, wet fingers digging through my windbreaker.

In the burst of strobe light, I saw a woman in a gaudy evening gown, her hair twisted up and styled as if she'd been on her way to a costume ball. Tears and the frigid water had drawn lines of the heavy mascara and eyeliner down her gaunt, pale face.

"Help me!"

A chain ran down from a leather collar with a metal box attached to it.

"Where's the way out?" I shouted back over the roar of the wind.

"Get me out!"

"I'm trying! You have to tell me—"

"He's gonna kill us!"

"How many people are in here?"

"Four! There's a girly in the cage!"

I got closer, caught a glimpse of her chest. Hanging around her neck was an engraved plaque, the writing edged with frost.

CIRCLE 2: LUST
You have to accept the fact that part of the SIZZLE of sex comes from the danger of sex. You can be overpowered.

I recognized the Camille Paglia quote, as I'd read all of her books, but I didn't understand its significance in this case.

"What's your name?" I shouted at the chained woman.

"Patricia Reid!"

"How did you get here, Patricia?"

"What?"

"How did you get in this room?"

"I was on the bus!"

"What bus?"

"The bus!" she said, nodding frantically.

I remembered Andrew Z. Thomas's website, ALONE-AGAIN posting in the forum.

Luther can do anything. He once swallowed a bus.

"What bus?" I screamed, but my words were drowned out by a sound that surpassed even the roar of the wind.

A deep, awful creaking.

Metal grinding against metal, like the sound of an old, rusty gate being opened.

Or a new, frozen gate.

A way out?

Patricia turned toward the sound, her face barely visible in the fleeting streaks of blue light that resembled lightning through the fog.

Up to this moment, the screams had been difficult to hear against the backdrop of wind and whatever machines were producing it. But the scream that rose up twenty feet away hit me loud and clear.

I'd never heard anything like it.

Human. Female. Beyond terror.

And so much pain in it.

A sharp, rusty taste coated the back of my throat.

I had started to open my mouth to ask Patricia if she knew the way out when I saw something slowly emerge out of the icy fog.

My first thought was *Luther*, but this couldn't possibly be him.

This thing was huge, moving on all fours, lumbering like a bear...

Holy shit.

Not like a bear.

This thing *was* a bear.

The wide, waddling beast stalked toward us with strings of bloody drool escaping its jaws, which still chewed on something.

From fifteen feet away, it looked enormous.

No black or brown bear. This had to be a grizzly.

Patricia hadn't said there was a *girly* in the cage. She'd said *grizzly*.

Luther had actually gotten a grizzly bear.

Patricia bolted off into the fog, the coil of chain at my feet unwinding, and then I heard a cry and a thump as it arrested her forward momentum and slammed her to the floor, the chain taut.

The bear took notice of her, its giant head swiveling her direction, and then rushed forward three steps and pounced.

It clamped its jaws around Patricia's neck as her limbs flailed around her.

There was a terrible *CRUNCH*, and then Patricia was still.

The bear put a paw on her chest, tugging its head back, ripping her throat open. Then it stared back at me.

In the oncoming gust of wind, I could already smell the odor of its musk—wet fur and pungent urine and fresh blood.

I backpedaled into the mist, slowly at first, not wanting to incite a chase, but the bear accelerated to a lope, its great haunches pumping up and down, and I thought, *I can't believe I'm going to die like this. I'm from Chicago, for chrissakes.*

The bear stopped.

In that erratic blue light, I could see its black nose wrinkling, catching competing scents in the swirling dark. The fur all down its neck was matted and slicked with gobs of gore.

I kept retreating, one step at a time, my heart thundering in my chest.

The monster lowered its head and looked at me, staring for a long, eerie moment through those beady eyes—eyes that reminded me of a pig's. Around its neck was a thick, leather collar, with a metal box attached to the underside.

Then its head dropped, and I had a terrible premonition of what was about to happen.

I was right.

It charged with the deadly speed of a rolling barrel, surprising me that something so massive could move so fast.

I whipped around and ran as hard as I could, full bore into the freezing wind, one hand cupping my stomach as ice pellets drilled my face, my body. I couldn't see a goddamn thing, even when the strobe sliced through the cloud.

If I'd blinked at the wrong time, I would've missed seeing the ladder.

Just caught a glimpse of it ten feet away out of the corner of my eye.

I turned and sprinted toward it, crashing into the old metal hard enough to bruise my arms.

It rose straight up the brick into darkness, and I grabbed the rungs above my head, hoisted myself up onto the freezing, lowest rung, and began to climb.

The bear crashed into the ladder with enough force to set the whole thing shaking.

I glanced down, saw it rear up onto its hind legs, roar, and swipe one of its claws, just missing my right leg but tearing the ladder off the lower prongs that bolted it into the wall.

I tightened my grip as the ladder shook, but kept climbing, now twelve feet off the ground, which was becoming lost in the swirl of fog and wind below.

The bear was gone.

I clung to the rungs, my legs shaking with exhaustion and fear. The ladder led to a hatchway, secured with a rusty padlock. Not the exit.

I had no desire to go back down onto the floor, but I couldn't stay on this ladder. Already, the joints in my hands had begun to tighten, fingers going numb from the cold.

The noise of the wind machines was softer here, and the visibility better.

I looked around. When the strobes flashed, I thought I saw a door twenty-five or thirty yards away. I also saw two other people, chained to opposite walls. A woman and a man.

I didn't recognize the man and was again selfishly relieved it wasn't one of my friends.

Nothing else to do...

I descended.

Ten rungs put me back on the floor.

The grizzly roared, but I couldn't pinpoint its location or distance amid the gusts of wind. I heard another terrified cry for help—a cry that was silenced in midbreath. Patricia had said there were four people in the room. By my count, the bear had already gotten three.

If I was to save the fourth, I needed a weapon. Maybe there was one in the next room.

I must've pulled a hamstring running because I felt a twinge down the back of my left leg as I jogged toward the door, pushing through thick clouds of fog and a torrent of sudden wind that nearly knocked me on my ass.

Breathless, I stumbled into the door, grabbed the handle, and turned it down.

Nothing happened.

I waited for another moment of darkness to pass, and when the next burst of light came, I saw the keypad. It had been installed upside-down.

Punched in 666, waited for the green light, but it blinked red instead.

Had I keyed it in wrong?

I tried the number again, made sure I got it right, and got another red light.

Think, think, think.

Shit.

It's upside down. The number 6 upside down is 9.

I tried 999.

Red light.

What was I missing?

There'd been a plaque in that house that exploded. CIR-CLE 1: LIMBO 666.

There had also been a plaque in this room, around Patricia's neck. But it hadn't contained any numbers on it. Just the word SIZZLE in capital letters.

I heard the grizzly growl again.

Closer than before.

Followed by another agonized scream. The final victim.

Final, except for me.

No time to stand here and brown my pants. I needed to keep moving.

I trailed one hand across the brick and started walking along the wall.

With Luther in my ear, I'd been distracted on my approach to the warehouse and had no real concept of its dimensions.

It seemed to take years to reach the intersection with the next wall. I turned the corner, waited for another burst of light, and saw smooth, unadorned brick for the next fifteen yards—no sign of another plaque anywhere.

I picked up the pace, jogging now, the pain in my hamstring expanding and intensifying.

A new scream grabbed my attention, and I stared out into the raging wind and ice, saw a half-second glimpse of the illuminated grizzly feasting on someone thirty feet away, its jaws buried deep in their chest.

The next decent jolt of light glimmered off something shiny hanging on the wall up ahead.

I reached it but had to wait ten seconds for enough light to read by.

It wasn't a plaque. It was a sign that read HARD HAT AREA.

I turned to head back to the door and found the bear standing between me and the wall where I needed to be.

This time, I didn't wait for the charge.

This time, I just turned and ran like hell in the opposite direction, pain in my leg be damned, kid in my belly be damned, veering away from the wall, into the fog, passing through a heavy spray of super-cooled water droplets blowing hard into the side of my face.

A cluster of objects loomed straight ahead, and I threaded my way through ancient oil drums, risking a glance back over my shoulder to see the grizzly inside of twenty feet and closing fast.

I pushed over every drum I passed, and the boom of hollow barrels crashing to the concrete floor added the sound of thunder to the chaos all around me.

Cutting a hard left, I plunged into the howling mist, no walls, no door in sight, heard the bear careening through the oil drums behind me, and hoped I'd bought myself a few extra seconds.

I had no idea if I was even running toward the exit now, felt more like I was flying through an electrical storm.

My shoes suddenly lost traction on the concrete, but instead of falling, I managed to torque my feet to the side and slide. Glancing down at what I'd run through, I saw that I was skidding across a pond of red.

I fell onto one knee, feeling warmth soak into my pants, the warmth of someone's blood. Incredibly, I'd wound up back at the upside-down panel.

Behind me, a roar.

The grizzly within a few yards.

I stared at the keypad, tried 666 again.

Nothing.

999.

Nothing.

The strobe light flashed, throwing up the giant shadow of the bear across the door. It was so close I could sense it, though I dared not look.

SIZZLE.

That was the only capitalized word in the Paglia quote.

Why had it been capitalized?

And then it came to me. Luther had studied the killers I'd chased. He obviously knew about Mr. K, and letters that looked like numbers had been an integral part of that case.

SIZZLE.

If you looked at it upside-down, it would be the numbers 372215.

I typed the numbers in.

Green light.

Heard the deadbolt turn.

The bear bumped me from behind, its cold, wet nose pressing into my back.

I spun around, its face right at my chest.

It sniffed my belly.

No!

NOT MY BABY!

I cocked back my hand, and smacked it across the snout.

"BAD BEAR!"

The bear stepped backward, its ears flattening against its skull, and for a moment it looked like a giant, scolded puppy.

Then I grabbed the handle and scrambled through the door—

—slamming it behind me just as the bear pounded into it with a gigantic shudder.

Luther

He watches Jack on the monitor, tinted green from the night-vision camera.

That was a close one.

In his hand, Luther clutches the master remote control. His finger had been hovering above the button that would have detonated the explosive collar on the bear. Several times, he'd almost pressed it. Much as the bear had cost him, Jack was more valuable. The goal is to teach her something, not kill her.

Although there is a very real possibility, which he has to acknowledge, that it could ultimately come to that.

There were several close calls, and it has been quite exhilarating to watch. But as Luther had hoped, Jack prevailed.

Time to make it harder for her. He presses the microphone button, activating her headpiece.

"Nice job with Teddy, Jack. I commend you. Was I seeing things, or did you get maternal there for a moment? The mother wolf, protecting her pup?"

"I'm done playing games with you, Luther."

"No. Actually, you're just getting started. Do you see that water tower, a hundred yards ahead of you?"

"Yeah."

"I need you on top of it. There's a ladder at the base."

"No way."

Luther has anticipated this. He leaves the control room, walking toward the seventh circle where Phin and Harry wait.

"I suppose I can't force you. But maybe I can persuade you. Who would you like me to burn first, Harry or Phin?"

Jack's voice comes so low it's hard to hear. "Leave them alone, Luther."

"Then do what I say. Climb to the top of the water tower, or you can listen to me roast both of them alive."

Jack doesn't say anything for a moment.

Finally, she utters a defeated, "Fine. Just don't hurt them."

Luther smiles.

It would have been a shame to play that card this early. No doubt Jack would have been horrified listening to her friends fry.

How much worse it will be for her when she stands in their circle of hell and is forced to *watch* them fry.

Jack

It was cool outside, but a welcome relief from the frigid temperature of the bear cave.

I reached the outskirts of a metal fence topped with razor wire, which enclosed the base of the water tower.

"You seriously think I can climb over that, Luther? You do realize I'm eight and a half months pregnant."

"Walk around to the other side. I've cut a hole."

I circumnavigated the fence, moving over pieces of broken glass that crunched under my tennis shoes.

When I finally arrived at the opening, I stopped. He'd cut a segment out of the fencing three feet across and four feet high. I ducked through and walked the last few yards to the tower's base.

It was an older structure, the kind that looked like a rocket ship—big metal cylinder on stilts with a pointed cone roof. A walkway circled the perimeter of the tank. The four metal struts stood bolted and buried in a foundation of crumbling concrete. For some reason, I'd expected a spiral stairway that would access the tank at the top of the tower, but there was only a narrow ladder whose bottom rung stopped six feet above the ground. A rope ladder extended down from this lowest rung, bridging the gap. It swayed in the breeze.

I froze, my stomach coiling into knots.

"Luther, please."

"Start climbing."

"I can't."

"I'm getting bored with threatening your friends."

"I can't do this."

"Fair enough."

"Wait."

He snorted. "Make up your mind, or I'll start—"

"Just give me a second," I said.

Walking over to the rope ladder, I took hold of it, thinking of the oft-repeated story of Chinese women in the rice paddies, working hard up until they gave birth, then clutching their newborns to their breasts and going right back to work.

If they could do it, why couldn't I?

I stared up the ladder, felt butterflies swarming in my lower intestines, and then something like an electrical current shot all the way down the length of my legs and through to the tips of my toes.

The ladder must have soared between seventy-five and a hundred feet into the sky, which seemed to be no more than a half hour away from full-on dusk. The low deck of clouds streaming over the tank spit a steady drizzle of cool rain, and though I couldn't be sure, I felt certain the tower itself was swaying. Imagined I could hear the rusty metal creaking.

"Luther—"

"You have seven minutes to get to the top, or I execute someone you love. And the fun part is that you'll get to hear it all. Their last seconds. I have a recorder so you can hear it again and again and again."

I shut my eyes, trying to steady the pounding of my heart. I hated heights. Despised them. For my forty-eighth birthday, Phin had taken me downtown to a Brazilian steakhouse called Brazzaz. But before dinner, he'd cajoled me into riding up to the Willis Tower's Skydeck. On the west side of the tower, four glass balconies had been installed, which allowed sightseers to step out over the street and stand on glass with traffic moving like Hot Wheels beneath them on Wacker Drive, thirteen hundred feet below. I'd known it was sturdy, known that no insurance company in the world would issue a liability policy on such a tourist attraction if it hadn't been safer than sitting at home on your sofa, and yet—

—I'd declined to step out.

Some primal siren in the back of my brain had physically stopped me from walking out onto the glass.

Phin, of course, had taunted me mercilessly.

And now—

"What's the holdup?" Luther purred in my ear. "Is the fearless Jack Daniels a little bit afraid of heights?"

A little bit? Try a lot.

"Better get going."

I reached out and grabbed the swaying ladder, the rope damp.

Heaving my pregnant ass onto the lowest rung, I began to climb, the rope ladder stretching under the strain of my weight, the metal rungs above me creaking and groaning.

I took it slow, one rung at a time, the protrusion of my belly adding another element to the challenge.

By the time I reached the first metal rung, I had warmed up from the bear cave and was sweating freely.

The metal was cold and wet, the rungs barely more than a foot wide, and the moisture on my palms made it difficult to get a secure grip.

But I didn't think. I just climbed, adopting a side-stepping technique since my baby bump made climbing straight on impossible.

Five rungs up, the vibration of my weight caused the entire structure to shudder—a subtle, horrifying vibration I could feel in my bones.

I went on, refusing to look down, maintaining a laser-focus on the next rung, the next step, clearing my mind of all other thoughts and distractions.

Halfway up, I stopped. Not out of fear—I hadn't dared to look down though I could feel the gaping space all around me—but out of pure exhaustion.

"How we doing?" Luther asked.

"Just catching my breath."

"No rush, but you have three minutes. I must admit, I'm sort of hoping you don't make it."

Sweat ran down my face into my eyes, and I blinked against the sting.

I went on.

One foot up.

Next foot up.

One hand on the rusty metal of the next rung.

Next hand on the rusty metal of the next rung.

Lather.

Rinse.

Repeat.

It would've been monotonous if each step didn't require more energy than the last.

If I didn't seem to be getting heavier the higher I climbed.

If one mistake wouldn't result in my death.

"You have one minute remaining," Luther said.

I got my feet onto the next rung and reached up without looking.

My hand passed through air, and a jolt of stomach-churning fear shot through me. I clutched the ladder, my legs quivering with strain and panic.

The next rung above my head was missing—looked like it had simply rusted away and fallen off.

"Forty-five seconds."

I didn't even realize I was doing it until I found myself staring down the length of the ladder, eighty feet to the tower's concrete base.

The world fell away and rushed toward me all at once, and I was struck by the sickening sensation of falling.

I clung tighter to the rungs and shut my eyes as Luther laughed and said, "Thirty seconds, Jack. If I'd have known this was so scary for you, I would have chosen a taller tower."

Go, Jack. Right now. Go. Go. Go. You have to do this.

I reached up, my fingers grazing the next intact rung, got a white-knuckled grip and pulled myself up, barely managing to get my feet over the two-foot gap to the next step.

"Twenty seconds."

I climbed as fast as I could manage, no luxury to pause between rungs now.

"Ten seconds."

Three rungs above me, I could see the railing and the catwalk that encircled the base of the water tank.

"Five seconds."

I fought my way up the last few steps, and grabbed hold of the railing, trusting it would hold my weight—it had to— and hauled myself up onto the catwalk and rolled over onto my back, staring up into the darkening sky as specks of water dotted my face.

Luther spoke into my ear again, but I was gasping so loud I couldn't hear him.

After another twenty seconds of panting, I told him, "I missed what you said."

"I said you made it, Jack. Congratulations."

I rubbed my belly and then used the flimsy railing to haul myself up into an awkward sitting position, my legs spread. The catwalk spanned twenty-four inches, and from my vantage, a hundred feet above the ground, the view of Luther's concrete kingdom was impressive.

Row after row of decrepit factory homes.

A six-story housing project, long abandoned.

Factories and warehouses as far as I could see—big brick monstrosities with smokestacks and vacant parking lots that had once teemed with cars, now reduced to sprawling, concrete deserts.

It was a wasteland.

No sign of life or industry or movement as far as I could see, save for a low skyline a mile, maybe two away, accompanied by the distant hum of automobiles.

It might as well have been a thousand miles from where I sat, utterly helpless, utterly at Luther's mercy.

"Up, Jack."

I struggled onto my feet, my legs weak, extremities tingling.

A soft, mechanical buzzing above my head drew my attention.

I looked up into the eye of a camera.

Luther

He reaches out, touches her face on the screen, says, "Smile."

Jack

I didn't smile at the lens pointing down at me, hanging just above the spot where the catwalk intersected with the ladder.

Beneath the camera, I spotted another brass plaque, the only thing on this tower not encrusted with rust:

CIRCLE 8: FRAUD 911
"If I believed that my reply were made
To one who to the world would e'er return,
This flame without more flickering would stand still;
But inasmuch as never from this depth
Did any one return, if I hear true,
Without the fear of infamy I answer."
Inferno, Canto XXVII

A noise on the other side of the tank drew my attention from the plaque—sounded like a chain dragging across the catwalk's metal grate.

I couldn't tell from which direction it was coming, my vision blocked by the curve of the tank.

Now something vibrated the catwalk—footsteps approaching me.

"What is that, Luther? Are you up here?"

He didn't answer.

"Luther?"

The footsteps closed in, now just around the corner on my right. I squared up and backed slowly away, arms coming up instinctively, the fight-or-flight response kicking my adrenaline into overdrive.

A small, wiry woman with silvering hair walked into view.

She wore a tracksuit like mine and held the biggest folding knife I'd ever seen. No, actually I had seen this one before. McGlade had one—it was a Cold Steel Espada with a curved, nine-inch blade. He'd carried it around for days, obsessively flicking it open like some knife-wielding badass, until it had slipped out of his grasp and stuck blade-first into his 70-inch LED flat-screen.

Luther said, "She wants to live, Jack. Very badly. I told her if she killed the person who came up the ladder, I'd let her go. I will keep my promise, and I've convinced her of this. The only way out is to kill her first."

"I won't do this," I said, backing away.

"Then just stand there and let her hack you to bits."

The woman was still approaching, something predatory in her eyes, a detached gleam that hinted she was going to try something.

Holy shit.

It must have hit her at the same moment it hit me, because we both stopped in our tracks and our mouths fell open.

"Do I know you?" I asked.

"I'm wondering the same thing."

Her voiced sealed it for me. Pure Manhattan.

"Cynthia Mathis?" I asked. "Andrew Z. Thomas's literary agent?" I recognized her face from the photo on her blog.

"Yeah, who are you?"

"We spoke on the phone several days ago. I'm Jack Daniels."

Her eyes widened.

"Not quite as pretty in person," she said.

As if she were the one to talk. Her blog photo was at least twenty years out of date.

"I'm not exactly made up. And well..." I patted my belly. "A little bit pregnant at the moment."

"He's listening to us right now," Cynthia said.

I nodded, noticing that she also wore an earpiece.

Tear trails carved down through the makeup on her face like ancient riverbeds. If she'd been hysterical before, which I imagined she had, she seemed to have steeled herself for something. There was a hardness to her that went far beyond negotiating book deals. I wondered how long he'd left her chained to the top of this tower to prepare herself to kill. Hours? A day? She looked soaking wet and cold as hell.

Her eyes cut to the knife, then back to me.

"I'm just going to be straight with you, darling...may I call you Jack?"

"Sure."

She stood ten feet away, shifting her weight back and forth between the balls of her feet like she was readying herself to receive a tennis serve.

"He's going to kill me, Jack. Unless I kill you."

"How?"

She touched something around her neck which I had overlooked. A collar—a smaller version of the one I'd seen on the bear.

"I've been up here for a long time waiting, playing it through in my mind. He didn't tell me it was you coming, but you know what?"

"What, Cynthia?"

"It doesn't matter, darling."

"Why's that?"

She edged forward, the chain scraping on the grate behind her. "I'm a year from retirement. I have grandkids, Jack. A husband. We were going to the south of France for the summer. I'm not going to die here. It's you or it's me. And it won't be me."

"Listen to me, Cynthia."

"What?"

"We can find another way."

"What way?"

"I don't know, I just—"

"He's in my head right now," the woman said. "He's urging me to do it. He's saying he'll kill me if you're still here in sixty seconds."

"Give me the knife. We can't let him—"

"Jack, he's going to kill me in less than a minute."

She was psyching herself up for this—I could see it in her eyes.

"Cynthia..."

Luther in my ear: "Get ready, Jack. She's gonna make a run at it. I would've armed you, but I didn't think it'd even approach a fair fight, considering your training and her advanced age. This is one tough broad, though. A shark when she has to be. Watch yourself."

Mathis came a step closer, holding the knife in both hands like it was a sword. And the blade was damn near long enough to qualify as one.

"I'll help you get out of the chain," I said, but even as the words left my mouth, I knew Luther would kill her if I did. Her, or someone I loved.

"What do you want out of this, Luther?" I asked as the older woman moved in.

"I want to see you kill her."

"You know that's not going to happen."

"Then she'll kill you. She'll kill your child."

As if on cue, my baby began to fidget. I reached down, felt her pushing outward, a little bump—her foot—through my windbreaker

"I'm sorry, Jack," Cynthia said.

But she didn't sound sorry.

Cynthia dashed forward—three quick steps, with one hand on the railing, the other grasping the giant knife.

Wasn't exactly a shock, but I could tell Mathis had never held a blade before.

This was a good thing for me, because when it came to surviving a knife attack empty-handed, there was no foolproof system.

The best option was to run, if you could. Next would be to get something between you and the blade.

I couldn't do either, which left two choices. Immobilize the knife hand, or strike.

Working against me was my pregnancy and exhaustion, and worse, that I wasn't facing some puny switchblade. If Mathis got lucky, this folder could conceivably take a limb off.

She closed the five feet between us faster than I expected, stood sideways with her left shoulder facing me, and lunged, the big blade coming straight toward my stomach.

I staggered back, breathless, more than a little stunned at how close the tip came to my bulging belly.

"You better take this seriously," Luther said.

I'd barely recovered before Mathis came at me again, this time with a wild, downward slash. With the darkness quickly falling, I didn't trust my eyes to judge the distance, so I scrambled back as the tip slashed inches before my eyes.

Mathis seemed to be getting more comfortable in her role as attacker.

As she righted herself, an idea came to me—I might not even have to touch her.

I turned and ran as fast as my chubby legs could carry me, shoes threatening to slide on the wet metal grate.

Mathis pursued, her footsteps pounding the catwalk behind me, but my fleeing had taken her off guard, and I had a couple steps' head start on her.

I came around the other side of the water tank and spotted exactly what I'd hoped to find—the bolt attached to the chain, which hooked to the collar around Mathis's neck. I squatted down, fighting a bout of dizziness, eyes burning with sweat, as she stormed toward me, slashing like a swashbuckler.

I grabbed the chain and wrapped it around my forearm as she drew within five feet.

It was the only time in months I could remember being thankful for gaining all this weight.

I jerked the chain as hard as I could just as Mathis swung the blade.

Her head went back, shoes coming straight off the catwalk, and her shoulders slammed flush and hard against the metal grate, the breath bursting out of her lungs.

I hurried over and bent down for a hard, immobilizing palm-heel strike to the face, but I froze with my right arm cocked back.

The Espada lay beside Mathis on the catwalk, its blade blood-darkened.

Cynthia clutched her right side with both hands, groaning, like she was trying to hold something in. A steady stream of blood like a faucet not quite shut off trickled through the metal grate and fell in a shower of raindrops toward the concrete slab below.

Even in the low light I could see the blood was bright red. An artery.

I dropped to my knees. Her eyes were wide. Not with pain, but with surprise.

"I don't want to die."

I lowered my hands to her side and said, "Here, let me." When I applied the pressure, I could feel the blood pulsing between my fingers. Lots of it. She'd cut herself badly. I pushed harder and she cried out.

"She's injured, Luther."

"I know. Do you have any idea how much all of these wireless cameras cost me?"

"I don't give a shit about your cameras. She needs medical attention right now."

"How does it feel to kill her, Jack?"

"It was an accident. And she's not dead yet."

"But you're the one that did this."

"No, Luther. *You're* the one that did this. Help her. Please."

"See her knife? Toss it over the side of the tower."

I complied.

"Now step away from her," Luther ordered.

"She'll bleed to death."

"I promise you. She won't."

I hesitated, then took my hands off her pulsing wound, backing away.

There was a *CLICK*, then a *BANG!* like a gunshot.

Cynthia's head rolled off her shoulders and off the catwalk, smoke curling up from the remains of her collar.

"Explosives in the collar," Luther said. "Instant, and fatal. I told you she wouldn't bleed to death."

I felt like screaming, crying, and collapsing from exhaustion, all at the same time.

"Don't mourn her, Jack. She tried her best to kill you. Cynthia was always cutthroat in her career, always out for herself, but I never expected her to take it to heart like that."

"How is this crazy game of yours supposed to end, Luther?"

"It's a surprise."

"Maybe I'll surprise you, by jumping off this tower."

"No you won't, Jack. You're a fighter. I haven't broken you. Yet."

A disgusting waft that smelled like sewage swept over me.

"What is that?" I asked.

Already, I could see a viscous sludge creeping around the curve of the water tank across the catwalk, some of it dripping through the metal grate, most of it moving along at the speed of molten rock.

"I would get down off the tower if I were you, Jack."

"What is it?"

"What does it smell like?"

"Shit."

"Cynthia was at heart a flatterer. She exploited people with language. In the second bolgia of Dante's eighth circle, flatterers were steeped in human excrement, as Cynthia soon will be. I'd start descending if I were you."

I hurried back around to the ladder, dodging sewage that was streaming out of a pressure valve and expanding to cover the catwalk.

Using the railing, I carefully lowered myself down onto the ladder.

There was plenty of fear, but no hesitation this time. I descended as fast as I could manage and was halfway down when the first gob of excrement landed flush on the top of my head.

I only froze for a second, then continued to down-climb as sewage trickled down out of my hair, along the sides of my face, between my eyes.

It was raining now—a literal shitstorm—fat brown drops falling all around me, specking my arms and head, slickening the metal rungs. There was a temptation to look up, to see what was coming, but the prospect of getting any in my eyes—or worse, mouth—kept my head down for the duration of the descent, until I'd reached the tower's concrete base.

I finally touched solid ground, covered head-to-toe in human waste, and when I stepped off the lowest rung of the rope ladder, my legs gave out, and I collapsed onto the fractured concrete.

Every muscle in my body trembled uncontrollably, and I couldn't close my hands into fists—the tendons so stressed from gripping the rungs.

I lay on my side, moaning, and I could've stayed there for hours, but the sewage was dripping all over me.

I grabbed the rope ladder, used it to haul myself onto my feet. My knees quivering.

I gazed off toward the west as the sun sank over this corpse of a town, and felt my soul grow cold. I wasn't sure how much more of this I would be able to take, but I knew there was a lot more to come.

Luther had recreated Dante's Inferno, just for me.

And there were six circles of hell still left.

* * *

I stepped down off the tower's foundation and crawled back through the hole in the fence.

The rain had stopped, and in the puddles of standing water, I glimpsed unbroken reflections of the sky.

In the wake of the rain, water still poured out of a gutter on a building up ahead, and despite my complete exhaustion, I hobbled toward it as fast as I could until I was standing under the waterfall.

For several minutes, I let it pummel every square inch of my body until it had rinsed away the filth.

At last, I stumbled away, clean but soaking wet and already beginning to shiver.

In the last five minutes, the clouds had gone from pink, to purple, to blue, to a dark, steel gray that would be sheer black in a matter of minutes.

The prospect of being in Luther's playground after dark added an entirely different component to the terror.

"Can you still hear me? Does the earpiece still work?" His voice startled me.

"Yeah."

"See the factories in the distance?"

"Uh-huh."

"Start walking toward them."

The factories—what little I could see of them in the fading light—resembled a steampunk skyline. Soaring chimneys, vents, buildings behind buildings. A labyrinthine maze of vacated industry.

After five minutes, I emerged into a parking lot dotted with light poles, most of which had long since toppled or snapped in half, succumbing to years of rot.

The downed electrical wires lay serpentine and thickened with rust—long brown worms frozen mid slither.

An intense chill descended over me.

I felt a cold draft funneling through a tear in my windbreaker where Cynthia had sliced the fabric with the knife.

I was coming up on a three-story brick building—the first in a series of many which, from the top of the water tower, had appeared to interconnect.

"See the double doors?" Luther asked.

My heart rate quickened and it wasn't merely from the exertion.

"I see them."

"Head on through. Hope you remember the code from the water tower. Shame if you had to climb all the way back up there in the dark."

Donaldson

Earlier

He hurt.

He hurt like hell.

The pain meds they'd stashed away were supposed to last for two weeks. But it had only been two days and they had already gone through half of them.

They'd gotten in last night, cold and hungry, down to fumes in their gas tank. Once more they were forced to sleep in the car. Donaldson was constantly being woken by Lucy's snoring. It wasn't her fault—along with her nose, part of her septum was missing. Still, more than once that night he'd considered murdering her.

An especially pleasant thought, because not only would it slake the bloodlust that had been building up inside him for years, but it would also mean he wouldn't have to split the meds.

But he'd sat on the urge.

If everything went according to expectations, he'd get to kill someone today.

Kill someone in a much slower and more painful fashion than boring old strangulation.

Besides, in a twisted kind of way, that girl was growing on him.

Donaldson had never spent this much time with anyone in his entire life. Especially someone he understood on such a base level. He and Lucy had the same needs, same hopes, same fears.

It was truly a match made in hell.

When they woke up that morning, the duo spent the day exploring the deserted town. That fat bitch, Violet King, had sent them here, but hadn't been specific on where to go. So they had been driving around, cold, hungry, in pain, and growing increasingly frustrated.

By dusk, they hadn't found anything.

That's when they'd run out of gas.

Donaldson was revisiting his thoughts of strangling Lucy when they saw the explosion on the other side of town. It was followed sometime later by several gunshots.

They closed in on the action on foot.

"You're going too fast, D."

Lucy's limp had gotten worse, and if she moved any slower she'd be walking backwards.

"We're so close, Lucy. Don't give up now."

"I can't keep up."

"Then don't come," he snapped. "See if I care."

"D, please..."

Donaldson stopped. He'd never heard Lucy use the P word before.

He turned around, looked at her, saw the pain etched on her face—

—and he felt bad for her.

Donaldson couldn't remember sympathizing with anyone, ever. Countless people had begged him for mercy, and all that had done was turn him on.

But Lucy's "please" didn't arouse him. Instead, it made him want to help her. Comfort her.

How bizarre.

"Want to rest for a minute?" he asked.

She nodded.

They parked their sorry, lame, mutilated bodies on a decaying bus stop bench.

"Need more meds?" Donaldson asked.

"We're going through them too quickly."

"I know. But we can deal with tomorrow when tomorrow comes. *If* tomorrow comes. Let's worry about today, today."

They each dry-swallowed two Norco.

The rain had stopped and the sun was setting. It was almost pretty.

"What do you want to do, D? When this is over?"

"What do you mean?"

"I mean, what next? We're escaped fugitives, and it's not like we can blend into a crowd. We can't run forever, can't hide. They'll find us."

"Canada," Donaldson said.

"How are we supposed to make it on our own? Get jobs?"

"Why do you assume we'll be together?" Donaldson asked. It came out too harsh, not like he'd intended.

"You mean, when this is done, we split up?"

"We've been forced to work together, Lucy. Once we finish this, we can go our separate ways."

Donaldson waited, hoping she would object, wondering why he cared so much.

"If that's what you want, D."

It wasn't what he wanted. In fact, it was the last thing he wanted. He wondered why he'd said something so stupid.

"We'll, uh, talk about this later. Right now we have business to attend to. You up for it?"

Lucy nodded.

"Gonna be good to kill someone again, don't you think?"

She put on a pained smile. "Definitely."

They walked another block, their shadows growing longer and then disappearing along with the sun. The only flashlight they had was the novelty one, shaped like a frog, on the car keychain.

Donaldson was conflicted. He knew he needed to keep his mind in the game, on what needed to be done, but his head kept running through what he'd said to Lucy, over and over again. He needed to set it right. At the same time, a big part of him was worried she'd reject his offer. He had no idea why that scared him so much, but it did.

Donaldson cleared his throat, but the lump remained.

"Look, I was thinking. It probably is best if we work as a team. Stay together."

"You sure about that, D?"

"Yeah. We could hitchhike up to Canada, killing drivers along the way, taking their money and credit cards. When we get there, we get some fake IDs, saying we're citizens. They got socialized medicine. All the pain pills we want, courtesy of the government."

"I'd like that," Lucy said.

In the darkness, her hand found his.

Donaldson hurt.

He hurt like hell.

But right then, in that moment, for the first time in ages, he didn't mind the pain so much.

* * *

They pressed on for another ten minutes, their progress slow and interrupted by frequent rest breaks.

"D, look." Lucy was pointing toward a wide expanse of nothingness, dotted with the occasional tilting light pole—an abandoned parking lot.

"What?"

"You don't see her?"

He stopped and stared into the distance, and when he finally saw what Lucy was pointing at, he felt first a thrill, and then a pang of amazement. How the hell had his one-eyed partner spotted this from several hundred yards away in the semidarkness of early evening?

"It's her, isn't it?" Lucy said.

From this distance, neither the height nor the hair length and color would've confirmed it, but the woman's protruding belly certainly did.

A pregnant woman was limping across that parking lot toward a brick warehouse.

"Yep," Donaldson said, "that's Jack Daniels."

Phin

He heard a door opening, and then Luther Kite was standing in the dungeon room, staring at him and Harry.

"I'm a rich man," McGlade said.

"So am I," Luther replied. "You think your money means anything to me?"

"No. But it means a lot to me. I was hoping you'd let me go so I can spend my money on stuff. Like a vibrating stripper pole."

Luther's dark eyes settled on Phin's. "Does he always do that? Make jokes in times of crisis?"

"Yeah. All the time."

"Doesn't it annoy you?"

Phin stuck out his jaw. "Where's Jack?"

"She'll be by shortly, to watch you both suffer. I just want to do some last-minute tests to make sure everything is working properly. Those chairs you're strapped to are quite ingenious. They were designed to inflict pain of varying types. This control panel here," Luther walked up to a metal cart installed with a laptop, "can deliver heat, cold, pressure, electricity, perforation, and abrasion. In other words, you can be burned, frozen, shocked, cut, and scraped, in a variety of agonizing ways."

"Nice," McGlade said. "You get that at Psychos 'R' Us?"

Luther picked up two objects from the cart. He walked around Phin's back and placed one in his hand, and then did the same for Harry.

"This is how the game will work," Luther said. "We'll start with electroshock. You each hold a remote control with a button. If pressed, it will send electricity to the other chair."

Phin was suddenly seized by a white-hot jolt of pure pain, vibrating every nerve in his body.

It was over in an instant.

"Sorry, buddy," Harry said. "Just seeing if it worked."

Phin blew out a breath. "Goddamn it, McGlade."

"How bad was it?"

Phin blinked away the tears. "Bad."

Luther's mouth formed a thin smile. "Here's the game. Only one of the buttons will work at once. If you press your button, you'll shock the other person and stop the flow of electricity to your chair. Soon Jack will be watching you, from behind the Plexiglas there." Luther pointed to the far wall. "I want you to put on a good show for her. Show her who's stronger. Oh, and burning ash will be falling down on you the entire time."

"No contest," Harry said. "Phin's stronger. I cry watching reruns of *Family Ties*."

"Then Phin will take the suffering for both of you."

Phin steeled himself. That one-second electrical jolt was damn near the worst pain he'd ever experienced, and he and pain went back a long way.

But he'd spent over an hour trying to get McGlade to stop sobbing. Phin remembered the last time they'd been in this situation, with Alex cutting off McGlade's fingers.

Poor Harry had endured the worst of it that time.

Phin was prepared to take the worst of it now.

"Let's try it out, shall we?" Luther said, getting behind the control panel. "We'll start with you, Phin. And I must apologize in advance for pairing you with such a coward."

Phin took a deep, calming breath, and let it out slow.

"Harry McGlade is my friend," Phin said, his teeth clenched. "And he's also the bravest man I ever met."

"You mean that, buddy?" McGlade asked. His voice had gone soft.

"Yeah."

"You want to play this asshole's game?"

"Hell, no."

"Me neither. Ready on three?" McGlade asked.

Phin stared at Luther, and grinned. "Hell, yeah."

"One...two...fuck you, Luther...three!"

Phin began pressing the button rapidly, knowing McGlade was doing the same. That way, they both took intermittent, rapid shocks, neither of them bearing the brunt of it.

Still, the agony was blinding. Phin felt like his entire body was becoming a giant charley horse. But it was sporadic, not constant, only happening every other second.

He heard screaming, realized it was Harry.

When the screaming got louder, Phin realized he'd joined in.

"Stop it!" Luther yelled. "This isn't how the game works!"

McGlade began to shout, "THIS SUCKS! THIS SUCKS!" over and over, Phin figuring that he was going to bow out, forcing him to endure all the agony.

But, son of a bitch, Harry kept pressing his button.

And so did Phin.

Smoke rose from the chair he'd been strapped to, and his blood felt like it had begun to boil, but he wouldn't stop tapping that button.

He swore he'd die first.

McGlade had stopped his *THIS SUCKS* mantra and was now yelling out words between jolts and screams.

"PUT...A...LIGHT...BULB...IN...MY...MOUTH...SEE... IF...IT...GLOWS!"

Phin forced himself to smile, teeth clenched, eyes squeezed shut, the pain so bad he was heading toward a blackout, but he kept pressing that button over and over andoverandover until consciousness ceased.

Luther

First, Phin's chair shorts out, causing a small electrical fire. Then McGlade's follows suit.

Luther grabs the fire extinguisher under the cart and quickly puts out the flames. He needs these chairs to work. They're an integral part of the plan.

The duo has passed out, and Luther uses a portable oxygen cylinder filled with QNB gas to make sure they stay out for a while, strapping on the face mask and giving each a dose.

Then he frees them, pulling them onto the sandy floor and checking out his precious machines.

Phin's is fried, the circuit board melted.

Luther gives the unconscious man a hard kick in the ribs and then checks Harry's chair.

It still seems operational, thankfully.

Luther rubs his face, considering his next move. This was the Violence circle of hell, and the goal had been for Jack to watch her friends kill each other. Luther has put many people in these devices before, and they always made for a good, drawn-out show. Most people resisted at first, but they eventually broke and allowed their counterpart to suffer.

Apparently, he underestimated the bravery of these two men.

Especially McGlade.

Luther walks over, gives Harry a hard kick as well.

No matter. There will be time later to kill them both.

In fact, if things go well, he'll have the chance to watch Jack kill them both.

But first, Luther has to break her.

He goes to the control panel, putting the second device through the paces, testing to make sure it all works. Unfortunately, it has lost its ability to deliver electrical shocks.

That's okay.

It can still burn, freeze, stretch, cut, and abrade.

Luther knows he has to alter the course of Jack's journey. She was supposed to visit Violence next, but Luther supposes he can now save it for last.

After all, once he straps her to this chair, she won't be in any shape to do any more wandering around.

Jack

I reached the doors, typed in the code.

When the deadbolt retracted, I tugged them open.

Shit.

It was dark outside.

Inside...it was pitch black.

From what little light slipped in, I made out the faintest impression of a corridor.

Cracked and buckled linoleum flooring.

Walls streaked black with mildew.

Ceiling panels missing, exposing old ductwork.

And something just beyond the edge of visible light that I couldn't quite nail down.

"What are you waiting for, Jack?"

I stepped across the threshold but lingered in the doorway.

"There's no light, Luther."

"You aren't scared, are you?"

Through sheer force of will, I moved decisively over the threshold and got three steps in before I couldn't see anything anymore.

Total darkness.

Total silence.

"Luther?"

He didn't answer.

"Luther. I can't see a damn thing. Where am I supposed to go?"

I waited, both for him to reply and for my eyes to register some inkling of light, but neither happened.

Tightness was beginning to press down against my chest.

I rubbed my belly and said in my head, *It's okay. We're gonna be okay. He doesn't want to kill us. He doesn't want to kill us.*

Nothing to do but edge forward.

So slowly, painstakingly.

One step at a time.

My hands outstretched so I wouldn't walk into something.

Ten steps in, my left hand grazed a wall, and I kept it there, letting it trail along like a lifeline.

"Luther, what is this?" I asked. "What do you want?"

Received as a response only the echo of my voice.

Luther

He watches her through a hole in the wall, night-vision goggles presenting her in washes of gray and green.

Eyes sparkling like emeralds.

He can see her chest heaving in the darkness.

The fear in her face a profound and lovely thing.

One of the handful of times he did this before, a woman simply crumpled down into a fetal position and screamed until she lost consciousness.

But Jack won't do that.

Jack is afraid, sure, but she's in control of her fear.

He removes the goggles, puts his finger on the switch, and waits.

Jack

I stopped.

Breathe in, breathe out.

Breathe in, breathe out.

Gave my heart a chance to settle down.

In place of the terror, I conjured up the faces of Phin, Herb, and Harry. Imagined Phin sitting across from me at the end of my sofa, rubbing my swollen feet and telling me some story from his past with that mischievous glimmer in his eyes that I'd first fallen for while he hustled me at the pool hall. Saw Herb with donut crumbs in his walrus mustache, trying to convince me his newest diet was working. Harry—insane, stupid, offensive, wonderful Harry—trying to name my daughter after the newest trendy brand of vodka.

Let my affection for my boys carry me on.

Two steps later, I bumped into something and jumped back, stifling a shriek.

No, not something.

Some*one*.

The soft pliability of skin through fabric was unmistakable.

"Luther? Is that you?"

Still staggering back, I realized I'd let my hand lose contact with the wall.

Disorientation rushed in.

I wanted to grab the floor, so I didn't fall over, but I managed to stay in a crouching position.

"Who's there?"

No one answered.

I couldn't hear anything over the tribal drumbeat of my heart.

Tried to walk but collided into a wall.

Turned.

Started forward again.

Thinking I was heading back toward the double doors, but instead I stumbled into someone else, and as I screamed, it hit me.

Rot...decay.

Please no.

A rivet of blinding blue flashed in the corridor for a fraction of a second, and I felt my knees soften from abject terror.

Swaying men and women—perhaps a dozen of them—dangled from the ceiling in clear plastic body bags, their toes just inches off the floor.

"Is anyone alive?"

No response, and in the next burst of strobe light, I caught a glimpse through the plastic of the damage that had been inflicted upon them—gunshot and knife wounds. Blunt-force trauma to the head. Some of them leaked through rips in the plastic, the linoleum floor just ahead of me slicked with their blood.

I could feel the hyperventilation coming on, felt myself standing on precipice of a world-class, point-of-no-return freak-out.

No. No. No.

That's what he wants.

To see my fear.

To break me.

To hell with that and to hell with him.

I needed to keep going. For my friends. For my baby.

I had nothing to fear from the dead. The dead, I could handle.

I righted myself and forced my way through the hanging corpses which swung on their chains as I elbowed past, careful to avoid the puddles of blood, careful not to inhale the eye-watering odor of total putrefaction.

When I'd made my way through, I turned the corner, and the strobe shut off.

Darkness again.

I stumbled forward faster than before, hands outstretched, just needing to put distance between myself and those—

My knees bumped into something new.

It moved beneath me, crying out.

I stumbled back as the noise of metal crashing into metal hammered my eardrums like a peal of thunder.

A panel of soft, blue light glowed overhead.

I found myself in a room of solid concrete walls with the dimensions of a bathroom.

The panel of light shone at least ten feet above my head, and the walls rose another five beyond that before disappearing into darkness.

The door that had closed behind me was black and metal.

No handle, no keypad.

At my feet crouched an older woman in a gold ball gown covered in sequins that glittered in the pale light.

The first things I noticed were her fingers and toes—completely laden in bejeweled rings.

At least ten pearl necklaces encircled her neck, and her wrists and forearms, all the way up to her elbows, were practically encased with gold bracelets.

She cowered beneath me on a stone floor speckled with pennies.

The woman scrambled onto her feet, but she could only stand hunched over. A collar around her neck chained her to a black, cast-iron ball the size of a watermelon, with "100 LBS" printed on one side and "HUSBAND # 6" on the other.

I had to squat down to look her in the eye.

Older woman, but beautiful.

Face heavily made-up and tear-streaked.

"I'm Jack Daniels," I said. "What's your name?"

"Amena." Her voice was barely audible and raspy, as if she'd blown it out screaming.

"Did Luther put you in here, Amena?"

"I don't know his name."

"A man with long, black hair?"

"Yes."

Again, I surveyed the room, searching for something to break the chain, but found nothing on the smooth, concrete walls.

Not even a plaque, which worried me.

"Why is he doing this?" Amena asked.

"He's sick in the head, and this is how he gets off," I said, knowing he could hear.

I stared up at the walls again. This made no sense. There was no way out as far as I could tell.

Wait.

There.

I'd missed it in the dim illumination of the light panel, but there was an opening ten feet up. From where I stood, it looked like an air duct.

How the hell was I supposed to get up there?

"You have to get me out of this!" the woman screamed.

"I'm trying," I said. "Just give me a second to think."

Maybe I could stand on her shoulders, reach the duct that way. No, she'd have to stand straight and tall for me to even have a chance, assuming my pregnant ass didn't crush her.

And she was attached to a sphere of solid iron—she wasn't going anywhere.

I reached down and touched the cold weight that held her to the floor.

Gripping the chain, I gave it a tug.

Nothing moved, but my spine crackled like a bag of chips.

I tried to roll it, succeeded in budging it a whopping four inches.

"Is there a way out?" she asked.

"There's a vent ten feet up the wall. I'm thinking maybe there's a keypad inside of it that'll open this door."

"So get up there."

"I can't reach it."

"You stupid, bitch, help me!"

Something struck the top of my head and bounced off onto the floor.

It felt like a chunk of small hail, hard enough to smart.

What the hell?

I looked up just as another one pinged my forehead.

"Ow!" Amena cried.

Another one hit my hand, and as it fell to the floor and spun out, I realized what it was—

Pennies.

Copper pennies falling from above.

"What is it?" Amena said. "I don't have my glasses. I can't see."

"They're pennies," I said.

"What?"

"Pennies."

"Where are they coming from?"

"I don't know. Somewhere above us."

They were falling faster now—pounding the top of my head, some becoming stuck in my clothes, most bouncing off onto the stone floor, and filling the concrete cell not only with a raucous noise but with the stench of money.

The odor of rust and blood.

Already, the stone floor lay covered in coins and they were falling faster and faster, the air thick with them.

Amena yelled something, but I missed it over the tremendous noise getting louder by the second.

"What am I supposed to do, Luther?" I screamed, but if he answered I couldn't hear him.

Only the noise of the pennies raining down.

Intensifying.

"Pennies from heaven, Jack," Luther cooed in my ear.

Then the floodgates opened.

So many coins striking me, I could feel their accumulation on my back, my head, my shoulders. My shoes were quickly buried, now standing in four, five, six inches of copper, paralyzed, trying to comprehend what was happening, what I was supposed to do—

—and then I understood.

Oh, no.

I squatted down, the pain in my hamstring flaring, and shoveled the coins away from the cast-iron ball, which was already a third of the way buried.

I didn't know if she understood yet what was happening, what was going to happen, but I couldn't communicate it to her regardless through the hailstorm of copper.

Bending my knees, I heaved my weight into the ball, managed to lift it several inches, but by the time it came to rest, it was already becoming buried again.

I tried to heave it with every bit of strength I possessed.

Four vertebrae popped.

No way. Wasn't going to happen.

I locked eyes with Amena, saw the fear bleeding into hers. She knew.

"Help me!" I yelled at her.

The coin-depth was above my calves now, approaching Amena's waist. I dug furiously, clawing the pennies away from her as she strained to raise her head, but the chain prevented her from lifting it more than several inches above waist-level.

I wasn't stopping anything, the pennies falling impossibly harder, faster than I could bail them out around her.

In my ear I thought I heard Luther say, "Can you feel the change in the air, Jack?"

The metal rain continued to pound down on us.

My attempts to help Amena were futile.

She screamed, the side of her face inches above the pennies which were piled at least a meter high.

I had to keep moving my feet, staying on top of the rising pile to avoid getting buried.

I began digging under Amena's face, shoveling pennies aside, but there was simply nowhere for them to go as the level continued to rise. A block of coins slid down into the depression I'd made, filling it in, expanding and reaching her chin.

She couldn't lift her head another millimeter, face turning purple as she struggled against the chain, and then her screams went silent as the level of pennies raised above her mouth, then her nose, her eyes, forehead.

I clawed them away, my fingernails breaking, scratching into her cheek, and for a brief second, I exposed her mouth which had filled with coins and blood, eyes bulging beyond terror.

When they finally covered her head I let out a whimper. Then I began to focus on saving myself.

The pennies were accumulating too quickly. In the time it took me to lift one foot, the other was buried up to the ankle.

Soon, both ankles were buried.

I scooped up piles by the handful, throwing them over my shoulder, and once my feet could move, I scrambled up onto all fours.

It must have been as close a sensation as it gets to walking on water—the surface constantly changing and sinking, always threatening to drag me back under. I worked my way over to the wall and spread my stance, ever shifting as the coin-level rose, making me ascend, inch by inch, toward the air duct above.

I saw a hand rise up out of the pennies, reaching for the sky, for something, bejeweled fingers twitching.

I stepped into the middle of the room, got a decent purchase on the surface, and grabbed Amena's hand, squeezing for ten long seconds, the coins rising over my ankles, until her grasp went limp.

I didn't know this woman, but my eyes filled with tears in that awful blue light as the copper rain poured down on me.

* * *

In another three minutes, the pennies had lifted me high enough to climb into the air duct.

Just before squeezing myself through, I noticed something on the concrete above the opening to the vent.

A plaque:

CIRCLE 4: GREED

Here saw I people, more than elsewhere, many,
On one side and the other, with great howls,
Rolling weights forward by main force of chest.
They clashed together, and then at that point
Each one turned backward, rolling retrograde,
Crying, "Why keepest?" and, "Why squanderest thou?"

Inferno, Canto VII

I heaved myself into the air duct, wriggling my swollen belly along the metal, coins dropping out of my hair.

It was much darker in here, and the thunder of falling pennies behind me had begun to ease.

By the blue panel of light in that concrete room, I glimpsed the keypad up ahead.

I reached it, experienced a moment of terror when I remembered there had been no code on the plaque.

So I took a shot in the dark.

211—the police code for robbery.

Punched it in.

Green light.

The door opened and I heaved myself up into a wide air duct. I was still gasping for breath and fighting back wracking sobs that had come out of nowhere when Luther said, "You're uncharacteristically quiet, Jack...a penny for your thoughts?"

Luther

He misses her response entirely, his attention drawn to a panel of a flat-screen showing the pair of interlopers who have been wandering around his concrete barrens for the last twenty-four hours.

They're closing in on the warehouse, on all the action, on Jack.

Luther needs to handle this. Now.

But he can't leave Jack yet.

Not when one of his favorite circles of hell is coming up.

Jack

I calmed myself down, doing the Lamaze breathing I'd been taught in that one class I took with Phin. It was supposed to be a three-week class, but we'd never gone back, having endured too many questions about my age, including one young chick who asked if the Guinness World Record people had been notified.

It seemed so long ago.

Hell, it seemed like it had happened to someone else, in a different life.

I pushed away thoughts of the past, of Phin, and pressed onward.

Crawling while pregnant was like doing everything else while pregnant: slow and difficult. But I kept moving, shaking off the last few pennies stuck in my clothing.

When I reached the end, I pushed open a grating and edged forward.

Poked my head through.

Peered out.

A bare lightbulb dangled from the ceiling on a cord—the sole source of illumination.

This room was twice the size of the previous one, and I wondered how I was supposed to climb down until I fixed my sights on a series of iron bars which had been driven into the stone walls. Just within reach, they descended ten feet to the floor below.

On one wall I saw a black door with a keypad mounted to the wall beside it.

Standing vertically against the opposing wall—a casket-shaped object that appeared to be constructed of solid iron or steel.

I grabbed the closest iron bar and with considerable effort dragged myself the rest of the way out of the air duct. Then I eased my feet down onto one of the lower bars with an embarrassing grunt that made me thankful no one but a psychopath was privy to hear.

Four steps down and I was standing on a floor that resembled a metal grate.

My clothes were still soaked from the gutter-shower, my bones chilled, but this room felt warmer than the others.

Much warmer in fact.

Or maybe just a killer hot flash coming on.

I walked over and inspected the keypad and the door.

Then turned and crossed to the tomb.

Dark gray metal alloy, smooth, and with no defining characteristic beyond a new plaque, its casket-like shape, and the four-inch slot at head-level—

I startled.

—through which eyes watched me.

"Who's in there?" I asked, taking a step closer.

The eyes stared into mine, unblinking, and what struck me first was their kindness, followed by a second realization—there was no life in them.

The capillaries in the whites had long since broken up.

These eyes belonged to a dead man.

I backed away to let a little of the overhead light stream in. Through the slot, beneath the eyes, I saw a ruined face. Trails of dried blood running down the cheeks. The white and black of a clerical collar.

Luther had killed a priest.

Locked him in a tomb.

Why?

I noticed a plaque midway up the casket as another hot flash enveloped me. I'd suffered my fair share during pregnancy, but nothing as strong as this, strong enough to instantly pop beads of sweat on my forehead.

I read the plaque under the slot:

CIRCLE 6: HERESY
Can you take the heat?

No accompanying quote. No code.

The hot flash was getting worse, and it wasn't just in my face—it almost felt like drafts of heat were rising up beneath me.

I moved away from the tomb, fighting the kind of dizziness that precedes a heat stroke.

Steam actually lifting off my windbreaker.

I'd suffered through my fair share of hot flashes since becoming pregnant, but this was ridiculous.

The floor caught my attention.

More specifically, something under the grate.

Concentric circles were becoming visible—at first, just a dimly-glowing brown, but that turned amber, which quickly warmed into dirty orange. It reminded me of the burners on my stove.

And still, the heat continued to intensify, the brunt of it blasting the tomb like an oven—hell, it *was* an oven—fluids sizzling inside and the room filling with the smell of meat beginning to cook.

I rushed to the keypad.

Found it harder to gather my thoughts as the temperature spiked.

Okay, in the last room there was no code on the plaque, but a corresponding police code worked. So what's the corresponding police code for...intense heat?

Arson?

I wiped sweat out of my eyes and punched in 447.

Red light.

The temperature was rising faster now. I glanced over my shoulder, saw flames licking up at the priest's face inside the tomb. The smell in the room was beyond offensive—the odor of a human being turning to smoke and ash.

I tried something else.

Code for fire.

I'd been out of the game a while, and it took me a moment to recall, but I got it.

904.

Red light.

All right—scanner 11 codes.

Fire alarm...shit, what was it?

1170?

I gave it a shot.

A third red light blinked at me as I smelled the soles of my shoes beginning to scorch. The scent of burning rubber comingled with roasting BBQ.

Fire report.

1171.

Red light.

"Goddamn it!"

The heating element was turning a stronger orange, and I could feel the warmth in my wet socks, my swollen feet.

I was missing something.

Stumbling out into the middle of the floor, I studied the room once more as smoke poured out of the flaming tomb, filling my nose with a sweet, nauseating acridity.

What the hell was I missing?

I'd already made a close inspection of the tomb, but maybe I'd overlooked something when I'd first entered the room.

Through the smoke, I stared up at the air duct.

There.

I'd completely missed it.

The panel had closed back into place over the duct, and on its surface, I spotted a small circle with a silver perimeter and white interior that contained numbers and dashes.

A clock, perhaps?

No.

Of course—a thermometer.

But I was going to have to climb back up there to get a closer look.

I hurried over to the black iron bars that served as a ladder and reached for one at chest level.

The moment I grasped it, I screamed and withdrew my hands.

The metal was burning hot.

I glanced down at my shoes, where black smoke had begun to rise off the soles.

Any thought I might have had that Luther didn't want to kill me vanished in the fear of being cooked alive.

I tugged down the sleeves of my windbreaker, and used them as gloves to buffer the palms of my hands from the blistering heat.

Didn't hesitate, even though I didn't want to touch the hot metal again.

I began to climb, legs still screaming from muscle strain, but I didn't have the luxury to pace myself. Even with the windbreaker bearing the brunt of it, the heat was excruciating.

I reached the top rung in a matter of seconds, found it mercifully cooler than the ones close to floor-level. I held the bar with one hand, and leaned over to inspect the thermometer.

The circle was three inches in diameter, and the instrument had been attached to the panel with a magnet. I squinted, eyes burning from sweat and smoke.

It looked like a thermometer that belonged in a laboratory with a temperature range from –60°F to 500°F.

The needle nudged past 120°F as I watched it.

My sense of panic escalated with the temperature. So what did this mean? What did this have to do with giving me a code for the keypad? Would Luther actually let me die in here?

I leaned in closer as the rung I held approached a level of discomfort that would soon force me to let go.

I studied the brand name, the dashes, the numbers, the— There.

I had to squint to pull it into focus, wondering if it was my imagination, or if that was actually a thin, manmade dash next to the bold line denoting a temperature marking of 375°F.

Was this intentional?

The heat was becoming unbearable.

I swung back over to the ladder and descended back into a heat which crossed the threshold into lethal, feeling certain I couldn't stand much more than a minute at this temperature.

Flames shot out of the tomb.

The room had grown hazy with yellow smoke.

My shoes sizzled as I stepped down onto the metal grate, and one of my shoelaces which had come loose touched the floor and began to smolder.

I staggered over to the door.

As sweat poured down my face, I reached out for the keypad and punched in 3-7-5.

For a minute, nothing happened.

The heating element in the middle of the room now glowed bright orange, the priest in the tomb engulfed in flames, and the heat reached through my melting shoes, the soles of my feet growing hot, my nostrils burning intensely.

"Come on!"

Green light.

The deadbolt clicked.

The door swung back and a draft of the loveliest cold air I'd ever breathed swept into the room.

I pushed my way through and stumbled out of the sixth circle.

"Wow," Luther said. "That was hot."

For a moment, I thought I'd walked into another pitch-black room, but soon my eyes began to function.

"Nice work, Jack. Keep heading forward."

I smelled rain and heard everywhere the sound of dripping water.

I ventured a step forward. My shoes felt strange, the soles uneven, having melted and re-hardened.

A blister was rising on my right hand from grabbing the burning step.

The taste of the smoke still lingered in my nasal cavity, even after several deep breaths.

It happened all at once—the darkness divulged its contents.

Long conveyer belts.

Robotic arms that hadn't moved in years.

Giant machines. Drills. Presses. Planers.

Strong whiffs of old grease.

I stood at the far end of an abandoned factory, and through windows above, saw the orange glow of clouds tinting the night sky.

"Now what?" I asked.

There was no response.

I wondered if he was toying with me, or perhaps on the move.

I worked my way alongside a conveyor belt, passing what looked like the exoskeletons of cars. Wheelless, engineless shells rusted beyond recognition.

Halfway through the factory, I stopped, sat down on the forks of a broken-down forklift, and tried to catch my breath.

I cupped my belly in my hands, feeling a tide of tears coming on.

No time for that.

No time to break down and piece myself back together.

My friends needed me.

Even two minutes on my ass stiffened me up quite a bit and got the hamstring tight enough to strum. I limped on through the factory, finally arriving at a pair of double doors, uncertain if I was even heading in the right direction.

I pushed them open anyway.

Oh. Perfect.

Total darkness again.

I stumbled forward, my hands clutching the railing to a staircase, just as my right foot stepped out into nothing.

I followed it down, step by step, my hand gliding along the railing.

Reached the first landing.

Continued on to a second, still descending, losing all sense of direction.

I was on the verge of turning around, when my next step sank two feet into cold water.

Donaldson

They arrived breathless and groaning with pain at the double-doored entrance to the warehouse they'd seen Jack enter fifteen minutes prior.

"A keypad," Lucy said. "Bet these are locked."

Donaldson grasped the door with his claw like hands and pulled it open.

"Or not."

He stared down a well-lit corridor, Donaldson feeling a smile expanding across the wreckage of his face.

"Is that what I think it is?" Lucy asked.

"Oh yeah."

They stumbled inside, the doors closing after them, and pushed their way through the corpses that dangled from the ceiling.

"Someone's been busy," Donaldson said, pulling the Beretta out of his pocket as they continued down to where the corridor T-boned a shorter hallway.

To the right, the hall terminated at another black, metal door with a keypad mounted to the wall beside it. He limped down to it, tried the handle, but it was locked.

"This one's open!" Lucy shouted.

He turned, saw her standing at the other end of the hall, beside a door that opened into darkness.

Herb

A few minutes after Luther had led him to a cold room and attached a chain to the collar around his neck, Herb heard a woman's voice, a few meters away.

"Is he gone?" she asked.

"I don't know," Herb said. "I think I heard him leave."

He ached to pluck the thread out of his eyelids, or even rub them for some relief against the terrible sting, but his hands were still bound behind his back.

"Did he stab out your eyes, too?"

Herb shuddered. Whoever his companion was, apparently Luther hadn't given her the option of stitches.

"My name is Herb Benedict. I'm a Chicago cop. Who are you?"

"Christine. Christine Ogawa."

"Do you know where we are, Christine?"

"A man, he hijacked a bus, kidnapped all of us. We're in Michigan somewhere. Are more cops coming?"

"I don't know. How many people were on the bus?"

"Over forty. But..." Her voice trailed off.

"But what?"

"Not all of us made it."

Herb listened to the woman cry for a bit, unsure of what solace he could possibly give her.

"Why is he doing this?" she finally managed.

"He's insane."

"Before he...did...you know...to my eyes...he asked me questions about my weight. I think that's why he didn't kill me right away. He put me here instead."

"Are you overweight?"

"Yes. Are you?"

"I've never met a cheeseburger I didn't like."

"Cheeseburger. Oh, God. I know it sounds terrible, but I'm so hungry right now. I'm blind, and I'm probably going to die, but I keep thinking about food."

"Don't worry, Christine. I'll order us a pizza."

She let out a small laugh.

"You a pepperoni and sausage kind of girl?" he asked, trying to keep her mood up.

"I'm from California originally. I like pineapple and sprouts on my pie."

"That should be illegal."

She laughed again. "And tofu. Nice, roasted chunks of tofu."

"Sacrilege."

"There's a place in Arcadia called Zelo. They do a cornmeal-crust pizza with smoked mozzarella and fresh corn. It's so good...I...I..."

She went back to crying. Herb had no idea what to say to her. He felt like sobbing himself.

"We're going to die here, aren't we, Herb?"

Herb set his jaw. "I've been in some bad situations before. Some even worse than this. You can't give up hope."

There was a moment of silence. Herb tested the length of the chain around his neck by carefully walking forward until it went taut. The chain was thick, heavy, perhaps five feet in length, which was long enough for him to sit down. But he had no desire to do so. There was some sort of thick muck on the floor, and it was cold. Damn cold.

His mind began to go to bad places, think terrible things.

"What's your favorite thing to do, Christine?" Herb asked. "Favorite thing in the world?"

"I love to sing. I'm in the church choir."

"I'd be honored if you sang a hymn for me."

"Seriously? Now?"

"Absolutely. What's your favorite?"

"There are so many. But I really love the 'Battle Hymn of the Republic.'"

"Glory, glory, hallelujah, his truth is marching on?"

"That's the one."

"That's my favorite, too."

Christine burst into song. She had a powerful, beautiful alto, as fine as any he'd ever heard. He tried to pay attention, to lose himself in her voice, but then he began to think about Jack. Where was she? What was Luther doing to her?

Christine went into "Rock of Ages" without being prompted.

Herb backed up against the concrete wall, which was so cold it hurt his hands. He had to assume Jack was dealing with the same thing he was. The same, or worse. Ditto Phin and McGlade.

Luther had planned the cemetery abduction brilliantly. He obviously had other things planned as well. Herb cursed himself for being so easily misled. If they were in Michigan, like Christine said, there was no way the Chicago police would ever find them. No hope of rescue.

Christine was right.

They were going to die.

Donaldson

The warehouse was cold, dark, and endless.

He had a hunch Lucy couldn't see for shit, because she kept clutching onto his arm and stumbling into things.

There was a time he might have had a little fun with her. Ripped his arm free, gone and hid behind one of the massive machines. Watch her stumble blindly around into hard metal objects.

Okay, even now, that would probably be fun.

He chuckled at the idea of it.

"What, D?"

"Nothing?"

"You just laughed."

"Oh, I was just thinking of something."

"Fine, don't share."

He sensed the hurt in her voice, and suddenly the idea wasn't funny anymore.

They reached the end of the warehouse and arrived at a pair of doors.

Pushing his way through, Donaldson flicked on the froggy flashlight, swinging the weak beam across a stairwell that descended beyond the light's reach.

"Better hold on to me," Donaldson said.

Lucy clutched his waist.

For some reason, it felt even better than Norco.

Jack

My other foot slipped out from under me, and I was sliding down a steep, concrete embankment into a foot of freezing water, goopy mud sucking at my knees.

I scrambled up, gasping from the cold shock, spinning around and instinctively trying to climb through the darkness back up onto dry ground. But the concrete was slimy and I couldn't get any purchase on it.

I slid back down, the water to my calves and a putrid stench rolling off the top of it, almost like the gaseous emissions of a swamp. Decaying organic matter and human waste in competition for which smelled worst. I gagged, feeling my gorge rise, biting it back.

Either I was losing my mind, or something had changed in the last five seconds, because I saw a light that hadn't been there before. Some distance away—impossible to determine in the virtual darkness—the wavering of a flame.

I hesitated for a moment and then started toward it, wading through the frigid, stinking water, which now came all the way to my waist, each step a struggle as the mud suctioned my feet to the ground.

The noise of my splashing echoed through whatever room I'd entered—a bright, contained sound. Somewhere out in that blackness, away from the light, I thought I heard the sound of human groans.

The putrid water eased the pain of the blister on my right hand, so I trailed it underneath as I pushed on toward the light.

Drawing near, the water level dropped below my thighs, and then my knees, and then I climbed another concrete embankment and found myself standing on dry ground, legs coated in mud and worse.

A torch had been placed in a wall-mount, and beside it, in the flickering light, I studied another brass plaque.

CIRCLE 5: ANGER
While we were running through the dead canal,
Uprose in front of me one full of mire,
And said, "Who 'rt thou that comest ere the hour?"
And I to him: "Although I come, I stay not.
Inferno, Canto VIII

"Who's there?" a man called out to me from across the room, and I could hear the pain and the stress in his voice.

Instead of responding, I lifted the torch and carried it with me back down into the freezing swamp, the cold setting in again as the water rose back up above my waist.

Under the flame, the surface of the water was a glittering black. Like oil.

The voice called out again, "Who's there?"

"My name is Jack," I answered. "I'm coming to help you."

I still couldn't see a thing beyond the light's reach, so I used the direction of his voice to guide me.

Twenty feet on, shivering against the chill, my flame passed over a small island in the swamp. I stopped to stare. It couldn't have been more than fifty square feet, and the concrete blocks that formed it only rose an inch or two above the surface of the water.

Two people lay draped across each other on top of it, unmoving.

"Hello?" I called out to them. "Can you hear me?"

"They're dead," the man in the distance said.

"Are you sure?"

"Yeah."

"How?"

"He made them fight."

The firelight flickered off the wet steel of a blade still in the hands of one of the dead.

I held the torch closer, watched the light play off their faces.

Young men. Arms covered in gang tats.

Both wearing collars, which no doubt Luther had used to do his persuading.

I went on, and after another minute, the torch began to illuminate something straight ahead, the light glimmering off the chains that held a man crucified to a concrete wall.

"I see you!" I called out. "I'm almost there!"

My legs were cramping from the effort it required to move through the mud, but I persevered, waddling the last thirty feet, and then crawling up the concrete embankment to dry ground.

A tall, thin man stood before me, chained shirtless to the wall like something out of an Edgar Allan Poe story, completely covered in mud except for the whites of his eyes. He was standing, feet together, arms splayed out.

I knelt down on the floor and took a moment to steady my breathing.

Numbness streaking through my hands and feet.

I didn't know how much more of this I could take.

"Are you injured?" I asked.

"My shoulder...I think it's out of place. I don't know how long I've been down here. Do you have any water?"

I shook my head, realizing how thirsty I was as well. "What's your name?"

"Steve."

I looked him over, the thought occurring to me that none of the poor souls I'd encountered in these circles of hell had survived. Luther didn't want me to save them. He wanted me to watch them suffer and die. But Steve wasn't wearing a collar. I hoped this was a promising sign.

"I'm going to try and help you, Steve, but first I need to find a way out of this room. There should be a door and a keypad somewhere around."

I struggled up onto my feet.

His eyes had begun to shimmer with tears. "If you want to leave this room, you have to kill me."

"What are you talking about?"

"You have to kill me."

"I'm not going to do that, Steve."

"There's a bow saw hanging on a nail behind me."

"Steve—"

"You don't understand...if you don't do this, he's going to torture me to death. I've been on his machine. I can't go back."

"Listen to me—"

"Cut my throat, and then—" He gestured with his head. "—you can...you can open the door behind me."

I made out the faint outline of the rusty door he was chained across. The knob was near Steve's side.

Luther didn't want me to just kill Steve. His hands were chained on either side of the doorway. His ankles were chained together to the bottom of the door itself.

I couldn't open the door without hacking off Steve's arms or legs.

"No way," I said, taking a step backward.

"Please, Jack. I—"

"No!"

"—deserve this."

"No, you don't. No one deserves this."

He was crying now, breaking down. "I killed a man," he blubbered. "Three years ago. I've carried it around with me all this time, and now I just need you to know that I *want* this! I've thought about ending myself a thousand times, but I never had the guts."

"Well, I'm not going to do this. I can't, Steve."

"Do you understand what Luther will do to me?"

I'd killed before. But even with someone irredeemable like Alex Kork, it hadn't been easy. Not pulling the trigger. And not living with it after the fact. I couldn't imagine ever bringing myself to murder an unarmed man chained to a wall, no matter what he'd done in his past, no matter how desperately he was begging me to end him.

"Please, Jack!"

"Shut up for a second. Let me think."

I moved closer, studying the door. No hinges, so it pushed inward. I tried the knob, put some weight on it. The door moved an inch, the chain tightening around Steve's ankles.

"Can you hop backward?"

"I can't even feel my feet. They're so cold."

"I'm not doing this, Luther," I said.

My earpiece didn't reply. I looked around for a camera, saw one on the wall, ten feet up. I waved at it.

"You hear me, asshole? I'm not going to—"

Then the door behind Steve jerked inward, pulling him off his feet. Steve screamed, his weight falling onto his arms, his legs being pulled back. The door only opened a few inches, but an arm snaked through.

A man's bare arm, covered with scars.

It snagged the bow saw hanging on the door. Then two eyes peeked through the opening.

"Well, lookee here. It's Jack Daniels. Been a long time."

I didn't recognize the misshapen face. But the voice...

I could never forget that voice.

From the truck stop, years ago.

Donaldson.

"I've been dreaming about seeing you again, Jack. Of cutting off bits of your face and feeding it to you. And now, all that's between me and my dreams are a few limbs."

He brought up the bow saw, placing it through the crack in the door onto Steve's bare wrist.

I reached for the other end, my heart pounding in my ears, my baby kicking wildly, trying to pull the saw away, but the tug of war—the back and forth—that ensued was essentially doing what Donaldson wanted, cutting through skin and bone as Steve screamed, and then my legs went wiggly and the world began to spin and blackness crept into my vision.

No!

Not a seizure!

Not now!

I fell onto my butt...Steve's voice disappearing...the whole world disappearing...the dark swallowing me up.

Lucy

The man chained to the door died too fast. Without a tourniquet to stop the bleeding, he was unconscious within a minute and dead shortly thereafter.

Lucy had felt the old, familiar thrill at his cries, and a pang of loss when he finally stopped breathing.

It took her and Donaldson almost five minutes of sawing and pulling to get the door open, and there was no fun in it. By the time they were through, all Lucy wanted was a Norco and a nap.

But D had other ideas. He was standing over the unconscious pregnant woman, his scarred features twisted into a hideous grin.

"It's her, Lucy. It's Jack Daniels."

"We don't have time for this."

"Yeah, we do."

She touched Donaldson's arm. "We didn't come here for her. We only needed her to find that bastard who did this to us."

"So? This is like a bonus. An appetizer before the main course."

Donaldson descended with the saw, but Lucy pulled him back. He spun on her.

"What the hell? You getting squeamish on me?"

"Of course not. I'm tired, and in pain, and I want to save my energy for the man who tortured us and scarred us and turned us into...this." She spread out what was left of her hands.

"I want to kill Luther Kite as much as you do, Lucy. But we deserve to have a little fun. This one here, she's like a serial killer's dream victim. Doing her will be the highlight of my career."

For a moment, Lucy wanted to plead with him. To remind him of whom they were looking for, and why. But she saw the bloodlust in Donaldson's eyes, knew that there would be no talking him out of this.

"Fine," she said, releasing his arm. "Do what you want. I'm going to keep looking for him."

"What? You don't want to stay and help?"

"I want to save my energy. You should, too."

"You can watch, at least."

"She's not even awake, D."

He grinned again, raising the saw. "I know how to wake her up."

"Whatever. I'm leaving."

Lucy turned and hobbled back into the dark maze of hallways that had led them there. Over the past few hours, they'd stumbled across many dead, mutilated bodies. Their boy had been busy. It must have taken a long time to put all of this together.

She went left, then right, feeling along the concrete walls in total darkness. They'd found Jack by following her voice. With no sounds to guide her, Lucy had no idea where to go next.

Though she'd never admit it to Donaldson, Lucy was afraid. A minute after leaving him, she regretted it. While there might not be safety in numbers, she found comfort in D's company. But the more they saw of this place, the less Lucy felt they'd actually be able to do what they'd hoped. She felt overwhelmed. Outmatched.

They shouldn't be killing that cop. They should be working with her to find—

Then she heard it. Voices.

Donaldson.

And another man...

Oh, no.

Lucy fought the urge to run in the other direction. But she couldn't allow D to face that maniac alone. She followed the voices until she could make out the words.

"The gun in your pants. Take it out, slowly, and throw it into the water. Now."

There was a faint splashing sound.

"Now put down the saw and step away from Jack."

A clang of the bow saw being dropped on concrete.

Lucy crept closer.

"Where's the girl?"

"Go to hell."

A gunshot, followed by Donaldson crying out.

"I've got seven more bullets in this magazine. You think your leg hurts? I can do knees next. Or balls."

"You already cut off my balls, you son of a bitch."

Lucy turned the corner, until she was spying on them through the door, ten feet away. Her legs felt ready to buckle.

"Sorry. I forgot. We did have some fun times together, didn't we, Donaldson? I'm sure you aren't anxious to relive those times. Tell me where Lucy is, and I'll kill you fast. One in the head."

"I have no idea where she went. We split up when we escaped."

"Liar."

Another shot. Another scream. Lucy watched as Donaldson fell over and clutched his bleeding knee.

"Six bullets left. Then, when those are finished, I use the saw. Where is she?"

Donaldson spoke through clenched teeth. "She went to Canada. Heard it was beautiful this time of year."

Two more shots, in the same leg. Lucy flinched, and then peed herself.

It wasn't supposed to end like this.

Not like this.

She forced herself to take a step, to reveal her location. She couldn't bear to watch Donaldson suffer anymore.

Then she saw it. Though there was no way D could see her in the darkness, for the briefest moment he seemed to stare right at her. Deep into her eyes.

And he gave his head a slight shake.

Telling her not to come any closer.

Then, somehow, he struggled back up onto his feet.

"I saw the two of you on my cameras. I know she's here. I've put too much effort, too much money, into this production, and I can't have you two amateurs running around, mucking things up."

"Amateurs?" Donaldson barked out a pained laugh. "Let me tell you something, *Luther*. Me and Lucy forgot more about killing than you'll ever know. She told me all about you. You're not the real deal. You're a wannabe, going through the motions. You're the most pathetic asshole I've ever met."

Another shot, this one in the right arm.

Donaldson groaned, but he stayed on his feet.

Lucy's eye welled up with tears. She watched Luther approach her friend.

"You love her, don't you? I watched you both, walking hand in hand."

Lucy held her breath. She had no idea how D would answer, but all of the sudden it became very important to her.

"Yeah," D said. "I love her."

Lucy stifled a moan, her whole body shaking.

"Tell me, Donaldson. How does it feel?"

"You want to know how it feels?"

"Yes."

Donaldson laughed. It wasn't forced. It was genuine, a belly laugh, loud and long.

"I've spent my whole life on my own," Donaldson said. "Which is why it feels so good to have someone to watch my back. She's going to get you, you bastard. My Lucy is going to mess you up so bad—"

The shot sent a vibration through Donaldson.

When Luther stepped away, Lucy saw a dark swatch of blood expanding through the fabric around D's stomach, which he clutched in both hands.

Luther raised his right leg and kicked Donaldson in the chest, sending the man stumbling back into the water.

Donaldson's feet entangled, spun him around, and he plunged facedown into the murk, and slowly sank.

Lucy had to bite her wrist to keep from crying out.

Come up.

Please come up, D.

Please...

He didn't come up.

Lucy made her legs move, back into the dark halls.

The pain slammed into her, worse than anything physical.

Lucy's very soul hurt.

She needed to find a weapon.

She needed to kill that son of a bitch.

To make Donaldson's last words come true.

Donaldson.

The only man she'd ever loved.

Phin

When he opened his eyes, he was bound to a chair.

He hurt all over, but the worst was a pain in his right side. Felt like a broken rib.

He blinked, squinting in the dim room, and saw McGlade tied to another chair. It was made of steel and leather, built solid, high legs.

A bar stool. Not the horrible torture devices they'd been previously strapped to.

Phin didn't see any rope around Harry. He looked down at his own hands and saw his wrists were attached to the chair arms with plastic zip ties. His hands were bright pink and swollen. He tried to move his feet, realized that his ankles were similarly bound.

Phin pulled against the zip ties, testing their strength.

They were strong.

He tried to jerk against the chair, but it was strong, too.

Steel. Heavy, unyielding.

Then he twisted his wrists, seeing if there was any give.

None at all.

And if they weren't loosened soon, his hands would completely lose circulation and die. He already had that pins-and-needles sensation from the lack of blood flow.

"Harry! Wake up!"

McGlade grunted, and then his eyes fluttered open. "Tell me we got drunk and this is some lesbian hooker bondage thing."

"You used that joke already."

"Joke? Don't rain on my dreams, man. How you feeling?"

"Like fried shit. You?"

"I'm shocked. Heh heh. Get it?"

Phin looked around.

Unlike the dungeon atmosphere of the previous room, this one resembled an abandoned office. Desks, a few scattered chairs, and a lot of dust. Weak light filtered in through the open doorway, ten feet to his left.

"Your artificial hand is strong, right?" Phin asked. "Can you break your bonds?"

"It isn't working. That goddamn electric chair shorted out my battery. Also, I think my curlies burned off."

"Your curlies?"

"My pubes. My sack sweater. My dick fro. I can smell the burnt hair."

"Nice."

"On the plus side, I didn't wet my pants. Maybe I should have. It would have doused the briar patch flames."

Phin tried to rock forward on the bar chair. It scooted several inches across the tile floor, the chair's base wide enough so it didn't tip over.

"How about you?" Harry asked.

"Me?"

"Did you have a brush fire at the big dick corral?"

"Can we talk about something else?"

Phin jerked his body forward again, harder this time.

The bar stool moved forward almost a foot but then began to teeter. He shifted his weight back, balancing the chair out.

Tipping over would be bad. He wouldn't be able to get back up.

"I shouldn't have talked about peeing," Harry said. "Now I gotta pee."

"Think of something else."

"I can't. I close my eyes and I picture Buckingham Fountain. Except all the water is yellow."

Phin tried to ignore him. He scooted forward once more, gaining another half foot. His destination was the open door.

"My bladder is ready to burst. It feels like a basketball filled with urine."

Phin continued to slide across the floor, until one of his chair legs hit a snag. He looked down, saw a tile was missing, leaving an indent. He scooted backward, intending to go around.

"Where are you going?" Harry asked. "The bathroom?"

"I'm going through the door."

"Is there a bathroom through the door?"

"I don't know. But maybe there's something we can use."

"You know what I could use?"

A muzzle, Phin thought. But instead of speaking, he continued toward the doorway.

"A toilet," Harry said. "I could use a toilet."

"Can you do me a favor, Harry?"

"Does it involve me being quiet? Whenever someone asks me for a favor, that's usually the one. I talk when I'm nervous. And when I'm trying not to wet my pants."

Phin managed to get around the tile, but he was growing tired. Tired and worried. Sweat leaked down his face, stinging his eyes. He fought a growing sense of desperation. It was unlikely there would be anything beyond the door that could help them escape. Luther was too smart, too careful.

Phin shook his head like a dog, flicking off the sweat. He thought of Jack, of what horrors she was going through, and continued toward the doorway.

Mercifully, Harry had stopped talking and was imitating Phin's movements, following him in the chair. For five minutes, they scooted and grunted and strained and sweated, and then Phin finally reached the doorway.

The office let out into a short hall, where a single, bare lightbulb hung from the ceiling. The floor was concrete, and the corridor ended in a staircase, which descended into darkness.

"What's there?" McGlade asked from behind. "Tell me it's wire clippers and a urinal."

Phin didn't answer. He slid his chair into the hallway, a plan forming in his head.

"Shit," Harry said. "Are those stairs?"

"Yeah."

"How many?"

Phin counted. "At least fourteen. I can't see the bottom." He scooted closer to the top of the staircase.

"What the hell are you doing, Phin?"

"These bar stools are too solid to break. But maybe they would break if they fell from a certain height."

"So we're going to fling ourselves down a flight of stairs, with no protection at all for our heads and bodies, with the hope that the fall somehow breaks these chairs and not our much more fragile bones?"

"Yeah."

"Sounds good to me. You go first."

Phin took another scoot sideways, one of the legs sliding over the edge and suspending itself in midair. Going down side-first seemed smarter than headfirst, though *smarter* was perhaps an inappropriate term.

Though, even if he was terribly injured, or even killed, it was better than being tortured to death by Luther.

"If you die, it won't be in vain," Harry said. "Your corpse will break my fall."

Phin stared down, enveloped by vertigo. It wasn't that high, but tied to a bar stool, staring down at that unforgiving concrete, he was finding it difficult to summon up the needed courage.

"Just duck your head, close your eyes, and pretend it's a ride at Disneyland," Harry said.

"Sure. Donald Duck's Wacky Chair Roll."

"Chip and Dale's Crippling Plunge of Death."

"Mr. Toad's Instant Paralysis."

"It's a small flight of stairs after all," Harry sang. "Now hurry up so I can have my turn."

Phin took in as much air as he could and held it, tucked his chin to his chest, pictured Jack's face, and gave the chair one more jerk.

For a terrible moment he hung motionless, suspended on two chair legs, gravity undecided about the pivot point. Then, in agonizing slow motion, he pitched forward down the stairs.

He quickly lost his breath in an involuntary yelp of pure terror, and then his right shoulder came crashing down against the concrete. Before he could register the damage, his feet went up and over his head. There were thumps and cracking sounds, groans of metal, and one of his legs came free. But the stairs, and momentum, weren't finished with him, and he went into a second cartwheel.

A blow to the head made everything dizzier. Phin cried out once more, from pain and fear, helpless in the throes of gravity, and the stairs spat him onto the floor, where he skidded to a stop on his left side.

There was a great silence, the ringing in Phin's ears echoing into nothingness. He tried to wiggle his fingers, but didn't feel anything. Too numb.

Or maybe paralyzed.

"You alive?" Harry yelled from the top of the stairs.

"Yeah."

"Did it hurt?"

"Not one bit," Phin lied.

"It looked like it hurt. You break anything?"

"I don't know."

"Are you free?"

Phin tugged his arms. Both were still bound to the chair.

"No."

"You see a bathroom?"

"I haven't looked."

"Okay, here I come."

"Harry! Wait!"

But McGlade had jerked his chair over the edge of the stairs and began his tumbling descent, yelling as he fell. Energized by the fear of getting crushed, Phin kicked out both of his legs, realizing they were free, and pushed away from the bottom stair, frenzied to get out of Harry's way. McGlade's yells became high-pitched screams as he initiated his first cartwheel, his stool crumpling from the impact. Then he skidded down the last few steps headfirst, the screams continuing even after he hit the floor, mere inches away from Phin.

"AAAAAAAAH!"

"McGlade!"

"AAAAAAAAH!"

"McGlade!"

"AAAAAAAAH!"

"Harry! Shut up! It's over!"

The screaming stopped, and McGlade looked frantically around, finding Phin.

"I wet my pants," Harry said.

"Are you hurt?"

"I'm still pissing. I can't stop."

"Harry, are your hands free?"

Phin heard some shifting and a clang of metal on stone.

"I'm still going. Oh, the indignity, Phin. The indignity..." His voice trailed off.

"Goddamn it, McGlade! Are your hands free?"

"You might want to back away before the puddle reaches you."

Phin gave up. He shifted his body, wincing at all the new aches and pains, and managed to turn onto his knees. Forcing himself rigid, he snapped the seat off the chairback. His arms were still tied to the armrests, but he would be able to walk.

"Lemme help," McGlade said. He stood next to Phin, using his free hand to jam a broken metal chair part under Phin's wrist. With a quick twist, he broke the plastic zip tie.

"Thanks, McGlade. I could hug you."

"Don't. I'm not done peeing yet."

He handed Phin the metal rod, and then waddled off, bowlegged and squishing. Phin finished freeing himself and then sighted down the hallway. It ended in a metal door. He walked to it, wincing at the pain in his ribs, his shoulder, his right knee. The door was locked, but the frame was set in damp, crumbling concrete. Using the chair legs, it shouldn't take more than a few minutes to get out of there.

"Help me out, Harry."

"Almost finished. It's like a dam burst."

"You're still going? How big is your goddamn bladder?"

"Almost as big as my prostate. Do yourself a favor and don't live past forty-five."

Phin let out a short laugh. "Look on the bright side. At least you don't need to find a bathroom anymore."

Harry's face darkened. "Phin, let's get serious for a second. We're friends, right?"

"Yeah."

"We've faced a lot of bad stuff together."

"What is it, Harry?"

"I will give you twenty thousand dollars if you trade pants with me."

Phin smiled. "Get over here. Bring a chair leg. Let's kill that son of a bitch and go save Jack."

Jack

I startled myself awake, ready to fight Donaldson, or Luther, or anyone dumb enough to get too close.

But I quickly realized I was alone.

Alone with one corpse.

Donaldson was gone, and Steve lay in pieces, an expression of anguish frozen on his dead face.

The only one with a gun was Luther, so I quickly pieced together what had happened. Not liking his little horror show interrupted, Luther had taken Donaldson out of the game. Since Luther had left me alone, I could guess there was more for me to see and do.

How many circles in Dante's hell?

Nine.

I'd only seen six.

Enough for a lifetime.

I placed my palms on my stomach, pressing, trying to feel some movement in response.

There was none.

I rubbed harder, panic jolting through me, wondering if somehow, with all the stress, with the eclampsia, the baby had—

There. She pushed back.

Thank God.

I rubbed my finger along the bulge and felt her tiny little hand.

"It's okay," I told my little girl. "We're going to be okay. We're going to find your daddy and—"

"Good, you're awake. It's time to get moving."

I reflexively touched my earpiece.

"I'm done being the lead character in your sick little drama, Luther."

"But there's still so much to see. So much to learn. Get up and go through the door. You've got an old friend waiting for you."

"I'm also done listening to you and your bullshit."

I began to tug on the earpiece, felt my skin start to tear.

"Jack, don't you dare—"

It abruptly pulled free, stinging like hell, warm blood dripping down my neck. I chucked the earpiece into the water, gave the camera the finger, and got to my feet.

The doorway led to dark, concrete hallways that forked just ahead, and I stumbled along, tired, thirsty, hungry.

Angry.

Very, very angry.

Too many people had died so this maniac could...

Could what? Show me how powerful he was?

Frighten me?

Teach me the value of life?

I already knew the value of life. And seeing it wasted didn't make me value my own even more.

I may not have maternally bonded with my unborn child yet, but I had time for that.

I may have been treating the people in my life poorly, but I had some damn good excuses.

I may have been acting selfish, but I was entitled. I'd done a lot of good in this world. I'd taken a lot of bad people off the streets. And all I'd gotten in return were sleepless nights, guilt, and a lot of my friends and family hurt.

Truth told, I didn't like myself very much.

But that didn't mean I was lost.

Right?

I stamped my feet, which were cold and wet and losing circulation. Part of me wished I hadn't thrown away the earpiece. While I was sick of Luther being in my head, he no doubt would have told me which direction to go.

Then I heard it.

Voices.

Singing voices.

One of them familiar.

I followed the sound, trying to determine direction in the dark with all the echoes. The corridors were like a labyrinth, turning, splitting, dead-ending. It was slow going, but I made steady progress, the volume increasing until I turned down a hall with a door at the end.

I opened it, getting blessed with the third verse of "Michael Row Your Boat Ashore," stepping into cold muck, and seeing—

"Herb!"

"Jack!"

He was chained to the wall, one of those horrible explosive collars padlocked around his neck.

I hurried over for a quick embrace. He was even colder than I was, his hands tied behind him, but it was the warmest hug I'd ever received.

"Are you okay?" we both asked at the same time. It was followed by a mutual chuckle, which felt so good in the face of so much bad.

"Phin and Harry?" I asked.

I felt my friend's shoulders go limp. "I don't know. Haven't seen them. Haven't seen anything."

I held Herb at arm's length. "What do you...oh, Jesus. Herb..."

For the first time I noticed his eyes. Red.

Swollen.

Sewn shut.

"Got any Visine?" he asked.

I hugged him again, tighter this time. I needed to get him—both of us—out of there. I checked his back, saw his hands were bound with zip ties.

"My shoelaces," Herb said. "They're five fifty."

I nodded, kneeling into the freezing muck and spending a hard minute unlacing his shoe. The cord Herb used for laces was parachute line with a minimum breaking strength of five hundred and fifty pounds. When I had the cord free, I forced an end between his wrists, against the plastic, and then rapidly pulled the ends back and forth, essentially using it as a friction saw.

The zip tie broke within seconds.

Then we indulged in a real hug.

"Are you here to save us?"

I flinched, having forgotten someone else was in the room.

I turned and saw a stout woman, also wearing a collar. She had a tiny, almost beatific, smile on her round face. But her eyes...

Unlike Herb, Luther had blinded her permanently.

I braced against the horror and tried to sound positive as I said, "My name is Jack Daniels. I'm a prisoner here, like you. But I'll try my damnedest to get you both out of here. Was that your lovely singing voice I heard?"

"It was. Though your friend was doing pretty good on melody. I'm Christine Agawa. When I was younger, I used to dream that someday I'd be Cher. But now...Stevie Wonder, maybe?"

I already liked her.

"I always preferred Stevie to Cher," I said.

I let go of Herb and began to look around the room for a brass plaque. It was on the wall behind Christine, next to a keypad.

I trudged over to it.

CIRCLE 3: GLUTTONY
Where there's a will, there's a way.

I reread it again, but there were no numbers in the passage. I rubbed the back of my neck, trying to think.

"Herb, I need to punch in a code to open this door. There's a plaque here. It says, 'Circle 3: Gluttony, where there's a will, there's a way.' Any ideas?"

"A way?"

"Yeah."

Then Christine's collar began to buzz.

I whipped my head around, but only managed to say, "Oh no," before it exploded.

Luther

He's spent so much time planning this, considering all possibilities, all outcomes, that there have been very few surprises. He built in safeguards and backups in case anything went wrong.

The hardest thing to ensure was Jack's safety. Even with all she's gone through, Luther made sure he could help her at any given moment. The bear had an electronic collar, ready to blow if he took a swipe at her. The same with überagent Cynthia Mathis. The furnace and the pennies had cut-off switches, in case it got too dangerous.

When you spend years planning something, you tend to pay attention to the little details.

There were some unforeseen events. That idiot fangirl Lucy is still wandering around somewhere, but he'll take care of her like he took care of her oafish partner. Phin and Harry ruined one of Luther's submission chairs, but that was a last-minute addition anyway, since he hadn't even planned to abduct them.

Sometimes you had to roll with the punches.

Improvise.

He had expected, however, for Jack to pull off her earpiece at some point. Or for it to malfunction. As a redundancy,

Luther had the dozens of remote-control cameras in his playland all wired for sound. Speakers and microphones.

It will make one helluva movie when he edits all the footage together.

After blowing the fatty's collar, he hits the intercom button on his control panel.

"She died because you removed your earpiece," he says.

She would have died anyway, for another reason, but why not heap on the guilt?

Guilt will be Jack's biggest challenge in the months and years to come.

Or rather, not succumbing to it.

He watches the monitor, sees Jack staring up at him.

But she doesn't appear guilty.

Or frightened.

She seems pissed.

"Before this day ends, I'm going to kill you," Jack says.

Luther doesn't like this. He needs her humble. To understand what's happening, and why. Defiance cannot be tolerated.

But he knows how to make her grovel.

"You have thirty seconds to say goodbye to Herb," he tells her. "Then I'm blowing his collar."

Herb

The stitches in the eyes had been bad. Not just the pain, but the helplessness.

But Herb had managed, because there had also been hope.

Hope he'd get through this.

Hope he'd see another day.

See his wife again.

But hearing Luther's words over the sound system, the last of Herb's hope disintegrated.

He was going to die.

Such a terrifying, sobering, overwhelming feeling, knowing you were about to die.

That you'd soon take that final breath.

That everything you'd lived through and experienced had culminated in this final, terrible moment that would be your end.

But Herb summoned up some deep well of courage. So deep he didn't even know he had it in him.

Rather than fear his fate, Herb accepted it.

He accepted it with strength.

And dignity.

All there was left to do was say goodbye.

"Jack..."

"GODAMMIT, LUTHER! DON'T DO THIS!"

"Jack! Listen to me!"

"LUTHER!"

"JACK!"

He felt her grab his hand, hold on tight. "Herb, I'm so, so sorry..."

"Shhh. It's not your fault."

"Herb..."

He managed to smile. "These are my last words, not yours. Let me talk."

She hugged him. He gave her a brief hug back then pushed her away, fearful the explosion would hit her.

His lower lip quivered, but he managed to smile anyway.

"Jacqueline Daniels, I can still remember the day we met, in that morgue, all those years ago. I think I knew then what an amazing cop you were. It has truly been the greatest honor of my life to work with you. You've been the best friend I've ever had. I hope that someday you think as highly of yourself as I think of you, because in all the time I've walked this earth, I've never met someone as selfless, as brave, as loyal as you."

"Herb—"

"You're going to get through this, Jack. I know you will. And when you get out of here, tell my wife that my last thought was of her, and how her love for me made my last moments happy."

Jack let out a sob.

Then she said something Herb hadn't expected.

"No."

Herb made a face. "No? Are you kidding?'

"You can tell her yourself," Jack said. "Because, damn it all, you are not dying today."

Then Jack grabbed him, wrapped her arms around his shoulders, and pressed her neck up against his.

Luther

He frowns.

The heroic monologue Herb just orated had been moving and seems to have touched Jack deeply.

But she still refuses to submit.

Instead, she does something Luther hasn't anticipated. Something entirely unacceptable.

There is no way he can blow Herb's collar with Jack holding on to him like that. Though the shaped charge is pointing inward, the possibility of her getting hurt or killed is too great.

"Herb, I'm going to blow your collar in five seconds. If you care about Jack, you'll push her off you. Five...four...three..."

Luther watches as Herb tries to push Jack away.

She knees him in the balls, staggering the fat man sideways, but continues to hold onto him.

"Are you going to cling to him forever?" Luther asks into the microphone.

Jack doesn't answer.

Luther hisses out a deep breath. While it is gratifying to know that Jack has finally realized the value of her friends, this stunt brings the whole operation to a standstill. He supposes he could wait her out. Eventually she'll fall asleep. Or pass out from exhaustion or her eclampsia. Or he could bring in the last bit of QNB gas, even though he's been saving it for another use.

But these aren't best-case scenarios. Luther is anxious to get to the next phase and doesn't like the idea of waiting around for hours.

"I'll make you a deal, Jack," he says. "I'll give you the key to Herb's collar, but you have to follow my orders."

"No deal!" she yells.

Luther is surprised. "Then I'll leave you both in there for a few days."

"You don't want to do that. I could die. We both know you don't want that."

"So what is it you want? Surely you know I'm not going to let you go."

"I want the key to Herb's collar and your promise that you won't kill him."

Luther considers it. He can lie, of course, and kill him anyway. But if Jack is willing to make a deal, it shows compliance on her part.

Compliance is the first step to humility.

Besides, Herb might still be of some use.

"Done," Luther says. "It'll take me a few minutes to get there."

He goes to his key cabinet and finds one of the tiny padlock keys used for the collars, makes sure he's got a full magazine in his Glock, and then heads through the warehouse, past the cells containing the corpses of those who didn't work out.

He'll never tire of this place.

The smell of rust and mildew.

Of abandonment.

Perhaps one day, he and Jack will hunt in these warehouses together.

Five minutes at a brisk pace brings him to the gluttony door.

He unlocks it, his pistol at the ready.

Jack is still clinging to Herb. Luther considers trying to physically separate them. But that would mean getting in close, and both Jack and Herb are capable fighters.

He could just shoot Herb in the head, be done with it, but he needs Jack compliant for the next part of her journey, and right now, the threat of killing him is a more powerful motivator than if the fat man is dead.

But then, he still has Harry and Phin. They can be motivators, too.

Luther walks into the room, gets within three meters of the pair.

"Here's the key," he says, holding it up. "I'm going to toss it to you. Don't drop it in the muck."

He throws it, watches its arc, watches Jack snatch it in midair.

It takes a few seconds of fumbling for her to unlock Herb's collar.

"Okay, now step away from him," Luther orders.

Jack shakes her head. "You'll kill him."

"I said I wouldn't, if you agreed to follow orders. Now step away or I will kill him."

Jack hesitates, then steps away.

Luther aims at the fat man and fires.

Jack

"**N**o!" Herb pitched forward, falling into the mud. I rushed to him and kneeled down in the freezing slop.

"Goddamn it, Luther!"

"He's still breathing," Luther said. "I didn't kill him. But I will if you don't do as I say. Now get up and come with me."

"He needs a doctor!"

"He'll need a coroner if you don't listen. Start walking, Jack."

"I love you, Herb."

"I know," he groaned. "Right back at you."

I struggled onto my feet, which were going numb either from the cold, my eclampsia, or both. Luther kept his gun on Herb.

"Walk ahead of me. Don't stop."

I stumbled through the freezing mud, glancing every few seconds over my shoulder at Herb, keeled over on his side.

"Through the door."

I stepped over the threshold and had turned for one last glimpse of my friend when Luther slammed the door behind us.

I stood in a small, sterile room.

Whitewashed, concrete walls.

A tiled floor with a large metal drain.

I would've thought that of all the horrors I'd been exposed to in the preceding hours, nothing could've stopped me in my tracks and put the cold finger down my spine, but I was wrong.

In the center of the room stood a blue-padded table with armrests and—

Leg holders.

A birthing table.

"Get on," he ordered.

I didn't move. I couldn't.

"Climb onto the table and buckle yourself in. I'll do your last wrist."

I hadn't noticed the wrist and knee straps.

No.

I couldn't do this.

Then I thought of Herb, bleeding in the mud.

I walked across the room and did what I'd done so many times during the course of my pregnancy—heaved my fat ass up onto the padded seat and worked my legs into the stirrups. It was the second step that I had to force myself through—actually locking down the wrist and ankle bracelets.

"Damn, Jack," Luther said, cinching my right wrist tight. "I was sure I'd have to gas you to get you in this chair."

"I love my friends, Luther. You wouldn't know what that means—"

"Don't fool yourself into believing you know anything about me," he said, pulling on a rubber apron.

He brought out a rolling IV stand also mounted with a tray of medical implements, a handful of syringes, and several glass vials.

Sidling up to the table, he smiled down at me—looking so different without that sweep of long hair I'd come to expect and associate him with.

He laid the back of his hand against my forehead, and I tried to turn away, but it was no use.

"The great Jack Daniels. Finally in the flesh. You're quite beautiful."

"You're disgusting."

"Do you really want to make me angry? Now? When you're so vulnerable?"

"Let my friends go. Then I'll tell you what a sweetie you are."

He touched my cheek again, and I forced myself not to flinch. For the moment, anger was still overriding my fear. But I had no idea how long that would last. I'd never felt more vulnerable, and I knew it would only get worse.

"How are you feeling?" he asked.

"Terrible."

"You're what? Thirty-eight weeks along?"

"Yeah, why?"

"I think it's time we got this baby out of you. What do you say?"

"Get the fuck away from me."

"Now, now."

He lifted a syringe off the tray, jammed the needle into a vial.

"What is that?" I asked. I could feel my heart beginning to gallop.

"Pitocin."

I shut my eyes. This was a nightmare. Couldn't really be happening.

"It's a synthetic form of a naturally occurring hormone in your body—oxytocin. It's used to induce—"

"I know what it's used for."

"Your contractions should begin soon. Are you going to be able to push this baby out on your own in the next few hours?"

My eyes welled up, spilled over.

"Luther, for God's sake. Not like this."

"You're better than begging, Jack. Don't lower yourself to that kind of behavior."

He filled the syringe and set it aside.

Wrapped a blood-pressure cuff around my arm, inflated it, studied the gauge.

He shook his head. "Worse than I thought."

"What is it?" I asked.

"One seventy-five over one ten. No wonder you had a seizure." He undid the Velcro. "Now, I need you to hold still please."

Before I even realized what had happened, I felt the needle enter a vein near my wrist.

"I'm starting an IV. Don't struggle, Jack. Do you understand how completely your life is in my hands at this moment?"

A fear beyond the well-being of my friends, beyond my own safety, bore down upon me like the apocalypse. Through my own selfishness these last nine months, I'd missed it entirely.

There was a person growing inside of me.

A real person.

Precious. Helpless. Utterly innocent.

One who would someday walk and talk. Have likes and dislikes. Dreams and ambitions. A life of her own.

And her first seconds in this world might be in the hands of this maniac.

"Listen to me, Luther—"

"Don't talk, Jack."

"Are you going to hurt my baby?"

"No."

"You're lying."

"You'll have to trust me, Jack. You ready?"

"For what?"

"Labor."

He inserted the needle into the injection port.

"I'm giving you a big dose, Jack. I need you to be ready, because this is going to come fast and furious."

As he injected, I stared up into his black, dispassionate eyes.

"You're dehydrated," he said and pulled out a water bottle.

Until I saw it, I hadn't realized how thirsty I was. He held the nozzle to my lips and I sucked the water down until he took it away.

Three minutes later, it started.

The first contraction felt like a menstrual cramp right above my pubic bone, the pain all-encompassing, knifelike, hipbone to hipbone.

And from there, it got worse—a slow detonation in progress between my legs, and already I wanted to die.

I knew that induction had been a very real possibility considering my preeclampsia, but the fear of induction had been mitigated by the fact that my birth plan called for copious amounts of drugs. Through the course of my Internet research into what I was in for, I'd stumbled across numerous blogs written by women praising the virtues of natural childbirth. Of staying connected to your body through every contraction, every ounce of pain.

Those women were out of their minds.

My approach had been solidified months ago: stick a needle in my back and wake me up when the pain was over.

But that wasn't going to happen now.

No drugs, no epidural.

No doctor.

And to make matters worse, everything I'd read about induction indicated that Pitocin only increased the pain and intensity of contractions, as if they needed any help.

When the next contraction ended, I stopped screaming long enough to say, "Leave me alone."

He was standing beside me, holding a cold washcloth to my forehead.

"You're doing great, Jack. But you shouldn't push yet. If you do, this will take a lot longer."

"Get the hell away from me."

"Then you'll die, Jack. You and your little girl will die in this room."

"I need water."

He fed me another few sips.

"Oh, God. Here comes another one."

He reached out and offered his hand.

"Why are you being nice to me?" I asked.

"I have my reasons."

I refused to take his hand, instead making a fist.

Screamed as I stared into the lightbulb swaying gently over my head.

* * *

Thirty minutes could've passed.

Five hours.

A day.

Time had lost all meaning.

Between contractions, I raised my head off the padded chair and saw Luther standing between my legs with a knife, cutting away my pants.

"Am I close?" I gasped. I didn't want him anywhere near me, but I was faced with the horrible realization that I needed him.

I felt his fingers inside of me.

"Your water broke," he said, holding up his hands, his latex gloves glistening with amniotic fluid.

"Am I close?" I asked again.

He squatted down, this bastard staring between my legs, and I didn't even care.

Just wanted this baby out of my body.

It was such a burning need, it shut out everything else.

"You're close," he said, "so when the next one comes?"

"Yes?"

"Push with everything you've got."

* * *

It came.

I screamed.

I pushed and I pushed and I pushed and I pushed.

Nothing happened.

* * *

"You gotta give me another hard push."

I squeezed my eyes shut.

Imagined it was Phin in here with me.

Phin holding my hand, instead of me clenching my fist.

I pushed with all I had.

"One more, Jack! I can see the head!"

* * *

IpushedandIpushedandIpushedandIpushedandIpushed-
andIpushedandIpushedandIpushedandIpushedandIpushed-
andIpushedandIpushedandIpushedandIpushedand—

* * *

"Come on, Jack, don't you quit on me. You're almost there!"

Almost there.

Almost there.

How many times had he said that?

Was he doing something to me? Something that kept the baby from coming out?

* * *

I gathered up every last molecule of air I could force into my lungs and pushed. Pushed like my life depended upon it, because it did. I couldn't take another contraction. I had reached the end of my endurance. I would lie there and die after this.

And then it came—the ring of fire.

So perfectly named.

Ten seconds of agonizing, world-ending pain, Luther shouting, "She's crowning! She's crowning!" and then—

Release.

The sound of a baby crying.

I raised my head, and I stared down at Luther, holding in his arms a purple, squirming thing covered in white paste.

It looked hideous—

—and absolutely beautiful.

My baby.

Mine.

"Give her to me," I gasped.

He released my wrist restraints, said, "Open your jacket."

My fingers trembled as I found the zipper and tugged it down. I sat up and pulled my arms out of the windbreaker.

"Cut my bra off," I said. He came around behind me, and I felt the knife slice through the fabric. He pulled the sports bra away and laid my child on my chest.

The pain had vanished.

I was flooded with a rush of what could have been pure heroin it felt so good.

Joy bursting.

Eyes flooding.

"I'll give you both a minute," Luther said.

I didn't watch him leave, because I couldn't take my eyes off this perfect, precious angel in my arms. She stared up at me, red-faced, crying, mad, helpless, completely out of sorts.

"Hi, little thing," I said in a tone that sounded too high-pitched and saccharine to be mine.

She stopped crying and opened her eyes.

Phin's bright blue eyes.

Unbelievable.

My voice had calmed her. She recognized it.

I brought her to my breast, and it took her a moment, but she finally glommed onto my nipple.

"Are you getting anything?" I asked, cradling her tiny head.

She began to suck.

"Oh my, you're very good at that, aren't you? Yes you are."

I reached over and grabbed the windbreaker and covered her with it.

She stared up at me while she nursed.

The endorphin blast intensified.

Like nothing I had ever experienced.

Euphoria.

She nursed, and I stared and stroked her face with my finger.

"I'm your mother," I said. "But I bet you already know that, don't you?"

It occurred to me as I held her that even if we somehow escaped this, if I returned to Chicago with her and Phin, nothing would ever be the same again. And it wasn't the terror of the last day that was changing everything. It was her. In five minutes, this little thing had come into my life and stared into my eyes and turned me into a different woman. What had I feared? The loss of identity? My time? How stupid and selfish, because holding my child, watching her suckle, every doubt and fear I had about her vanished.

I fell, instantly, irreversibly, in love.

Phin

McGlade was chipping away at the concrete wall using the metal chair leg, giving it all he had, but Phin really wished he would step away for a minute.

Harry's wet pants were making Phin's eyes water.

"I got it from here, Harry."

"You sure? We're almost through."

"I'll finish. You go rest for a minute." Phin casually pointed to the other side of the hall. "Have a seat on the stairs back there. You've earned it."

"Thanks, buddy."

McGlade began to walk away, but then stopped and turned. "This isn't because I smell like piss, is it?"

Phin quickly shook his head. "No. Of course not. I can't smell anything."

"You sure? Even my socks are soaked."

"You're fine," Phin lied, turning away quickly so he didn't taste the air.

Harry walked off, and Phin noted with each step McGlade made a squishing sound. Finally able to breathe, Phin attacked the door with renewed fervor. Thirty seconds later he'd broken away the masonry around the deadbolt. One swift kick, and the door groaned open.

"You can wash leather shoes, right?" McGlade said. "These are Bruno Maglis."

"Bruno Maglis? I thought they were yours."

"Funny. They cost five hundred bucks. But if they smell like piss it will greatly reduce their sex appeal."

"Let's try to stop talking about piss for five minutes, okay?"

"Sorry," Harry said. "Didn't mean to piss you off."

Phin took the lead, heading through the doorway and into an unlit corridor. His head was still smarting from the fall down the stairs, and his right knee was beginning to swell up. He kept one hand on the wall, the other in front of him, moving as quickly as he dared. The walls were cold, concrete. Once again, Phin wondered where they were. Some kind of abandoned factory or warehouse? He stopped for a moment, letting his ears tune in to the environment. No traffic noises. No planes flying overhead. No people sounds at all.

Well, no sounds except for McGlade's squishy footsteps.

Phin sniffed the air, crinkling his nose. He smelled sewage.

"That wasn't me," Harry said. "I only went number one."

Phin guessed they were underground, either in or near the sewer. But his guess proved wrong when they came to another door, which opened up into a room filled with brownish, foul-smelling water. It stretched out for maybe twenty meters, a faint orange glow at the other side.

"Luther needs to clean his pool," Harry said.

"There's a light there."

"You're not thinking of going in that shit, are you? I already smell bad enough."

But Phin was already wading in. This wasn't the sewer line, or a cesspool. Phin knew this was created by Luther, for some deranged reason.

The water was cold, and Phin held up his hand and felt the circulating air. He listened for a moment, caught the hum of a large air-conditioner.

What the hell was this place for?

"I'm so sorry, Bruno," Harry wailed, trudging in after Phin.

The duo stuck to the perimeter. It took longer but wasn't as deep, not going higher than the thigh.

McGlade kept Phin company with a constant barrage of complaints.

"Ugh, you smell that?" McGlade said. "How many diseases you think are floating around in this slop, looking for hosts?

"It's a hot zone in here...

"A goddamn hot zone...

"...I can't remember if I'm up to date on all my vaccinations...

"...yuck, something solid just bumped me...

"...I think it was a snake...

"...a long, brown, stinky snake...

"...it was either that, or feces...

"...I really hope it was a snake...

"...ugh, it was feces...

"...or the snake was covered with corn...

"...I hate feces...

"...I really hate feces...

"...can you smell all the feces, Phin?"

"Harry, please, can you just be quiet for a few minutes? Please?"

"It's clinging to me, like I'm some giant shit magnet."

"McGlade..."

"Is it clinging to you, too?"

"McGlade!"

"Okay, I'll shut up."

It lasted all of twenty seconds before Harry said, "I think some splashed in my mouth."

But Phin was focused on the platform ahead of him.

A platform with a body on it.

He increased his speed, making it over to the concrete slab, to the dead man.

Harry said, "This guy was apparently late for something."

"Late?" Phin said, staring at the dismembered corpse.

"Yeah. He had to split."

"Sometimes I wonder how your brain works, Harry."

"I had to go out on a limb for that one."

The orange light was courtesy of a gas lamp in the wall. Next to it was a door. Part of a man still hung in the door-frame.

And then Phin saw it. Lying in the doorway, like a gray tongue.

A Velcro strap.

From Jack's shoe.

"Jack was here," he said, hurrying though the door.

More dark hallways, and the next few minutes were a rush of panic and hope. Jack was still alive. She'd been this way. They just needed to find her.

"Phin! Losing you in the dark, buddy!"

"I'm over here!" he yelled to Harry, not slowing down.

"Phin!" But it wasn't Harry. It was another familiar voice.

Herb.

"Herb! Keep yelling!"

Herb kept up the chatter until Phin came upon another cold room.

Herb was sitting in the muck on the floor.

Surrounded by blood.

Jack

My daughter was sleeping when the door opened and Luther walked in carrying a metal cylinder with a digital timer attached to the pressure valve.

The timer was counting down from eighty-five seconds.

He set it on the drain beside the chair.

"In less than a minute and a half, that canister is going to fill this room with QNB gas. It'll knock you out. I fear it will kill your little girl. When you were in the truck, she only got a tiny dose because she was still inside you. Now she'll get a full dose. Give her to me, and she'll be safe."

"You go to hell."

I tightened my grip on my daughter.

"Seventy-five seconds, Jack."

"Please, Luther, even you—"

"Even I, what?"

"You wouldn't do this to me. To her."

"You have no idea what I'm capable of."

I couldn't do it. I couldn't hand her over.

But the thought of watching her die in my arms was too much.

"When will I see her again?"

"Soon."

"When?"

"Fifty-five seconds, Jack." He eased forward, opened his arms.

"I can't," I cried.

"Give her to me or she'll die."

"I haven't even named her!"

"Give her to me or she'll die."

I closed my eyes. Luther was still talking, but I tuned him out, spent twenty seconds just letting my hand rest on her back, feeling the microscopic rise and fall as she slept in bliss.

How could this be happening?

"Thirty seconds, Jack."

I whispered into her ear, "Your mommy loves you so much. I'll see you again real soon."

And then I opened my eyes, couldn't see a goddamn thing through the sheet of tears, said, "She'll need to eat, and you have to keep her warm."

I felt Luther lift her off my stomach.

I wiped away the tears, watching him carry her toward the open door.

When he reached the doorway, he said, "Jack, you do know you'll never see her again, right?"

I screamed out as he shut the door after him—a broken, bleeding, croaking noise like a dying animal, like my heart being ripped out of my chest.

If I'd had a gun, I would've eaten it.

The human mind wasn't designed to withstand this level of pain.

Then I heard the hiss of gas escaping the canister, filling this room.

This room where my soul had been destroyed.

Herb

"Phin? That you?"

"I'm here, Herb."

Herb sensed Phin kneel next to him. "Are you bleeding?"

"A little. Shot in the leg. The bullet went through."

"But..."

"Most of that blood isn't mine." Before Phin could get the wrong idea, he quickly said, "Not Jack's either. Luther took her through the door behind me."

"Is that you, fat ass?" McGlade sloshed into the room. "Man, you are a sight for sore eyes. Oops. Hell. Sorry, Herb. He sewed them shut?"

Herb felt Phin's hand on his chin. "Why?" Phin asked.

"This is Dante's Inferno," Herb said. "I've been condemned to the third circle, gluttony, sitting in human waste, sightless."

"Nice," Harry said. "Phin and I were in the violence circle. We were forced to shock each other. Then we fell down some stairs and waded through a cesspool. A brown snake attacked me, but it wasn't really a snake. It was feces. You want me to help you with your eyes?"

Herb sighed. He didn't like McGlade, and though he'd only arrived a few seconds ago, Herb was already sick of him. "How? You got scissors?"

"You want help or not?"

On most days it took Herb a tremendous effort just to tolerate Harry. But right now he needed all the help he could get.

"What have you got in mind, McGlade?"

"Hold still."

Herb felt Harry take his head in his hands then lean in close like he was about to kiss him. But instead, he moved his mouth over Herb's right eye.

"Damn, McGlade, what are you doing?"

"It's cool. I can tie a cherry stem into a knot with my mouth. I'm good at this. Hold still."

"Yuck. Harry—"

"Stop moving. I don't want to bite your eyelid off."

It was gross, and weirdly intimate, but it didn't really hurt. In just a few seconds, Harry pulled away and said, "There. Nipped the knot off. Lemme do the other eye."

A moment later, McGlade was gingerly tugging the thread from Herb's eyelids.

Herb opened his eyes, which were swollen so badly they only parted a slit.

But, damn it, that was enough.

"Harry...I...I can't believe I'm saying this, but it's great to see you."

"Great to be seen," he said.

Herb was so grateful he was momentarily at a loss for words. "I don't know how to thank you."

McGlade grinned. "How about a blowjob?"

Herb grinned back. "I don't want one right now. But how about this?"

And then Herb did something he never thought he'd do, even if he lived to a hundred. Herb Benedict gave Harry McGlade a big hug.

"Thanks, Harry."

"No problem, Herb. I've been a jerk to you for years. Least I could do."

"Well, I owe you one, and—" Herb's nose wrinkled up. "Do I smell piss?"

"It's Phin," Harry said, pushing him away. "Now let's go get our girl back."

Phin was already at the door, tugging on the handle. When it didn't open, he put his good shoulder into it, which did nothing.

"Can you walk?" Harry asked Herb.

"I dunno."

McGlade stared at the bullet wound then pulled off his jacket. "Ralph Lauren," he said sadly. "Sorry, Ralph."

He tucked it under his armpit and tore off a sleeve, and with Herb's help tied it around his calf. Then he helped Herb to his feet, making him wonder if this was really McGlade, or some robot replica.

"Do you know the code?" Phin called to them.

"Read the plaque again."

"'Gluttony. Where there's a will, there's a way.'"

Herb had been wondering about that, and he had an idea. "How is *way* spelled?"

"W-A-Y."

But *way* was a homonym for *weigh*. Which made a warped sort of sense.

"I think it might be her weight," Herb said, gesturing to Christine's body. Seeing her for the first time, it was impossible to match up the corpse to that beautiful singing voice.

"How much you think she weighs?" Phin said.

Herb frowned. She was bigger than he was, but it was hard to judge.

"Start at three fifty," he said. "Then go up, a pound at a time."

Jack

Iawoke, thinking I was still strapped to the birthing table.
But this was something else.

Something worse.

I could feel a bunch of pads between my legs, the faint trickle of blood.

I squinted until the room came into focus. Beneath me lay a floor of sand. Motes of light floated lackadaisically down from the ceiling. When one of them landed on my leg, I gasped at the sudden burst of heat.

It was smoldering ash.

Raining from above.

On the wall, I spotted another plaque that read "CIRCLE 7: VIOLENCE." There was some writing below it that I couldn't make out.

I checked my bonds, saw my wrists and ankles were strapped to some sort of pulley-and-gear mechanism. To my right stood a metal cart with a control panel on top.

But I didn't care about where I was, or what was happening to me.

All I cared about was my daughter.

My daughter and my friends.

I heard a door creak open, strained my neck to see.

Luther walked in, tracking through the sand, and stopped next to the gurney, staring down at me.

"You're still bleeding a little, Jack, but I took the liberty of placing some pads down there."

"Where is she, you bastard?"

He scratched the back of his head. "Originally, Phin and Harry were in these chairs. They were going to torture each other to death while you watched. The fiery ash would have rained down on them. You would have begged me to stop. It would have been quite beautiful."

An ash landed on his arm, and he watched it eat a tiny hole through his shirt.

I clenched my teeth. "Where's my daughter?"

"She's gone, Jack. Maybe someday, when you're ready, I'll tell you what happened to her. But you aren't ready yet."

I was exhausted, emotionally drained, and hurt in a dozen places, but I pulled on those straps with more force than I'd ever used on anything.

They didn't budge.

"Anger isn't the reaction I'm after," Luther said. "You need to get past that."

"What exactly is it you want, Luther?"

Luther put his face close to mine, his dark eyes drilling into me.

"I want a partner."

I didn't respond, wondering what the hell he was getting at.

"I've embraced a side of myself that few even acknowledge exists," he continued. "A dark, black side. Over the years, I've met others who possess this darkness. Alex Kork was one of them. Tell me, what did you think of Alex?"

"She was psychotic. Like you."

He nodded. "But she had a spark to her, didn't she? I visited her in prison. We had a...*connection*. A connection that went deeper than anything physical, anything emotional. I think I can also have that connection with you."

I closed my eyes. It was half-past crazy in loony town, and I'd had enough. There had been too many nut jobs, with too many delusional fantasies. I wondered if I was some sort of maniac magnet.

Luther touched my eyelids, peeled them open. "Morality is an artificial construct. It is, admittedly, necessary for society, and for civilization to prosper. But even in the most civilized nations, murder and torture flourish. Man's inhumanity to his fellow man isn't the mark of a backwards society. It's the pinnacle of what society has to offer those who are superior."

"Yeah, I've read Nietzsche, too."

"But Nietzsche chickened out." Luther released my eyes. "He didn't have the balls to directly state what he was hinting at. Some men are meant to hunt and kill others for their own amusement."

"And you honestly think this is something I have in common with you?"

"You already hunt people, Jack. You've been doing it your whole career. But you always stop yourself once you get to the fun part. I've been trying to show you how to fully embrace the inner you. The predator."

"Alex was crazy. But you're flat-out batshit nuts, Luther."

"You're lost, Jack. Lost and you don't even realize it. Just like Dante. I was lost once as well. Even after I embraced my true self, I still needed direction. I learned a lot from others. Others like Alex. I met them. I studied them. I studied your very cases, learned all about the people you chased. I cherry-picked the things that worked, and then, as you can see, improved upon them. Hunters tend to have short attention spans and monovision. But I see things large-scale. I have scope. I don't mind delaying gratification for a while if it means a bigger payoff."

"Batshit nuts," I said.

"I felt as you do, once. But something helped me see the light." He smiled, and it was an ugly thing. "Pain, Jack. Pain is cleansing. Pain is clarifying. Pain is pure. It strips away everything. Dignity. Artifice. Morality. Pain allowed me to be born again, to become truly free." His voice lowered. "And it will do the same for you."

I shook my head. "No, it won't."

"Yes, it will. It's just a question of how badly and how long I'll have to hurt you. When I said something helped me see the light, would you like to know what I'm referring to?"

I didn't. I just glared at him.

He patted the contraption I was strapped to.

"My time spent in this chair changed me forever, Jack. I was just like you. Holding back the darkness inside of me. Just open yourself up to the possibility that you have no idea how depraved you truly are. This chair is going to change you."

"No, Luther. It may kill me, but it won't change me."

He scowled. "Listen very carefully, Jack. If you're counting on the possibility of death to get you out of this, you could not be more wrong. You think I would ever let you die? Everything you've been through here, I've been poised at every turn, ready to step in and rescue you. Ready to save you. You aren't going to die, Jack. Though you will wish for it. In fact, your desire for death will become all-consuming. It's the not dying that will bring about the change in you."

I felt a sickness rising up inside of me.

Born out of the fear of imminent pain.

"You're like a horse, Jack. Wild and untamed. Full of potential. But you're not broken. I have to tear you down to nothing and rebuild you. Your strength, what I love about you,

will endure. Will become even harder. Your weakness and failings will be utterly annihilated. If it takes days, that's okay. If
it takes weeks. Months. I've got all the time in the world, and
no one knows you're here. I'll bring in Harry, Herb, and Phin,
let you watch them suffer. I can even make you hurt them. Kill
them. We all have breaking points, Jack. Even you."

I stared, defiant. "You may break me, but I'll never become
what you are."

"You already are what I am. The faster you accept that, the
easier it will be. When you come out on the other end of this,
for the first time, you'll know true joy. You've been miserable
all your life, haven't you?"

I didn't know how to answer that.

"Admit it, Jack. You despise yourself. Your relationships
are all unhealthy. You ever wonder why so many people around
you get hurt? Ever stop to think that hurting them is what
you really want?"

"That's bullshit."

"Yet you keep doing it, over and over. Your friends and
family are always getting hurt, or dying. It must be because
you want it. And tell me something. When do you feel most
alive? Most vibrant? Most worthy? Isn't it when you're chasing some psychopath? Closing in on the kill? That's why you
became a cop in the first place, isn't it?"

I wasn't sure how to answer that, or even if I should. Luther
was twisting the facts in my life to fit his own warped view.

"You're bending to the constraints and confines of a society in which you're an alpha predator, and you need to break
free of that. Don't you want to be happy for once? To sleep
peacefully rather than toss and turn all night? You have a will,
and the sooner you learn to follow it, the sooner you'll reach
perfection. But enough talk. Let's get started."

Luther moved behind the wheeled cart, touching the controls.

"Unfortunately, Phin and Harry burned out the electroshock feature. I have the scene recorded, and I'll show it to you later. They suffered quite a bit. But that was nothing compared to what I'll do to you. Happily, the chair you're in has many other methods for inflicting pain. Why don't we start with, let's see...abrasion?"

"I just had natural childbirth, motherfucker. There's nothing you can do to hurt me."

Luther smiled his ugly smile. "Oh yes, there is."

I closed my eyes.

Pictured Phin's face.

My daughter's face.

My life.

It hadn't been a perfect life. That's for sure. But all of the psychobabble Luther spouted in his half-assed attempt to analyze me was wrong. Dead wrong.

I could admit to being unhappy. I could admit to putting in too much time at the job and not enough time into me. But those were my choices. My mistakes. And slowly but surely, I was learning from them.

I would never be like Luther.

Never.

No matter what he did to me.

Something in the chair beneath me began to hum.

"Are you ready, Jack?"

I opened my eyes.

Bored them right into his.

"We gonna do this, or are you gonna talk me to death, asshole?"

Phin

He punched in 4-2-2.

Nothing.

Maybe Herb's idea that the code was the dead woman's weight was wrong.

4-3-3.

4-3-4.

4-3-5.

Green light!

The deadbolt opened. When he stepped through the doorway and saw what was inside, something within Phin snapped.

He walked over to the birthing table slowly, reverently. There was blood on the stainless steel, a gooey mess of afterbirth attached to a cut umbilical cord. Phin saw the wrist straps, where the woman he loved had been tied down while giving birth to their daughter.

Phin tried to imagine the scene and then tried even harder to push it out of his head.

The sensation of hate welling up in him was so all-consuming, it threatened to overpower him.

He wanted to save Jack.

He wanted to save his little girl.

But most of all, more than anything, he wanted Luther's neck in his hands.

Phin understood violence. He'd been around it often, both on the giving end and the receiving.

But he'd never craved violence before.

Phin was going to tear that son of a bitch to pieces and smile while doing it.

"Oh...oh man. Phin...you okay, buddy?"

Harry came into the room, propping up a limping Herb. Phin ignored them, putting on a guise of control, searching for the exit to the room. When he found it, he began to run, leaving his friends behind, anxious to find Luther.

He tore through an open doorway, down a long passage draped in semidarkness.

A door stood at the far end, and Phin burst through it.

Saw Jack, strapped to one of those torture chairs.

Saw Luther, at the control panel.

Luther locked eyes with him, and Phin saw something in his eyes.

Fear?

Maybe. But also something else.

Something like resignation.

Phin launched himself at him.

Luther raised the gun.

Fired.

Missed.

Phin almost on him.

Firing again.

Phin feeling a tug in his right shoulder, but momentum kept taking him forward.

He swatted Luther's gun hand away.

Made a fist.

Put everything he had behind it.

The punch split Luther's nose like a rotten tomato.

Then Phin tackled him, pinning him to the floor, raining down blows in a frenzy.

Luther tried to raise the gun.

Phin caught his wrist, leaned down, and bit Luther's arm until he hit bone.

The gun skittered away.

Phin began to hit him again.

"Phin! Stop! You'll kill him!"

No shit, Jack! That's the point!

"Phin! Our daughter! He took her!"

Phin had been raising his fist for another blow, his knuckles bloody and on fire, Luther's face split open in half a dozen places—

—and Phin unclenched his hand.

Our daughter.

Killing Luther wouldn't make him talk.

Phin turned, stared at the chair Jack was in.

Now *that* would make him talk.

He moved to get off Luther, and then saw Luther's hand snake down to his belt.

Phin immediately immobilized the hand and watched Luther's puffy lips form a red grin.

It was a feint.

Luther's other hand had gone for a knife.

Silver, glinting in the light, a wicked curved blade.

It tore into Phin's side, piercing his kidney, the pain so unimaginable he couldn't even breathe.

He fell off Luther, the world swirling and fading away.

Luther

Turning onto all fours, he quickly looks for the fallen Glock. He spots it a few meters away.

He needs to kill Phin, if he isn't dead already. Or at least immobilize him.

But if Phin escaped, Harry may have as well.

Luther shakes his head, blood and snot and tears spraying off.

Pain throbs through his skull, but Luther ignores it.

Jack is yelling for her boyfriend, but Luther ignores it.

Harry bursts into the room, and incredibly, he's got Herb with him, but Luther ignores it.

Luther's entire world has come down to him and the gun.

Get the gun, regain control.

Then the game can continue.

The game *must* continue.

It is his life's work. His masterpiece.

It must be seen through to completion.

More yelling.

Someone rushing at him.

Luther, reaching for the Glock.

Smiling when he grabs it.

Then he turns around and starts firing wildly with one hand, slashing his Spyderco with the other.

Jack

This was worse than anything Luther could do to me in this chair, watching my friends go down.

First Phin.

Then Harry, in a spray of bullets.

Then Herb, falling to his knees.

I cried out, straining against my bonds. Luther finally ran out of ammo, and he stuck the gun in his waistband and began to crawl over toward Harry.

With the knife.

"McGlade! Goddamn it! Get up!" I screamed.

But Harry wasn't moving.

Luther got within ten feet of him.

Eight feet.

Crawling slowly.

Smiling.

Enjoying this.

"HARRY!"

"Jack..."

A whisper, at my side. I turned, saw Phin there, sitting next to me. There was a streak of blood across the floor where he'd dragged himself.

He reached up to the control panel, hit a button.

My arms and legs were suddenly free.

"Go be you," he said to me.

So that's what I did.

I stumbled off the table, dropping to all fours, looking for some sort of weapon. And I spotted one, under the chair.

An empty beer bottle.

Sam Adams Cherry Wheat.

I grabbed it by the bottleneck, pulled myself up to my feet.

Luther was almost on McGlade.

But I was on Luther first.

Using a golf swing, I put everything I had into the blow.

All the fear. All the pain. All the anger.

But more than that.

Luther had taught me something. But it wasn't what he wanted to teach me.

I didn't need Luther to know I had to treat my friends better.

I didn't need Luther to know I needed to treat myself better.

I didn't need Luther to know I would be a good mother.

Luther hadn't broken me. He'd simply taught me what Nietzsche already knew.

That which does not kill you makes you stronger.

The bottle hit his face with the crack of a Sammy Sosa homerun.

Glass shattered.

So did teeth.

Luther collapsed onto his side. I grabbed his knife. Knelt on top of his chest.

"Do it," he said. There were shards of brown glass where his teeth used to live. "You're just like me now, Jack. Kill me."

I felt the rage build up inside me. All the men and women this animal killed. All he put me and my friends through.

Teeth clenched, every muscle in my body bunched up, I brought the blade to his throat.

A lifetime ago, I'd had the chance to kill a dangerous psychopath but arrested her instead. Alex Kork. It was a decision I paid for dearly when she escaped and went on another murder spree.

But I didn't regret the decision.

I wasn't like Alex. Or Luther.

I wasn't a killer.

"I'm nothing like you," I said, tossing the knife aside.

Then I grabbed his head and introduced it to the concrete.

"I won't kill you, Luther." I bounced his head off the floor a second time. "But you will tell me where my baby is."

I slammed his head once more, his eyelids fluttering, pupils rolling up into the top of his head.

Then I patted him down, found his plastic zip ties, and bound his hands behind his back. Tight. I used three ties, just to make sure. I also bound his legs with four more, dragged him through the sand, and then used four more to attach his ankles to the metal leg of the torture chair.

This was one psycho who wasn't going to come back to haunt me.

I was going to haunt him, until he gave me my child.

I stumbled to Harry.

Checked his pulse.

Strong.

Looked for injuries, saw his head was bleeding.

Pushed away his hair, matted and stuck to his scalp, fearing the worst.

The bullet had grazed him, leaving a big gash, but had apparently bounced off his thick skull.

Went to Herb.

Checked his pulse.

Weak.

Two shots in the stomach.

I touched his belly, and Herb groaned.

"I'll get help," I told him.

He smiled weakly. "Jack Daniels saves the day again."

"We can figure out who saved who when we're all out of here."

Then I went to Phin.

My man was sitting up, clutching his side.

He also smiled at me. "That's my girl."

I felt his pulse.

Weak.

"I'm so sorry, Phin. For everything."

"How's the baby?"

My eyes teared up.

"Beautiful. She has your eyes."

He reached up, clutched my hand. "We'll find her."

I nodded, a lump in my throat. "I love you, Phin. I love you so much."

"I love you too, babe."

"And I love all of you!" Harry had woken up. "Even you, fat ass."

Somehow, we all managed to get to our feet, clutching each other, supporting each other, limping and crying and ragged and battered and shot and needing urgent medical attention.

But not broken.

Goddamn it, not broken.

We got out of the Violence circle, stumbled down a dark hallway as one, like some dysfunctional, lopsided machine, and came to another iron door.

There was a plaque on it.

CIRCLE 9: TREACHERY
He from before me moved and made me stop,
Saying: "Behold Dis, and behold the place
Where thou with fortitude must arm thyself."
Inferno, Canto XXXIV

I was hesitant to enter, ready to backtrack and find another way, sick to death of Luther's games. But there could be more innocent victims inside.

I pushed open the door.

This room wasn't elaborate like the others. In fact, it looked more like a large storage closet than a circle of hell.

No wind. No freezing muck. No fire. No human waste. No pennies. No bears. No electricity.

Just a single man, chained to the wall, a gag in his mouth, surrounded by reams of eight-and-a-half-by-eleven-inch paper—pasted to the walls, stacked at his feet, sheets of it even stapled to his chest and legs.

One word repeated on every single page, across what must have been thousands and thousands:

```
lutherlutherlutherlutherlutherluther-
      lutherlutherlutherluther...
```

The man was naked, emaciated, covered in scars.

His gray hair and beard were long.

He was unconscious.

Somehow, I knew who it was, even though he looked nothing like his book jacket photo.

It was the author. Andrew Z. Thomas.

I left the boys and walked up to him, removing the ball gag.

He had no teeth.

"We're going to help you," I said, but he was unconscious.

I tugged on the chains. Solid.

"We're gonna have to find something to get these off."

Herb and Phin elected to stay with him, not being able to handle stairs. McGlade went with me, and we found the control room after thirty minutes of searching.

It looked like a high-tech television studio. Monitors covering three of the walls, all hooked up to cameras in each of Luther's circles and throughout the town. On one of them I noticed a Greyhound bus, parked in a warehouse. I searched each in turn, looking for my daughter.

Didn't see her. But she had to be close.

She had to be.

"Found the key box," McGlade said. "And lookee here."

On a table was a giant pile of wallets, purses, and cell phones. I spotted my iPhone case immediately and turned it on, thrilled to have three bars of signal strength and full 3G. Using the Maps application, I found my exact location. We were in Dirk, Michigan, outside of Detroit.

I dialed 911, identified myself, and asked for cops, search teams with dogs, and several ambulances.

"Anything else?" the awed operator asked.

"Better send animal control, too," I told her. "There's also a grizzly bear."

"A what?"

I hung up, going back to studying the screens, trying to think like a psychopath, like Luther. He'd planned for me to give birth there. Waited for me to get to full term. Built a birthing room for me. He must have had plans for the baby.

He must have.

So, goddamn it, where the hell was she?

"Oh, shit," Harry said.

I saw he was looking at one of the monitors.

The one labeled VIOLENCE.

I saw the torture chair. The broken bottle. The streaks of blood on the floor.

But Luther was gone.

PART III

Jack

I only slept because they gave me something, and when I jerked myself awake it was in a panic that I was still in Luther's chamber of horrors.

But a quick look around confirmed that I was still in the hospital.

Afternoon, as evidenced by the sun streaking in through the curtains.

I glanced at the clock next to the TV and confirmed it. Ten after three.

I absentmindedly patted my belly, surprised that it had gone down.

When I remembered what had happened, the hurt came back.

"Hey!"

An old, armed Detroit cop guarding the outside of my door peered in at me, different guy from last time I was awake. Shift change must have occurred.

"My baby," I said, my voice cracking. "Did they...?"

"Still looking," he said. "We got fifty guys there, but the area is huge. We'll find her."

"Did you check Luther's footage?"

"The video files are encrypted. We're working on that, too."

I allowed myself to be devastated for a few seconds, then pushed it deep inside. Depressed, exhausted, hurt as I was, I needed to pull myself together, to bring my A game.

I blew out a stiff breath. "I'm Jack Daniels, by the way," I said. "Thanks for watching over me."

"Not a problem. Name's Richie. You need anything, just let me know."

I rubbed the sleep out of my eyes, still struggling to push away the dread.

I needed out of that room.

I needed to be with my friends.

I swung my legs over the side of the bed, smoothing down my hospital gown over my legs. There was a pair of paper slippers on the floor, and I stood up and slowly slid my feet into them. I was still woozy. From the drugs.

From everything that had happened.

"I don't know if you should be getting up, Lieutenant."

"I'm not a cop anymore. And I'm going to see my friends. Know where they are?"

"Two doors down. I'll show you."

He led me down a bright, antiseptic hallway.

I moved in a slow shuffle, feeling a lot like a balloon that had all of its air let out. Richie was talking to the cop stationed outside the door, and I poked my head inside the room.

Harry and Herb occupied beds next to each other, which I immediately thought was a big mistake. But, incredibly, they weren't at each other's throats. In fact, they were both smiling and engaged in what appeared to be amicable conversation.

"Hey, boys."

I walked in, hugged them each in turn.

"Hey, Jackie," Harry said. "Herb didn't know I had club box seats at Wrigley Field. We're going to a game next week."

"Who is?" I asked.

"Me and Herb."

I eyed Herb. "You're going to a Cubs game with Harry?"

"Yeah. We've put our differences aside and realized we have a lot in common. We both like baseball. And hot dogs. And Neil Diamond. And microbrew beer. Harry's actually a pretty cool guy."

I glanced down at Herb's chart, looking for mention of a head injury.

"We'd invite you to come along," Harry said, "but it's a guy's night out. Bros before hoes. Right, big dog?"

"You know it."

I watched, astonished, as they bumped knuckles.

"Explode it!" Harry said.

They touched fists again, and then each made a *POW* sound as they opened their hands in a mock explosion.

I felt like rolling my eyes but didn't want to be the gray cloud in their sunshine parade. "Where's Phin?"

"ICU," Herb said. "His surgery took longer than ours."

"I got fifteen stitches," McGlade said, smiling proudly. "Herb got thirty. Fo' knucks, big dog! Holla back!"

They bumped fists again.

"Explode it!" Harry said.

Once more, with a *POW*.

I thought I liked it better when they hated each other.

Scratch that. I was positive I liked it better.

"Phin okay?" I asked.

Herb nodded. "They saved his kidney. Six hours under the knife, but he's doing fine."

"It's okay," Harry said. "He's got a spare one. Apparently he's some kinda genetic freak who was born with two kidneys. Phin's the man, dog. Bust the rock!"

They tapped knuckles again.

"Explode it!"

POW.

I would have told them to get a room, but they already had one.

"I'm going to check on him," I said, leaving them alone with their guy love.

My cop escort tailed me to the ICU, which required an elevator ride up to the seventh floor. Phin also had a guard in front of his door who wouldn't let me through until I lied and said I was Phin's wife.

Phin was asleep, a tube up his nose, his color pallid.

When I kissed his forehead, he opened his eyes.

"Hey, you," he whispered.

"Hey. How you feeling?"

"Groggy. But strong. Did they find...?"

I shook my head, a tear raining down my cheek. "Not Luther, or our daughter."

I reached down, held his hand, squeezed it. He squeezed back.

"Harry and Herb?" he asked.

"I think they're going to start dating."

"How are you, Jack?"

I pursed my lips together, because I was afraid I'd start sobbing if I spoke.

"That man," Phin said. "The one Luther had chained up. Maybe he knows something."

I nodded, wiping away a tear with the back of my hand. "I should go be me?" I said.

"No one does it better, babe."

I gave Phin another kiss, this one on the cheek.

Then I shuffled off to talk to Andrew Z. Thomas.

Lucy

Earlier

She walked into the waiting room of the ER.

Eyes instantly upon her, and why shouldn't they be?

Her housedress practically shredded and reeking of dried sewage from her romp through Luther's playhouse. And she looked like...

Well, she looked like what she looked like.

She limped up to the admit window and waited for the nurse to notice.

The older woman behind the glass didn't even look at her, just said, "Fill out the intake form, bring it back to me."

Lucy leaned in close to the glass, stared at the woman with her single, functioning eye, said, "Hey. Emergency here."

The old nurse finally obliged her and registered a beat of shock and horror at Lucy's hideous visage.

Already, blood was running down Lucy's skinny legs and pooling at her feet.

Lucy held up her three-fingered claw and then lifted her dress over her head, exposing the skin-graft seams she'd ripped out in the parking lot, figuring her only sure shot at an admit would be copious amounts of blood.

She heard an "Oh my God," from one of the other patients in the waiting room.

Heard the nurse pick up the phone and call for a gurney, stat.

Lucy had thought she'd have to fake losing consciousness, but she apparently had done too good a job, possibly ripped out too many seams, the blood flooding out of her faster than she'd planned or anticipated.

A swirling dizziness sapped the strength from her legs, which buckled.

She was out before she even hit the floor.

Jack

Richie led me down past the nurses' station to a room at the end of the wing, where another guard stood watch in front of a room I knew must belong to Andrew Z. Thomas.

The guards must've known each other because they bumped knuckles but thankfully restrained themselves from exploding. What was up with guys and doing that? Maybe I didn't get the memo because I didn't have testicles.

My guard said, "What's the hap-hap, Tone?"

"You know, just pulling the door duty. All's quiet."

"Same here. And I like it quiet. This is my last day, man. Retirement, here I come."

"You and the missus buy that beach house in Florida?"

"You betcha. Gonna spend my golden years fishing for hammerheads and drinking rum punch."

"Who's this, Richie?" Andrew's guard motioned to me.

"I'm Jack Daniels," I said, extending my hand.

"Officer Tony Satori. Pleasure to meet you."

"Is he up?" I jerked a thumb over my shoulder. "I'd like a few words."

"Doc said no one goes in."

"It's okay, Tone," Richie said. "She's the one who saved him."

Tony sized me up. "Yeah. You used to be that cop, outta Chi-town."

"Used to be," I said.

"Sure. Go on in. You want us in there with you?"

"I outweigh him by fifty pounds. I think I'll be okay."

Richie nodded, and I entered the room, closing the door behind me.

Andrew was lying in bed, the covers tucked under his bony arms. They'd given him a haircut and shaved off the Rip Van Winkle beard, but that only made him look even more like a corpse. His eyes were closed, and I immediately felt like I was attending a wake rather than visiting a live patient.

"Mr. Thomas?"

He opened his dark eyes. "What year is this?"

I told him.

"I've been gone a long time," he said. Not a trace of self-pity or bitterness.

"I'm sorry about what he did to you."

He made a small motion that might have been a shrug. "You reap what you sow."

"Do you know who I am?"

He nodded, so slowly I figured it must have hurt him to do so. "I overheard some of the police talking. They filled me in. I have you to thank, they tell me."

But he didn't thank me. He didn't say anything.

"He has my baby," I finally said.

"I heard that as well."

"Do you know where she is?"

"No."

I tried a different tract. "You know him. Probably better than anyone else. What do you think he did with her?"

"I don't know. I've seen him do terrible things. Many of them to me. He has no empathy. No mercy. He's the perfect killing machine. I have a pretty active imagination, but I could barely comprehend the depths of depravity he reached."

Thomas wasn't helping me. In fact, he was creeping me out.

I wondered if the years of abuse and captivity had destroyed his mind.

What was I thinking? Of course they had. This guy actually knowing something was beyond a long shot.

But a long shot was better than no shot at all.

"If you have any ideas about what he did with my little girl, I'd like to hear them."

"I have some ideas. Like putting your baby on a skillet, the stove turned on low. A newborn couldn't flip out of the pan. Just slowly cook, screaming, wondering why this terrible thing was happening after nine months of floating in bliss."

I was so revolted, so outraged by the suggestion, that I almost struck him. I had to remind myself that this guy was insane, had endured things no one should have ever been forced to endure. It wasn't his fault.

"I'm..." I pushed it back. "I'm sorry to disturb you, Mr. Thomas."

I turned, ready to get the hell out of there.

"Hold on," he called to me.

I stopped. Waited.

"Try to think like him," Thomas said. "He wants to hurt you. Right?"

I nodded.

"What would hurt you more? Him killing your baby? Or him keeping your baby alive?"

I had no idea. They were both too horrible to comprehend.

"If he kills her, it'll be a one-time pain. But if he keeps her alive...sends you photos every once and a while...perhaps photos of the terrible things he's doing to her...wouldn't that hurt more?"

I felt the tears coming. "Yes."

Thomas spread out his palms.

"Then that's what he'll do."

I was about to reply when I noticed Thomas's fingers for the first time.

The tips were missing.

And I knew what that meant.

Luther

He shuts off some moronic game show playing on the television and climbs out of bed, padding to the bathroom. The mirror reveals the truth.

He's hideous.

A swollen, discolored, scabby face. Split lips. A nose packed with cotton.

The contact lenses and the black wig are gone, and for good measure he also shaved his head in a gas station bathroom a few miles outside of Detroit.

Luther opens his mouth, wincing at the missing teeth, the black and scarlet gums.

He looks like a Halloween jack-o'-lantern.

But it's the perfect disguise, ideal for hiding in plain sight. He almost wants to thank Phin for it.

Perhaps he will. Phin is just one floor above him in the ICU.

Luther was admitted into the hospital in the wee hours of the morning. He had to endure a clumsy doctor's attempt at stitches, a CT, and an X-ray, and after three hours of waiting and testing was diagnosed with a concussion.

That's courtesy of Jack. He plans on visiting her as well.

Earlier, with the use of a wheelchair the helpful nursing staff provided him, Luther found Jack's room, along with Herb's and Harry's, Phin's, and Andrew's. Each had an armed cop guarding their door. It had taken Luther a few late-night phone calls to find out which of Detroit's many hospitals they'd been brought to, but he'd hit the jackpot on the fourth try.

He isn't concerned about being spotted—his own dead mother wouldn't recognize him with all the swelling. And the best thing about wearing a memorable outfit—cowboy boots, black jeans, long hair—is that people tend to remember that more than actual features.

Being the object of a statewide manhunt, Luther figures the safest place to be is hiding right under their noses.

Besides the four cops on guard duty, there are two more downstairs, and various cops and Feds are constantly coming and going. On one of his excursions, Luther overheard one of Jack's doctors talking to the Sheriff's Department, explaining she wouldn't be fit to answer questions for at least another day.

The doctor was wrong.

Jack would *never* answer any questions.

"Goodbye, Luther," he tells his reflection. "It was fun being you."

Luther climbs into his wheelchair, drapes a blanket over his lap, and once again sets off prowling through the halls. It doesn't take him long to find a janitor's closet, and when he's made sure no one is looking, he pops in and quickly finds what he needs.

Next stop is locating a laundry cart.

He waits for an orderly to pop into a room to change sheets, then helps himself.

Finally, it's a quick elevator ride to the ICU floor.

As he hoped, there are new cops on duty. There's been a shift change, which means there won't be another for a few hours.

Perfect.

Unfortunately, along with Phin's guard, Andrew now has two. Luckily, they're on opposite sides, not within each other's line of sight. From eavesdropping on fifteen seconds of their banter, he picks up on their names.

Tony and Richie.

Luther rolls slowly past Andrew's room, taking a surreptitious glance through the window of the closed door, and realizes the reason for the double guard.

Jack is in there with him.

He continues to roll down the unit, stopping at the men's restroom door. He makes a pathetic show of trying to open it, then casts a glance at the cops to see if they're watching.

They are.

"Can I get a little help here?" he calls out.

After a brief discussion, one of them, the larger, older one—Richie—walks over.

Luther slides his hand under the blanket, opening the Harpy folder.

The cop pulls the door, and Luther says, "Thanks, Officer. Look, this is really embarrassing, but I'm going to need some help getting out of this chair."

"I can call an orderly for you."

"I don't need you to undress me or set me down, just a quick pick-up under the armpit. Please. This is an emergency. I don't want to have a code brown in my chair, if you know what I mean."

For a moment, it looks like the crusty son of a bitch is going to refuse to help a desperate, injured man, but then he holds up a finger to his partner and pushes Luther into the bathroom.

It's empty, as Luther had hoped. Richie the Good Samaritan pushes Luther to the handicapped stall and holds the door open for him. He positions the chair next to the toilet.

"Okay, just grab me under the arms," Luther says. He reaches up around the cop's shoulders, palming the Harpy with the blade pressed flat against his wrist.

As soon as the cop lifts, Luther jams the hooked blade into the back of his neck, tearing hard to sever the vertebrae.

The effect is immediate. Richie falls, instant quadriplegia, the blood spurting away from Luther.

Abandoning the cop and the wheelchair, Luther wipes off the blade with some paper towels, and then sticks his head out of the bathroom door.

"Your buddy fell over!" he calls to the cop standing in front of Andrew's room.

Tony hurries over, unsnapping his holster on the way.

Luther ducks behind the door as the cop bursts in.

This one is less trusting than the first, and immediately swings his pistol up to where he thinks Luther would be.

But Luther expected the move and is crouching below the arc of the weapon. He slashes upward with the Harpy, under the cop's groin, severing the femoral artery so deeply the blade grazes bone.

He's a dead man walking, but he's still a threat until he bleeds out, so Luther drops the knife and puts both hands on Tony's gun, trying to twist it from his grasp.

The cop is strong, and for a few seconds Luther worries he might lose.

Then shock begins to set in, and by the time the cop decides it's time to call for help, Luther has both his gun and the knife and he silences the call with a slash across the throat.

Moving quickly now, fearful someone will walk in, Luther hurries to his wheelchair and takes the yellow stand from the seat, the one he liberated from the janitor's closet. He places it outside the door and then peels off his spattered gown and goes to the sink to clean up the blood on his hands and arms.

Suitably blood-free, he dons the cop's utility belt and then slips on the hospital gown he pinched from the laundry cart.

Luther has no plan to get Jack or anyone else out of the hospital, because he doesn't plan on getting out himself.

Breaking Jack hasn't worked.

His years of careful planning, ruined.

If he gave it too much thought, the disappointment would crush him. But he can either bitch and moan or relish the last ten minutes of his life.

All that's left to do is kill everyone and go out in a blaze of glory.

He picks up the cop's fallen gun, a .40 SIG Sauer. Checks the magazine.

Thirteen rounds.

Luther goes back into the stall, checks the other dead cop's gun. A 9mm Beretta.

The .40 is better.

More stopping power. And he can't shoot for shit lefty. Much better to have the Harpy in his free hand.

For detail work.

Lucy

They redid her skin-graft seams and transfused a couple pints of blood, and now Lucy rested comfortably in her room.

There was a psych consult scheduled to happen within the hour, based on her reported inability to recall her name or anything further back than waking up in front of the automatic doors to the ER.

But she wouldn't be here for that.

There were a few old friends up in ICU whom she just couldn't wait to see.

She climbed down out of bed and limped out into the corridor.

A quiet afternoon on her floor. Reminded her of the prison hospital, those days with D which she'd now—so strange to think—remember fondly, with a tinge of sadness even.

Lucy wandered down the hallway toward the elevators across from the nurses' station.

No one noticed her, the nurses buried in chart work.

She punched the UP arrow and waited for the doors to split.

Stepped inside when it arrived, glad to see the car empty.

She hit number seven, the ICU floor, heard footsteps coming quickly out in the hall, a man's voice asking for the elevator to be held.

"Too late," she said, as she jammed her deformed finger into the CLOSE DOOR button.

She was just exiting the elevator when she saw a cop run into the washroom. Lucy watched for a moment, wondering what was happening.

A minute later, a patient stuck his head out and placed a stand outside the door.

DO NOT ENTER, RESTROOM BEING CLEANED.

Lucy had a hunch what was going on. Could she really have gotten this lucky?

Her hunch was confirmed a moment later, when the patient strolled out of the bathroom by himself.

His face was badly swollen, but Lucy knew who it was.

She knew it deep in the bones she still had left.

Jack

The door opened, and I turned, expecting to see Richie and Tony, but stood face-to-face with a monster instead.

I didn't recognize him at first—his face so swollen and distorted.

But the eyes revealed him. The color had inexplicably changed from black to bright blue, but the intensity remained.

They'd contained some element of play in the few horrific moments we'd shared previously, but now they were all rage.

Luther Kite stepped over the threshold and came into the room, closing the door softly behind him with one hand as he pointed a gun at me with the other.

For a long moment, no one spoke.

Luther's breathing was accelerated, from what I could only imagine was the exertion it had taken him to get past the two cops. I yelled for them.

"Hello, Jack. Tony and Richie aren't going to answer."

"Where's my daughter?"

"You're going to die not knowing."

He was twitching, and I recognized the look. His calm demeanor was gone. This was a man on the edge, ready to plunge over.

I held up my hands, trying to buy some time. If he'd killed the cops outside, replacements would come. "You need me, Luther. You want me. You think I'm going to—"

"I'm over you, Jack. We could've been amazing together, but you and your friends screwed everything up. My God, how I'd love to spend several weeks killing you, but we'll just have to make our brief time together count."

He pulled a knife out of his pocket.

I thought quickly. Like all of the serial killers I've known, Luther was a grandiose narcissist, his ego off the charts. He chose me because he thought, in some warped bastardization of logic, that I'd appreciate his genius.

"You took his fingerprints," I said, spreading my hands. "So the evidence had both your prints and Andrew's prints on them. To make it look like you were killing together."

Luther paused. "How'd you figure that out?"

"His are gone. You must have snipped them off. What did you do with them?"

Luther smiled. "Tanned them and then glued them on a pair of leather gloves. Important to keep them oiled, so they didn't crack and dry up."

Keep him talking, Jack.

"Why?" I asked. "Why frame Thomas?"

"Horror writer turns from writing about murder to actually doing it. Interesting story, don't you think?"

"Were you ALONEAGAIN as well?" I asked, thinking back to the Andrew Z. Thomas message board and the reviews of his books on Amazon.

"You saw those? I hoped you would. But then, you don't miss much, do you, Jack? But you did miss something. Maybe even the biggest secret of them all. Unfortunately, you're going to die without ever finding—"

The door busted in.

I turned, expecting cops, but it wasn't the police.

Instead, a horribly disfigured woman stood in the threshold clutching a gun in a three-fingered hand.

I'd never met her, but I knew this was Lucy. Donaldson's partner.

For a second, it looked like she and Luther were going to shoot each other. But neither made a move.

"There's another cop on the ward," Lucy said. "We fire, no one gets out alive."

"What makes you think I want anyone to get out alive, Lucy?"

"Don't be stupid, Andrew. You're too self-absorbed to want to die here."

Andrew?

And then it hit me.

The pieces all coming together at once.

Andrew's missing fingerprints.

Luther's contact lenses and wig.

The odd ALONEAGAIN comments.

How he'd lured the agent, Cynthia Mathis, to Michigan.

The reason for putting Thomas's books in the bodies.

The maniacal obsession with Dante.

Holy shit.

The man I'd known as Luther Kite was really Andrew Z. Thomas.

I looked at the bed. At the emaciated man lying there.

That wasn't Andrew Z. Thomas.

That was...

"Hi, Luther," Lucy said to the man on the bed. "Been dieting, I see."

"Do we know each other?" he asked.

"I've had some cosmetic work done since I last saw you back at that convention. I'm Lucy. Remember? You got me out of that jam."

The man on the bed—the real Luther Kite—smiled a hellish, toothless smile. "I remember, angel. Good to see you again. Is Andrew here responsible for your appearance?"

"Mine and yours."

I turned and stared at...what was I supposed to call him?

"You're the writer," I said to the man pointing a gun in my face. "You're Thomas."

"That was a lifetime ago. I don't write anymore. I pursue different forms of artistic expression. As you so well know, Jack."

"How?" I asked. "How did this...?"

"Luther," Andrew said, pointing his knife at the man on the bed while the gun stayed on Lucy. "He broke me. Just like I was trying to do to you, Jack. That was seven years ago. There was torture, of course. But the thing that changed me was what he made me do to Violet."

I recalled Violet King. The burn scars on her arms.

"You did that?"

Andrew nodded. "Luther told me if I did, he'd free her. But then I got the upper hand. I gave as good as I got, didn't I, Luther?"

"Yes, you did, Andrew. And then some. You've become quite accomplished. You're a better me than me."

I chanced another nervous glance at the door, wondering where the hell the cops were.

"It's so strange, Jack," the real Andrew said. "Suddenly realizing you have these...appetites, but not knowing how to satisfy them. I didn't have the benefit of starting young, learning as I went along. I had to take a crash course in becoming a predator."

His eyes were glazed, manic, like someone on speed. I thought about making a try for the gun, but his finger was tight on the trigger.

"So I studied other killers," Andrew continued. "Studied their methods. Tried them on for size to see if they fit. I spent many long, intimate hours with Luther, picking his brain, coaxing out his secrets. In order to drain his bank accounts—his family was quite rich—I had to impersonate him. And I found that I liked it. Stepping into his cowboy boots and black jeans, putting on the wig and the contacts, sucking those god-awful Lemonheads he likes so much. I realized the best way to be me was to be him. So we switched places. Let him be Andrew Z. Thomas, and then I could be Luther Kite."

This guy wasn't just broken. He was wrecked beyond repair.

"Look, Andrew," I said, "we need to—"

The shot was so sudden I didn't know where it came from. A bright muzzle flash, the smell of gunpowder.

It was followed by another, and another.

Andrew crumpled on the floor, both knees blown out, his gun arm disabled, his curved knife skittering under the bed, Lucy standing over him, aiming a 9mm at his stomach.

"You used to be my hero," she said. "I once drove six hundred miles to see the famous mystery writer Andrew Z. Thomas. Just to get an autograph. I used to be beautiful. And you turned me into a freak."

Andrew groaned on the floor, struggling to reach his gun.

"This is for Donaldson," she said, shooting him between the legs.

"Lucy!" I yelled, taking a step forward. "Stop it!"

"Back it up, lady." She pointed her gun in my face while Andrew groaned and writhed on the floor. "I'll deal with you in a second."

I held out my hands. "He'll rot in prison. You don't have to do this."

"Actually, I do."

Where was that goddamn cop? "Please, Lucy. He took my baby."

"Sucks to be you."

"Lucy!"

The gun went back to Andrew. "Should have finished me off when you had the chance," Lucy said.

"See...you...in hell," Andrew croaked.

"Hell doesn't exist, you dumb ass."

She shot him in the head as he cowered beneath her.

"No!" I rushed forward.

Before I got to her, Lucy turned the gun on me again. "And now, for the encore."

"Don't," Luther rasped, trying to sit up in bed. "She saved me, Lucy. Let this one go."

"I've heard about her. Supposed to be a real badass. Why take a chance? You sure?"

"I'm sure."

Lucy bent down, tugged the pair of handcuffs off of Andrew's utility belt, and then forced me at gunpoint toward the open door leading into the bathroom.

"Get in the shower, Jack."

I stepped inside, and she tossed me the cuffs. If she'd killed me at that moment, I wouldn't have cared. When Andrew died, so did my hopes of finding my daughter.

"You know what to do," she told me.

"Lucy—"

"Bitch, I am running out of patience."

I snapped a bracelet onto one wrist and clamped another to the shower handrail.

Then Lucy disappeared back into the room. I couldn't see what she was doing, but it sounded like Luther was struggling up and out of bed. I heard her say, "They're going to be here any minute."

"Hold on. Push me to the bathroom."

Lucy appeared in the doorway, Luther in a wheelchair. He stared up at me, his eyes black as night.

"Andrew lost his humanity," he said. "But not completely. That's why he failed. He left too many survivors. Survivors have a way of coming back and biting you in the ass."

"Do you know where my baby is, Luther? Please."

He paused, said, "Andrew always regretted what he did to Violet. To Violet and her son. That's how a lot of us go astray. We all break things. But sometimes..." His tongue shot out, licking his thin, pale lips. "Sometimes we try to fix the things we broke."

My last glimpse of them was Lucy pushing him away.

Then the door opened and shut, followed by shouts and another gunshot, causing my heart to skip a beat.

Phin's guard?

Had he gotten Lucy?

Had she gotten him?

Or...God forbid...one of my boys?

I didn't call out. There was no point. The shots had been heard by everyone in the adjacent floors, and word would be spreading fast around the hospital.

Less than a minute later, Harry and Herb were in the bathroom, both holding guns.

"Phin?" I asked.

"Safe," said Herb. "You got a dead cop outside the door. Place is going crazy. What the hell happened?"

"Find a handcuff key." I held up my arm, frantic to be freed. "We need to get out of here, Herb. I think I know where my baby is."

* * *

After hearing Andrew's story, it made perfect sense.

There was a risk to not calling the authorities first. A risk that weighed heavily on me during the long car ride. I didn't want the SWAT team storming in, guns blazing. I'd seen that end badly before.

I just had to keep telling myself that my baby was safe, and that I'd get her back unharmed.

The boys had insisted on coming with me, even though they were in bad shape. The hospital made us all sign release forms saying we left against doctors' orders. Phin was especially fragile, but keeping him away from going after his daughter was like holding back a flood with a single sandbag.

The drive was made both bearable and unbearable by Harry and Herb singing old Neil Diamond songs, egged on by their newfound bromance and some heavy-duty narcotic painkillers.

It was cute at first, but after the fifth rendition of "Song Sung Blue," which neither of them knew completely, I was grinding my teeth hard enough to crush granite.

When we finally got to Peoria, I checked to make sure the cylinder of my Colt was full, even though I hoped I wouldn't need it.

"Harry, Herb, the back. Take one of the universal keys. Phin, you should wait here."

"Like hell."

"You just had major surgery."

He rolled his eyes like that was no big thing and then grabbed the other key.

The four of us extricated ourselves from my Juke and converged on the residence of Violet King.

It had to be her.

Andrew had been sending her his royalty checks.

Andrew had felt responsible for the loss of her baby.

Andrew must have had help to get out of those zip ties, and although the Detroit PD still hadn't decrypted any of the footage he recorded, I knew in my gut who'd helped him.

The Sam Adams Cherry Wheat bottle had been the clincher.

And my hunch proved correct when I got up to the front door and heard the wonderful, musical sound of a baby crying.

Phin had stitches, and I wasn't faring much better, so we brought along two universal keys—a paint can filled with concrete. One swing at the latch and the door burst inward.

We rushed in.

Violet was on her couch, my daughter cradled in her arms. She stared up at us, surprised.

The surprise quickly melted into sadness.

"Andy didn't kill you all at the hospital," she said.

"No. He didn't." Neither Phin nor I had drawn our weapons. "You're the one that helped him escape."

Violet nodded, her eyes welling up. "After what he did to me, he owed me. Is he dead?"

"Yeah."

Another nod. "Was it those two? Lucy and Donaldson?"

"You sent them?"

I heard the sound of the back door breaking in.

"I told them they could kill Andy, but only after I got the baby." Violet glanced down to look at the child in her arms. "She's beautiful."

"I know."

Phin stepped forward, reached out his hands. Violet hesitated.

"She's not yours," I said. "She's ours. Please don't make this messy."

After a tender finger stroke across the cheek, she handed the baby over, and Phin snuggled her up in the crook of his arm.

"Hi, there," he said. "I'm your dad."

"Got her!" I yelled. Herb and Harry stampeded in a moment later.

We all watched Phin hold her, everyone quiet for almost a minute, no sounds but our breathing and the crying of my little girl.

The crying eventually gave way to cooing.

"There are diapers upstairs," Violet said. "Bottles in the fridge. I didn't hurt her."

"I know," I told her.

"I'd never hurt her."

"I know."

Herb called the police.

I walked over to Phin, and he put his free arm around me. We both stared at our child.

I couldn't explain it, but somehow, I felt whole.

"We still haven't named her," Phin said.

"I've been thinking about that. Your last name, Troutt, really sucks."

"Tell me about it."

"And Daniels is from my ex-husband. So I think we should pick a whole new name for her."

"What have you got in mind?" he asked.

I looked beyond the baby, to Violet's table, still stacked with empty beer bottles.

It had been her Cherry Wheat bottle, back in Michigan, that I'd hit Andy with. That had saved my life back in the Violence room.

It had saved all of our lives.

"Let's call her Samantha," I said.

"Samantha?"

"Samantha Adams."

Phin held me tighter. "I think it's perfect."

"Sam Adams?" Harry said. "Hell, yeah!"

"Nice," Herb said.

We held Sam until the cops arrived and arrested Violet.

Then we held her all the way back home.

Epilogue

"The Guide and I into that hidden road
Now entered, to return to the bright world;
And without care of having any rest
We mounted up, he first and I the second,
Till I beheld through a round aperture
Some of the beauteous things that Heaven doth bear;
Thence we came forth to rebehold the stars."
DANTE ALIGHIERI, *THE DIVINE COMEDY*

Jack

I signed for the next-day FedEx package and eagerly opened it while still standing at my front door. There was a note next to the baggie.

Nice rock. I had it professionally cleaned.
Will FedEx your dog back tomorrow. —Duffy

I took the engagement ring out of the bag and stared at it. The midafternoon sunlight caught the facets on the diamond and made it sparkle like a disco ball.

"Who was at the door?"

I turned, saw that Phin had come up behind me.

"I'll tell you later. Right now, I need you to drive me someplace."

He raised an eyebrow. "Where?"

"City Hall. If we get the marriage license today, we can be married by tomorrow."

Phin's face lit up. "I'll go put Samantha in her carrier."

"Wait. First, I need you to put this on me." I held up the ring and my left hand. "Please."

Phin came over. He touched me so gently I got a lump in my throat.

"Jacqueline Daniels, will you make me the happiest person on the planet?"

"No," I said.

"No?" His features went from soft to confused.

"I'll marry you, Phineas Troutt. But it won't make you the happiest person on the planet." I smiled, my eyes getting misty. "You'll have to settle for second happiest."

Then he slipped the ring on my finger and kissed me, and in that single, magical moment, I became the woman I had always wanted to be.

In the past, my job had defined me.

Then my relationships had defined me.

But now I was ready to define myself.

I was ready to like myself.

I was ready to be happy.

Phin hustled off to get our daughter. His kiss lingered, making me smile. I stared at myself in the hallway mirror and almost didn't recognize my reflection. That woman was so relaxed. So content. So sure of herself.

That woman was me.

Andrew Z. Thomas had wanted to break me. He'd tried his best.

But I wasn't broken.

For the first time in my forty-eight years, I was fixed.

Officer Knight

They'd been searching the warehouses and factories all day, coming across one horrific scene from hell after another.

Bodies everywhere.

No survivors.

What kind of a monster had dreamed up and actually built a place like this?

What kind of a mind?

This was hell on earth. No other adequate description.

Knight wondered how he was going to sleep tonight, how he could look into the faces of his children after seeing a place like this.

He could sense sessions of therapy in the not-too-distant future.

First the water tower.

That freezing room where a bear had mauled those poor souls to death.

The gluttony room.

And now this...a warehouse filled with muck and freezing water.

Two dead bodies out on a small island in the middle of the swamp.

And near where he stood, one man dismembered, one of his wrists still dangling from a chain attached to the door.

Then a bald man in bib overalls, legs still floating in the water, his torso draped across the concrete shore.

If he was honest, Knight didn't know how much more of this he could take. It was only his second year on patrol, but they'd called in everyone to canvas this nightmare world for survivors.

He flipped open his notepad and wrote a brief description of the warehouse and the number of victims: four.

Maybe there were more submerged in the muck, but the divers would have to find them. No way in hell was he going to wade out into—

The guy in the overalls coughed.

Holy shit.

Knight jammed his notepad into the pocket of his parka and hurried over to the edge of the water.

He knelt down, grabbed the man's hand.

"You okay there, buddy?"

There was no response, but the man was definitely breathing.

Knight rolled him carefully over. Gunshot wounds to his legs and arms.

One in the gut.

Oh God—his face. This man had been burned as well. The closer Knight looked, he saw scars over every square inch of his body.

And yet...he was breathing.

He'd held on.

"I'm here, buddy," Knight said. "We're gonna get you out of here. Get you all the help you need."

Knight's heart was swelling. He'd actually found a survivor. He was going to save this man's life.

He keyed the mike on his shoulder, tried to keep his voice steady as he spoke, "This is Knight in warehouse three. I've got a survivor, repeat, I've got a survivor. Multiple gunshot wounds, lacerations all over, but a steady pulse. Need EMT assist immediately. Over."

As Knight waited for the cavalry to arrive, he sat down beside the mangled, scarred wreck of a human being whose name he didn't even know.

He held the man's hand. He prayed for him. He told him again and again that everything was going to be all right.

"You're going to get through this, buddy. You're going to get the very best medical care."

The ruin opened its mouth and said in a raspy voice, "Norco?"

"Absolutely. We'll get you out of here, shoot you up so you won't feel any pain."

Knight couldn't be sure, but he thought he saw the man smile.

Luther

"How are you feeling?" Lucy asked.

"Better every day. You're an angel for taking care of me like this."

"I'm one damned ugly angel."

"No, you're not, Lucy. You're beautiful. So beautiful." Luther offered a toothless smile. "Come here."

Lucy limped over to him. She held his skeletal hand in her claw. Before escaping the hospital, Lucy had the foresight to rob the pharmacy. They had enough pain medication to outlast a nuclear winter.

"I have a contact," Luther said. "He can set us up with some fake IDs. Good ones, enough to travel with. We'll leave the country for a while. Go south. Relax. Heal. Have some fun."

"Why Mexico?"

"Because they aren't so uppity about murder in Mexico. We could kill a lot of people before anyone even notices."

Lucy smiled. "Seriously?"

The real Luther Kite nodded.

He felt that feeling again.

That special feeling that had lain dormant during his many years of captivity.

"Little girl, I have a lot of catching up to do."

THE END

The Crouch/Kilborn/ Konrath Universe... Six Decades of Mayhem

Want to read every book, novella, and short story in the Crouch/Kilborn/Konrath Universe in chronological order?

Here's how you do it...

ALL CAPS = Novels
Italics = Novellas and Short Stories Contained within SERIAL KILLERS UNCUT

A Watch of Nightingales by Blake Crouch (1969, Orson Thomas, Andy Thomas)

A Day at the Beach by Blake Crouch (1977, Luther Kite, Maxine Kite, Rufus Kite)

A Pitying of Turtle Doves by J.A. Konrath and Jack Kilborn (1978, Donaldson and Mr. K)

The One That Stayed by J.A. Konrath (1983, Charles Kork, Alex Kork)

A Night at the Dinner Table by Blake Crouch (1984, Luther Kite, Maxine Kite, Rufus Kite)

Cuckoo by Blake Crouch (1986, Luther Kite, Rufus Kite)

SHOT OF TEQUILA by J.A. Konrath (1991, Jack Daniels, Tequila)

A Wake of Buzzards by Blake Crouch and Jack Kilborn (1991, Orson Thomas, Donaldson)

A Brood of Hens by Blake Crouch (1992, Orson Thomas, Luther Kite)

A Glaring of Owls by Blake Crouch and J.A. Konrath (1993, Orson Thomas, Luther Kite)

A Murder of Crows by Blake Crouch and J.A. Konrath (1995, Orson Thomas, Luther Kite, Charles Kork)

Bad Girl by Blake Crouch (1995, Lucy, Orson Thomas, Luther Kite, Andy Thomas)

DESERT PLACES by Blake Crouch (1996, Andy Thomas, Orson Thomas, Luther Kite)

The One That Got Away by J.A. Konrath (2001, Alex Kork and Charles Kork)

LOCKED DOORS by Blake Crouch (2003, Andy Thomas, Luther Kite, Violet King, Sweet-Sweet & Beautiful)

An Unkindness of Ravens by Blake Crouch, J.A. Konrath, and Jack Kilborn (2003, Luther Kite, Alex Kork, Charles Kork, Javier Estrada, Kiernan, Isaiah Brown, Donaldson, Mr. K,

Swanson, Munchel, Pessolano, Jack Daniels, Tequila, Lucy, Clayton Theel, Barry Fuller, Sheriff Dwight Roosevelt)

WHISKEY SOUR by J.A. Konrath (2004, Jack Daniels, Charles Kork)

The One That Didn't by Blake Crouch and J.A. Konrath (2004, Luther Kite)

FAMOUS by Blake Crouch, (2004, Lancelot Blue Dunkquist)

Break You by Blake Crouch (2004, Luther Kite, Andy Thomas, Violet King)

BLOODY MARY by J.A. Konrath (2005, Jack Daniels, Barry Fuller)

RUSTY NAIL by J.A. Konrath (2006, Jack Daniels, Alex Kork)

SNOWBOUND by Blake Crouch (2007, Javier Estrada)

DIRTY MARTINI by J.A. Konrath (2007, Jack Daniels)

Truck Stop by J.A. Konrath and Jack Kilborn (2007, Donaldson, Jack Daniels, Taylor)

Serial by Jack Kilborn and Blake Crouch (2008, Lucy, Donaldson)

Killers by Jack Kilborn and Blake Crouch (2008, Lucy, Donaldson, Luther Kite, Kurt Lanz, M.D.)

A Schizophrenia of Hawks by J.A. Konrath and Blake Crouch (2008, Luther Kite, Alex Kork)

AFRAID by Jack Kilborn (2008, Taylor)

DRACULAS by Jack Kilborn, Blake Crouch, Jeff Strand, and F. Paul Wilson, (2008, Clayton Theel, Kurt Lanz, M.D.)

FUZZY NAVEL by J.A. Konrath (2008, Jack Daniels, Alex Kork, Swanson, Munchel, and Pessolano)

ABANDON by Blake Crouch (2009, Isaiah Brown)

CHERRY BOMB by J.A. Konrath (2009, Jack Daniels, Alex Kork)

TRAPPED by Jack Kilborn (2010, Taylor)

ENDURANCE by Jack Kilborn (2010, Sheriff Dwight Roosevelt)

SHAKEN by J.A. Konrath (2010, Jack Daniels, Mr. K, Luther Kite)

Lovebirds by J.A. Konrath (2011, Lucy, Donaldson)

STIRRED by Blake Crouch and J.A. Konrath (2011, Jack Daniels, Luther Kite, Andy Thomas, Violet King)

RUN by Blake Crouch (2013, Kiernan)